REG

Bride

Michelle Styles

MILLS
BOON

First Published in Great Britain 2017
By Mills & Boon, an imprint of HarperCollins*Publishers*
1 London Bridge Street, London, SE1 9GF

ISBN: 978-0-263-92377-3

52-0217

Our policy is to use papers that are natural, renewable and recyclable products and made from wood grown in sustainable forests. The logging and manufacturing processes conform to the legal environmental regulations of the country of origin.

Printed and bound by
CPI Group (UK) Ltd, Croydon, CR0 4YY

A REGENCY

Collection

Hattie Wilkinson Meets Her Match

Born and raised near San Francisco, California, **Michelle Styles** currently lives near Hadrian's Wall with her husband, a menagerie of pets and occasionally one of her three university-aged children. An avid reader, she became hooked on historical romance after discovering Georgette Heyer, Anya Seton and Victoria Holt.

Her website is www.michellestyles.co.uk and she's on Twitter and Facebook.

Chapter One

End of June 1816—the Tyne Valley, Northumberland

A stifled noise, halfway between a giggle and an excited gasp, caused the Honourable Harriet Wilkinson to halt in her march back to the ballroom. Her entire being tensed. She knew what that sound signalled— in Summerfield's small card room, someone flirted with ruin.

'None of your business, Hattie Wilkinson,' she muttered. When had she become a censorious busybody poking her nose into other people's lives, rather than someone who understood a ball held the possibility of romance? Today was no time to start, and particularly not at a ball to celebrate the first anniversary of Waterloo.

Another trill of laughter sounded. 'That is highly amusing. Why should I ever feel in danger with you?'

Hattie sighed. Turning her back on an unknown couple was one thing. Turning her back on her high-spirited niece during her first foray into polite society was quite another. Far too much was at stake. Livvy with her clear blonde looks, graceful manner and more than adequate dowry had the potential to be a huge success in the London marriage market...if she was allowed to make it that far.

Hattie leant forwards and rattled the door handle.

'I wonder,' Hattie declared in a voice loud enough to wake the dead, 'where on earth have my gloves gone? I suspect I left them in the card room earlier. I had better check.'

She placed her lace gloves in her reticule, counted to ten slowly and flung open the door. The snug room with its artfully arranged tables, high-backed sofa and small fire in the marble fireplace was the sort of room that could offer privacy, especially as there was an unseasonable chill in the June air. In the centre of the room, her sixteen-year-old niece stood closer than strictly proper to a gentleman in evening dress.

Hattie pointedly cleared her throat. 'Excuse me, but I have mislaid my gloves.'

The couple sprang apart. Hattie noted Livvy's bright pink cheeks and mussed lace. Silently she thanked her guardian angel that it was she who had happened on the couple rather than one of the old cats who prowled the corridors searching for the latest tittle-tattle.

'This is Mr Hook, Aunt Harriet. He and I...' Livvy flushed scarlet. 'That is—he's a visitor to Northumberland and...'

'I'm looking for my gloves. Have you seen them, Livvy dear?' she asked brightly, ignoring the way Livvy quickly attempted to straighten her bodice and how young but dangerous Mr Hook appeared with his London-cut frock-coat and tousled Corinthian-styled hair. The time for a lecture on propriety, the necessity of maintaining one's spotless reputation and not settling for the first man who pays you a bit of attention was due later after Hattie had extracted Livvy from this tangle.

'You must know the ones I mean, Olivia,' she continued. 'The lace ones which your dear mama gave me for my birthday.'

'Your gloves, Aunt Harriet?' Livvy did an impression of a trout, repeatedly opening and closing her mouth.

'I think they might be in here. I was…' Hattie paused, trying to think up a reason why she might have been in the card room earlier. Her mind refused to yield the excuse. She opted for a brilliant smile. 'Olivia dear, would you mind helping me to search?'

Livvy behaved like any sixteen-year-old and rolled her eyes. 'If I must, Aunt Harriet, but honestly…'

'I positively insist. I am all sixes and sevens. Balls and me…well, the least said about my nerves the better.' Hattie waved a vague hand, well aware that Livvy had no idea about her normal behaviour at balls and quite probably considered a twenty-seven-year-old aunt bordered on senility in the general course of events.

A crease formed between Olivia's brows and Hattie could see the desire to appear older warring with her natural inclination to stay with her new swain. 'Yes, you are always like this at balls. When did you last have them? Think carefully now.'

Hattie's shoulders relaxed. Livvy had taken the bait, even down to spouting the exact words she always used with her nieces. The next stage of operation commenced now—gently guiding Livvy back to the ballroom with no moonlit detours.

'And you will do the usual and help me to look.

Your sharp eyes are so much better at finding things than my ageing ones.'

Hattie waited for Livvy's agreement. Slowly and steadily she would prise Mr Hook from Livvy's life before he did any lasting damage. Unlike Livvy, she knew precisely the pitfalls of London gentlemen who made extravagant promises. Whilst she had avoided ruin seven years ago, she had been unable to avoid the heartbreak that goes with discovering one's beloved had, in fact, been another woman's beloved at the same time. Livvy would not suffer that fate. None of her nieces would. Silently Hattie renewed her determination.

'Perhaps your aunt left them in the garden,' Mr Hook said in a falsely concerned voice. 'We could investigate, Miss Parteger.'

'What a splendid idea.' Hattie clapped her hands and fixed Livvy's would-be seducer with a stern eye. 'You may search the garden, Mr Hook, while dear Olivia and I search the library, drawing room and the card room. Make sure you leave no stone unturned in your quest to find my gloves.'

Mr Hook gulped twice and scampered out of the card room faster than a fox with the sound of a hunting horn ringing in his ears.

The sound of slow clapping filled the room.

Someone is here! Livvy mouthed, turning redder than a beetroot. A cold shudder snaked down Hattie's back. She'd once been a carefree girl like Livvy. But after succumbing to the advances of a dashing soldier, she had been hustled into a quick marriage, a marriage she had considered romantic beyond her wildest dreams until she had discovered the sordid truth after his death. Even now the humiliation of her discovery caused the bile to rise in her throat. Livvy deserved better.

'Bravo! Bravo!' a rich masculine voice called out. 'A truly stunning performance.'

'What are you doing here, sirrah?' Hattie demanded, brandishing her reticule like a sword towards the sofa. 'Listening into others' private conversations? Show yourself.'

The man rose from the sofa with a book in his hand. Hattie swallowed hard. He was the sort of man to make the pulse beat faster—crisp black hair with brooding dark grey eyes combined with broad shoulders and a lean frame. His face was saved from utter perfection by the presence of a nose which had obviously been broken several times in the past. 'One could hardly help overhearing. You are the one who should be apologising for interrupting my reading and sending my godson on a pointless game of Hunt the Gloves, but I shall forgive you if you beg prettily.'

'Aunt Hattie?' Olivia tugged at Hattie's hand as she started to back out of the room. 'It's Sir Christopher Foxton.'

Christopher Foxton. The name thudded through Hattie. The entire village had been gossiping about him for weeks, ever since it became known that he'd finally decided to visit Southview Lodge. About how he'd beat a man near to death over a game of cards and while the man lay recuperating had stolen his mistress and his fortune. How he was unbeaten in the ring, daring to fight bare-knuckled with the best of them. But mostly how because of his breeding, good looks and personal charm, every door in London was open to him and how various mamas predicted that they would capture him for this or that daughter, even though his mistresses were reputed to be some of the most sought-after courtesans in London.

The amount of sighing and speculation over him had reached such epidemic proportions that it seemed all anyone in the village could speak about was Sir Christopher and his exploits.

Hattie raised her chin a notch and met his intense gaze head-on. He had another think coming if he expected her to beg his forgiveness, prettily or not. She was immune from such men and their superficial charm.

'Where are my gloves, then, if I have sent your god-son on a pointless game?' Hattie cried, exasperated. Confessing her rescue mission was out of the question. She'd rather face a gaggle of gossips dressed only in her chemise and petticoat than reveal her true purpose to this…this rake!

'Your gloves are in your reticule.' Sir Christopher held out an uncompromising hand. 'Allow me to demonstrate, my dear lady.'

'There is no need. And you will call me Mrs Wilkinson. I am not your dear or anyone else's dear or any other endearment you care to mention.' Hattie clutched the reticule to her chest. Panic clawed at her stomach. The gloves! How could he know? How would he twist the discovery?

'There is every need, *Mrs Wilkinson*.' Sir Christopher's tone hardened to well-tempered steel. 'Your reticule.'

Silently Hattie passed the beaded reticule over to him. Their fingers brushed and a single tremor of warmth ran up her arm. Ruthlessly, she suppressed it. A delayed reaction to all the gossip about his private life, that was all.

He weighed the reticule in his well-manicured hand as if trying to decide what to do. She prayed for a miracle and that he might suddenly reveal a handkerchief. He opened it and withdrew a pair of lace gloves with mulberry bows tacked to the cuffs.

'Very pretty they are, too. Or perhaps you have another pair and keep these for emergencies.'

'They are mine,' Hattie ground out, silently wishing him, his dark brooding eyes and his infuriatingly superior expression to the devil. 'I obviously forgot where I had placed them. I thank you for your assistance.'

'Always happy to oblige a lady.' He made an ironic bow. 'But you owe me a forfeit for finding them.'

'A forfeit?'

'The next dance.' Kit Foxton concentrated on Mrs Wilkinson. The woman with her carefully coiffured crown of blonde braids and severe dress needed to learn a light romance at a ball was something to be desired rather than condemned.

'Olivia, close your mouth,' the overbearing Mrs Wilkinson declared. Her skirts swirled as she turned, revealing surprisingly shapely ankles. 'Sir Christopher found my gloves. We shall be returning to the ballroom. Behave as if nothing has happened. Say nothing about this incident. Ever.'

'Such a simple stratagem, but I found your gloves.' Kit clenched and unclenched his fists. Mrs Wilkinson appeared to believe that she had the right to pass judgement on others' behaviour and to fashion the world how she wanted. He looked forward to proving her wrong. 'You may have them back once the forfeit is properly paid.'

Mrs Wilkinson gave a pointed cough. 'Olivia, the ballroom! Now!'

'What are you afraid of, Mrs Wilkinson? Why are you running when it is you who started this game?' he called out. 'Your reputation being ruined? It takes more than a few moments of pleasant conversation to sully a reputation as you must know.'

She froze, slipper dangling in mid-air. 'My reputation has never been in danger. Ever.'

'I'm pleased to hear it.'

She slowly turned to face him with her hands balled on her hips, blue-green eyes flashing with barely suppressed fury. 'It never will be. I would thank you to remember that.'

'You want to dance with my aunt? But she is a widow of seven years!' Miss Parteger clapped her hands together.

'Dancing is not forbidden to widows,' Kit said. A widow. Why did the knowledge not surprise him? The only shock was that she must have once experienced romance.

Kit frowned as Mrs Wilkinson turned her head to glare at her niece and he saw her long swanlike neck. The curious dead part of his soul that had been part of his existence for a year stirred and moved. Mrs Wilkinson had possibilities.

'We appear to be in a bit of a tangle here,' Mrs Wilkinson said, putting her hand on her hip. 'You will cease your funning this instant, Sir Christopher, and return my gloves.'

'They are safe in my care until the forfeit is paid. To the victor, the spoils.'

'Just wait until Mama hears about this,' Miss Parteger said, clapping her hands together. 'She will be at sixes and sevens with excitement. Aunt Harriet has a beau. Finally.'

'I would suggest, young lady, that you hold your tongue about this adventure.' Kit gave a cold nod. Mrs Wilkinson had lost. He knew it and, more importantly, she knew it. She would yield to his suggestion.

Miss Parteger blinked rapidly. 'Why?'

'Because if you don't, it will reveal you were somewhere where you shouldn't have been and your trip to London might become a distant dream,' Mrs Wilkinson replied without missing a beat. The colour drained from her niece's face. 'And, yes, Sir Christopher, I will dance with you, but it must be the next dance. I want this fanciful forfeit finished and this entire episode an unwelcome memory as soon as possible.'

Kit resisted the temptation to crow. There was no point in grinding one's opponent into the floor like his father used to. Kit didn't require abject humiliation, just total surrender.

Kit held out his arm and smiled at the overly confident Mrs Wilkinson. A waltz in this backwater would be too much to hope for. A simple quadrille which would allow him to put his hands on her waist was all he desired. Mrs Wilkinson needed this. She would thank him for it…later. 'Our dance awaits.'

As Hattie set foot in the ballroom, flanked by Livvy and Sir Christopher, the music ceased and the mass of humanity seethed around the dance floor as people exchanged greetings and partners.

Hattie breathed deeply and released Sir Christopher's arm. Tonight's adventure was finished. A solitary quadrille with Sir Christopher to prove her point, and she'd be finished. The dance would prove useful if Livvy was unable to resist confiding her adventure. She would merely claim that Sir Christopher had requested a dance and she'd agreed. No one needed to know the precise circumstances.

'Shall we?' She gestured with her fan towards the middle of the dance floor, well away from the chandelier and its dripping wax.

'This dance? Don't you want to know which one it is?'

'Why wait? Or are you a coward?' she called out. 'I wish to get this forfeit over.'

She was halfway across the dance floor when the master of ceremonies announced that the next dance would a German waltz. Hattie halted. A waltz? The next dance couldn't be a waltz. They never waltzed at Summerfield. A waltz would mean being in Sir Christopher's arms, looking up into his dark grey eyes. Impossible!

'It would appear I was wrong. It isn't a quadrille, but a waltz.' Hattie shrugged a shoulder and attempted to ignore the ice-cold pit opening in her stomach. 'Fancy that.'

'Is a waltz problematic?' he asked, lifting a quizzical brow, but his eyes gleamed with hidden lights.

'Such a shame. We agreed to a quadrille.' Hattie gave a falsely contrite smile. Escape. All she needed to do was to escape. He wouldn't come after her. He wouldn't create a scene. 'It has been a pleasure, Sir Christopher.'

She dropped a quick curtsy and prepared to move towards where Stephanie sat, surrounded by the other matrons, surveying the dance floor.

Sir Christopher reached out and grasped her elbow, pulling her close to his hard frame. 'Not so fast. We have an altogether different agreement.'

She tugged slightly, but he failed to release her.

'Have you gone mad? What in the name of everything holy are you doing?' she said in a furious undertone. 'All I wanted to do was to rescue Livvy from your godson. Nothing more.'

'You promised me the next dance, Mrs Wilkinson. A German waltz is the next dance.' He tightened his grip, sliding it down her arm until her hand was captured. He raised it to his lips. 'I hope you are the sort of woman who keeps her promises.'

Hattie hated the way his velvet voice slid over her skin, tempting her to flirt with him. Her traitorous body wanted to be held in his arms. But that would lead to heartbreak. She'd sworn off such men for ever. She concentrated on all the gossip about him—the women, the duels and the gaming—but her body stubbornly remained aware of him and the way his fingers held her wrist.

'I implied, rather than specifically promised. There is a difference,' she said, looking him directly in the eyes. 'You of all people should know the difference.'

'An implied promise remains a promise.' His full lips turned upwards. 'Consider what might have been, Mrs Wilkinson, before you reject me entirely.'

Hattie studied the wooden floor, scuffed with the

marks of a hundred dancing slippers, and concentrated on breathing steadily. Her entire being longed to say *yes*. Charm, that's all it was, just as it had been with Charles. Once she allowed herself to be swayed, she'd lose everything.

'I suspect you say that to everyone.' She gave a light laugh and her pulse started beating normally again. 'You've never seen me waltz.'

'Ah, you don't know how to waltz. You should have said rather than stooping to subterfuge.'

'Waltzing reached Northumberland several years ago.' Hattie put her hand on her hip. Talk about assumptions. Did she really look like a frumpy wallflower? When had that happened? 'I can and do waltz when the occasion demands. I simply prefer not to waltz right now.'

'Unfortunately, we can't always get what we want, Mrs Wilkinson. Here all I had intended to do was to dance with you. However, if you insist, we shall have a flirtation in the garden. My late uncle always said that northern women were bold, but until I met you, I had no idea.'

'Do such remarks cause the ladies in London to swoon at your feet? Up here, you are more likely to get a slapped face.'

'It is one of my more endearing traits. Impossible, but with a modicum of wit,' he said, giving her a hooded look. 'But will the lady waltz? Or is she a coward with two left feet?'

'I'll waltz with you, if only to prove you wrong about my dancing ability,' Hattie ground out.

'Hand on my shoulder now and we shall begin.'

His tone became rich velvet which slid over her skin. 'I promise you a dance to remember.'

'Are you a dancing master now? Is there no end to your many talents?'

'I endeavour to give satisfaction, particularly to the ladies.'

'Proprieties will be observed, Sir Christopher.'

'Did I suggest otherwise?' Kit stopped. The instant his hand had encountered hers, he'd felt an unexpected and searing tug of attraction. For over a year, he hadn't felt any attraction and suddenly this. Why her? Why this widow with an over-developed sense of propriety and hideous hairstyle? He had made it a policy not to be attracted to respectable women ever since Brighton.

'I'm pleased we hold the same view.'

'What can I ever have done to result in your censure?' he murmured, slightly adjusting his hand so it fit more snugly on her slender waist. Kit gave an inward smile as they circled the room. Mrs Wilkinson's lesson was proving more enjoyable than he first considered. He inched his hand lower. She gave him a freezing look and he returned to the proper hold.

'Your reputation preceded you, Sir Christopher.'

Kit could easily imagine what the village gossips were saying about him and his wicked past. There had been a time when he hadn't cared or appreciated what life could offer. He had gambled and whored with the best of them. He fought bad men with his bare hands. All that had ended a year ago when his best friend gave up his life for him and he'd become one of the walking dead.

'You have been listening to common tittle-tattle. That should be beneath you,' he said.

She tilted her head to one side and gave an unrepentant smile. 'When someone as notorious as you comes from London, his antecedents are discussed. It is the way of the world. Mr Hook is your protégé. He follows your methods, but fortunately for my niece, I happened along rather than one of the Tyne Valley gossips. Olivia will not suffer the fate of so many of your women.'

A blaze of anger went through Kit. She'd judged not only him, but also Rupert, on the basis of a few pieces of tittle-tattle. He renewed his determination to ensure that a full and complete flirtation happened. 'I'm no saint, Mrs Wilkinson, but neither am I a black-hearted villain. I have never ruined a débutante or indeed participated in the ruining of a débutante. Neither have I ever seduced a woman from her children or her husband. It is against my creed.'

'But they said...I'm sure...the stories...'

'Yes, I know the stories, but more importantly I know the truth. Do you? Have you ever been misjudged?'

She dipped her head, showing her intricately braided hair. Only the smallest curl dared escape. 'Perhaps I have been over-hasty in my judgement. I will accept your word that you would have said something if I had failed to come into the card room. And I'm wrong to punish you for another's actions.'

'Apology accepted. Shall we start again and endeavour to enjoy the dance?'

He pulled her waist closer to his body so that her skirt brushed his legs. Her hand tightened about his. His breath caressed the delicate curve of her shell-like ear. Her shoulder trembled under his fingers. He smiled inwardly. A little romance always brightened everyone's life. He looked forward to discovering Mrs Wilkinson's hidden depths.

'Will you give me a chance to prove the gossips wrong?' Kit asked quietly. 'Will you dance with me again or, better still, take a turn about the garden where I can plead my case?'

He waited for her breathless agreement.

'This is where the dance ends,' she said in a voice that left no room for dissent. She gave a small curtsy. 'We would hardly wish to cause a scandal. We are only strangers after all.'

'I must become a friend and discover what sort of scandal you have in mind,' Kit murmured. 'Be reckless. Further our acquaintance. You intrigue me.'

'One dance will have to satisfy you, Sir Christopher.' She stepped out of his arms. 'I bid you goodnight.'

She strode away, her hips agreeably swaying and her back twitching. Kit frowned. He had nearly begged for her favour. He never begged. His skills were rusty.

He patted his pocket where he'd placed the gloves. Their little romance was not over until he decided. Mrs Wilkinson had a lesson to learn and she would learn it…thoroughly. 'Until the next time, Mrs Wilkinson. Sweet dreams.'

Mrs Wilkinson paused, half-turned, then, appearing to think better of a retort, she resumed her march in double-quick time as if the devil himself was after her.

Chapter Two

'You left Sir Christopher Foxton standing on the dance floor even though the dance hadn't finished!' Mrs Reynaud said with a stifled gasp as Hattie reached the end of her highly edited tale the next morning. The sunlit parlour with its dimity lace curtains and artfully arranged ornaments was a world away from last night's splendours of the ballroom.

'It was the right thing to do.' Hattie reached for her teacup. There was little point in telling Mrs Reynaud about how her legs had trembled and how close she'd been to agreeing to his outlandish suggestion of a turn about the garden. She knew what he was, why she couldn't take a chance with him and still the temptation to give in to his charm had been there. Even after all she'd been through with Charles and his unreliability, a part of her had wanted to believe in romance and she refused to allow it to happen.

'Do you know you were the only lady he danced with all night?'

Hattie set the cup down with an unsteady hand. She could hardly confess to have been aware of Sir Christopher in that fashion. 'How do you know that *on dit*?'

'My maid had the news from the butcher's boy this morning,' the elderly woman said. 'Your waltz is the talk of the village. I've been in a quiver of anticipation. Thank you for telling me what truly happened, my dear. It makes my mind rest easier.'

Hattie kept her gaze focused on the way her papillon dog, Moth, was delicately finishing her biscuit, rather than meeting Mrs Reynaud's interested gaze. The whole point of the story was to enlist Mrs Reynaud's advice about Livvy's behaviour and how best to approach the talk she knew she'd have to give, rather than discuss her near-flirtation with the village's current most notorious resident.

Why was it that women lost their minds as soon as Sir Christopher's name was mentioned? Her sister had gone fluttery when Hattie returned from the dance floor, demanding to know how Hattie was acquainted with Sir Christopher. Hattie glossed over the card-room incident and Stephanie appeared satisfied.

'It was a waltz, nothing more,' Hattie said finally, seeking to close the matter. 'We had a brief verbal-sparring match. He dislikes being bested, but the game has ended. Honours to me.'

'Do you know how long Sir Christopher will be in the neighbourhood?' Mrs Reynaud handed Moth another biscuit. The little brown-and-white dog tilted her head to one side, waiting, but after Hattie nodded gobbled the biscuit up.

'He failed to confide his intentions.' Hattie stroked Moth's silky ears. Moth had come into her life just after Charles's death and for many months was the only bright spot. 'It has taken him over a year to visit his inheritance. Our paths won't cross again.'

'Predicting the future is always fraught with danger, my dear.' Mrs Reynaud brushed the crumbs into a pile for Moth. 'It does my heart good to hear news of him after such a long time, even if it's only for a short while.'

'Are you acquainted with him, then?' Hattie stared at the woman.

'I knew the family years ago. His late uncle arranged for me to have the lease on this house.'

'Perhaps he will call on you once he realises you are here.'

The colour faded from Mrs Reynaud's face, making the pockmarks stand out even more. 'My dear, I...I have changed a great deal since we last encountered each other.'

Instantly Hattie regretted her words. Over the last two years since Mrs Reynaud had taken up residency in the tiny cottage, she'd become accustomed to Mrs Reynaud's ruined features. 'An old friend never looks at faces. They are pleased to renew the friendship.'

'I doubt that he will remember me, whatever the state of his manners,' Mrs Reynaud said, raising a handkerchief to her face. 'Pray do not bother him with an old woman's remembrance of a past acquaintance. I was wrong to mention it. Ever so wrong.'

'Very well, I won't insist.' Hattie buried her face in Moth's fur. What was she doing, clutching at straws, searching for a way to encounter Sir Christopher again? Had her experience with Charles taught her nothing? A few minutes waltzing with a confirmed rake and she behaved worse than Livvy. 'It is a moot point as our paths are unlikely to cross.'

'Are you that ignorant of men? He forced a forfeit and waltzed with you and only you.'

'He did that for…for his own purposes,' Hattie explained. 'They say his mistresses are the most beautiful women London can offer. Why would he be interested in someone like me and my few charms?'

'You underestimate yourself, my dear, and that borders on foolishness.' Mrs Reynaud held out her hand. 'I merely wanted to point out that having done your duty to your fallen hero and mourned him properly, you can start to live again. But if your heart is for ever buried with your husband and you are one of the walking dead, then so be it. A pity with you being so young.'

Hattie swirled the remains of her coffee. Living again. She thanked God that Mrs Reynaud didn't know what her husband was truly like. The extent of his perfidy and hypocrisy had only emerged after his death.

Before then she had considered that she had a blissful marriage with someone utterly reliable and steadfast. She'd had no idea about his other family or the debts he'd run up. Thankfully, the woman in question had been discreet and she'd managed to scrape together the required amount. But no one else knew. She had her pride.

Sometimes she felt as if she was still living a lie, but she couldn't confess the full horror. Not now, not ever. It remained her problem and she didn't want false sympathy.

She opted for a bland, 'I hardly know what to say.'

'A light-hearted flirtation never did anyone any harm. Allow a little romance into your life. You're a handsome woman and should be aware of your power!

You should celebrate being alive, rather than running from it.'

Hattie focused on the tips of Moth's ears as Moth snuffled crumbs. Flirtations could harm people, if they believed in romance. That lesson was etched on her heart. 'I'll bear that in mind, should ever the question arise.'

'Oh dear, I fear I've shocked you. It's what comes from living abroad for such a long period.' The corners of Mrs Reynaud's mouth quirked upwards. 'You'll get over it in time and forgive me, I hope. I do so look forward to your visits. They are always the highlight of my day.'

'I should go to Highfield and see how Livvy fares before I go back home,' Hattie said, plopping Moth into the now-empty basket. Moth gave a sharp bark and placed her paws on the rim.

Although she loved her sister and nieces and nephews, Hattie maintained her own establishment—the Highfield Dower House at the edge of the Highfield estate. Her old nurse Mrs Hampstead served as her housekeeper. Close enough to be on hand if there was a crisis, but far enough to maintain her own life.

She had come to Northumberland shortly after Charles's death was confirmed. Her mother had died of a fever a few months before and her father of a broken heart, a week before Charles's things arrived.

She'd always been grateful neither of them knew of Charles's perfidy. She couldn't have hidden the truth from her mother.

When Stephanie's plea for help came, Hattie had considered it better than staying in London with her brother, the new viscount, and his wife. She had discovered a peace in Northumberland that she hadn't considered possible.

'You spend far too much time running around after your sister and her brood. She uses you as an unpaid lackey.'

'There may be flowers or notes,' Hattie said at Mrs Reynaud's look. 'And don't worry, I will tell you everything about Livvy's progress when I next visit. I think you are right, a quiet word and then tales about the wonders of a London Season should suffice.'

'Come tomorrow. I will regale you with tales about how I escaped from the harem. Lots of danger and excitement.'

A great longing to see far-flung places and experience life swamped Hattie. When she was a little girl, she used to watch the ships on the Thames and swear she'd go abroad some day. But the furthest she'd travelled was to Northumberland and now that had become home.

Now that Stephanie's children were nearly grown, she could start thinking about travelling. Doing things for herself rather than for others, but she still had to be aware of how her actions could affect the family. Outward appearances were everything. 'Did you really escape?'

'I feel the sheikh desired me more than I desired him. I was a great beauty once, you know.'

'You still have a beautiful soul, Mrs Reynaud.' Hattie covered Mrs Reynaud's hand and ignored the tear that trickled down Mrs Reynaud's face.

'You have no idea the mistakes I have made and how I've paid for them.' Mrs Reynaud's gnarled hands fumbled for a handkerchief. 'Sir Christopher... Remember, I specifically want to know when he departs from the neighbourhood.'

Hattie firmed her mouth. She wouldn't enquire into Mrs Reynaud's reasons, but she suspected they would both be relieved when he went. 'If I learn any more news about Sir Christopher, I'll tell you. I promise.'

The gravel crunched under Hattie's feet as she marched towards Highfield's rose garden. Despite the pile of unopened cards and several bouquets littering the drawing room, her sister and nieces were entertaining gentlemen callers in the rose garden.

Hattie knew she should have come earlier, but she had wanted to visit Mrs Reynaud and get her opinion before she acted. Surely Stephanie could cope with Livvy's high spirits for a few minutes? When the time was right, she intended to have a quiet word with Livvy. Romance at a ball was all well and good, but some day, you had to wake up and face the harsh reality of the morning after when the evening prince turned out to be an unreliable toad.

Moth gave a sharp bark, indicating she wanted out of the basket. Hattie set the basket down. Moth gave Hattie a quizzical look and wandered off to investigate the garden, but came racing back almost instantly and sat at Hattie's feet. Straight behind her strode Sir Christopher, his black coat and tan breeches gleaming in the sun. A gentleman caller with a difference.

'Ah, I had wondered if you were going to grace us with your presence, Mrs Wilkinson, before I managed to wear out my welcome.'

'Sir Christopher.' Hattie hoped any high colour would be attributed to her walk, rather than his nearness. Mrs Reynaud had put ideas in her head about flirtations. Not precisely true. Her sleep had been filled with dreams of them dancing where Sir Christopher spun her round and round as Charles stood in the shadows.

'Is the miscreant dog yours?' he asked. 'I caught her attempting to dig a hole in the borders. She is hardly bigger than a cat.'

'Yes, Moth is mine. She is a papillon.'

'A trained killer, rather than a butterfly.' Sir Christopher bent down and tickled Moth under the chin. Moth lifted her chin a notch higher before rolling over and exposing her belly. Moth gave a little whimper of pleasure as Sir Christopher obligingly stroked her belly.

Hattie belatedly realised she was staring and turned towards a stand of deep-blue delphiniums. 'An unexpected pleasure.'

'My godson was anxious to call on Miss Parteger, but my true purpose involves you.'

'Me?'

'The return of your gloves.'

Hattie winced. The gloves. How had she forgotten he had retained them until the blasted forfeit was over? 'Where are they?'

'Your sister has taken possession. She expressed surprise that you were so careless with her birthday gift.'

'It was good of you to return them.' Hattie kept her gaze carefully on the gravel path, rather than meeting his intense grey eyes. 'I'm sure my sister will hand them to me. She is very trustworthy in that regard.'

'I assumed they were precious to you. You were

very concerned when you mislaid them earlier in the evening.'

'That had a different purpose, as you rapidly guessed.'

'I know, but you neglected to finish your forfeit and collect your gloves. What does this say about you?'

Hattie winced, knowing she'd been the one to make the mistake and leave the dance floor so abruptly. She'd been foolish to give in to her anger and to forget that he held the gloves hostage last evening. It wasn't his fault that she'd once believed a night's romance at a ball would last for ever. All Sir Christopher had required was light conversation during the dance and a polite goodbye, something seven years ago she'd have done without considering the consequences. Instead she had behaved like the worst maiden aunt, storming off as if he had attempted to make love to her on the dance floor. 'The dance was over.'

'We shall have to examine another forfeit for leaving me bereft on the dance floor.'

'Have you spoken with your godson about his behaviour?' she said more tartly than she intended as she tried to banish the sudden image of Sir Christopher kissing her. She would not be agreeing to any sort of renewed forfeit.

'Rupert now understands the necessity of behaving properly if he desires to further his acquaintance with your niece. Your niece is very adept at the use of her fan. He had considered that she was older.'

A cold shiver went down Hattie's spine. She could just imagine. She knew all about Livvy's fascination with fan language for flirtation purposes. She'd warned Stephanie about it weeks ago. Obviously nothing had been done. The problem was how to discuss Livvy's use of the fan without revealing where she had been. 'Livvy is impetuous, but innocent. It was a game to her, to see if she could. Nothing more.'

His shadowy grey eyes locked on to hers. 'And was it a game for you, bursting in on them? Attempting to find evidence of a flirtatious game gone too far? Or is any flirtation too far for you?'

'My niece's reputation is paramount.' Hattie hugged her arms about her waist and tried to control the shiver. 'And anyway, why are you wandering about the grounds on your own?'

'Your sister is playing the chaperon while I attempt to find the cedar of Lebanon. As Rupert has decided he wants to do more than play infantile fan games with your niece, he needs to make a favourable impression on your sister.'

'Have you found the tree?' she asked brightly.

'I was on my way when your dog discovered me.' He checked his fob watch. 'A quarter of an hour to make a good impression is all Rupert requires.'

'You need to find the tree before your time is up. Truth in all things.'

'We reach complete understanding at last, Mrs Wilkinson.' A smile tugged at his features. 'It is part of my creed.'

Hattie shook her head. His charm was lethal. She was certain most women discounted his words and only focused on the seductive warmth in his voice. Listening to him, it was easy to understand why he enjoyed such a reputation with ladies. But she knew the trick—the words, not the tone, were important.

'You're going in the wrong direction,' she called as he started going towards the boating lake.

'Am I? How remiss of me.' A dimple shone in his cheek. 'Perhaps you will be kind enough to show me the proper way, Mrs Wilkinson? Getting hopelessly lost could ruin the entire matter. Consider it a fair exchange for leaving me on the dance floor.'

'When you put it that way, how can I refuse? Find the tree and all obligation will end.'

'Something like that,' Sir Christopher murmured.

Hattie placed her gloved hand on his arm. Every inch of her being hummed with awareness of him and the tantalising sandalwood scent he used. A pleasant conversation would not harm anyone, particularly as she remained in control. Mrs Reynaud was right. It was about time she started living, rather than hiding behind her widowhood.

'We should take the left-hand fork here,' he said.

She glanced at him under her lashes. His entire being radiated smugness. 'You engineered this walk! You know precisely where the tree is. Stephanie gave you directions.'

'Walks are more pleasant if there are two people, even if one of them has tendencies to be sharp-tongued.'

'I'm not. What is the point of having a mind if I can't speak it?'

'Never apologise. Women fall over themselves to falsely compliment me. You make a change.'

'Why were you in the card room?' she asked to keep her mind away from the potential rocky subject of comparing her to other women. 'You hardly seem to be the shy and retiring type. Were you waiting for a lady to appear? One of those who fall over at your compliments? Surely you can confess all to a sharp-tongued widow like me.'

He stopped abruptly in front of a spreading oak. All humour vanished from his countenance. 'You continue to do me a disservice, Mrs Wilkinson. I only ever pursue one lady at a time.'

The butterflies started beating inside her. *One lady at a time*. He had sought her out after the dance when he could have sent the gloves.

The news made her blood fizz and tingle.

She removed her hand from his arm and took a gulp of life-giving air. She was not going to start to believe in the illusion of romance again. Charles Wilkinson had for ever cured her of that. Sir Christopher had an ulterior motive, but he would be disappointed. She would show him that at least one woman would not tumble into his bed with the merest crook of his finger or a seductive laugh. Two could play this game. He would learn a lesson.

'Is that the only explanation I will get?' She forced her voice to sound playful. You'll trap more flies with honey than vinegar, she reminded herself.

'You require more?'

'The mystery intrigues me. Did you see the fan play between Mr Hook and my niece and know where the proposed liaison would happen?'

'I was not playing an errant knight. Alas.' Kit stopped and stared out into the garden with its low hum of bees and faint birdsong rather than at the soberly dressed woman who stood next to him. The scene contrasted so much with the thick mud and scent of gunpowder that had filled his nostrils a year ago. The feeling of being truly alive washed over him again.

The circumstances, rather than the company. Kit forced the brief panic down his throat. After his mother's departure when he was four and his later experience in Brighton, he'd vowed never to care about a woman. In any case, Mrs Wilkinson was far too severe for his taste. She wanted an explanation, she would get it. That would be an end of the matter.

'A year ago last Thursday, I attended a ball in Brussels. It was all gaiety, but like many other men I had to leave early. We went from the Duchess of Richmond's ballroom to the mud and stink of war. I returned, but many of my comrades didn't.' He waited for her to take the hint and politely change the subject.

'You were at Waterloo? As a soldier?' she asked, her eyes growing wide and luminous under her bonnet.

'I was at Waterloo,' he confirmed.

'No one ever mentioned you being in the Army. Not a single word.' She turned her head and all he could see was the crown of her impossible bonnet and the back of her shoulder.

'Does it bother you?'

'It is unexpected. I have heard stories…'

Kit could well imagine what was said of him. And for the vast majority of his life, he hadn't cared. It was far better to be thought heartless than to be ridiculed as someone whose mother couldn't love him, who had left his father because of him.

After Waterloo, it had changed. Brendan Hook had thought him a good enough friend to die for. London and his former pleasures lost their allure.

'It doesn't matter what others think. It has never

mattered,' he said. 'The battle only occupied a few hours of my life. Being in the Army lasted a few short weeks and then I went back to my usual haunts.'

'You are wrong to minimise it,' she said, turning back towards him. 'Very wrong. You played a part in a great victory. People will be celebrating Waterloo for years and you can say that you were there.'

Kit regarded her earnest face with its English-rose complexion, gazing up at him. She possessed a delicate beauty, he realised with a start. He wondered how he'd overlooked it before. But the highly conventional widow was also not his type.

Kit was very strict about the women in his life and his rules surrounding them. They asked for no more than he was prepared to give. They were experienced and knew the rules without them being clearly stated. He always ended it before emotions were involved.

Mrs Wilkinson was trouble, but he was also loath to leave before this lesson in mild flirtation finished.

He turned the conversation to more mundane subjects as they continued towards the tree. To his surprise, the conversation about gardens was far more enjoyable than he had considered possible at the start of the journey.

'Behold the tree. We can turn back now,' Mrs Wilkinson said as they rounded a bend.

'Yes, the tree. It is a magnificent sight.'

A gentle breeze moulded her skirt to her remarkably fine legs. Mrs Wilkinson possessed a far better figure than he'd first imagined. Kit struggled to keep his gaze on her face and not wonder why she had failed to remarry. None of his business.

'You keep changing the subject.' She laid a gloved

hand on his arm. 'Why keep your service a secret? Weren't you supposed to be there?'

'I rapidly acquired a lieutenant's commission in the Life Guards once I heard of Boney's escape and was lucky to get that. Everything was snapped up in days. The whole of London society seemed to be in Brussels last year. A number of friends couldn't even get a commission, but they came anyway. They got out when the fighting got too hot and left it to the proper soldiers.'

The green in her eyes deepened. 'But you stayed until the end. You didn't run, even though you are determined that I should think the worst of you. If you had run, it would have been the first thing you said.'

'I know how to be a soldier.' Kit's shoulders became light. Even without his saying it, she believed he'd done the right thing. He hated to think how few people ever believed that of him. It mattered. 'Eton prepares one for it.'

The memory of those long-ago days swept over him. Back then, he'd thought himself capable of anything. In his final year, he'd believed himself in love and that Constance Stanley would marry him once he asked her.

His illusions were shattered when he'd arrived at her house unexpectedly with the engagement ring in his pocket. He'd overheard her assessment of him as the son of two wicked people and how her family needed his money and how she'd feared that she would have to marry a devil. He had stepped out of the shadows. Constance's shocked face had said it all. All of his father's warnings thudded into him. He bid her and her companion good day and gave the ring to the first beggar woman with a baby at her breast that he saw.

Never again had he allowed himself to contemplate

marriage. Never again had he allowed a woman to get close, preferring to end the thing before it happened. Kit had a variety of presents he'd send—a bouquet to end a flirtation, a strand of pearls to end a brief but hugely enjoyable weekend, sapphires to end something longer.

Mrs Wilkinson turned her back on him and walked with quick steps over to the cedar. She stood there, unmoving for a moment, her brows drawn together in a frown. He waited for her to make a remark about the weather or society.

'Why aren't you down in London? With Rupert's father?' she asked.

He turned from her and stared towards where the great cedar towered over the garden. Everything was so peaceful and still, except for the distant cooing of a dove, calling to its mate. No danger here. This was the England he'd fought for, not the bright lights of London. He wanted that peace that had eluded him. He wanted to show that he had changed and that he did deserve a future, a future that he did not intend to squander. 'Rupert's father died.'

'I didn't know. I'm sorry for you and for Mr Hook.'

'False sympathy fails to matter. You never knew him.'

'You're wrong. Any man's death should be remarked on and he was your friend. You must miss him,' she said with an intense earnestness. 'When did you decide to come up to Northumberland?'

'When I was on the battlefield, surrounded by men dying on either side, I swore that next year I would be somewhere which epitomised what I was fighting for.' The words came from deep within him. He wanted her to understand that on the battlefield he'd decided what was important and how his life needed to change. She, of all the people he'd met recently, might understand and the very thought unnerved him. 'I thought of the fair, the Stagshaw Bank Fair, and how it is held every year on the fourth of July.'

Her dusky-rose lips turned up into an incredulous smile. 'You are asking me to believe that you decided to come to Northumberland when you were at Waterloo? I can think of a dozen other more likely places that should have sprung to mind.'

'It seemed as good a place as any to my fevered mind. When I was a lad, my uncle brought me here. The day has long stood in my memory. He bought me a wooden jumping-jack.' He shook his head.

There was no need to explain that it had been the first time since his mother's departure that he'd received a gift or anyone had taken notice of him beyond cuffing him on the ear. He'd kept that jumping-jack for years, hidden in his handkerchiefs so that his father would not stumble across it and destroy it.

'It seemed like a place worth fighting to see again. I said as much to Brendan, who was on my right—*there will be time enough to reminisce as the years go by, but next year I would be up in Northumberland and would go to the fair.* He agreed to go with me.'

'And that is why you and Mr Hook are here,' she breathed. 'To honour your vow.'

Kit closed his eyes and said a prayer for Brendan's soul. He had said enough. She didn't need to know the rest. He'd asked Brendan to exchange places with him because he thought he'd get a better shot. Brendan had agreed with a laugh and a clap on his back. The next thing he'd heard was the soft thud of a bullet hitting Brendan in the chest. Brendan's last words were about his son and his hopes for Rupert's future. Kit had promised and he intended to keep that promise.

'But he would have been here. We made a vow together.'

'Is it why Rupert is with you? To fulfil his father's vow?' She tilted her head to one side. 'It would appear that I misjudged Mr Hook. There are not many men who would have done that.'

'His mother died soon after he was born.' Kit stared at the grass. There was no need to explain that Rupert's mother had been a courtesan and they had only married on her deathbed, at Brendan's insistence. Seventeen and a widower with a baby. Brendan always claimed his heart had died with the woman. Kit tended to counter that at least he had a heart. 'Rupert's grandmother took charge of the boy, but she died shortly after hearing of her son's death. I promised her that I'd make sure her grandson would become the fine man that his father wanted him to be.'

He willed her to understand his reasoning.

'I hope the fair lives up to your expectations.'

He forced a smile. 'I'm sure it shall. Anyway, I was invited along with Rupert to the ball, but I found I needed time alone to reflect, particularly as they had played a reel that I remember from the Duchess of Richmond's ball. I went to the card room for a few moments and found a book. You know what happened next.'

'I'm sorry for not believing you.' She took a step closer to him. Her dark-red lips softly parted.

'It doesn't matter.' He knew he lied. It mattered

more than he wanted it to. 'It is in the past. I rarely think about the past.'

'It was my fault. I rushed away from the dance floor,' she whispered, putting her hand on his arm. 'We should have had the second dance. I would have if...if I'd realised about your past.'

'Never do something because you feel sorry for a person.' He covered her hand with his. Their breath laced. He knew that all he had to do was to lean forwards a few inches and her mouth would yield. He was surprised that he wanted to. But for the lesson in flirtation to be complete, the movement needed to come from her. He'd be magnanimous in the lecture which he gave her later.

'Aunt Hattie, Aunt Hattie! I know you are here. Moth found me. We have visitors! You will never guess. Livvy has an admirer!' a young voice called.

Mrs Wilkinson jumped back and her cheeks flamed bright red. 'I need to see my niece. You do understand the propriety of the thing.'

Kit forced his hands to his sides. His little lesson in flirtation was proving more enjoyable than he'd considered. He would see where the game led. 'No one is preventing you.'

Chapter Three

Hattie picked up her skirts and ran to the rose garden, not daring to look behind her and see if Sir Christopher was following. If Portia hadn't shouted, she would have kissed him. Her lips ached with longing. It went against everything she had promised herself and yet she didn't feel ashamed, only disappointed. The next time... Hattie stopped and pressed her fingers to her temples. There would be no next time. Sir Christopher had explained why he was in the card room. The matter was finished. She'd survived. Hattie picked up speed as if the devil himself was after her.

As she reached the rose garden, Portia hurtled into her, throwing her arms about her. 'You will never guess who is here!'

Hattie disentangled herself from the hug and regarded her favourite niece who was four years younger than her sister, Livvy, and still far more interested in four-legged creatures than young men. Her pinafore had a series of smudges and a solitary wisp of hay clinging to the hem. Hattie knew despite her mother's orders Portia had spent time in the stables, helping out.

She always kept a tit-bit in her pocket when Moth

came to call. It was no surprise to Hattie that Moth had gone wandering off to find her treat, but a small part of Hattie wished she hadn't and that she and Sir Christopher had remained under the cedar tree. Alone.

'Sir Christopher and Mr Hook,' Hattie answered, putting away all thoughts of kisses from Sir Christopher. It wasn't going to start.

If she ever was attracted to any man again, it would be to someone who was steady, sober and scandal free, someone who was completely different from Charles Wilkinson. Not someone who lived and breathed sin. If Charles Wilkinson had a dark wild side which no one knew about until it was too late, then Sir Christopher was midnight-black wild through and through. She forgot that at her peril. Sir Christopher was not a man to be relied on. A man whose wit and conversation were to be enjoyed rather than to be thought of as a life's partner.

'Sir Christopher wanted to return my gloves from last night and Mr Hook came along for accompaniment.'

Portia's plump face fell. 'You knew? How!'

'Aunts know these sorts of things. Little birds.'

'I've the honour of being the little bird,' Sir Christopher said, coming to stand by her, a bit closer than strictly proper. His stock was ever-so-slightly undone and she glimpsed the strong column of his throat. Hattie hurriedly pretended an interest in the roses. 'Your aunt met me, Miss Portia, and kindly showed me the cedar of Lebanon's location.'

Portia beamed back at Sir Christopher, her entire countenance lighting up under his voice's spell.

'There, you see,' Hattie said, putting an arm about

her niece's shoulders and turning her away from Sir Christopher. 'All is explained.'

'How did you find the cedar tree, Sir Christopher? Does it approach the magnificence of your boyhood home or surpass it?' her sister, Stephanie, called out from where she sat in the rose garden with a silver teapot by her side. On her other side perched Mr Hook, looking much like an overgrown schoolboy. Livvy appeared all young innocence in her light-blue muslin gown, but the tips of her ears glowed pink. Hattie hated to think how quickly that sort of innocence vanished.

'I found what I was looking for, yes.' Sir Christopher gave Hattie a searing look.

Hattie resisted the temptation to explore the renewed aching in her lips. No one could brand with just a look. She clenched her fists. She was not going to behave like a fool again. Heady romance was an illusion that she could ill afford.

'I discovered Sir Christopher and kept him on the right path.' Her voice squeaked on the word path. Hattie cleared her throat. 'It was the charitable thing to do.'

Stephanie, who looked like an older and plumper version of Livvy, held out the gloves with a superior smile. 'How clever of you to visit this morning, Hattie…particularly as Sir Christopher thought you'd be here. I wonder how that came about?'

A distinct air of accusation rang in Stephanie's voice. She thought Hattie had arranged all this! Sir Christopher wore a smug expression as if it was precisely the outcome he'd hoped for. Hattie shifted uneasily. Why did he want anyone to think they had a flirtation? She could hardly be the type of woman with whom he generally flirted.

'I'll take possession of them. They have caused a great deal of trouble.' Hattie plucked them from Stephanie. A faint scent of sandalwood caressed her nostrils. She hurriedly stuffed them in her basket. When she arrived back at the Dower House, she would put them in her bottom drawer, never to be worn again.

'You really are too careless, Hattie. Those gloves were a *gift*. I spent hours getting those bows correct. First you mislaid them at the ball and then you place them in the basket all higgledy-piggledy.' Stephanie carefully poured a cup of tea. 'You were always the careless one of the family. When will you ever grow up and take responsibility for your actions?'

Sir Christopher cleared his throat. 'I was grateful for the excuse to call.'

'Will you and your godson be in the Tyne Valley long?' Stephanie asked in a speculative tone.

'It depends on a number of things.'

'It will depend on Aunt Harriet, that is what Sir Christopher means,' Portia said, bristling with self-importance.

'What on earth are you talking about, Portia?' Stephanie asked with an arched brow.

'Aunt Harriet is in the midst of a flirtation with Sir Christopher,' Portia burst out, her entire being quivering with excitement. 'Last night in the card room at Summerfield as well as today beside the cedar. Livvy told me. She swore me to secrecy, but that's why Sir Christopher kept the gloves. Why will no one tell the truth?'

'Out of the mouths of babes,' Sir Christopher said in a low tone.

'Next time I want to go, Mama. Things happen at balls. Please, Mama. Pretty please.'

'You are twelve, Portia,' Livvy replied with crushing firmness. 'You have years to wait.'

Portia stuck out her tongue.

'Portia, you know it is wrong to repeat tales, particularly highly embroidered ones,' Hattie said before either of her nieces uttered another damning phrase or their squabbling descended into all-out war. 'Sir Christopher has returned the gloves and seen the famous tree. His time will be required elsewhere. Do not seek romance where there is none, young Portia.'

Sir Christopher showed no inclination to take her hint and to depart. If anything, he seemed to be amused at her discomfort. He sat down and accepted the cup of tea that Stephanie held out. 'Fascinating place. Northumberland. My godson and I look forward to attending the Stagshaw Bank Fair.'

'Oh, the fair. Of course, I should have guessed the reason for you being here.' Her sister leant forwards. 'Mrs Wrigglesworth said it true when we first heard of your arrival—Stagshaw Fair attracts all sorts of people. Everyone had wondered. But hopefully having seen the delightful entertainment Northumberland has to offer, you can be persuaded to stay longer.'

Hattie bit her lip. Stephanie was up to something. She could feel the sense of impending doom creeping up her spine. She dismissed it. Stephanie knew of Sir Christopher's reputation. She'd never dare.

'I'm sure Sir Christopher is fully capable of finding entertainment to occupy his time,' Hattie said, seeking to end the discussion. 'We mustn't presume, Sister.'

'My godson and I would be delighted to take a full

part in the village life while we are here. The estate I inherited has been neglected for far too long. And the company is utterly charming.' He inclined his head. The twinkle in his eyes deepened. 'We should go for a picnic out to Stagshaw to see what it is like before the fair. A local guide would prove of great assistance.' His voice became silken smooth. 'Would tomorrow suit, Mrs Wilkinson?'

Hattie's mouth went dry. There should be a thousand different reasons why she should refuse, but she heard herself say, 'Tomorrow would be wonderful.'

'Then it is all settled. Tomorrow at noon.'

'We will all go.' Hattie looked at Livvy, who suddenly straightened her back and blushed a violent pink at the hopeful glance Mr Hook gave her. Now that she knew Mr Hook was properly interested in making an honourable offer she was prepared to help. They did deserve a chance to get to know each other better, properly supervised. A picnic was hardly a debauched party. 'Livvy and Portia love picnics. It will make for a splendid expedition. You were saying just the other day, Stephanie, how we ought to picnic more often now that the fine weather had arrived.'

'Then it is settled. The day will be much brighter for the presence of all the ladies here.'

'Oh dear!' Stephanie banged her cup down. 'Tomorrow is no good at all. Far too much is on. Livvy and Portia have their dancing class. And I will be required at the Corbridge Reading Rooms. Colonel Cunningham will be thrilled to learn that we now have the world expert on newts in our midst. An illustrated lecture must be organised before Mr Hook departs.'

'Please, there is no need,' Mr Hook said, turning a

violent red. 'It is nothing. My research is at an early stage.'

'I disagree, Mr Hook.' Stephanie raised an imperious hand. 'You mustn't be allowed to hide your light under a cloak of false modesty. You've informed me about your prowess and this must be shared with the neighbourhood. Immediately, before the schedule is cast into iron. There is a committee meeting tomorrow which I must attend.'

'Stephanie!' Hattie glared at her sister. Stephanie enjoyed the kudos of being on the village hall committee, but hated actually doing any work. She always produced the flimsy excuses to avoid the meetings where events like lectures were decided. 'We're talking about an invitation to a picnic, rather than this summer's lecture series schedule, which was decided weeks ago.'

'You must go of course, Hattie. You gave your word.' Stephanie waved a vague hand in the air. 'I feel certain that Sir Christopher and his godson understand why I must decline. Mr Parteger told the Colonel the other day that the lecture series was looking a bit thin. And the Colonel had the temerity to blame me. Schedules are made to be altered.'

Mr Hook turned a sickly greenish-yellow. 'I've not lectured before. I've no plans.'

'Then you must start. How else will you get on in this world? Mr Parteger has always said that we must have educated men as Livvy's suitors.'

'In that case, I...I would be honoured.' Mr Hook mirrored a tomato for colour.

Hattie curled her fists and attempted to ignore Stephanie's triumphant look.

'Of course, I will go on the picnic.' Hattie turned

towards Sir Christopher. 'I would be delighted to accompany you and Mr Hook. Mr Hook can plan his lecture there.'

The flecks in Sir Christopher's eyes deepened. 'The picnic will be all the more memorable for it.'

Kit relaxed against the carriage seat, going over the morning events. It had unfolded differently than he'd planned, but not disastrously. After the picnic, he decided, he would send the flowers. He wanted to see Mrs Wilkinson fully blossom and realise the error of her censorious ways.

If he stopped prematurely, she would revert and cause her nieces problems. The lesson needed to be learnt thoroughly. Kit enjoyed the sense of goodness which radiated from his decision to take Mrs Wilkinson on the picnic.

'Do you care to explain precisely what happened while I was exploring the garden, Rupert?' Kit asked to keep from thinking about the precise shape of Mrs Wilkinson's mouth. 'How did you end up with a possible lecture engagement for a subject that you have never professed an interest in? Do you even know what a newt looks like?'

Rupert tugged at his neckcloth. 'Of course I know what a newt looks like. They are a type of amphibian, have four legs and a tail.'

'Is there some reason for Mrs Parteger to suspect that you are a world expert on newts?'

'I needed to say something to mark me out from the crush.' Rupert's ears turned pink. 'Miss Parteger is an angel. Two more bouquets arrived when you were touring the garden. I was desperate. Then I remembered how Miss James's father dismissed me as a know-nothing. It was not going to happen again. My tongue rather ran away with me. Newts were the first thing to pop in my brain.'

'You are now committed to giving a lecture about a subject you know nothing about. How is that going to impress anyone?'

'But I love her! I want to be with her. I know you will think me mad, but it is how I feel about her.' He thumped his chest. 'Sometimes, you know in here. The instant you see her. It was as if I had been waiting all my life and she walked into the room.'

Something inside Kit twisted. Rupert had no idea about love. It was calf-love like he'd experienced with Constance, something that burned bright and fierce and vanished. And when it went, it hurt like the very devil. Every boy goes through it in order to become a man. And now he was a man, he protected that vulnerable bit of him so he would not get hurt again.

'You don't know what you are saying, Rupert. You hardly know her. How long will it last? Do you remember what you said about Miss James?'

'That was different.' Rupert flicked his fingers. 'I was merely a boy of nineteen.'

'You are only twenty!'

'What were you like when you were my age?'

'Young and foolish. Luckily your father stopped me before the folly went too far.' Kit shook his head. Never again would he allow a woman to share his secrets. All Constance had done was to mock him about his parents' scandalous past. 'I thanked him for it later.'

'Do you ever see her?'

'Who?'

'The woman who broke your heart? The one my father used to mention in his cups.'

'Your father was right. My broken heart lasted until the next dance when I found another lady who welcomed my attention.' Kit forced a laugh. His heart had been broken long before when his mother refused to look at him, despite his pleading, as she went out the door and his life. He'd settled for something less and kept his patched-up heart protected.

'Surely your heart was truer than that!'

'What heart? Didn't you know I'm heartless? How many women have despaired of taming me and thrown the accusation at me when I ended the affair?'

'My father didn't think that. He used to say—'

Kit held up his hand, stopping Rupert's words. 'Whatever he said, he said in confidence. Your father had a unique way of looking at life.'

'I wish he was here,' Rupert whispered.

'Your father asked me to look after you.' Kit glanced up at the carriage's ceiling, regaining control. 'I'm offering my advice. You keep your word. If you are determined to give this lecture, you study. My uncle did have an interest in amphibians and his papers and books are in the library. They should be enough to enable you to give an account of yourself. And you never make a false claim again. Lying never makes for a happy relationship.'

Rupert hung his head. 'Now you are committed to going on a picnic with The Widow.'

'Which I plan to enjoy.' Kit frowned. The lesson in flirtation was going better than he'd hoped. It would be one that Mrs Wilkinson would not soon forget. She might not thank him for it, but her two charming nieces might benefit. 'I could not have arranged matters better.'

'You and Mrs Wilkinson…but she is so old.'

'She is younger than I am.'

Rupert screwed up his face and stared out the window. 'I had always thought…they tell stories about you and the beauties. Mrs Wilkinson will never be a toast of London.'

Kit tapped his fingers together. He refused to indulge in speculation about Hattie Wilkinson's beauty. Rupert would not understand that it was precisely the point. Hattie Wilkinson possessed a refreshing charm that hadn't been powdered and primped to an inch of its life.

'One final lesson for today, Rupert. Never discuss a lady. Ever.'

'What precisely is going on, Stephanie?' Hattie asked once her nieces had been otherwise occupied with refurbishing their bonnets. For the first time in a long while, Livvy had expressed an interest in improving her mind, but the suggestion had been firmly quashed by her mother.

'Whatever can you mean, dear?' Stephanie looked up from where she was sorting out a variety of ribbons. 'I do hope you are not going to be tiresome, Hattie, and ruin your chances again. Simply because you had a wonderful marriage that was cut cruelly short does not mean you will not find happiness again.'

Hattie sighed. Her decision not to tell anyone about the full extent of Charles's betrayal did make for awkward moments. Stephanie refused to believe that her marriage was anything other than breathtakingly romantic. And this was the second lecture she had received today about making more of her life. Why didn't anyone understand that she was content as she was?

'This is Sir Christopher Foxton! Are you aware of his reputation? Marriage won't be on offer, if he has anything beyond mere politeness in mind.' Hattie clasped a hand to her chest and tried to regain control of her emotions. 'There, are you satisfied? I've said it. He is notorious in the extreme. He will be after more than an innocent conversation.'

'Why did he visit me and take pains to be correct?' Stephanie rolled her eyes. 'He brought the flirtation out in the open rather than hiding it behind closed doors. No man wants to remain a bachelor for ever.'

'You are mistaken, Sister. Some men are determined to remain bachelors. They are far from safe in carriages or conveyances of any kind. And Sir Christopher is first amongst them.'

'Sir Christopher seems very pleasant, rather sweet.' Stephanie crossed her hands in her lap and gave one of her Madonna-like smiles, which always grated on Hattie's nerves. 'On the other hand Mr Hook was painfully ill at ease. He droned on about his blessed newts. I doubt he even knows what women are.'

'You dislike Mr Hook's shyness?' Hattie stared at her sister in astonishment. She had anticipated Stephanie's objecting to Rupert Hook on the grounds of his association with Sir Christopher, but not because of his timidity. 'I believe you're wrong about the man. He has an abundance of confidence.'

'I dare say he will do for a chaperon for this picnic of yours or you can take Mrs Hampstead if you wish to have conversation on subjects other than amphibians. The man will not be moved. I did try.'

'Surely it is better for Livvy to realise what a bore Mr Hook is rather than to sigh for the love of his fine eyes. You can allow Livvy to accompany me,' Hattie said firmly, giving her final argument.

'Hattie, I do despair. Livvy is too young for such things.' Stephanie made a superior clucking noise. 'Sir Christopher Foxton pursues you. You should allow yourself to be caught and then force the marriage. It is how it is done.'

'You've muddled everything, Stephanie. The visit was about Mr Hook properly courting Livvy, rather than Livvy arranging clandestine meetings with her fan.'

'Pshaw!' Stephanie slammed her hand down on the table. 'My little Livvy would never do such a thing. Besides, Mr Hook was not acquainted with Livvy until today. Sir Christopher formally introduced him.'

With a heavy heart, Hattie rapidly explained the events of last evening, emphasising that Sir Christopher had only danced with her to prove a point about making assumptions. A forfeit, nothing more and then she'd left him standing on the dance floor.

'According to your tale, Sir Christopher was already chaperoning. Why was he there if not to ensure that nothing untoward happened to my dear girl? I do declare that people have done him a grave disservice in the past. He is the most perfect of gentlemen. I refuse to hear another disparaging word said against him.' Stephanie leant forwards and gestured with her fan. 'That is the end of the matter. Sometimes I worry that you became a walking ghost after your husband died.

Why not enjoy the fun of a mild flirtation? After all, it is not as if you don't know where the boundaries lie.'

Hattie pinched the bridge of her nose. The conversation was starting to spin out of control. She refused to confess after all these years. At first it had been far too hard and Stephanie had never enquired. Her throat had swelled every time she thought about Charles and how he'd used her, how she'd stood mourning at his grave, bereft, and then had discovered about his other family, the woman he'd loved. And she had felt so stupid.

Her whole idyllic life had been a lie. Never again would she make the mistake of loving someone who could not love her back. Her blood ran cold every time she considered it.

'You would have to ask him why he was in that card room.'

'And you should ask yourself why he chose to dance with you and then to invite you specifically on a picnic. Now shall we speak about the colour of ribbon you will wear on your bonnet to this picnic?'

Hattie ignored Stephanie's peace offering. 'Why do you want me to go on this picnic alone? Do you truly want me to ruin my reputation?'

'You are a sensible widow of twenty-seven who learnt your lesson years ago. If it had been anyone but Charles in that summer house, I shudder to think what would have happened. He worshipped the ground you walked on back then… It was utterly romantic. Your wedding when you fainted at the altar was so…so special. Then he had to leave to go to the front and wrote you such beautiful letters. They made me weep when you showed them to me.'

'Yes, I was lucky there.' Hattie fought to keep the irony out of her voice.

Stephanie smiled. 'I want you to have your last chance at a second marriage. Go on the picnic with Sir Christopher without distractions.'

'Livvy and Portia are not distractions.'

'I, too, remember last year when Portia put the lizard in Dr Hornby's tea. He had planned to propose to you that day. Portia and Livvy never gave you that chance.'

Hattie hid a smile. It had taken her the better part of three hours to capture that lizard. 'It happened for the best, Sister.'

'Hmmph.'

Stephanie in these moods was insensible to reason and ever likely to come up with more transparent schemes for entrapping Sir Christopher into marriage. Hattie gave an involuntary shudder.

There was no hope for it. She refused to sit here and allow herself to become embroiled in one of Stephanie's projects.

She would have to go and explain to Sir Christopher the dangers. He had to understand why the picnic and any hint of intimacy was an impossibility. And she had to do it before she lost her nerve.

Hattie clicked her fingers. 'Moth, we are going.'

Her sister's face creased. 'Hattie, I am only doing this because I love you and want you to be happy. You need someone in your life. You looked happy when you arrived in the rose garden. Your cheeks were bright pink.'

'I like my life with Moth, with Mrs Hampstead and with you and your children.' She raised her chin. She refused to go back to that needy deluded girl who believed romance happened when two people's glances met across a crowded room. Going on a picnic with Sir Christopher was not going to happen.

'Hattie…'

'It satisfies me. Do not tell me otherwise.' Hattie hoped Stephanie believed her words because she was less than sure.

Hattie stood in the gloomy panelled hall of Southview Lodge. A variety of stuffed birds peered down at her. All the way here, she had planned her speech. Somehow it seemed right to explain the situation in person rather than writing a letter. Sir Christopher had to know what Stephanie was trying to do and why it would never work. The solution had come to her as she tramped home over the fields. Sir Christopher needed to know about her sister's machinations.

She had deposited Moth with Mrs Hampstead before driving the governess cart to Southview. She intended on handling this problem on her own without interference from Moth and her penchant for investigating.

'Mrs Wilkinson, what a pleasant surprise.' Sir Christopher came out of his study. His stock was undone and he was in his shirtsleeves. His black hair swooped down over one eye. Despite her intentions of being aloof, a curl of warmth twined its way around her insides.

Hattie inclined her head and was pleased her straw poke bonnet shadowed her face. 'Sir Christopher, I do hope you will forgive the intrusion.'

'I wasn't expecting any visitors. My uncle's affairs

are in a bigger tangle than I had anticipated. He appears to have used a code…' He ran a hand through his hair, making it stand on end. 'But as you are here, you must stay and have a cup of tea. Come into the drawing room.'

'My sister was rude in proposing that Mr Hook lecture,' Hattie began before she lost her nerve. 'Take no notice of her. She became dreadfully confused and believes Mr Hook is a shy newt-fancier who needs bringing out.'

'Is this a problem?'

'Is he…a newt-fancier? A world authority? He appears awfully young for such a thing.'

The corners of his mouth twitched. Hattie risked a breath. She might not have to confess about Stephanie's other machinations after all.

'Rupert confessed. He misjudged the moment. Rupert shall be spending all his time studying the habits of newts until the lecture. He should know better than to lay false claim.'

'He doesn't know.' Hattie clapped her hand over her mouth. 'Oh dear. Just before I left the Dower House, Livvy arrived, looking for books on amphibians.'

Their shared laughter rang out.

His eyes turned sober. 'You didn't come all the way here simply to tell me about Rupert's folly. Out with it, Mrs Wilkinson. What else was your sister attempting to do? Why must I be wary?'

Chapter Four

He knows. Hattie's heart sank. Sir Christopher had known about Stephanie's intention all along. She twisted the handle of her reticule about her fingers and wished she was anywhere but here in Sir Christopher's hallway. She had made a mistake in thinking he was naïve or at best unaware. He was no fool, but a hardened and experienced rake. He must have foiled hundreds of marriage schemes in his lifetime.

Her first instinct was to slink away, but she had started so she had to continue—no matter how much she wanted the ground to rise up and swallow her.

'My sister wishes to play the matchmaker. You and I.' Hattie tried for a sophisticated laugh, but it came out strangled. 'How ridiculous! Anyone can see how ill-suited we are. I like to speak my mind too readily and you…you…well, you have a certain appetite for life.'

A flash of something—sorrow, disappointment?—crossed his face, but it was gone before she could really register it was there and his face became a bland mask.

'I would have used a different word,' he said.

'Stephanie refused the picnic invitation so that you would be forced to take me on my own. She knew I would never be rude and find a threadbare excuse to call it off.'

'Why did she think her being there would be an impediment?'

'My sister unfortunately recalled that I once used my nieces to sabotage her previous efforts.' Hattie knew her words were coming much too fast, tumbling over one another like a cart picking up speed as it careened down a perilous slope. 'A childish trick. I should have seen the possibility before it happened and saved everyone the embarrassment. What I was thinking…who knows?'

'Perhaps you were thinking that a picnic with me would be a pleasant way to pass an afternoon.' His grey eyes flashed. 'A picnic, Mrs Wilkinson, is not an invitation to a debauched party. Nor is it a prelude to sticking your neck through the parson's noose.'

'The expedition should be called off. Immediately.'

'Why?'

'Because it will encourage Stephanie and her folly,' Hattie said weakly, trying not to think about the way his mouth looked or how his eyes sparkled. A note giving a bland reason would have been simpler.

'I'm more than delighted to be spending time with you, Mrs Wilkinson. The arrangement suits me very well.'

'Does it?' Hattie gulped. She refused to consider that Sir Christopher might actually be attracted to her. The notion was completely absurd. She lacked the attributes that men like him prized. He had an ulterior motive. He had to. Her head pained her slightly.

'Had I thought you'd accept without your family for chaperons, I'd have proposed the current arrangement in the first place. For Rupert it was desolation but for me it is serendipity.' He lowered his voice. 'I take it you will bring your dog as a chaperon. It is always best to have a solitary chaperon…it provides cover.'

'My husband died at Talavera, Sir Christopher.' Hattie focused on a picture of an English castle which hung on the wall behind his right shoulder. It was easier to say the words when she wasn't looking at his face. She tightened her grip on her reticule. She refused to tell him the truth about the sham of a marriage and her humiliation, but he had to understand that whatever game he was attempting to play stopped here. 'I have no wish for another.'

'Marriage has never been one of my aspirations, Mrs Wilkinson. My parents were exceedingly unhappy. I trust you understand me.'

Hattie gave a little nod. She had thought as much, but the plain statement caused a tiny bubble of disappointment to flood through her. Just once she would have liked to have been wrong and for Sir Christopher to have had honourable intentions.

A tiny voice in the back of her mind whispered that he was the sort of man to make a woman believe in romance. She ignored it. That sort of thinking belonged to another woman. She knew what her responsibilities were. She liked her life as it currently was. She knew what was important to her. Free love was for women like Mrs Reynaud and her sheikh, not her.

'Thank you for being frank, Sir Christopher.' She met his gaze full on, never flinching or wavering. 'I must also inform you that I've no intention of our acquaintance becoming more intimate. I enjoy my current reputation and wish to maintain it. In the circumstances…'

'More intimate?' His grey eyes became flecked with a thousand lights. 'You do like putting the cart before the horse, Mrs Wilkinson. Most women wait to be asked. I shall allow you the opportunity to change your mind should the subject ever come up.'

'I find my sister's attempts at matchmaking intensely irritating.' Hattie quickly concentrated on the black-and-white tiles of the entranceway, rather than giving in to the temptation to drown in his eyes. 'Her schemes made my life a misery throughout the years until I found a way to halt them. Why should I have to seek another husband? There is no law against being a widow.'

He tilted his head to one side, his eyes coolly assessing her. 'Your husband must have been a lucky man. To have someone so devoted after his death.'

'He was a man in a million.' Hattie attempted to look pious and sorrowful. She had already had her folly with Charles. She had swallowed whole the lies of instant adoration, love and eternal devotion that dripped from his lips that night in the summer house.

She had continued to believe in the false illusionary world where she was the very heart of his universe until she had sorted his private papers, which arrived after his death. The stark black ink tore the illusion from her soul.

It was then she learnt what he truly thought of her, how another woman had had his regard and his joy at the birth of his son, a son he'd fathered after their marriage. That had been the hardest thing—reading about his joy at the birth and knowing how much she'd longed to have a child.

'I have no desire to change your mind. I only wish to go on a picnic with you.'

'And I should accept your word?' she asked. 'Without questioning it?'

His eyes flashed. 'I may be many things, Mrs Wilkinson, but I am no liar. Nor do I take advantage of unwilling women. Nothing will happen on this picnic that you do not desire.'

'Then I have no choice but to accept your assurance that the picnic will be between friends.' Hattie hated the way her heart jumped. The gloomy mood that had plagued Hattie on the way over vanished. Sir Christopher wanted to go on the picnic with her, despite knowing about Stephanie's machinations. She swallowed hard. Stephanie would not give up. The picnic would only embolden her. 'What am I to do about Stephanie? I've no wish for you to become burdened or embarrassed.'

He took a step closer. 'A determined matchmaker needs to have a concrete reason to desist. You and I know of her intent and we can counter it…if we work together. If done properly, your sister might learn a valuable lesson. The world needs fewer meddlesome matchmakers. We will be doing a service to society.'

'Why are you willing to do this?' Hattie put her hand to her throat. She could see the sense in Sir Christopher's scheme but… She shook her head. 'You gain nothing.'

'Except the pleasure of your company for a few hours.' His eyes danced with a myriad of greys.

Hattie attempted to control the sudden fluttering of

her insides. Mrs Reynaud had been completely wrong. Like most men of his ilk, he was probably attracted to sophisticated ladies of the *ton* or courtesans, rather than twenty-seven-year-old widows who were long on the shelf. 'I hope the company will suffice, then.'

'And now you have given me a further purpose. You need to be able to live your life free from your sister's interference. You should not have to worry about her matchmaking simply because you wish to enjoy the banter and repartee.'

'I welcome your assistance,' she whispered and held out her hand.

'You have it. To confounding the matchmakers, my intelligent friend.' His fingers curled around hers. Strong and firm. She swayed toward him, lips parting.

Somewhere in the bowels of the house, a clock chimed the quarter-hour. She let go abruptly, aware that she had held his fingers for a breath too long. She forced her mouth to turn up. He thought her intelligent, but unappealing. It reminded her of Charles's journal. *My new wife is a sensible choice, but far too intelligent for my taste.* Just once she wanted to be thought of as fascinating. A tiny piece of her had wanted Mrs Reynaud's scandalous suggestion to be true and that he'd pull her towards him and kiss her thoroughly.

She had entirely misread the situation earlier. A small shudder ran down her spine. She had nearly kissed him under the cedar. And now again here— just after she had proudly proclaimed no interest in marrying again! When had she become forward? And what if he thought she was an advocate for free love?

How embarrassing would that have been! *Poor silly deluded Hattie. Always gets it wrong.* Another of Charles's entries in his journal. She knew what she wanted from life and being one out of many women was not for her. 'I thank you for the compliment.'

'And you will come on the picnic with me? As a friend?'

He leant close and his breath laced with hers, doing strange things to her insides. He smelt of sandalwood and the faint tang of wood smoke. All she had to do was to lift her mouth a few inches. A slight tilting of her head was all it would take, except he wasn't interested in her, not in that way. Hattie concentrated on breathing, slowly and steadily, controlling her desire.

'I'd like that, Sir Christopher. True friendship is beyond price.'

'Kit. We are friends and intimates, Hattie.' His voice rolled her name.

'Very well, Kit.' Even saying his first name seemed intimate and wicked as if she was slowly but inexorably sliding towards the sort of woman who did indulge in serious flirtations. 'It took me three months before I dared think of my husband by his first name, let alone call him by it.'

'Then it is just as well that I'm not your husband.'

'Until tomorrow.' Hattie hated the way her blood leapt. She could stop any time she wanted. Going on a picnic did not mean she was going to become his mistress. It took more than a solitary picnic to ruin a reputation.

Kit made certain that he gave the appearance of relaxing back against an oak tree as he finished his share of the picnic, but his entire body was intensely focused on where Hattie Wilkinson sat, blithely eating strawberries. Her hair today was in a loose crown of braids with a few tendrils kissing the back of her neck.

The picnic had been far more pleasant than he'd anticipated. The conversation with Mrs Wilkinson had ranged from a mutual admiration of Handel and loathing of sopranos who added trills to arias to the games of chess and cricket. Mrs Wilkinson, he discovered, was a keen bowler and took pride in her ability to take wickets.

Having concluded the debate about the correct way to bowl off-side, Mrs Wilkinson reached for the few remaining strawberries in the dish.

'How did you guess I adored strawberries? Normally Livvy or Portia eat their fill before I get a chance to have more than one.'

'Another reason to be pleased you came without them.' Kit pushed the dish towards her. He'd nearly accomplished his mission. Mrs Wilkinson had blossomed. Perhaps it was as simple as her needing to understand that life went on without her husband. He hoped the man had deserved her devotion. He wondered how any woman could be so devoted? He doubted if any woman would shed real tears for him. Crocodile tears because he was no longer picking up the bills, but not real ones that came from deep within.

'One more, then.'

'You mustn't be shy. Take as many as you want. They are begging to be eaten.'

'When you put it that way, how can I refuse?' She gave a quick laugh and brought a berry to her mouth. Her teeth bit into it and the juice dribbled, turning her lips bright red. Kit silently handed her a handkerchief and indicated towards her chin.

She hastily scrubbed her face. 'Honestly, you would think after all these years I'd learn. How long has it been that way?'

'Long enough. You look delightful.' He leant back against the tree, put his hands behind his head and savoured the moment. 'This picnic is supposed to be about enjoyment.'

'And you think eating strawberries in the sunshine is a suitable pastime?'

'None better.' He shifted so his legs were stretched and struggled to remember the last time he had felt so content. There again, he found it difficult to remember the last time he had taken a woman on a picnic. The women in his life were far more inclined towards intimate late-night suppers, silken sheets and expensive presents. He had rarely wanted to talk to any of them about matters beyond the bedroom.

With Hattie Wilkinson, he wanted to hear her views. He enjoyed debating with her and disconcerting her in order to win.

A tiny frown appeared between her brows. 'I would have thought a man with your sort of reputation…'

'Simple pleasures are the best ones.' He reached across and popped the last strawberry into her mouth.

She half-closed her eyes and a look of supreme pleasure crossed her face. 'Those are exceptionally good strawberries. Don't you agree, Mr Hook?'

Full of more than his fair share of cold game pie, watercress sandwiches, fruit cake and elderflower cordial, Rupert sat with his head in a book about newts, mumbling about amphibians and their feeding habits and ignoring Hattie's attempts to bring him into the conversation. Mrs Hampstead, Hattie's housekeeper, likewise ignored the conversation and knitted.

It would be easy to do this every day.

Kit inwardly smiled at the thought—the great *bon vivant* Sir Christopher Foxton indulging in rustic pleasures. He could imagine the caustic remarks. He should end the flirtation now, before he was tempted to enjoy it or, worse still, repeat it and start to count on it. Counting on women for anything beyond the basics was a bad idea. He'd learnt that bitter lesson long ago. His mother had turned her elegant back on him and never attempted to make contact with him after she left.

Kit struggled to his feet. His mother, her lack of care and her penchant for scandalous behaviour were far from suitable topics for conversation or thought on this glorious day.

'Is there something wrong?' Hattie asked at his sudden movement. The light in her eyes flickered and died.

'Shall we explore the area to work off some of the lunch? You may have eaten the strawberries, but I had game pie,' Kit said, gesturing towards where the busy coaching inn stood.

Physical activity was what was required. It would keep his mind from wandering down unwanted paths. After today, there would be no more picnics with Hattie Wilkinson. This was about a lesson in short flirtation rather than a prolonged friendship.

'There is nothing much here,' Rupert said unhelpfully, looking up from his book. 'Just some empty fields.'

'When you see the two crossroads, there is little

mystery as to why the fair is held here,' Kit continued, giving Rupert a meaningful glare. 'Do you know how long the fair has been going on, Hattie?'

'Since time immemorial,' Mrs Wilkinson replied, dusting her fingers with a white handkerchief.

She leant back and the bodice of her gown tightened across her breasts. In other women, he'd suspect that it was done deliberately, but with Hattie, he was sure it was unconscious. All too often recently, his life had been filled with women who knew what they were on about and sought to accentuate their sexuality, leaving him cold.

'There are some Roman remains just to the north of the inn. We could walk there.' Her long lashes fluttered down, hiding her expressive eyes. 'It is possible they had a fair. I've never really considered it.'

The tension went out of Kit's shoulders. Virtue radiated from every pore. He could end the flirtation there. Something simple and it would be over. It was better to be done now, than to risk liking Mrs Wilkinson. They had no future. She'd never agree to an affair and he had no wish to become respectable.

The thought sent a pang of unaccustomed melancholy through him.

'The perfect destination for an afternoon stroll.' He made a bow. 'If you are up for exploration and exercise...'

Mrs Wilkinson stood up and shook her skirts. Her carefully arranged crown of braids slipped to one side. With a laugh she brushed the grass stains from her skirt.

He considered his last three mistresses, all high-stepping courtesans, and if they would have reacted so favourably to a picnic or to eating strawberries or, worse, having any of their immaculate clothes soiled. The thought of the hysteria, shrieks and sulks which would have ensued made him shudder.

'Shall we all go and explore? Mrs Hampstead and I will take the rearguard while you and Rupert…'

'I do believe Mr Hook can stay with me,' Mrs Hampstead said, looking up from her knitting.

'But why?' Hattie tapped her fingers together. 'I can remember you always proclaiming about the virtues of a walk.'

'I wish to find out about newts and I have seen enough stone to last me a lifetime. Why a bunch of old stones provides such amusement I'll never know. But I know all about you and your walking, Miss Hattie. You were never able to sit still as a girl and you've never changed,' Mrs Hampstead said with a placid smile. 'Walk off your energy with Sir Christopher. You are a grown woman, not an impetuous girl of sixteen. I trust your judgement, even if you don't.'

Rupert turned a dull purple and swallowed rapidly. 'I'm sure you will find the subject quite dull, Mrs Hampstead. That is to say—a walk will do everyone some good.'

'Not at all. It will do my bones no good to go clambering over rocks and stones.' Mrs Hampstead patted a place beside her. It amused Kit that so many people in Mrs Wilkinson's life seemed to think a bit of romance would do her good. 'I have an enquiring mind and Miss Parteger came over yesterday to specifically ask about the subject. She assures me that you are a great authority. You are going to give a lecture in Corbridge and she plans to sit in the front row listening.'

'Miss Parteger said that? She plans to?' Rupert dropped the book and the page flopped open to lesser spotted newts and their habits. He hurriedly shut it and his face grew even redder. 'Of course the lecture was pure speculation on her mother's part... I mean, if called upon, I will be delighted to lecture. I believe I can give a convincing lecture...on newts.'

'It is good to see that you are willing to rise to the challenge, Rupert,' Kit said, looking at his protégé. Rupert was learning to honour his commitments and hopefully to think carefully before laying claim to any prowess again. He would repay his debt to Rupert's father.

Rupert ducked his head. 'I would endeavour to do my best.'

'Practice always makes perfect.' Mrs Hampstead fluffed out her skirts. 'Mr Hook, I've waited a long time to hear about such things and I trust you will oblige me.'

'You will have to imagine the illustrations.'

'I have an adequate imagination.' Mrs Hampstead reached for another ball of wool. 'I told Dr Hornby that last year when he did his lecture on battles in the Bible. My imagination is more than adequate for the task required. What are you two waiting for? Go and enjoy yourselves.'

Kit exchanged an amused glance with Mrs Wilkinson. She gave a little shrug as if to say she knew about the stratagem.

'Shall we leave Mrs Hampstead and Rupert to their discussion? I fear I don't find newts as fascinating as Rupert currently does.'

'I'm sure Moth would enjoy the exercise,' Mrs

Wilkinson said, snapping her fingers towards where Moth lounged in the sun.

'I believe Moth would like to stay as well. The summer sun is a bit hot for her.' Mrs Hampstead gave Hattie a significant glance. 'You can tell us all about the ruins when you return. Take your time, my dear. We will be here when you return.'

Hattie concentrated on smiling sweetly rather than screaming. The disease of matchmaking appeared to be highly contagious. First her sister, and now Mrs Hampstead felt she should be encouraging Kit with a view towards matrimony. She shook her head. The man had dodged more marriage traps than most. Besides, he was a person to be enjoyed, rather than to lose one's heart to.

A walk alone with Kit—the very prospect was enough to set her nerves jangling like some young débutante's.

There again, sitting in the blanket, gazing at his regular features and listening to his voice rumble over her had done nothing towards eliminating the attraction she felt for him. Familiarity was supposed to breed contempt…when in this case all it bred was the desire to be kissed. She clenched her fists.

She refused to start believing in romance again. It led straight to heartache.

Hattie picked up her parasol and hoped that Kit would not see her heightened colour and attribute it to the wrong reason. 'A walk will be just the thing.'

'You obviously haven't informed your house-keeper about our arrangement,' Kit observed when they reached the small pile of stones which marked the remains of Portgate.

Hattie stumbled over a stone. They had covered the ground between the picnic and the ruins in silence. She'd kept thinking up topics for conversation and rejecting them as unsuitable. She'd finally settled on the weather when, without warning, he mentioned the very topic she wished to avoid—the blatant attempts at matchmaking.

'What sort of arrangement do you mean?' she asked, attempting to stay upright.

'Our friendship. Or is everyone chronically addicted to matchmaking in Northumberland?'

'In my defence, I tried to warn you.'

'Surely you confided in someone about this? Women always confide in their female friends.'

She glanced upwards to see how he felt about it, but the planes of his face gave no clue. Her heart sank. Of course, he could scent matchmaking wiles. Such men always could.

Her grip on the parasol tightened.

'Mrs Hampstead used to be Stephanie's nurse as well as mine. They remain close. If I want to fool my sister, I can hardly confess to Mrs Hampstead. You do understand my reasoning, don't you?'

'Perfectly.'

Hattie shook her head. Even the thought made her blood run cold—confiding in Mrs Hampstead. The fewer people who knew about her arrangement with Kit, the better.

'All I can do is to apologise.'

His eyes widened. 'Why apologise? None of it was your doing. And I do think I am old enough to see through a simple matchmaking stratagem. I'd have hardly remained single for this long if I didn't. It amused me to see it happen. Do you think she will tell your sister?'

'Yes, of course.' The words tasted like ash in her mouth. Hattie pulled her bonnet forwards. She hadn't asked for Livvy to list her shortcomings this morning—passable figure, too long of a nose and far too inclined towards sarcasm. And she failed to smile enough.

'All we are doing is going for a walk, Hattie. Relax and enjoy the moment. Nothing untoward will happen. Nothing to cause adverse comment.'

Hattie hated the butterflies which had started beating in her stomach and the way her jaw hurt from trying to keep a smile. This going for a walk alone was a poor idea.

If anything it emphasised that she wanted to be with him as more than a friend. She liked thinking of herself as independent and not needing a man, but right now all she could think about was how alone she was and how his arms felt when they waltzed.

'It was sweet of Livvy to ask Mrs Hampstead about newts,' she said, attempting to keep the subject away from the matchmaking scheme.

'Rupert is learning a valuable lesson in the folly of trying to please people.'

'Please people?' Hattie stopped beside a large pile of stones. 'It certainly backfired on him. Livvy still likes his well-turned calf muscles, but if his object was to impress her mother, he singularly failed. He is about to endure a baptism of fire. They still speak about the great Hollingbrooke disaster from '98 when Mr Hollingbrooke tried to give a lecture on the history of lime kilns and people began to throw rotten fruit.'

He reached out and caught her elbow. 'Hattie.'

'We have exhausted the subject, yes, I know.' Hattie gulped air. She babbled when she was nervous and today was no exception. 'You have no interest in the great Hollingbrooke disaster and it was wrong of me to bring it up.'

'Hattie,' he said again. He stood looking at her with his top hat pushed back, giving him a rakish look. 'I didn't go on this picnic to discuss my godson or his prospects. I came because—'

'We don't need to discuss why,' Hattie broke in before he could finish. The last thing she wanted to hear was his proposal for confounding the matchmakers. She needed to end this now, before she started to enjoy his company. She refused to go back to that naïve girl whom Charles had taken advantage of. 'When we return to the picnic, it will appear that we had a quarrel. The nature of said quarrel will be highly trivial, but on an important point of principle. I will inform my sister that we will have fallen out of civility with each other. After that we become civil but distant acquaintances. The only thing I need from you is to decide how long we stay out here. I'm sorry if my words are blunt, but there you have it.'

She waited for him to agree. Or to at least comment on her rudeness. The solution had come to her in the middle of the night, when she had awoken from a dream about his mouth against hers.

'Hattie.' He took a step closer. She became aware of his elusive scent and the way his stock was intricately tied. It was one thing to make plans to counter a dream Kit and another to be confronted with the living and breathing man.

Her mouth went dry. His eyes were a luminous grey and his face seemed suddenly intense and serious. She knew she ought to pick up her skirts and run like the very devil was after her. She stood still. Behind her, some bird burst out into a trill of song.

'Kit,' she breathed.

He lowered his mouth and his lips lightly brushed hers. The kiss, if you could call it that, was over in a breath.

Hattie fingered her lips. They ached slightly. Two bits of knowledge hammered through her. First she wanted to be kissed again, more thoroughly and second, perhaps more importantly, he was attracted to her. The realisation made her wary, in case she had mistaken it. 'What…what was that for?'

'You wanted a reason for us to fall out of civility. I gave you one.' He snapped his fingers. 'I refuse to apologise. It was the most agreeable part of my day so far. What happens next is up to you.'

Hattie nodded, and attempted to ignore the way her heart thudded. 'You expect me to pick up my skirts and run as if the devil is after me?'

He tilted his head to one side. The grey in his eyes deepened. 'Did I mistake the moment?'

'You have a funny idea of women.'

A dimple showed in the corner of his mouth. 'You don't think it was enough. You want more.'

'I am made of sterner stuff and fail to wilt when someone seeks to mock me. In any case, a simple quarrel over the Romans would have sufficed.' Hattie concentrated on a particularly nondescript piece of rock.

Her mouth ached and she knew she wanted more, but that went beyond the bounds of propriety. She refused to get herself into a situation where she jeopardised her reputation. 'Your choice of topic leaves a lot to be desired.'

'You want to be kissed again. Immediately and more thoroughly.'

'You are being ridiculous.' Hattie pressed her lips together and attempted to banish the strange quivering in her stomach. 'I never said anything of the sort.'

'You told me to pick the topic and I have. It is far better to fall out of civility over something like a kiss than over anything else.'

'The question of whether or not I want to be kissed by you is inappropriate.' She crossed her arms over her breasts and tried to ignore the way they felt. 'Completely and utterly inappropriate. I could hardly confess to Stephanie that I fell out of civility because of a kiss! Imagine the commotion.'

'But you do want to be kissed.' He cupped her cheek with firm fingers. She fought against the impulse to turn her face into his palm. 'It is in your eyes.'

'In my eyes?'

His thumb traced the outline of her mouth.

'And your lips.'

He lowered his head. This time his kiss was slow and coaxing. Instead of merely brushing her lips, he tasted and explored. Slowly and steadily. Tiny nibbles at her lips made her stomach contract and warm pulses shoot through her.

Hattie brought her hands up and rested them on the solid broad cloth of his coat. His hand moulded her body to his. At the insistent pressure, her lips parted slightly and she tasted the cool interior of his mouth. Nothing in her life had prepared her for the sensation rippling through her. It made the memory of Charles's kisses seem like poor milk-water.

He groaned and deepened the kiss, drank from her. His hand tangled in her hair, pushing her bonnet off her face. He rained kisses down her cheeks, her eyes and her nose before returning to plunder her mouth.

Hattie allowed herself one more heartbeat of pleasure. She felt ridiculously feminine and pretty, someone to be cherished. Cherished?

The thought poured ice water into her veins. She refused to become like one of those women who fell at his feet. She was never going to become another notch, to be enjoyed and then tossed away. She had been there with Charles and never again. No romance required.

She beat her hands against his chest. Instantly he loosened his arms. He looked down at her with a quizzical expression in his eyes.

She stumbled backwards and attempted to breathe normally. Her body protested at the sudden rush of air between them. She knew her eyes were too large and her lips too red. She grabbed at her bonnet and tore a ribbon. It lay glistening in her hand, mute rebuke of what she'd done.

Anger at herself, at him and at life in general washed over her. After all her promises, all she had been through, the first man with a reputation crooked a finger and she behaved like a babbling schoolgirl. This stopped before it ever started.

'That should never happen again. Ever!' she said when she had regained her balance. 'I forbid it!'

Chapter Five

'Forbid?' Kit watched Hattie through narrowed eyes.

Hattie's breath was far too quick and her eyes were huge blue-green pools. It took all of his self-control not to pull her back into his arms. His response to her was entirely unexpected. Ever since Waterloo, nothing— not even with the most experienced courtesans London could offer was there any excitement or response, but one gentle brush of his lips against hers and his body started to rage out of control. He'd kissed her again to make sure and had nearly fallen off the edge.

He wanted to drink from her mouth and leisurely explore the contours of her body. Silently he willed her to come back into his arms and to allow the kiss to develop further. With a great effort, he concentrated and brought his breathing under control.

'You only needed to tell me to stop,' he said when she continued to stand away from him, looking at him with those huge eyes. 'And I will, if that is what you truly desire.'

'I should never have done something like that. I'm not like that. I'm not given to...'

'I'm very honoured.' Kit clung on to his sanity. She

was frightened of her response. Intellectually he should have expected it, but it still hit him in his gut. She had enjoyed the kiss until she had started thinking and remembering that she was a respectable person.

'All I know is that it must not happen again. I'm not that sort of a woman. I'm a widow who has responsibilities. I'm not looking for a quick tumble in the hay.'

'Do you see any hay around here?'

Hattie gave an impatient stamp of her foot. 'You know what I mean!'

Hattie took a step backwards, half-stumbled on a rock and tumbled down on her bottom. She gave an exasperated cry.

'Do you need help?' Kit held out a hand to help her up, but she ignored it and scrambled to stand up.

'I can manage on my own. I always do.'

'Your bonnet is crooked.'

'Is it? I...I hadn't noticed.'

Kit reached out and straightened her straw bonnet, placing it firmly on her head, pulling it forwards so she was once again the perfectly proper woman he'd first met. He should say the words he'd planned to end it, but they stuck in his throat. He wanted more of her. He wanted to see if the promise in the kiss held true, but he knew he'd have to go slowly, coax her and discover why the physical frightened her. He wanted to see what would happen when she fully gave in to the passion that simmered under the surface.

'There, no one will guess. Your armour is back on.'

'Armour?'

'To keep you safe from the world's scrutiny. No one will remark if that is what you are afraid of.'

'Nothing. I am not afraid of anything.' Her words

were barely audible as she half-turned from him. 'It has to be this way for both our sakes.'

Kit allowed his hand to drop to his side. Not only did her body have to crave his touch, but her mind as well. He wanted her to want him as he wanted her. He'd felt the passion in her kiss. He wasn't ready for the flirtation to end. He wanted it to continue and for them to explore this white-hot spark that flickered between them. He'd be a poor person if he gave up at the first hurdle. 'I'll respect your wishes, but will allow you the luxury of changing your mind.'

A long sigh escaped her mouth before she straightened her back. 'I can't. I won't. It ends here. It has to. Things like this don't happen to me.'

'Denying your passion won't bring your husband back.'

'You seek to discomfort me. Never mention Charles Wilkinson again. He has nothing to do with this. He died seven years ago.' She wrapped her arms about her waist. 'That…that demonstration of your prowess was totally unnecessary.'

Kit clung on to her response as a dying man might cling to a wooden spar. She didn't say unwelcome. He hated that it mattered and that he wanted her to want him. Silently he cursed her husband and what they must have shared. He'd never had to compete with a ghost before.

He could just imagine the upright Army hero who had won her. Someone who had more to offer than he ever could. A sudden irrational hatred of the man filled him.

'Why did you do it, Kit?'

'If we intend on falling out of civility, I wanted it

to be for something real,' he said lightly, pushing the unaccustomed jealousy to one side. He never examined the past. 'The truth is far easier than a lie. The mealy-mouthed kiss earlier was nothing, but this, this will make the falling out worthwhile.'

The colour rose in her cheeks, rivalling the dusky pink of her lips. 'Just so you understand, there can be no future.'

'I try never to look to the future,' Kit said stiffly. 'And I never regret the past where women are concerned. It helps.'

She clasped her hands together so tightly he could see the knuckles through her gloves. 'Just know that I have no intention of becoming somebody's mistress. Anyone's mistress. I wouldn't want to soil…to soil my spotless reputation.'

'We are friends.' Kit bit back the words that he didn't want her to become just anyone's mistress—he wanted her to be *his*.

It would be laying claim to her. He'd never laid claim to anyone. To claim someone meant that you cared. And if you cared, you got hurt.

'We should go back to the picnic.' She turned away from the ruins. 'Mrs Hampstead may need rescuing from Mr Hook's lecture.'

'We should indeed.' Kit put his hand in the small of her back. 'Careful. The path is unsteady.'

'I can walk on my own.' She made no attempt to move away.

'Sometimes everyone needs help.'

'I'll remember that.'

'You appear far more serious than I intended,' Kit remarked when they neared the picnic area. Rupert's voice declaiming loudly about the sleeping habits of the great crested newts punctuated the air. 'What have I done to cause the frown besides kissing you?'

'I was considering how to break the news to my sister of our incompatibility so I can prevent further meddling.'

'Surely the kiss is excuse enough?'

Her hand flew to her mouth. 'There is no need for anyone to know about the kiss. I have no plans to tell.'

'Honesty is always best.' Kit stifled a smile. The kiss had caused her to go off balance by a bit, but she hadn't fully capitulated. A wise man knew when to retreat and when to advance. He'd pursue her slowly and see what happened, but first he'd give her the protection she craved. 'We quarrelled and you see no way to mend the quarrel. You are far too distraught to talk about the quarrel because it was over a trifling matter.'

'That excuse might do.' She gave a heart-stopping smile. 'It will do very well indeed.'

Kit raised two fingers to his hat. They said that there was a first time for everything, but he had never considered that he'd be involved in this—pursuing a woman by giving her advice on how to break up with him. Quarrels were made to be mended. He would see this one was. 'Until the next time.'

'Will there be a next time?'

He leant forwards and brushed her cheek with his forefinger. 'You can count on it.'

Reasons why she was not interested in Kit Foxton...

Hattie read down the list of reasons, starting with his notoriety and his lack of reliability and ending with the taste of his kisses making her unsettled. She frowned. The taste of his kisses was not something she wanted to consider. With a furious stroke of her pen, she crossed it out.

'There you are, my dear,' Mrs Reynaud said, bustling into the drawing room of the Dower House. Unlike the day before, which had been bathed in brilliant sunshine, a steady rain fell, adding to the general air of gloom.

Hattie nearly dropped her pen in surprise. She was hard pressed to remember when Mrs Reynaud had last come calling. Hattie slid a piece of paper over the list.

'Is something the matter, Mrs Reynaud?'

'I feared something had happened to you,' Mrs Reynaud explained in a rush as she removed her veil, depositing it on an armchair. 'You failed to stop by this morning. There were things I wished to discuss with you. The picnic you had yesterday with Sir Christopher...did everything go as you would wish?'

'I went on a picnic. For the most part, it was highly pleasant. Mr Hook practised his proposed lecture and sent Mrs Hampstead to sleep. I ate my fill of strawberries for once as neither Livvy nor Portia were there.' Hattie folded her hands in her lap and tried to keep from looking at the list. 'There is little to discuss. A typical picnic. Nothing exciting. No handsome highwaymen or rescuing distressed maidens like you always seem to be encountering.'

'No picnic is typical if it involves Sir Christopher.' Mrs Reynaud lifted her chin. 'Your sister quite bristled with importance when she called yesterday. You dined with Sir Christopher Foxton. Your sister has expectations, great expectations. Left to her own devices, I believe she would be calling for banns. Do you have expectations, my dear?'

'My sister came to see you,' Hattie said slowly. How many other people had Stephanie happened to tell? Expectations indeed! Silently she offered up thanks that she had already dispatched her note to Kit, severing any connection. It had come to her last night. After the kiss they enjoyed, sending a letter was her only course forwards, but it had to be carefully worded, coded without appearing to mention That Incident. She had retained a copy to show Stephanie when she appeared, but she didn't want to appear too eager to share the news.

'Mrs Parteger required urgent advice about Mr Hook and her eldest.' Mrs Reynaud narrowed her eyes. 'I believe you mentioned something about me knowing Sir Christopher…'

'Only in passing.'

'It was many years ago.' The elderly woman fluttered her hands as two bright spots appeared on her pockmarked cheeks. 'I wouldn't want Sir Christopher to feel that I claimed an acquaintance. And I have no knowledge of Mr Hook's antecedents in any case.'

'Stephanie should never have bothered you with such a trivial matter. I fear she wanted to gossip about the picnic.' Hattie leant forwards and lowered her voice. 'No doubt she neglected to mention that Sir Christopher invited the entire family, but she declined, preferring to concentrate on arranging a series of lectures.'

'No, your sister never mentioned that.' Mrs Reynaud gave a merry trill of laughter. 'I thought Colonel Cunningham had charge of the lectures this year because it was something your sister loathed. Indeed, we very nearly did not have any lectures last year because your sister forgot.'

'Stephanie changed her mind. She thinks Colonel Cunningham needs some assistance now.'

Mrs Reynaud's eyes danced. 'Fancy forgetting that piece of information about who was originally invited. It puts the invitation in a different light.'

'My sister is rather inclined to make overmuch of the matter.' Hattie stood up and faced Mrs Reynaud. The sooner she stopped the gossip, the better for all concerned. 'The matter is now closed.'

'The matter with Sir Christopher or Mr Hook?'

'Both.' Hattie remembered the uncomfortable way Mr Hook had shifted in the carriage and how Mrs Hampstead had confided that she doubted anyone, even Livvy, could sit through something that dull and tedious. It was better for all concerned if they drew a line under the entire episode. 'Livvy might suffer for a few weeks, but London gentlemen never stay. It is no good hoping they will. They never do. I will inform Stephanie and the lecture can be postponed before real harm is done. I would hate for anyone to be disappointed.'

Mrs Reynaud tilted her head. Her sharp eyes assessed her. It seemed as if her gaze bore into her soul. Hattie toyed with her pen as her cheeks flamed.

'He kissed you. More than once, I reckon,' Mrs Reynaud said in solemn tones. 'It is far from a crime and occasionally most enjoyable. You were discreet. Yes. Yes, that goes without saying. You are the sort of woman who would be discreet. It was always part of my trouble when I was young and foolish. I forgot to be discreet.'

Hattie put her hand to her throat. How had Mrs Reynaud guessed? Nearly twenty-four hours later, and there should be no mark on her. Hattie glanced down and saw the word kiss, underlined, rather than scratched out. She moved the piece of paper more firmly over the list.

'We quarrelled. I doubt he will kiss me again. Nor would I wish him to.' She tilted her chin upwards. 'I sent him a note explaining the situation. It is impossible. He is impossible.'

'Why did you do that if you wanted to end it?'

Hattie put her hand on her stomach and concentrated on keeping her shoulders straight. She could hardly explain that she saw herself becoming like the woman whom Charles had loved, living on the margins of society, and for the first time it had tempted her.

'Because I have Livvy and Portia's reputation to think about,' she said firmly. 'How could they make the matches they need if their aunt is pilloried for being wicked? Sir Christopher does not believe in marriage. His parents had a dreadful one, I believe.'

The colour drained from Mrs Reynaud's face. 'He spoke to you about his parents and their marriage?'

'Only briefly to explain why he intends to remain unwed.' Hattie resolutely did not look at her list.

'People should not visit the sins of one generation on the next.'

'It was a brief interlude and now it is over.' Hattie walked over to the window and looked out over the garden with its gravel paths and roses. Off to her left, she could just make out Highfield's chimneys and the great cedar of Lebanon. This was home and safe. She was not prepared to risk her heart again. Charles had seen to that. Life would have been much easier in ways if Kit had been the marrying kind, but he wasn't. His honesty made her decision easy. 'I love the girls like my own and I would hate anything I did to ruin their chances of a good marriage.'

Mrs Reynaud made an impatient noise. 'Stop using them as shields to stop you from living. You are as bad as a foolish débutante who believes that a man's promise in a summer house offers a life of undying romance.'

'The heat of the moment overcame me, but I recovered before any real harm was done. He accepted my verdict.' Hattie pressed her hand into her stomach. Even a day later, the intensity of the final kiss made her senses reel. She had been so close to giving in completely. And she knew the next time she kissed Kit, she'd lack the will-power to stop. A very large part of her had wanted to drown in that kiss and blot out any memory of Charles's rough love-making. And she worried that it made her very wicked indeed, whatever Mrs Reynaud might say.

'As you say, it is all over. Then no harm is done.' Mrs Reynaud came over to her and put her hand on Hattie's shoulder. 'In my experience with men like Sir Christopher, they wish to be the one to end things. Formally. Informally is quite another matter.'

'This time it will be different,' Hattie said decisively as she gave Mrs Reynaud a copy of the letter. 'I was very firm and unyielding.'

'And you are prepared for the consequences, my dear?' Mrs Reynaud handed the letter back to Hattie. 'If Sir Christopher is half the man I have heard him to be, he will not give up at the first hurdle. He will see your letter as a challenge, an invitation to raise the stakes.'

'A challenge?' A pulse of warmth went through Hattie. 'You're wrong. He will see the logic of my argument. After all, it is not as if it were a serious flirtation.'

Kit tapped the note with his forefinger. The various scrawled words leapt out at him. Faint aromas of Hattie's jasmine scent permeated the paper and forcibly reminded him of how her lips had yielded. How she had forgot herself and given in to the passion for a moment.

Hattie had put her case for breaking with him in flowery language which did not detail the situation. She regretted that they were incompatible and that the picnic had proved a great trial. From now, they would have to be distant friends.

'Liar,' he whispered. 'All a quarrel means is a chance to become closer. You want this friendship. And I'm going to prove it to you. I do not quit over a simple misunderstanding. Or a baseless fear.'

Kit held Hattie's note over a candle and watched it smoulder and burn to ash. Over? It wasn't over until he ended it. He made a point of it. No woman had left him since Constance and she had begged in the end to return.

He paused. Hattie wasn't like any woman he'd been involved with before.

It didn't matter. He refused to allow Hattie to end it on such a slim pretext. No woman had ever written to him like that. And Hattie certainly had not kissed him like they would not suit. He had allowed her a chance to raise her drawbridges and retreat. But retreat was not for ever. The next stage needed to begin. Today, before she had a chance to think.

'You wanted to see me, sir?' Johnson, his valet, appeared in the doorway.

'I find I require my evening clothes after all today.'

'You are going out?'

'The musicale in celebration of Waterloo awaits.'

'Sir?' Johnson struggled to keep his face blank. 'You loathe such things. Tuneless playing.'

'I shall go and enjoy myself. Where was that note from Mrs Parteger? After all, I do have an invitation. A seat has been saved.'

'You were wrong to send that letter discarding Sir Christopher.' Stephanie sank down next to Hattie in a flurry of feathers and ruffles.

'This is not the time to discuss it, Stephanie,' Hattie said through clenched teeth. She had to wonder how much Stephanie knew of the contents. 'The concert to celebrate the deliverance from Napoleon is about to begin.'

'You always do such things to me. At least this time, hopefully I learnt about it early enough.' She glanced over her shoulder. 'Oh dear!'

'I have no idea what you are talking about, Stephanie.' Hattie slid towards the vacant chair on her right. Stephanie's feathered turban kept tickling her nose. The last thing she needed now was a frank-and-public discussion about her severing relations with Kit. 'What is the problem?'

'Maria Richley has waylaid Sir Christopher.'

Hattie fought against the inclination to turn her

head. She had counted on Kit not appearing at this concert. 'Really? I wish her the joy of it.'

'I feel certain that the Widow Richley will not squander any opportunity. No…hush.' Stephanie laid a proprietary hand on Hattie's arm. 'All might not be lost, Hattie. Be civil if he approaches.'

'You are making it seem like I am younger than Portia.'

A trill of laughter cut through the musician's tuning. Hattie turned her head. Maria Richley clung to Kit's arm as if she were drowning. Over the heads of the other concertgoers, Kit nodded directly at her. A sardonic smile curled on his lips. He leant down and said something to Maria Richley, which sent the woman into further peals of laughter.

Hattie forced her eyes forwards. She crumpled the music programme in her hand. It was none of her business if he chose to enjoy Maria Richley's favours. All it did was to confirm that she'd been correct in the first place. That man was trouble.

Only she wished that he had not stood quite so close to Maria Richley.

Her view was suddenly obscured by a large expanse of black broad cloth.

'Mrs Parteger, Mrs Wilkinson…if I may squeeze in? You have a free seat, I believe.'

Hattie shrank in her seat. She was now going to have to spend several hours trapped between Stephanie's headdress and the vicar, Dr Hornby's, bulk. The perfect way to spend an evening. No doubt Kit would have secured a place with plenty of space for Maria Richley.

'Doctor Hornby.'

'Your sister said that you would be here, Mrs Wilkinson. How delightful to see you again.' Doctor Hornby gave a jowly smile. 'I'm looking forward to the planned lecture series now that it is finally settled. You will come to my lecture on the problems of mapping the Holy Places in two weeks' time?'

Murder, Hattie decided, was too humane a punishment for Stephanie. She needed to be tortured slowly. 'I look forward to it.'

'My dear Mrs Wilkinson, you do me such honour.' Doctor Hornby made a grab for her hand and froze. His face became a mottled purple.

'Are you well, Dr Hornby?'

'Perfectly fine. I must leave you ladies.'

Hattie had half-turned and saw Kit glowering. He gave her a cold nod. 'As long as you are certain.'

'On second thoughts, I do believe Miss Gormley has saved me a seat. I would hate to disappoint her.'

'I understand completely.'

Hattie drew in a breath of air and concentrated on steadying her pulse. She resisted the urge to turn around and see Kit's reaction. They were finished, and she was not going to be kissed again. Ever. The thought made her unbearably sad.

'If you will excuse me…I believe this is my seat.' Kit pushed passed her and sat down in the chair Dr Hornby had just vacated.

'I hadn't realised it was spoken for.'

'It was.' He turned his back on her. 'Mrs Parteger saved it for me.'

Stephanie developed a sudden interest in her programme and ignored Hattie's sudden jab to her side.

* * *

Hattie spent the entire concert busily trying to ignore his very existence. And failing. She rejected a number of possible conversation topics but finally settled on a polite discussion of music. She'd demonstrate to Stephanie and Kit that she bore no ill feeling. The remainder of the concert was spent in happy contemplation of what she would say.

When the concert was over, he stood up.

'It has been a pleasure, Mrs Wilkinson, Mrs Parteger.'

Before Hattie could utter another word, he was gone.

'You could have done more, Hattie. I am highly disappointed in you.'

'He nearly cut me dead.'

'You were the one to send the letter. Ill timed and ill advised. I was attempting to mend bridges. Sir Christopher is a neighbour.'

He'd only sat with her to prove a point. Stephanie in her misguided way had given him an opportunity. Hattie narrowed her eyes. 'If you ever do that again, Stephanie, I will create a scene and, more than that, a scandal. How would you like me to be embroiled in a scandal?'

'Some people are entirely too touchy.' Stephanie gave a loud sniff. 'Very well, you will hear no more from me on the subject. I entirely wash my hands of you, Harriet Wilkinson. I hope you enjoy your widow's bed.'

'I find it utterly comfortable. Far better than my marriage bed,' she muttered under her breath.

* * *

'Aunt Hattie, it is his carriage. I know it is,' Livvy breathed when Hattie turned the governess cart into the Corbridge High Street the morning after the concert.

'Whose carriage?' Hattie asked absently as she brought the cart to a halt outside the ironmonger's. Her dreams had been confused last night after the concert. Twice she had woken with her mind full of thoughts of Kit and the way his lips had moved over hers. She should have said something before he left. It was quite possible he considered that she had a part in that saving of a seat débâcle. She couldn't decide which was worse—Stephanie's behaviour or the fact she had been supremely aware of him.

Today was a day for concentrating on the jobs that needed to be done before the Stagshaw Bank Fair, rather than considering what might have been. Once the fair was over, he'd depart the neighbourhood and she would not have a constant reminder. She could get over this attraction.

'Whose carriage, Livvy?'

'Sir Christopher's, of course!'

Hattie ignored the sudden fluttering in her stomach. She had made the correct decision. She'd no other choice. Any lady would have done the same thing. 'I wasn't aware that you ever paid much attention to carriages.'

'It has butter-yellow wheels and is quite new. Mr Hook told me all about it. Sir Christopher purchased it once they arrived in Newcastle by packet boat.'

'Other carriages have butter-yellow wheels,' Hattie said, more to control her own sudden onset of nerves than Livvy's. After the concert where he'd barely spoken to her, she wasn't entirely sure what to expect.

Livvy kicked the board under her seat. 'Can I go to the circulating library?'

'May I. Where are your manners today, Livvy?'

'May I go? Portia, you will come with me.' Livvy grabbed her sister's arm. 'Aunt Hattie, surely you can't object if I have a companion. I wish to improve my mind.'

Portia gave an indignant squeak.

Hattie pinched the bridge of her nose. 'I thought you wanted to go to the haberdasher's for more ribbon.'

'I can do that after. Please. I want to see if the latest by the author of *Waverley* is there. And Papa wants a book on animal husbandry. He wants to settle an argument with Colonel Cunningham. I will catch you up in the haberdasher's.'

Hattie gave a weary wave. It would make life easier if neither Livvy nor Portia accompanied her on her errands, particularly when she needed to find out if indeed the firebox for Mrs Belter's cook stove could be repaired as Mr Ogle had promised weeks ago or if she'd be better investigating the range of stoves at the Stagshaw fair for Mrs Belter. The fair did represent an opportunity to buy a wider range of goods than were generally available in the Tyne Valley.

She watched the pair for a few steps and decided that they would be all right. Livvy could not get up to any mischief at the circulating library and the probability that Mr Hook was actually there was slim. The back of her neck crept. The last person she wanted to encounter was Kit and if Mr Hook was in the library,

Kit would not be far behind. And she certainly did not want to explain about the concert.

She stepped into the ironmonger's and collided with a solid expanse of chest. Hattie inhaled the sandalwood scent. Strong fingers caught her elbow and steadied her.

She hurriedly took a step backwards out of the shop. She ducked her head, hoping that he wouldn't see her flaming cheeks. 'Sir Christopher. This is most unexpected.'

'Mrs Wilkinson.'

Hattie shifted in her boots. Of all the people! This time she refused to be cut. 'I wanted to make sure Mr Ogle had finished a job for me.'

'It is your habit to enter establishments without checking to see if anyone is coming out?' His grey eyes danced.

Her heart did a little flip. He wasn't angry with her. He was flirting with her as if the breach never happened.

'Yes, I mean, no. I was thinking of other things.'

'Obviously of great import.'

'Domestic triviality.' She squared her shoulders. This encounter would not throw her off balance. She had made her decision, but it did not prevent her from being civil. 'You understand how it is.'

'Wool-gathering,' he said decisively. A smile tugged at his lips. 'It is a bad habit. You neglected me dreadfully during the concert.'

'You left straight after the concert.' She pulled at her gloves, straightening the fingers. 'I wanted to thank you for rescuing me.'

'Rescuing you?'

'From Dr Hornby. He can be difficult to sit next to.'

He tilted his head to one side. 'It was my seat. Your sister signalled to me when I came in, I thought you knew.'

'Obviously I was mistaken.' Hattie picked at the seam of her glove. She wished she had thought of that scenario. She should have guessed something like that had happened. Stephanie could be singularly stubborn. 'Despite my best efforts, my sister harbours hopes.'

'If he bothers you again, let me know. Simply being the vicar does not give him the right to touch people.'

Hattie glanced up quickly. 'You saw that.'

'I happened to look over. Even if it had not been my seat, I would have done something.'

'You would have?'

'You are the only true friend I have in the neighbourhood.'

'You plan on staying in the neighbourhood?' Hattie gripped her reticule tighter. He was going to stay for longer. A mixture of fear and excitement vibrated through her. She would have to see him again and again, but on what terms? Friendship was the only sensible course. She had to think about safeguarding her reputation.

'I am undecided about what to do with the Lodge.' The tone in his voice seemed to indicate something troubled him more than the Lodge.

'And will you be doing up your tenants' houses?' Hattie asked, trying to steer the conversation away from their friendship.

'They appear to be in good order. My uncle may not have cared for his own comforts, but he did make sure that his tenants all had a roof over their heads.'

Kit drew himself up to his full height. 'I do employ the same estate manager. No one has been to me with complaints about him.'

She thought about Mrs Reynaud and how she had mentioned him. It would be the perfect opportunity for them to renew their acquaintance. 'Perhaps your tenants might like to meet you. People like the personal touch rather than being treated like a component in one of those new-fangled machines. You hardly want to be considered aloof.'

He quirked his eyebrow. 'Are you seeking to teach me my duty now, Mrs Wilkinson?'

'No. It was merely a suggestion. I believe they feared you would never arrive.'

'Sir Christopher, there you are.' A trilling voice called behind Hattie. 'Mama and I thought we had lost you. I should be most distressed if that happened.'

Miss Dent and Maria Richley. How many other women after that? Hattie ground her teeth. Had he lied when he said that he only pursued one woman at a time? Kit knew what he was on about. She shouldn't have to spell out how tenacious the Dents could be. He had the perfect right to see anyone he wanted.

'Miss Dent, I was endeavouring to follow, but circumstances dictated otherwise. Please go on to our arrangement. I will follow you shortly.' He inclined his head. 'You must excuse me, Mrs Wilkinson. We must continue this highly interesting conversation some other time. I did promise Miss Dent that I would join her father for a cup of coffee in the Reading Room. He apparently knows a good joiner and the staircase at the Lodge will have to be replaced.'

Hattie kept her head up. It was not as if she had

any claim on him. She had made her choice the other day. And if anything, her encounter showed that she was wrong to suspect his hand in Dr Hornby's odd behaviour.

'You are busy, you should have said. The social whirl surrounding this year's fair has been phenomenal. I've no wish to keep you…from your duties.'

'I'm never too busy to speak with a friend.'

'I thought…' She attempted to focus on the coal scuttles, grates and variety that adorned the walls of the ironmonger's rather than on Kit's face.

'We remain friends.' There was no mistaking the finality in Kit's voice. 'We may have quarrelled, but it is settled now. What is friendship without quarrels? Life would be very dull indeed.'

The air rushed out of her lungs. He was determined to ignore her letter. It shouldn't make her heart feel so light, but it did. 'Yes…yes, of course.'

His smile brought sunshine into the gloom of the ironmonger's. She wasn't going to ask for more than he could give. She knew what he was. He was precisely the same as Charles and if she ever forgot that for a moment, she'd lose her way. She was not going to be betrayed like that again. 'I knew you'd see it my way.' His smile increased as he rocked back on his heels. 'I burnt your letter. It held little of value.'

'You burnt it? Did you even read it?'

'I know why it was written, Hattie. And you are wrong to be afraid. I wanted to let you know that.'

She was conscious of staring at him for a heartbeat too long, of drinking in his features. She was very glad now that he hadn't read the pretentious twaddle.

It didn't change things. Serious flirtations were out. The risks were too great. 'I'm not afraid.'

'That is good to know.'

'There are things I must do.' Hattie forced her chin upwards so she looked Kit directly in the eye. Here she retook control of the conversation. 'Mr Ogle was going to fix Mrs Belter's firebox. It needs to be done or I shall have to order another stove at the Stagshaw fair.'

'Who is Mrs Belter?'

'One of my brother-in-law's tenants. Stephanie can't be counted on to ensure my brother-in-law knows how they are doing. Over the years, I took the responsibility on. It keeps me out of mischief and makes everyone's lives happier.'

'Far be it from me to keep you from doing anything.' He put two fingers to his hat. 'Until the fair, Mrs Wilkinson.'

Hattie put a hand to her head as she stepped back into the shop. He probably thought her sighing from love just like Miss Dent and Maria Richley. She gave a little smile. The next time she encountered him, she would not feed his self-importance. *Until the fair.* Had she agreed to meet him? Did he think they were going to meet? Impossible! She had to find him and tell him that it was not going to happen.

Hattie hurried back out of the ironmonger's. Her feet skittered to a stop.

Kit stood facing the door, arms crossed. He raised an eyebrow and inclined his head. She curled her fists. He knew she'd appear. He had waited for her to appear. Silently she cursed for behaving precisely as he thought she would. Seven years after Charles's betrayal and she acted worse than Livvy.

'Is there a problem, Mrs Wilkinson?'

'I...that is...' The words stuck in her throat. She swallowed hard and tried again. This time she stuck her chin in the air and took refuge in her dignity. 'I had no plans to see you during the fair.'

'But you have no objections, should it happen?'

Hattie waved her reticule in the air in a gesture of magnanimity. 'If it happens, I will not cut you.'

'You have relieved my mind.' His eyes danced. 'The thought has kept me awake in recent nights. What could be worse than being cut by Mrs Wilkinson at the Stagshaw fair? How can I prevent it?'

Hattie allowed her hand to drop to her side. All the pretence flowed out of her. 'You are laughing at me. You think me a censorious widow who has forgotten what it is like to be alive.'

'Not at all. I'm not given to flights of fancy. I do have the honour of having been on a picnic with you. I have heard you laugh.'

'Then what?' She found the answer mattered suddenly.

The dimple in the corner of his mouth deepened. His gaze seemed to pierce her very soul. 'I'm merely welcoming our return to friendship. Nothing more. Your servant, Mrs Wilkinson. Stop being so hard on yourself.'

Chapter Six

'Hurry up, Livvy,' Hattie called from the governess cart just after ten on the fourth of July. 'You don't want to be late for the fair. Your mother and father left over an hour ago.'

Portia had run over and clambered immediately in, but Livvy slowly picked her way across the puddles, holding a white parasol over her head. Hattie wanted to get out of the governess cart and bodily pick her up. All night she had thought about Kit and how she'd behave during the fair. They were friends. The fact that she kept remembering the kiss they had shared was her problem.

'Isn't the sun fierce this year?' Livvy said, finally getting into the cart. 'You will freckle, Portia, if you don't pull your hat forwards.'

Portia stuck out her tongue and pushed the straw bonnet back.

'If there is any bickering, you can stay at home.' Hattie gave the reins a shake and the horse started off smartly. All she could hope was that the day improved. This was the sort of thing she loved—being with her nieces. Except today, it felt a bit like everyone took her for granted. There was a question of how she greeted Kit as she had not bothered to inform Stephanie about the precise ending of hostilities. 'I mean it, Portia and Livvy. I want no repeats of last year.'

'You can't do that!' Portia's eyes went wide. 'I have been waiting for oranges and gingerbread for ever so long. Whenever I'm feeling sad, I tell myself—oranges and gingerbread lumps as big as hats at the Stagshaw fair. Somehow it makes everything seem more bearable.'

'I am sure there will be time for both oranges and gingerbread...provided you both behave yourselves.' Hattie concentrated on navigating the rutted road. The short journey to Stagshaw was fraught with difficulty after so many carriages and carts had churned up the road. The last thing she needed was a broken wheel or to get stuck in the mud. She had taken pains with her dress and had tried out a new hairstyle. 'I've saved some pennies for you. Shall we see how many squares of gingerbread we can eat?'

'Can I use the money towards a pair of Hexham Tans?' Livvy smoothed her skirt and tilted her chin. From where Hattie sat, it appeared that she was striking a variety of poses, trying them out to see which suited her best by looking at her shadow. Hattie remembered the phase all too clearly. 'I would like a pair of gloves more than anything and I have almost enough. I've saved my Christmas and birthday money especially.'

Portia snorted. 'You mean you are hoping to run into Mr Hook and don't want your face grubby. Personally I fail to see what the fuss is about. He doesn't appear to know much about newts. I asked him about the toads in our garden when we ran into him at the Halls' At Home. And he kept primping his curls when he thought no one was looking. The tousled look.'

Livvy rolled her eyes. 'There is a difference between toads and newts, Portia. Any fool knows that.'

'Will he be giving the proposed lecture before he departs? I understood they were only staying for the Stagshaw fair,' Hattie asked, attempting to keep her voice casual. Her mind raced to think about whether Kit had actually said they were staying or if today was truly going to be goodbye. Her heart sank. She wasn't ready to say goodbye.

'It depends on what Colonel Cunningham decides, but I plan to sit in the front row when it happens.'

'Livvy, we weren't going to speak about meeting Mr Hook in the High Street. Mama said. Sir Christopher would barely speak to Aunt Hattie at the concert. They have fallen out of civility and it is all Aunt Hattie's fault. Her best chance for marriage in years is gone.'

Livvy clapped her hands over her mouth. 'I'm so sorry, Aunt Harriet. I understand now about the sorrows of the heart.'

'Is there a particular pair of gloves you want or are you going to look over the stalls?' Hattie asked, silently damning Stephanie. Sorrows of the heart and Kit being a good marriage prospect indeed. She was not wasting away for love or looking for a loveless marriage with a charming but unreliable man. The only person who would see the irony was Kit.

'Oh, I thought I would wander up and down the stalls until I found the one I wanted.' Livvy gave an elaborate shrug.

'Does your mother approve of your plan? You are hoping to meet Mr Hook.'

'Mama fails to understand.' Livvy bent her head and fussed with her lace gloves. 'I'm sixteen, but I also have a brain. I want to go to London and have a Season. I'm not about to do anything foolish.'

'You did go into the card room.'

'Mr Hook explained that it was not my best idea, but how else could I meet him?' Livvy screwed up her nose. 'Sir Christopher gave him a talking to. Being young is no reason to be ignorant of society's pitfalls.'

Despite her earlier misgivings, Hattie was impressed. Mr Hook had obviously considered his position and decided that he wanted to court Livvy. She might not agree with everything, but the light romance would not put anyone in danger. 'I agree with Sir Christopher.'

Livvy clapped her hands together. 'Why did you have to fall out of civility with Sir Christopher? It makes everything much more difficult. Mama has taken against Mr Hook for some unknown reason. And now they say Sir Christopher has taken up with one of the Dent sisters. The elder one who has the annoying laugh. And the younger one probably will get her claws into Mr Hook.'

'I heard that it was Maria Richley.' Portia put her hand over Hattie's. 'We weren't meant to tell. Mama made us promise.'

Hattie pasted a smile on her face. Stephanie obviously knew that Portia would be unable to keep a secret and had primed her. After the incident at the musicale with the seating arrangements, she should have guessed that Stephanie was not going to give up her matchmaking scheme easily. Still the gossip caused a slight jealous twinge and that surprised her.

All in all it was safer if no one knew about her renewed friendship with Kit. Hattie forcibly turned the subject away from Sir Christopher and back towards safer subjects like gloves, gingerbread and the possibility of exotic animals.

The odour of spice and citrus fruit mixed with animal and overlaid with sawdust took Kit back to his childhood. He could remember every step of the fair even though he had not been in twenty-five years. The stalls looked tantalisingly familiar—here one for London Spice and there another selling oranges. Still further on were the stalls devoted to all manner of pots and pans. It appeared as if a large tented city had sprung up overnight. Kit struggled to see the windswept field where he and Hattie had picnicked only a few days before.

The memory of waiting outside the ale tent and hoping that his uncle would not turn out like his father sliced through him. *Your father has it all wrong, Kit. Bad blood doesn't mean you have to be bad. Damn your mother to hell. Never wait on a woman.*

Kit frowned and pushed the memory away. Over the years he'd perfected the art of not thinking about the past and only living in the present. And the present meant deciding what to do about Hattie. He wasn't ready to face that…yet, and it was unlike him to be mealy-mouthed. He would end it after the fair. The gift he gave her would be special, but in keeping with their relationship. The weight on his shoulders eased. He was going to do the right thing.

'Do keep up, Rupert,' Kit said as Rupert endeavoured to linger at the gun stall and then at Moles Swords where the latest models were hung with precision and a crowd of ten deep stood. 'You purchased a sword before we left London. Maybe now you will understand why I urged you to wait. Moles always brings out its new range for the Stagshaw fair.'

Rupert put down the rapier with a loud sigh. 'You are right. Nothing, not even a sword, can give me pleasure when the sight of my beloved is denied.'

'Petulance does you few favours,' Kit murmured. 'You were the one to get into this muddle. Women should be enjoyed, not mooned over.'

Rupert gave a glance behind him and his entire countenance lit up. 'Miss Parteger is at the glove stall, right when she said she would be. You are wrong, Kit, some women you can count on.'

Kit tensed. Hattie stood next to Miss Parteger, seemingly absorbed in choosing a pair of butter-yellow gloves. Her straw bonnet trimmed with green ribbons made a pleasant contrast with her round gown. Not a London sophisticate, but refreshing, someone who was comfortable in their skin. Was it just the novelty of freshness that intrigued? Kit frowned. It didn't matter. He would return to London soon and the flirtation would be over.

'Shall we go and investigate the famous Hexham Tans?' he said.

As he approached, Hattie looked up. Her straw bonnet framed her face, shadowing her features and making her look far more desirable than the majority of women of his acquaintance.

'Are you buying gloves?' he asked after they had exchanged pleasantries.

'Livvy is. She desires a new pair and they always do specials on fair days. She is looking at the other stalls, but I always come back to Hedley's. There is a certain something about the way they soften the leather.' She stretched out her hand. 'I can't make up my mind about whether the butter yellow or light tan is best.'

'For riding?'

'General purpose.'

He looked down at her hands. Her fingers were small and slender, but there was a certain indomitable strength in them. She was the sort of woman who would bend, but not break. 'Can a lady accept gloves from a gentleman or would it be too intimate a gift?'

Her eyes twinkled, warming him. He found he'd missed the barely suppressed humour. 'I suspect you already know the answer.'

'A pity as those butter-yellow gloves suit your hands perfectly.' He waited for her to agree. 'It is a fair day after all and the normal rules don't apply.'

'I would hate to cause talk. And you make your rules as you go along in any case.'

'Not all my rules. Some are immovable.'

'But most of them. It lulls people into a false sense of security.'

'Is it my fault if they wish to be lulled?'

Hattie stripped off the glove and handed it back to the stall owner with a decided shake of her head. As she began to make a pile of the various other gloves, Kit signalled first to the stall owner and then to Rupert, handing the stall owner some money. He'd give Hattie the gloves when the time was right.

'Is the fair everything you hoped at Waterloo?' she asked, glancing up just after he had completed the transaction.

'It is everything I remember, but it is as if I am looking through a Claude glass rather than actually being here.' He gave a laugh. 'Perhaps I need a guide.'

Her hand brushed his as she reached for the next set of gloves. 'Is there anything missing? Something that would help make the day perfect?'

Kit contemplated saying her exploring the fair with him, but decided that it would be revealing too much. He opted for something safer, less declaratory. 'I need to find a toy manufacturer.'

Her hands stilled. 'What sort of toys? Dolls? Wooden tops? You hardly seem like the child-loving sort.'

'Jumping-jacks—little men or women with a string you pull. I had one from the fair when I was a young boy. My uncle bought it for me.' Kit gazed over her shoulder and knew it would help ease the unsettled feeling if he could find the stall. It would reassure him that there was nothing magical about the stall. The jumping-jack was just that, a wooden toy. 'I wanted to see if such a creature still existed. The stall holder had a humpback and a hook nose, but he made the most wonderful wooden toys.'

Her mouth became a perfect O. 'You had one as a boy. From this fair. It is why you wanted to come back here?'

'That's right,' he agreed, surprised that she had guessed. 'My uncle gave me one as consolation.'

'Consolation? That is a strange word to use. Why did you need consolation? Had someone died?'

'I had waited outside the ale tent for hours.' Kit clamped his mouth shut. He had explained too much already. He remembered thinking that he'd meet his mother. Of course she had never appeared. He'd blocked the memory until now. The last thing he wanted was to discuss his mother, particularly not with Hattie Wilkinson. He'd already revealed more about his past than he'd intended. He never spoke about her. It saved having people look at him with pity.

'You won't find one on this row.' Hattie's brow knitted. 'The toy manufacturers are two rows down, near the London Spice merchant. I think I know the one you mean. I used to buy my nieces and nephews toys from him when they were little.'

'It sounds straightforward enough.' Kit touched his hat. He silently thanked her for not pursuing the topic. 'Rupert…'

Rupert had wandered down the stall and appeared to be in earnest discussion with Miss Parteger over a pair of gloves. Instantly he broke off the conversation and stood up straighter. Rupert appeared to have taken their conversations to heart. Kit gave a wry smile. Then he *was* Brendan's boy and Brendan could always be counted on to do what was right.

'I'm about to go that way after Livvy finishes and I return her to her mother.'

He caught her hand. 'And you won't lead me astray?'

She tilted her head to one side. Her eyes danced with mischief. 'I can show you if you like. As for leading you astray, I fear you went from that path long ago.'

Kit laughed. A heartbeat later, Hattie joined in.

The sound of her laughter made the whole day seem brighter. Kit knew he would get his way. He'd enjoy today and finish the flirtation before it started to mean anything. It was better that way. He'd retrieve the gloves from Rupert later and send them with a note before he left for London. And he would leave for London, once his business here was finished.

'That would be perfect. With you by my side, Mrs Wilkinson, I know I shan't lose my way.'

'I'll tell Livvy to hurry up. She has lingered far longer than I thought she would. Portia and Stephanie went off to buy oranges over an hour ago.'

'Rupert can look after your niece. He is quite safe.'

'Are you sure? The memory of the card room lingers.'

'He has grown on this trip. You must take my word for it.'

'I shall.'

Kit called to Rupert and told him to take Miss Parteger back to her mother without stopping for refreshment on the way. His godson blushed a deep scarlet.

'Very neatly done.'

'I like to think so.' Kit tucked her hand in the crook of his arm before she had a chance to pull away. 'What is the wagering that they do stop? Maybe not for refreshment, but to watch a Punch and Judy show or one of the other entertainments?'

'Just so you know, I never bet on a sure thing. It takes the fun out of it. Everyone should have a little romance in their life. It will be harmless.'

'You surprise me, Mrs Wilkinson. I was willing to wager on you not understanding about young romance except I make it a policy never to wager on a lady, only with her.'

Her eyes turned cloudy and something close to sorrow tugged at her mouth. In that instant, Kit hated her late husband. Seven years and he retained a hold over her. 'You are wrong about that. I understand about romance and its perils all too well.'

'Is this the one you want? Now that we are finally here.' Hattie held up a red-coated jumping-jack.

'And whose fault is that?'

'Yours, I believe.' She gave a light laugh, basking in the warmth of his smile. 'You kept seeing another stall you wanted to investigate.'

'It has been an age since I've been to a fair. I wanted to make certain things were here.'

'Including having a go at the ha'penny man?'

'I did win.'

The toy stall had proved more difficult to find than she thought it would be, not the least of which Kit seemed intent on taking the most circuitous route. Not that she had strenuously objected. She had enjoyed talking with him and laughing. They seemed to share the same sense of humour. They were friends, nothing more. It could never be anything more.

She refused to go back to the girl she had once been, and in any case, Kit had been clear about his views on marriage. She wished that she could be like someone in Mrs Reynaud's stories, but there were considerations. She shivered slightly, remembering how Charles's mistress had said that they were more alike than she thought.

To banish the unwelcome memory she blindly reached for another toy.

'Do you like this jumping-jack? Personally I think

he has a roguish smile, just the sort of thing for a man like you.'

'It will do.' His hand closed over it. A sudden fierce longing crossed over his face. 'The one I had as a boy had a dark-green coat with white trim.'

'You must have loved it.'

'It meant a lot to me once. It was about my only toy.'

Hattie's heart bled for the lonely boy that he must have been. 'Your only toy?'

'My father didn't hold with such things, but as it was a present from my uncle, he allowed me to keep it.'

'Then it was good that you loved it so much.'

He tilted his head to one side. 'I suspect you find it strange. But my father had his own views on life.'

'Not at all. Just tell me that he died a lonely and bitter old man.'

He lifted an eyebrow. 'Why?'

'It saves me from having to kill him. Children should have toys. There is time enough to be grown up.'

'My father would not have agreed. Boys need to learn to be men. My father was a hard man.'

'But you are not your father.'

'I'm grateful you realise that. I try not to take after either of my parents.'

Hattie relaxed in the sunshine of his smile. A sharp longing sliced through her. If only… Hattie pushed it away. It was far too late for regrets. She was not the type to indulge in casual affairs of the heart. She had her responsibilities and duties to think about. This had to be the last time she indulged in a flirtation with Kit.

'The jumping-jack will be a present from me,' she said, taking control of the conversation.

His eyes narrowed. 'Are jumping-jacks different than gloves?'

'Jumping-jacks are better given as gifts. Every child since time began knows that. It adds to the magic.'

'I agree.' There was a catch in his voice and he turned his face from hers.

'Is something wrong?' She laid her hand on his arm. 'Kit, explain. We are friends. I want to know.'

He turned back towards her. His eyes held a distinctly sultry look which caused a warm curl to wind its way around her insides. 'I normally never let my lady buy me anything.'

A warm shiver went down her back. She envied the unknown lady who would be his. A longing to feel his lips against hers and the touch of his hand against her skin filled her.

'But I'm not yours, am I?' she returned more tartly than she had intended. 'It is a gift from a friend, nothing more.'

His eyes bore into her, searching down to her soul. Hattie returned his gaze as steadily as she could, hoping he didn't see the white lie.

'I stand corrected,' he said finally. 'In that case I shall be delighted to accept the gift. Child that I am.'

'Play with it wisely. It is what I always tell my nieces and nephews when I give them a toy,' she joked after she had paid the wizened toymaker.

Keep it light. She needed to keep it light. She gripped her reticule tighter. Their time was coming to an end and she didn't want it to.

She could easily imagine what one of his London mistresses would be like—the highly sophisticated way she'd laugh and how her gestures would be perfectly poised. Everything she wasn't and could never be.

'I intend to treasure it.' Kit tucked it into his breast pocket. 'It should be safe there. Thank you, Hattie. It is a first being given something like this from a woman, but then you are unique.'

Hattie dipped her head. There was a wealth of meaning in those words. If she wasn't careful, she would start wanting to be kissed again. And that would be a very bad idea. 'I should get back to the family. Livvy and Portia will be wondering what has happened to me.'

'Surely they can spare you for a while longer yet? There must be some part of the fair you haven't explored. Perhaps you'd like your fortune told. There are always gypsies at fairs like these.'

'I'm not overfond of fortune tellers. My husband used to enjoy such pastimes.'

'And you gave them up as frivolous on his death.' He held up his hand. 'Say no more, Hattie. Your past defines you.'

'That is not it at all.'

'Why can't you linger with me a while? We won't have our fortune told. We can enjoy the fair in other ways.'

'They count on me. I don't know where I'd be without them.' A sudden chill passed through Hattie. She'd been so close to agreeing. She needed to keep this friendship light and easy, but not lose sense of what was truly important in her life, permanent and lasting—her family. 'It helped so much to have them near after Charles's death. They restored my faith in humanity.'

'You should try living for yourself more.'

'It's funny...that is precisely what Mrs Reynaud said.' She straightened her back. 'You mustn't worry. Once they are grown, I intend to travel the world, really travel. There are so many places I long to see. I make a list every year. I only stay in Northumberland because Stephanie and her girls can't cope without me.'

'Mrs Reynaud?' A puzzled look came on his face and he seemed to go rigid. 'Do you know someone called Reynaud?'

'An elderly lady. One of your tenants. At Pearl Cottage.'

'None of my tenants is called Reynaud. I would know.'

'Perhaps she used a different name.' Hattie gave a little shrug. 'Her agreement was with your uncle. I think she knew your family when she was younger.' Hattie lowered her voice. 'She has led an exciting life and doles out tales of her wickedness. Stephanie doesn't entirely approve of her, but I enjoy her company.'

Kit's face became carved out of stone. All humour and goodwill had vanished. 'I can't remember ever meeting a Mrs Reynaud. What does she look like?'

'She says she is much altered. A few years ago before she came to the Tyne Valley, she suffered from smallpox and totally lost her looks. Recently she has become more of a recluse than ever. Mrs Belter told me that she had refused to come to the fair because the children might point their fingers and call her a witch.'

Kit tapped his fingers together. He looked her up and down in an assessing sort of way. Hattie was aware of the simplicity of her dress and the fact that it was several seasons old. He must consider it hopelessly naïve and unattractive. He took a step closer to her and his eyes became almost feline.

'I agree with her assessment, whoever this Mrs Reynaud is. You should have a life, Hattie, and let your nieces lead their own.' His hand slid down her back and his breath tickled her ear. 'It is your life to live. You only have one. Seize it.'

'I don't understand what you are saying.' She hated the way her voice caught. Her lips ached as if he had kissed them again.

'I think you do.' His voice rolled over her, silently urging her to move closer. Seductive in the extreme. 'I think you understand me very well. We could be good together.'

Hattie pulled her hand away. She pressed her fingers to her temples and willed the siren call to be gone. She knew what he was asking and she also knew she wasn't ready. Not today and probably not ever. She had to leave now and not look back.

'Hattie?'

'When I require your advice, I'll ask,' she said stiffly. She had nearly done it and she couldn't. She'd hate herself later if she embarked on an affair. She wasn't going to be like…like her late husband's mistress. She shuddered, remembering the time she'd visited and how awkward it had all been. She had to stay with where she was safe. She started to walk away from Kit.

'Where are you going now?' He reached her in two strides and put his hand on her elbow, bringing her against his body. 'I didn't think you were given to false modesty, Hattie.'

'Stephanie will have created a small camp for us near the black-faced sheep. She worries about my brother-in-law becoming lost and so they go back to the same place every year.' Hattie jerked her arm away. To think how close she had come! Poor deluded Hattie had nearly done it again. Been swept away on the romance and forgetting the cost. 'They will be wondering where I am. It was bad of me to go off like this.'

The dimple shone in his cheek, highlighting his lips. 'Your brother-in-law gets confused?'

'It is the one day of the year that he spends time in the ale tent. Stephanie refuses to go in, but always waits to take him home.' Hattie gave a careful shrug, but she was aware of how near he stood and where his hands were. Her sister and brother-in-law were very different but they did seem to have a happy marriage, something that was for ever going to elude her. All she wanted to do was to find a quiet place and regain control of herself. She'd been so close to giving in to temptation. It had been seeing the longing in his face when he held the jumping-jack in his hand which had nearly undone her and made her think that he might want something else. 'It is an arrangement which has served them well.'

'Shall I walk you there? Fairs can be notorious for drunks and others making a nuisance. Allow me to keep you safe.'

'I can find my own way.' Hattie used her reticule as a shield. 'The fair has so much to offer. You must try the ale tent yourself. If you find my brother-in-law, remind him that we are expecting to go home at a reasonable hour rather than at eight when the fair finishes. Please let me go, Kit.'

'Independent to a fault.' He held up his hand and his eyes became steely grey. 'I understand.'

Hattie didn't flinch even though she was dying inside. 'It is the way I like it. Independent but respectable. I can't have it any other way.'

'Because of your husband's memory?'

'Do not bring my late husband into this.' A cold chill went down her spine. She couldn't lie about Charles. Not to Kit. The thought stunned her.

'Let me know if you ever feel lonely.'

'I bid you adieu, Kit. I'll understand if you have to go back to London suddenly.' She made an expansive gesture as her insides wept. 'I hope this is everything you wanted.'

His hand curled about hers and then let go. 'Thank you, Hattie…for my jumping-jack.'

Hattie forced herself to walk away without looking back. It was one of the hardest things she had ever done, but she knew it was the right thing. Kit suddenly appeared to be taking liberties, to misunderstand why she'd purchased that stupid jumping-jack. She was safer on her own.

Chapter Seven

Walking away from Kit was the right thing to do, Hattie thought as she strode away from where he stood. To stay would mean giving in to temptation and starting to believe that there was something between them. She had nearly cried when he told her the story about the jumping-jack and then he became so cold, practically accusing her of trying to interfere. And then he'd made the suggestion and it changed everything. She was not going to tumble into bed with him. Ever.

Hattie pushed past the gawkers around the find-a-penny man and the farmers and their wives outside the exotic curiosity stall. She resisted the temptation to turn around and see where Kit was.

A gypsy cart had become stuck in the middle of a boggy bit. Hattie attempted to squeeze around the back, ignoring the gypsy woman who offered to read the pretty lady's fortune. When she was a little girl, Mrs Hampstead used to tell stories about how gypsies spirited people away, over and over again because Stephanie loved being scared. Even now, Hattie was not entirely comfortable around them. They were harmless for the most part and a simple 'no' generally sufficed.

A gypsy man with a scarlet bandana and a gold earring loomed up in front of her, asking if she wanted a bit of lucky heather.

Hattie shook her head 'no', picked up and hurried off in the opposite direction.

By the time she'd recovered her composure, she realised that she was in completely the wrong place, close to the rough end of the fair where the cockfighting and bear-baiting happened, with no easy or straightforward way to get to where Stephanie had set up camp.

She wished she had taken Kit's offer to escort her back but that would have only prolonged the agony. It was over and done. She could go back to her dull, unexciting life.

'Hey, watch where you are going.' a man shouted at her and she managed to duck before she was hit by a large metal trap.

'That was far from my fault,' Hattie muttered and turned down another row of stalls. These were devoted to all manner of farm equipment. She turned another way and heard the cries of a cockfight. She could never understand why anyone would think such a thing was entertainment.

She rubbed her hand over her face. Several painted women sauntered passed, with swinging hips and fixed expressions. The distinct odour of stale alcohol choked the air.

Hattie picked up her skirts and began to hurry towards the ale tent. It was early enough so there should not be too great of a problem. But once there, she'd get her bearings. Stephanie was going to be annoyed.

She could handle Stephanie, but she knew if anything had happened to Livvy or Portia, she'd never forgive herself.

What could she have been thinking about, going off with Kit like that? She'd abandoned Livvy for nothing but her own pleasure. Hattie quickened her steps. *Idiot. Idiot. Idiot.* Her boots seemed to pound out the words. Hattie reached for a handkerchief and covered her nostrils.

'What's your hurry, my dear?' A rough hand grabbed her elbow. Her captor sported a purple scar stretching from the corner of his right eye to his nose. Two more men stood behind him, egging him on. 'We can have some sport with this one.'

'I am not your dear.' Hattie drew herself up to her full height and gave her most imperious stare. The last thing she wanted to show was fear, particularly not to a man who looked the worst for drink. It was all a misunderstanding. 'Unhand me and allow me to go about my business unhampered.'

'Pardon me for breathing.' His hand loosened. He said something in an undertone to his loathsome companions.

A nervous trembling filled Hattie's limbs. It was that easy. Mrs Reynaud was right. A positive attitude could work miracles. Her virtue was her shield.

She started to move on, slowly and sedately, but purposefully. The men were drunk. They'd leave her alone. Once she'd returned to Stephanie, she was never going to hanker after travelling or adventures again.

'Give us a kiss. Proud lady.' Another hand caught her upper arm. The stench of sour ale and tobacco filled her nostrils. This time she was pulled back against his fat chest.

'Let me go.'

Kit let Hattie walk away into the crowd. It had all gone wrong when she'd mentioned the name Reynaud. Stupid, really. There were hundreds of people with that name. It wasn't Hattie's fault that his mother had abandoned him for a Frenchman named Jacques Reynaud. The woman in question was probably another innocent caught up in the mess his mother had left behind.

He'd taken the crude and insulting way out, using his seductive voice to make suggestions, making her unsure. He'd known that she'd leave. Coward that he was. And all because of a name from the past that should no longer have any power. He was a man, not a youth who had been teased endlessly about his mother and her morals. Disgust filled him. He knew the proper way to act in society. But it was better this way. Their friendship had to end before…before he started to care.

He curled his hand about the jumping-jack and regarded the various faces of the farm labourers and other men. The noise from the ale tent had increased. Hattie might think that she didn't need his help, but he was not about to abandon her. Not when it was his fault to begin with.

He watched her take a wrong turning and then followed a few paces behind. Once she was back with her family, he'd relax and she'd cease to be his problem.

He lost sight of her when she rounded the gypsy caravan. Kit went down one aisle and then another, but nowhere did he see Hattie's back. He started to circle around towards the ale tent, ignoring the shorter route by the cock and bear pits. Hattie with her strict sensibilities would never go there.

Let me go.

Her voice floated on the air.

Kit broke into a run. Near the cockpit, he saw her, surrounded by a group of farmhands who were the worse for wear with drink. Several of them gave coarse laughs and called out obscene suggestions.

Hattie's hand beat against the largest one's chest. Her straw bonnet had slipped off her head and lay abandoned in the mud. Kit cursed. Her predicament was all his fault.

He knew the dangers that a fair could bring and he'd been the one to allow her to wander about on her own. His mistake and he always owned up.

He glanced around. Four against one. The odds were not good, but he refused to stand by. Going and fetching the parish constable was not an option. But if he started something, others would join in and lend a hand.

'Unhand that lady!'

'Mind your business. We are having a bit of sport.'

Kit clenched his fists. His eyes flickered from face to face, memorising their features. He'd lost count of how many fights he'd experienced, but he knew how to fight and he was sober. 'I doubt that is possible. She is with me. I look after my own. Unless you want to be seriously injured or worse, let her go now.'

The mountain of a man loosened his grip on Hattie. The primitive urge to tear him limb from limb filled Kit. He struggled to keep his temper. Cool and collected won fights—giving in to anger resulted in errors. He'd learnt that back at Eton when he'd tried to defend his mother's name.

'Who will stop me? You? On your own? I have won my last six bouts in the ring.'

A would-be pugilist who had had far too much to drink. Kit stifled a laugh. It was going to be easier than he thought.

'It is a serious mistake to doubt my ability. My pugilist ability is renowned in London. Ask at any pub about Kit Foxton and see what they say.'

The mountain scratched his nose. 'It ain't known up here.'

'We could have a bare-knuckle fight if you wish, but allow the lady to go about her business,' Kit said in a deadly voice.

'And you think to come from London and tell us our ways.'

'You should respect your betters.' The blood pumped through Kit's veins. He looked forward to the fight. To do something. 'Shall we have at it, here and now?'

The mountain shoved Hattie away from him. Kit breathed again. 'If you wish.'

'Kit…' Hattie was suddenly very afraid '…he has a knife.'

'Go, Hattie. Get help. This shouldn't take long.' He turned his head slightly and felt the first punch graze his temple. 'You shouldn't have done that. I don't mind a fair fight, but not an unfair one. We start when we start and not before.'

He landed a punch squarely in the fat farmhand's middle, brought his knee up and connected again. The man countered with a wild stab, but the knife missed by a hairbreadth. Kit punched again, harder, and the man collapsed on the ground. When the man was down on the ground, Kit stamped on his wrist and the knife dropped from his grip. Kit kicked the knife away.

'Playing with knives can get you hurt.' Kit picked him up by the lapels. 'Are you ready to begin our fight?'

The man grunted and wildly flailed his arms. Kit landed a blow on the man's jaw. The man gurgled slightly and lay back. Kit lowered him to the ground. It was easier than he thought. Kit dusted down his breeches and turned his back on the prone man. 'Does anyone else have a quarrel with me?'

The three men looked at each other and began to back away. Cowards.

Kit gave them a look of utter contempt. 'Next time, give the ladies more respect.'

'I ain't finished yet, Londoner.' A fist came out of nowhere, landing in the middle of Kit's back.

Kit crouched and began to fight in earnest as blow after blow rained down on his head. Somewhere in the distance, he heard the sound of a parish constable's whistle.

The world turned black at the edges and a sharp pain went into his jaw, swiftly followed by a pain to the back of his head.

'All my fault, Hattie, I didn't mean to frighten you,' he murmured. The world went black.

Hattie swallowed the scream and rushed over to where Kit lay in the dirt, heedless of the way her skirt swept into the thick mud, ready to defend him, now that he was defenceless.

She put her hand on his chest. He was still breathing. The attackers had either run off at the sound of the whistle or lay on the ground, groaning. The fight was over. Kit had won, but at what cost? He couldn't be seriously hurt because of her folly, could he?

Hattie offered a silent prayer. She didn't care what happened to her reputation or anything else as long as Kit was all right. This entire mess had happened because of her pride and her fear. She knew where the blame lay and she wanted to make amends. A shiver went through her.

'Come on. Kit,' she said. 'We need to get you to the doctor.'

Kit mumbled incoherently and failed to rise.

'Here now, what is going on?' a burly parish constable demanded, bustling up. He gave another loud toot on his whistle. He started in surprise. 'Mrs Wilkinson, what are you doing here? Messed up in this nonsense? It isn't a sight for a lady such as yourself. Where is your family? Someone should be looking after you. It ain't safe around here. Here is where the gaming happens. And the cockfighting. Your brother-in-law should have known better.'

Hattie heaved a sigh of relief. Mr Jessop was the parish constable for St Michael's, rather than being from one of the other parishes. It made things much easier. She stood up and faced him.

'I made a mistake and turned the wrong way. Thankfully, my guardian angel was looking after me and sent a protector.'

'Where is he?'

'There on the ground. Sir Christopher Foxton.'

Mr Jessop gaped. 'Sir Christopher Foxton? He is involved? This is bad, very bad.'

Hattie noticed the other men turn white and start to edge away. A group of farmhands stood solidly behind Mr Jessop, preventing them from leaving.

'These men attacked me and Sir Christopher defended my honour, Mr Jessop. What you see is the aftermath of battle, which I am delighted to say Sir Christopher won.' Hattie rapidly explained the situation, giving an account that was accurate in all the particulars but skated over some of the details. There was no need to tell the constable about the quarrel which preceded the event. All he had to know was that Sir Christopher had defended her honour with great vigour.

'In broad daylight?' The parish constable's eyes widened. He drew himself up. 'What is the world coming to? You should have stayed to the main part of the fair, Mrs Wilkinson.'

'They were insensible with drink.' Hattie pressed her hands together and tried to keep her limbs from trembling. 'It is lucky Sir Christopher happened by when he did.'

'Do you wish to press charges?'

Hattie regarded the patch of spreading red on Kit's chest and the way his face was swelling. A primitive urge to see the men hanged filled her. She pushed it away. 'You must do as you see fit, Mr Jessop. It was a fight, but it is also the day of Stagshaw fair. You will have to speak with Sir Christopher when he is in a better state.'

'I see, Mrs Wilkinson. No doubt there will be a few

sore heads in the morning. A spell cooling off over in Hexham gaol will do them good.'

'I wish to get medical help for Sir Christopher before anything else happens. Sir Christopher's well-being is the most important thing.'

Kit mumbled something. Hattie bent down. 'What is it you want to say?'

His fingers curled about hers. 'Don't leave me,' he murmured in a broken whisper. 'Please stay…please, I beg you.'

Hattie's heart flipped over. She smoothed a lock of hair from his forehead. He'd risked his life for her. All this had happened because she had decided to take offence at his flirtatious comments, comments which were not meant to be taken literally. She had behaved worse than an aged maiden aunt. He wasn't asking her to stay for ever, just until he recovered. 'Yes, I'll look after you. I promise. I've no intention of leaving you.'

He gave a crooked smile and closed his eyes. 'Good.'

She held his hand, waiting until he became calm and his breathing regular. After what Kit had said, her decision was surprisingly easy. It didn't matter that Stephanie would be terribly shocked. Stephanie would get over it. One simply did not turn one's back on someone who had risked his life for her.

'His lordship can't stay here,' Mr Jessop said. 'It's not right.'

'I will take Sir Christopher back to the Dower House where he can be properly nursed.' Hattie stood up. 'I would appreciate the doctor arriving there as soon as possible. I will want several stout men to help me to get him into the governess cart.'

'Back to your house, ma'am? Are you sure that is wise?'

'I pay my debts, Mr Jessop, and I owe this man a huge debt. You send Dr Gormley to me once he has been found.'

'It is fair day, Mrs Wilkinson.' Mr Jessop rocked back on his heels.

'You may try the ale tent or, failing that, machinery exhibition. The good doctor is as fond of inventions as the next man.'

Hattie waited, trying to keep her gaze steady. Surely Mr Jessop was going to assist her, rather than throwing up roadblocks?

Mr Jessop nodded and gave the orders. 'It is my profound regret that this happened. We run a clean fair. It must be ten years since anything of significance has happened.'

'I know you do. It wasn't your fault.' Hattie bent down and shook Kit's shoulder. 'Kit, can you walk or do you need to be carried?'

'Give me your shoulder, Hattie, and I'll walk. I can do anything if you help me. I can do more things if you'd kiss me.' The words were a bit slurred and Hattie wondered if he'd hit his head in the fight. The Kit she was used to would never say such a thing.

Mr Jessop, she noticed, had studiously averted his eyes. So much for her hope to keep anything with Sir Christopher private—the gossip would be all over the fair within minutes. 'If you are sure you don't need us for anything else, I will get him back to my house. I believe he has hit his head.'

'I'll help you, ma'am, in case he falls like,' a thin farmer said. 'Way aye, I saw the whole thing and one of them brought a walking stick down on his head. 'Tweren't right, that. The man's a hero. It weren't many men who'd do something like that.'

'We will haul this lot up in front of the magistrates come Monday morning,' Mr Jessop declared.

'I will be happy to give evidence,' the farmer said. 'And me lad as well.'

Hattie felt the tears well up. She hadn't expected any assistance and now it seemed people were queuing up to support her.

'Let me know if his condition worsens,' Mr Jessop called out as she started the slow march towards her governess cart with Kit's heavy weight leaning on her shoulder.

'Obviously.'

Was what she was doing the right thing? Hattie gave a small shudder when she thought about Stephanie, but that couldn't be helped. She'd given Kit her word and she intended on keeping it. They were friends.

Please let him be all right. That was all that mattered.

Chapter Eight

Kit woke with a start from confused dreams about Hattie, his uncle and various jumping-jacks. A single candle shone by the bed and there was an engraving of some biblical scene hanging on the opposite wall. The room was small and austere, a sickroom and utterly unfamiliar.

His entire body ached and his right eye was swollen shut. And he was dressed in a voluminous nightshirt, unlike the sort he normally wore. His head ached like the very devil.

He searched his mind, trying to figure out how he'd arrived here. The events of the afternoon came flooding back. As far as bright ideas went, taking on four men was not one of his better ones. But try as he might, between landing the first punch and to just now, his mind was a blank.

He put a hand to the back of his head, probing. A huge pain shot through him, blinding in its intensity. He'd obviously banged his head. But beyond a few aches and pains, he would survive. There was no reason to stay here, helpless and at the mercy of some unknown quack.

He swung his feet over the side of the bed and started to push his protesting body to a stand.

'Oh, no, you don't. You are to stay in bed and get well.' Cool hands pushed him back down on to crisp linen sheets. He turned his head in case his fevered mind had conjured her up.

The candlelight made her blonde hair shine and highlighted the hollow at the base of her throat. An angel. No, an angel would not wear a sprigged muslin. An angel would be dressed in flowing robes. It was Hattie in the flesh and blood. Her sewing had fallen to the floor as she stood to enforce her command. The sheer domesticity of the scene made him want to weep.

He rubbed his left eye and tried to open his right to make sure he wasn't dreaming. He could not remember the last time when someone volunteered to look after him. Since an early age, it had always been someone who was paid and done out of duty, rather than for any other reason. A sense of great humbleness filled Kit. Hattie had done this for him.

'Where am I?'

'At my house.'

'Your house?' Kit searched his mind, but the big black well prevented him. 'What am I doing here? The last thing I remember is getting into a fight with a stubborn drunk.'

'You are to stay in bed until the doctor says that you can rise.' She crossed her arms and glared at him. 'I'd be grateful if you obliged me in this if nothing else.'

He tried to catch her hand before remembering how she'd walked away from him and settled for clutching the sheet instead. He refused to beg. He had deliberately driven her away.

'Hattie? Why am I here? How? You live miles away from Stagshaw. The last thing I recall is the fight near the cockpit. And that drunk with his paws on you.'

'Not too far.' She turned her face from him, revealing her slender neck. 'I had them bring you to my house. It seemed the best place. A bit closer than Southview. I was being practical after...after the fight. You couldn't be left on your own, waiting for the doctor to show up.'

'I thank you.'

'It was the least I could do in the circumstances. I'd do it for any wretch who risked their neck to save me.'

Kit swallowed with difficulty. She'd had him brought here out of duty. 'Why?'

She stood up without speaking and moved over to the right, away from his vision.

'Why, Hattie? There must have been a dozen other places I could have gone.'

'You were injured trying to save me. It seemed to be the Christian thing to do. I could hardly count on your valet or Mr Hook to look after you properly.'

'Beggars can't be choosers. I shall put my faith in your nursing skill.' He hated how his heart thumped. He knew it for a lie. He couldn't think of anyone he'd rather have nursing him and it frightened him. She'd forgiven his outburst without him doing anything.

'It is good of you to accept what is going to happen.'

'You haven't given me much choice.' He lay back on the pillows and breathed in the lavender scent. The smell reminded him of when he was a young boy in his room back in Hampshire, safe and secure without a care. He could almost picture the scene with the fire blazing and his nurse sitting, knitting socks, while a kettle hummed in the background.

'You were in no fit state.'

'My head pains me.' Kit tore his mind away from the memory. He always swore that he'd never voluntarily think about his childhood, and certainly not with a great longing. He must have hit his head far harder than he'd thought.

Hattie laid a cool cloth on his forehead. 'Is that better?'

A warm glow flooded through him. Despite her words dismissing him earlier, Hattie had stayed by his side. More than that, she'd obviously insisted that he was carried to her house. She'd publicly declared their friendship, after telling him that they were finished. Women were a different species entirely. He reached out his hand. 'You need not have done that.'

'Allow me to make my own decisions. I prefer to have my conscience at rest than worrying over your health.'

Kit struggled to upright. He clutched the blanket to his chest and tried to make sense of the turn of events. Nothing, simply flashes of voices. However, with each breath, he found himself more distracted by the way Hattie's hair curled about her shoulders and the shadowy place at her throat. 'Did you undress me? How did I get this nightshirt?'

A merry peal of laughter filled the room. 'You may stop looking shocked. You would think you were unused to a woman's attentions. It is not as if I haven't seen the male form before.'

'Hattie!' He pulled the collar of his nightshirt up.

'The doctor did it for me.' She shook her head.

'He wanted to examine the wound to your chest, but it turned out to be just a light cut. But your shirt is ruined. I found one of my late husband's nightshirts. It seemed sensible. Sleeping in one's clothes is hardly advisable at any time, but particularly not when one has been injured.'

He collapsed back against the pillows. He should have expected respectability from her. It was wrong that he'd briefly hoped that she'd been unable to resist taking a peek. 'The ruffian managed to miss. Sometimes my luck astonishes me. He must have been unable to see straight.'

'There was a deflection, something was in the way.' She sobered and her teeth worried her bottom lip.

'Out with it. Let me know the worst.'

'I'm afraid the jumping-jack took the brunt of one knife blow and then you managed to twist the knife out of his hand.'

Kit fell back amongst the pillows. Had the jumping-jack not been in his breast pocket, the knife would have sliced through his chest. A cold shiver went through him. 'Obviously a good-luck charm. I intend to keep it.'

'I'll get it for you.' She handed him the remains of the jumping-jack and shook her head. 'I don't think it is worth saving.'

'I must be more sentimental than you.' He smiled up at her. 'I think it is worth keeping.'

'That is your choice.'

'I shall treasure it always. Generally I take better care of my gifts than this.'

Her lips parted as if she was about to say something, but thought better of it. 'You need to rest. The doctor left some more laudanum for you.'

Kit shook his head. He felt as if he had been run over by a cart and then stamped on, but he could manage. If he drank the laudanum, the dreams about his childhood would start again—a figure in a blue dress smiling down at him, laughing at her boy, asking him to be brave.

He forced a wry smile and hoped Hattie would believe him. 'I dislike having my wits clouded. I've endured worse pain.'

'It is here if you change your mind.' She put a small glass beside the bed. He was aware of the intimacy and how her hair fell about her shoulders.

Gingerly he felt his jaw, sore but unbroken. He wanted her, he wanted to feel her move under him and catch her soft sigh in his mouth as she surrendered to the heat and passion. But he also wanted to hear her laugh, see her smile and above all he wanted to talk to her.

'Is there some reason why you are nursing me?' he asked in case she decided to leave.

'Instead of Mr Hook?' Hattie leant forwards and tucked the bedclothes about his body. Impersonal, but intimate at the same time. Her round gown gaped slightly and he caught a glimpse of the shadowy hollow between her breasts.

He tore his mind away from such thoughts. Hattie nursed his broken body out of compassion and duty. The fact that he noticed her considerable assets showed him that death would have to find another victim. He'd recover. It was merely his blinding headache that bothered him.

'If you like, Rupert could have done it.'

She laughed. 'He appeared distinctly ill at the prospect of blood. I'd no wish to torture him.'

'And Johnson, my valet?'

'Your valet was no use. Last seen in the ale tent, according to Mr Hook, rather the worse for wear.'

Kit silently blessed Rupert's quick thinking. If they had found Johnson, he would not be here. And despite everything, he was glad to be here. In this room. With Hattie. He valued her friendship. He groaned, remembering the taste of her mouth. He wanted to taste it again, particularly now.

At her look he said, 'I gave him the day off. It is his to use as he pleases.'

'You are a generous employer.'

'I can afford to be. Johnson's ability with boot polish and the starching of neckcloths is second to none.' He watched her, waiting for the slightest hint of what she was thinking, if she was aware of him as he was of her. 'No doubt he will turn up early in the morning with a suit of clothes. Johnson takes his job very seriously.'

'It is good to know. I will leave a note for Mrs Hampstead so she isn't surprised.'

'You still haven't said. Why did you insist on bringing me here?'

'You saved me from those drunken men and I'm determined you will be nursed with all care and attention.' She dipped her head. 'Too many people in my life have died who were not nursed properly. It was time to make sure it didn't happen again.'

Her husband. It was painfully simple to guess who she wasn't naming. Kit hated the twinge of jealousy he felt for Charles Wilkinson, the hero of Talavera. He had to be slipping. He prided himself on not caring about anyone's past or who they had loved. It was only the present that interested him. Ever. Except Hattie's past interfered with his present. She had the capacity for life.

He breathed in and his ribs ached.

'Then I'm grateful,' he said stiffly. 'You mustn't feel you should sit up with me. It will take more than a few knocks on my head to kill a reprobate like me.'

'You always insist on painting yourself blacker than you are.'

'I will not have you thinking I am better.'

'It was my fault that you were involved in the fight. I do pay my debts, Sir Christopher, and I owe you a great one.'

Kit watched how her slender fingers moved in the candlelight. She no longer wore a wedding ring. 'I enjoyed the fight for the most part. It suited my mood.'

'You enjoyed it?' She blinked rapidly. 'How could you enjoy something like that?'

Kit closed his eyes. It had felt good to work off his excess anger. He wanted to show her that he could do something for her and he had. The bruises and cuts were superficial. 'There's a certain amount of satisfaction in seeing someone get what they thoroughly deserve. He should never have done that.'

'But you are hurt. You didn't have to.'

'What would you have used—your elbows?' It was far harder to remember how Hattie looked, than to think about the way his hands and face hurt.

Her jaw became set. 'I can look after myself. I've been doing it for a long while now.'

'And I've been worse.' He forced his face into a ghost of a smile. 'Nothing appears broken. I will mend.'

'You will mend because I intend on making certain that you do.'

'Well, I feel that my presence is an imposition. And you even have me dressed in one of your husband's nightshirts.' Kit hated that he sounded so ungrateful.

'He never wore it.' Shutters came down on her eyes, instantly hiding her soul from him. 'Somehow, I never could get rid of the linen. I found it when I got out the sheet for the bed. It seemed the ideal opportunity to put it to practical use.'

It annoyed him that even after all this time, she still mourned her late husband. He was under no illusion that when he left a woman, within a few months she had forgotten him. Sometimes the bed they had shared was barely cold before another entered it.

He certainly made no effort to remember any of them. There might be tears for a little while, but ultimately they both went on their respective ways. It was the way it had to be. Remembering never did anyone any good.

Kit refused to think about the little boy he'd been, crying for a mother who never came. A mother who never came not because she was dead and living with the angels, but because she had left, unable to stand living with him. He had crouched down on the landing when his nurse thought he was in bed and had heard everything, seen everything. Silently he had willed his mother to glance up at him and stop. She kept walking with a handkerchief pressed to her face. She had been the most beautiful thing in his life and then she was gone, no more than a memory.

'You must have been very close.' He choked out the words, tearing his mind away from the unwelcome thought. He must have hit his head far harder than he'd considered. Normally he had no trouble in forgetting his mother. The illusion of her exquisiteness and delicacy had been well and truly shattered when he discovered a pile of old newspapers, complete with the criminal conversation trial of his mother, detailing her lovers. 'That much is clear.'

'Why would you say that?' Hattie clenched her hands together so tightly he could see the white knuckles. Her eyes glittered in the candlelight.

Silently Kit prayed that there wouldn't be tears. He hated tears. He'd lost count of the crocodile tears various women had shed in order to gain some trinket or another.

'You always look away when you speak about him.'

'We weren't close.' Her hesitant voice trembled with barely suppressed passion. 'I found out after he died that I never really knew him at all.'

'I'm sorry.' To his surprise, he meant it. 'A wife should know her husband. They should not have secrets.'

'Don't be,' she snapped and then appeared to recollect where she was. She sat up straighter and smoothed her sprigged muslin. She continued in a self-deprecating tone. 'I used to be very naïve and believed because a man told you that he worshipped the ground you walked on that he meant it.'

'He didn't?' Kit put his hands behind his head. The news that Charles Wilkinson was not a paragon made things easier.

Hattie was silent for such a long while that he wondered if she'd fallen asleep. Then, when he was about to whisper her name, she slowly began to speak.

'He had an adored mistress and a scattering of illegitimate children. Born before and after our marriage. I was the socially acceptable wife.' Her hands shook and she clasped them together until her knuckles shone white as she choked out the words. With each trembling syllable, the words sped up until they became a raging torrent. 'He feared if he married the woman he truly loved that his father would cut him off without a penny. It would not have been so bad if I had known how he felt, but I had no inkling. It came as a great shock.'

She finished on a half-laugh combined with a sob.

A coward. Powerful and primitive urges filled Kit. He longed to wring his neck for making a woman like Hattie suffer.

'So it was an arranged marriage?' he asked, trying to understand why someone who was so passionate had opted for something as bloodless as an arranged marriage.

'It was a marriage because he took me out to a summer house and whispered sweet nothings, swearing eternal devotion.' A single tear tracked down her cheek. She brushed it away before he could capture it. 'I was in love with the romance of it all. My husband knew the right words to woo me. I only discovered the truth after it was far too late.'

'On your wedding night?'

Her throat worked up and down. Her entire being vibrated with anguish. 'Worse, after he died. Stupid fool that I was. I swallowed his lies whole, never questioned. He was away, fighting, most of the time.'

'You never questioned or you didn't want to question?' he enquired.

She gave a sickly smile. 'It made it easy to keep my illusions. I lived for his letters. They were so sweet and so full of promises.'

'Were you in love with him?' He held up his hand, appalled that the question had slipped out. 'That was bad of me. I apologise. I have no right to ask.'

She turned her blue-green shimmering eyes to him. 'Sometimes I wonder if I ever loved him or just the idea of him,' she said in a deadly calm voice which contrasted with her earlier anguish. 'When I found out about his perfidy, I discovered that I couldn't tell anyone about the truth of the marriage.'

'Why?'

'I've my pride. I paid his debts and settled his other loose ends in the most expedient fashion. Then, Stephanie needed help and so I gave it, selfishly gaining a new start to my life where no one could pity me.'

'And no one knows about it? Not even your sister?'

'You know now.' She wiped her eyes with fierce fingers. 'I didn't want you to have some mistaken idea about my marriage. Or how I might feel about my late husband.'

Kit's heart leapt. Her marriage was far different from the one he'd imagined. He wasn't competing against some perfect ghost, but rather she'd been damaged in some way because of her late husband's heavy-handedness. It put the kiss they had shared in an entirely different perspective.

'I'm sorry,' he said. 'I had no idea.'

She dipped her head. Her hands were folded in her lap. 'You can't lose something you never had.'

He watched her without saying anything, but he could see she was teetering on a knife's edge. He doubted that she would have shared this information even a few hours ago. The fight had changed everything. He was very glad it had. The minor discomfort of a few bruises and pulled muscles was nothing compared to the relief of not competing against a ghost.

'What would he have wanted for you?'

'What he would have wanted is no concern of mine.' She shook her head. 'Stephanie keeps telling me that he'd have wanted me to marry. Charles Wilkinson was a dear friend of my brother-in-law's. Every time she brings the subject of remarriage up, I become more determined to stay a widow.'

'You are allowing him to define you.'

'I beg your pardon.' Her nostrils quivered like she was a wild deer, catching the scent of a hunter.

'You devoted your life to making Charles Wilkinson seem respectable. Why on earth did you do that?' Kit asked, keeping his voice soft and steady. He wanted to release her from the prison she'd encased herself in. Misplaced guilt. She had sealed herself off from love and desire. She denied her passionate nature. 'Where has that led you? Are you any happier for it?'

'Since when did my happiness become any of your concern?'

'Since I decided to fight for you. What happened, happened, Hattie. You can't change it, but you can stop allowing your life to be defined by it. It is not good to live in fear. You are a passionate woman. Why must you shut yourself off from life?'

'I will accept that you have no idea what you are saying due to the laudanum.'

Before Kit could protest she stood up and walked out of the room. Kit clenched his fist and slammed it down on the bedclothes. Since when did he break his rules about non-interference? It was better to allow her to go. Her life was nothing to do with him. She should be able to lead the sort of life she wanted, even if it was limited.

He should be thanking his lucky stars for the narrow escape. There could never be a future with her. He shuddered with the memory of the taunts he'd suffered, and the way respectable women had turned away from him in his youth after they had found out The Scandal.

Hattie laid her fevered cheek against the cool plaster of the hall and attempted to regain some measure of control. Her hand trembled so much that the wax spilt, burning her wrist. She set the candle down on the floor and forced herself to breathe in deeply.

She had made a mistake, a colossal mistake. She'd vowed never to speak about her husband's betrayal. Ever.

Now she'd confessed the bald truth to a man who was little more than a stranger, simply to keep from confessing how she felt about him!

What was worse—he'd said the things she had known in her heart. Every single word was true as much as she might wish it were a lie. She had allowed herself to be defined by Charles and what he'd done. She had hated what he'd done to her, but everyone considered her to be the grieving widow. How could she besmirch the memory of a hero? She'd used it as a way to lick her wounds for years but it was hypocrisy of the highest order. She had stopped living. Her dreams were just that—dreams.

Neither did she want everyone to know of her humiliation. Even now that burning sense of shame filled her. She hadn't been able to keep her husband happy. He had secretly laughed at her feeble attempts. His mistress had taken great delight in showing her the letters. She knew nothing about making love. Sensible and unattractive, lacking any real fire or passion. She'd longed to scream that he was wrong. But how could she when she had lived her life without passion?

Hattie hugged her arms and sank down to the floor. She wanted to feel passion, the real sort, the feeling-utterly-alive sort that she had felt when Kit kissed her at the Roman ruins. She had never had that all-consuming feeling before. She wanted to be alive, instead of existing.

When she had discovered the mistress's address, she had visited her. Hattie had not wanted Charles's miniature, but throwing it on the fire had seemed less than charitable. She had packed it up along with a few personal items so that the children would have something to remember their father by. Afterwards, Hattie had been sick in the street. The obvious love that woman had for Charles contrasted with her infatuation and fantasy of the perfect marriage.

All she'd wanted to do was to run away and hide. And she had—all the way to Northumberland. She'd been successful as well.

Undone by a man's nightshirt. How pathetic was that?

Hattie pressed her hands against her eyes and tried to control the shaking in her limbs. She refused to cry after all this time. Not again and most definitely not over him.

It had been a mistake to insist that Kit return to the Dower House, rather than allowing the doctor to look after him. And then she had further compounded the mistake by sitting up and watching him sleep.

What he must think of her! She hardly knew what she thought of herself! All she knew was that she could not have gone on with the pretence that somehow she had loved Charles with a deep and unyielding love when he'd asked.

She wanted to cleanse the knowledge of him and their marriage from her soul. She wanted to live her life rather than being defined by the old one.

Hattie stood up straight, and brushed the tears from her eyes. 'I'll live. Whatever happens. No one is going to laugh at me again. At the same time as writing me letters of sweet promise, Charles mocked me in those to his mistress. She showed them to me. Sometimes even now, I wake up in a sweat remembering the phrases. That stops now. I start living the life I was meant to.'

She picked up the candle and started down the hallway to her room. Kit did not need her to play nurse. She was through with being pathetic. She would be strong and aloof. She'd do her duty. And then she'd start to follow her dreams.

'Hattie? Harriet? Wait.'

She continued to walk towards the stairs, pretending she had not heard him call. The great Kit Foxton could survive the night without her panting over him, like some love-starved widow.

'Wait.' The note of despair tore at her heart.

She half-turned and saw him standing in the doorway of the sickroom with tousled hair and a shadow of beard on his chin. The voluminous white nightshirt revealed his muscular calves and bare feet. And where on any other man it would have looked ridiculous, somehow, on Kit, it highlighted his absolute masculinity.

'You were supposed to stay in bed.'

'You were supposed to stay by my side.' He gave the semblance of a smile. 'Looking after me. My nurse flees—what choice do I have but to go after her?'

Despite her misgivings, a hot spark smouldered its way around her insides. She wanted to touch his skin and see if it was silky smooth. If she took one step towards him, she'd be in his arms. She curled her hand into a tight fist about the candlestick and turned away from the enticing picture.

'It is late. Back to bed with you,' she said over her shoulder. 'And if I don't get some sleep, I will be in no fit state tomorrow. Tomorrow is sure to bring a steady stream of visitors, well-wishers and the downright curious. Your exploits will be picked over for days to come. The talk of the village.'

'I prefer to think of it as heroics. Don't disabuse me of the notion.'

'Heroics, if you must, but now is not the time for you to be up.'

'I wouldn't be if you acted sensibly and stayed. I believe I offended you. It wasn't my intention.'

'It is nothing to do with you. Nothing at all. I'm tired. I need to rest.' Hattie concentrated on keeping the candle steady. 'If you need someone, I'll wake Mrs Hampstead.'

She hoped he thought her voice stern and unyielding. To her ears, it sounded hopelessly breathless.

'Come here.' His voice allowed for no refusal.

Hattie took a step towards the stairs. Her stomach tensed. If she started towards him, she'd be in his arms, begging for his touch. And she already knew that was a hopeless cause. 'That wouldn't be a good idea.'

'I've gone beyond what you consider a good idea or not, Harriet.' He ran his hands through his hair. 'Come here. Let me see your face. All I can see is the light from the candle.'

She wiped the back of her hand across her eyes and straightened her skirt. He was too far away and the candlelight hid her upset state. 'No one calls me Harriet.'

'I know. It is why I am doing so.' He held out his hand. 'I've no wish to frighten you. Come back and talk to me.'

'Why should I?'

'I had no idea about your husband's betrayal. I thought your prim reserve was from a different cause. I'm sorry.'

'It served my purpose.' Hattie raised her chin. 'It is the first time I could speak of it.'

'Are you crying over him?'

'I shed my last tear for him a long time ago.'

'Then why the tears?'

'Because I've wasted my life.' When she said the words, she knew she meant them. They had sprung from a place deep within her. She'd wanted to erase all trace of Charles from her life, but she hadn't done. For too long she had been hiding, fearful of the long shadow. 'It is not what I wanted. I had so many plans. I've done none of them.'

His hand closed about hers and gently took the candlestick from her. 'You will burn your hand.'

'I already have.' She gave a shaky laugh. 'It is fine. I won't set the house on fire.'

Rather than letting her go, he pulled her to his hard body. 'Silence. Perfect silence.'

He bent his head and captured her lips, demanding a response. Hattie opened her mouth and tasted the sweet interior.

A deep and dark fire welled up inside her, blotting out everything else. She twined her hands about his neck and held him close, allowing her body to say things that she didn't dare. His mouth travelled over her face, softly nuzzling her cheeks and temple. 'Hush now.'

A soft moan escaped from her throat. With the last vestige of common sense, she put her hands on his shoulders and created a space between their bodies. 'I ought to go.'

'Why did you bring me here?' he said, sliding his hands down her back and cupping her body to his.

'I told you. Because I wanted to make sure you lived. You saved me and my honour.' Hattie kept her head up and looked him straight in the eye, attempting to ignore the fire blazing in her nether regions. If she wasn't hanging on to him, she'd fall. Her legs had become wobblier than jelly.

'It is poor excuse. We have gone beyond such things.' He traced the outline of her lips. 'Whatever you do, give solid reasons, rather than mealy-mouthed excuses.'

He placed a kiss in the corner of her mouth.

'Why do you think I brought you here?'

'Because you craved intimacy. You wanted more to your life than a solitary kiss in windswept ruins.' His fingers touched her face, gentle but at the same time wildly exciting. 'You wanted it as badly as I do. You have been driving me mad with longing, Harriet. The things I want to do with you.'

She turned her face to his palm. She was tempted to pinch herself to see if she was awake or if she had somehow fallen asleep and was dreaming. 'Did I?'

'You do.' He put his hands on her shoulders. His face turned grave. 'I'm not making promises that I can't keep, Harriet. You understand that. It is about living in the moment with no regrets. I can offer you a summer and that is all.'

'I'm aware of the rules of engagement, as it were.' She tucked her head into her chest, torn between a longing to put her head on his chest and listen to his heartbeat and the instinct to flee. He wasn't offering anything honourable, only pleasure and only for the summer.

There was nothing wrong with taking her pleasure. She was a widow, rather than a débutante in search of good marriage. Sir Christopher was notoriously single. With discretion all things were possible.

'A summer affair sounds intriguing, but we must be circumspect,' she said quickly before she lost her nerve.

He raised an eyebrow. 'Bringing me here is circumspect? The story will be all around the village before morning.'

'I brought you here because you were injured.'

Hattie tilted her chin upwards to show she had considered the potential for disaster. 'I was doing my Christian duty. No one dare gainsay that.'

'You kissed me all the same. And shall do again, I wager.'

A single finger lifted her face so she was staring directly into his eyes. His lashes were far too long and pretty for a man, she thought abstractly. She wasn't in love with him, not in the way she had thought she'd been in love with Charles. She desired him and his touch. Her heart was safe, more than safe. Passion might burn white-hot, but it rapidly turned to ash. She knew not to want for ever with this man. She'd settle for living in the moment for this one summer. 'Then we are agreed.'

'Until the summer ends.' He bent his head and softly kissed her lips. This time, the kiss was less fierce. It was a gentle heart-stopping persuasion. His mouth pressed kisses against her eyes, her nose and trailed down to her ear. Hattie knew that Charles had never kissed her like this. These kisses were about giving pleasure and healing.

She twined her arms about his neck, pressing her body against his. Hattie opened her mouth and allowed her tongue to tangle with his. In that kiss, all her fears and regrets fell away and all she knew was the feel of his lips against hers.

Her hand mimicked his and slid down the length of his torso. Instantly he stiffened.

'Is something wrong?'

He groaned in the back of his throat and put her from him. His face contorted in pain as he rotated his shoulder. 'I'm sorry. It is worse than I thought.'

She clapped her hands over her mouth. She'd been so intent on assuaging her own anguish that she'd forgotten about his very real pain. 'You are hurt. You have no business being up and about. This should never have happened.'

'I'm very glad it did.' He gave a ghost of a smile. 'I couldn't pass up the opportunity. You must never cry alone in a corridor again.'

'You should have done. The last thing I wanted to do is to cause you to get worse.' She felt the hot tears prick the backs of her eyes. 'You are the one who is supposed to be recovering from a terrible fight. You shouldn't have to comfort me because of something that happened seven years ago.'

'Allow me to be the judge of that.'

'You are to get back in bed.'

'And you shall join me in a bit of bed-sport?'

Hattie knew her face flamed. 'Mrs Hampstead will be up soon. We need to be discreet.'

She found it hard to believe that she was even discussing the possibility…of an affair.

'I would love to make love with you, Harriet. Right here and right now, but…it wouldn't be wise. My body aches too much.'

'The last thing I want to do is hurt you.' She looped her arm about his.

'It was worth having that fight simply to have you kiss me properly. I intend to hold you to your promise.'

'Which promise would that be?' Her voice sounded hoarse and seductive, foreign to her ears.

He smiled down at her and then immediately winced, going pale.

'You are to stay in bed tomorrow and I will have no excuses.'

'You are a saucy wench, Harriet. Ordering me to stay in bed, while your mouth is cherry ripe.' He gave her a hooded look. 'What else do you intend?'

His using her full name made her seem special and different from the Hattie who had been at the fair, but she also recognised the teasing note. She had never been teased in this way before, or indeed felt comfortable enough to tease back. A ripple of contentment went through her.

'I thought all fallen women were bold,' she retorted.

'You haven't fallen yet… It is not anyone else's business. It will stay that way if we are discreet.' He twisted a lock of her hair about his fingers. 'Reputations can be protected. I intend to do all that is in my power to be discreet and to prevent speculation.'

'I know. You can't promise…but you will try.' Her insides twisted. Open her mouth and insert her foot. She wanted this. She wanted that dark heat from earlier to consume her. Charles's love-making had been perfunctory and tepid to say the least. Even his early kisses in the summer house had been respectful. If she had known what it was like to be kissed by a master, maybe she would have stopped it. Hattie squeezed her eyes shut. No regrets. Ever. 'After you recover…'

'After I recover, we will take up where we left off. I want you, Hattie. That wanting is not going to go away. Trust me.'

She half-opened her eyes. He was looking at her with an intent gaze, but she could also see the pain in the way he held his mouth. 'I trust you.'

He dropped a kiss on her nose. 'This is where you

leave me. If you stay, I will want to make love to you and my mind may be willing, but my flesh is weak. When we make love I want to be strong. I want to give you pleasure. Immense pleasure.'

Her stomach tightened at the thought. He was interested in her pleasure, not just his own. She tried and failed to imagine having this conversation with anyone else. 'I…I don't know what to say.'

'Run along before I change my mind and do something we both regret.'

'I promised to stay.' The words escaped from her mouth. She swallowed hard and tried again in a calmer tone. 'At least allow me to see you back to your bed.'

'When? When did you promise?' The colour drained from his face, leaving him pale and tense.

'At the fair, you asked me.' Hattie blinked rapidly. Somehow she had made a mistake and she wasn't even sure what it was. She felt sick. If he hadn't requested her to stay, she'd never have confessed. She should have thought that it wasn't anything but a plea for the hurt to be gone. 'Surely you remember? You must remember.'

His gaze became troubled. Slowly he shook his head. 'Everything remains hazy. It remains a blank. You mustn't take what I said literally.'

'I brought you here because you asked me to stay with you.' Hattie's heart pounded. He didn't remember when he'd gripped her hand. It had seemed so important to her and he'd forgotten.

'I can take responsibility for myself tonight. I want you to dream of me in what little is left of the night.'

'And afterwards…'

He cupped her face with his hands. 'I want you,

Harriet Wilkinson, never doubt that. I want to make long slow love to you and show you how good it can be between us.'

Chapter Nine

Kit woke in the early hours of the morning and lay, gazing up at the ceiling. His entire body ached from the fight, but also with desire for Hattie. It unnerved him.

He kept willing himself to remember all the events. He couldn't have asked Hattie to stay. He never did things like that. He never tried to compromise anyone else's freedom in that way or put demands on them. Asking someone to stay would mean he had feelings for Hattie and he always made a point to end a relationship then. He refused to allow himself to be hurt.

What was worse was that he distinctly remembered speaking about his father. Kit had spent several years forgetting about him, his quick fists, the never-ending stream of perfumed women and his refusal to allow them in his life. He took pride in the fact that his fortune had not come from his inheritance, but from shrewd business decisions.

In his mind he went over the kisses in the hallway. None of them was supposed to happen. He had gone out to comfort her and to make sure that she wasn't hurting. And he'd nearly ended up seducing her. He should give her up. But having tasted the pure honey of her mouth, he knew he wanted more. It had infected him the first time he'd kissed her at the Roman ruins. He'd thought the feeling would diminish, but it had only grown stronger.

He knew she'd only kissed him out of a need to stop thinking. But he was very glad she had.

Now he was going to have to consider how to put things to rights and conduct their summer affair.

Discretion was called for and, as much as he might not like it, he had to take the hard decisions now. When autumn came, it would end, but Hattie would need to be protected. For once he was going to do this right.

Hattie sat in the dining room, staring at her half-eaten breakfast. Moth lay under the table, waiting for crumbs.

She had gone to bed, but had lain fully dressed, waiting to hear the slightest movement from the sick-room. Mrs Hampstead had appeared about six and told her to sleep.

'I came as soon as it was practicable, Hattie. These scrapes you do get in. I declare you are worse than the children.' Stephanie strode in, every inch the outraged matron.

Hattie dropped her piece of toast and stared at her sister. Silently she thanked her guardian angel that Kit remained upstairs, asleep in the sickroom. She swallowed hard to get rid of the tightness in her throat. 'Stephanie. How good of you to call and at such an early hour. It is not even ten.'

Stephanie towered over like some avenging angel from the inquisition. The ribbons on her bonnet trembled. 'Is it true that you insisted on bringing Sir Christopher here after what happened? Have you taken leave of your senses? Never mind the village, the entire Tyne Valley and possibly all of Northumberland are speaking about the fight and the aftermath. Your behaviour, Hattie, has been much remarked on.'

'No, I had my senses fully engaged. Sir Christopher had just rescued me from what is delicately referred to as a fate worse than death. I had no intention of leaving him to bleed on the muddy ground. Would you have done that?'

'You owed him nothing.'

'We shall agree to disagree on that. I always pay my debts.' Hattie gave a small shudder as she recalled how the drunk had pawed her and how his fetid breath had smelt. She hadn't been strong enough to fight him. 'He saved me and was injured, probably badly injured. Doctor Gormley has diagnosed a mild concussion at best. What sort of person do you take me for to put some form of mock refinement before my duty?'

'Surely Dr Gormley would have taken him in?'

'It was two hours before Dr. Gormley was found in the ale tent. I do not think he could have seen straight to sew stitches. And you know that his housekeeper is rather too fond of whiskey to be fully trusted.'

'It would appear that I misjudged matters,' Stephanie mumbled, sinking down into a chair. 'You were attacked. He saved you. Of course, it was right and proper in those circumstances to behave in the manner you did. I will make the appropriate people know how proud we are of you. It should stop the worst of the gossip.'

'You have indeed.' Hattie crossed her arms. She clearly recalled the enlightening conversation she'd had with Portia and Livvy on the way to the fair. Stephanie's meddling and interference stopped now. 'You rushed in without waiting for an explanation, Stephanie. However, if I had decided to utterly ruin myself, that would have been my business.'

'You won't be ruined. I will force him to marry you if needs be,' Stephanie declared. 'You can count on me.'

'How?'

'I will think of something.' Stephanie's ribbons swayed as her face took on a defiant air. 'I'm not a woman without influence. Mr Parteger will ensure the right and proper thing is done.'

'You mean a duel.'

'If called upon, my husband will be happy to defend your honour.' Stephanie put her hand to her mouth. 'But I doubt it will come to that. Sir Christopher will see the sense in my argument.'

Hattie shuddered at even the merest suggestion of a duel between Kit and her brother-in-law. In her mind's eyes she could see her brother-in-law's rather rotund figure lining up to face Kit's rather more athletic form. She was torn between laughing and crying at the prospect. She leant down and stroked Moth's ears, regaining some semblance of control.

'I would hardly want Mr Parteger fighting a duel over my reputation. Besides, it is utterly pointless and unnecessary. Nothing happened. How could it? Sir Christopher was insensible most of the time. You worry needlessly. Mrs Hampstead is here and you know what an ogress she can be. I remember when you were courting. You used to complain bitterly about Mrs Hampstead poking her nose into the drawing room.'

Stephanie readjusted the ribbons of her bonnet and gave a pained expression. 'Are you willing to give me an assurance that nothing untoward happened last night?'

'When have I ever done anything that was in the remotest way indiscreet?' Hattie sat back in her chair and waited, swallowing her other caustic retorts. Patience was required with Stephanie, not barbs.

'You have changed your hair. It is softer. Suits your face.'

'I thought I'd worn a crown of braids long enough. I like the ringlets.' Hattie tilted her head and regarded her sister through narrowed eyes. Stephanie had to be redirected before she started asking awkward questions. 'You are changing the subject, Stephanie. It generally means you are losing the argument.'

'You always look for the ulterior motive. I noticed it and I like it. I can also guess the reason.' Stephanie reached over and squeezed Hattie's hand. 'I'm your sister. I care about you, but you need to be careful. Sir Christopher has a much different stamp than your dear, but now long-departed, Captain Wilkinson. You were always too reckless, Hattie, even as a girl. I can't help fearing for your reputation. I want to make it right for you.'

Stephanie was worried about her. She was tempted to tell her that Sir Christopher was a man of entirely different sensibility than Charles, but it would leave her open to questioning and, having faced one storm last night, she knew she couldn't face another. And she had to wonder how much Stephanie knew or guessed. Her husband had been a friend of sorts to Charles.

'Mrs Wilkinson was merely doing her Christian

duty,' Kit's lazy voice said from the doorway before Hattie could think up a coherent answer. 'Surely no one would stoop so low as to accuse a woman who is doing her Christian duty of untoward behaviour?'

Stephanie gave a little panicked cry and ducked her head. Hattie saw him, standing in the doorway, dressed in his clothes with an intricately tied neck-cloth. He carried his body stiffly as if badly bruised. Her heart gave a little skip and she was pleased that she'd changed into her dimity with the tiny blue flowers embroidered on it. Portia always declared that it was her favourite dress as it made Hattie look sparkly.

From Kit's grim expression as he bent down to greet Moth, she had to wonder how long he'd been standing there and how much he'd heard.

Stephanie cleared her throat several times, obviously having the same concerns as Hattie. Hattie fought the temptation to laugh.

'Sir Christopher, you are up… That is to say—this is a most unexpected development. But welcome. A welcome development. Dear Hattie is such a good nurse. Quite devoted to it.'

'Then you will agree I was in good hands.'

'Very good hands.' Stephanie turned several deeper shades of plum. 'You are dressed, Sir Christopher.'

'He could hardly come down in a borrowed night-shirt,' Hattie said crossly. Stephanie had no right to be quizzing Kit in this manner. And Kit had no right to be up. Her carefully arranged plans of going up to see him after breakfast when she looked fresh and lovely were in smithereens. 'Really, Stephanie, you do spout some nonsense.'

'My valet arrived very early this morning with my

clothes. I believe the ride over from Southview did him good. Cleared his thick head. He spent rather too much time in the ale tent yesterday.' His smile failed to reach his eyes. 'He wished to make amends and brought fresh clothes.'

'You are able to move about?' Stephanie gasped.

'The doctor advised strict bed rest.' Hattie put her hand on her stomach and wished she hadn't eaten that square of toast. Kit was dressed as if he was preparing to depart. Did he regret their late-night conversation? Had she dreamt it?

'I don't care a fig for the doctor's advice.' His deep-grey gaze met hers. 'I do, however, care about your reputation. I came to the same conclusion as Mrs Parteger. It is commendable but unwise to have me as a guest when Johnson is more than capable of looking after me.'

'And your plans?' Hattie tapped a finger on the table top. Everyone had neglected to consult her. Surely, at twenty-seven, she was more than capable of making the correct choices?

'I shall journey slowly and sedately back to the Lodge in my carriage.' He gave a crooked smile. 'You may direct all well-wishers there, but you must under pain of death retain any strengthening concoctions such as calves'-foot jelly. The very thought turns my stomach.'

'Allow me to be concerned about my reputation,' Hattie said between gritted teeth.

'Nevertheless, my mind is made up. Johnson should be returning with the carriage within the hour.' He inclined his head. 'I do hope there is some chocolate. I would hate to leave without partaking of breakfast. I trust that meets with your approval, Mrs Parteger?'

Without waiting for an invitation, he came in and took a seat opposite Hattie. She carefully poured him a cup of chocolate. He took it, but made sure their fingers briefly touched.

'Did you pass a comfortable night?' Stephanie asked.

'Mrs Parteger, the doctor gave me laudanum to make me sleep. I remember little, except I woke completely refreshed and a new man. One might say that the fight did a powerful amount of good.' He saluted Hattie with his cup of chocolate. 'Improved my mood no end.'

Hattie took a hasty sip of her coffee and burnt the roof of her mouth. He couldn't have forgotten their kiss? She had made a positive declaration and now he'd forgotten it. How like her luck. She tried to think about how to best approach the matter, but her brain seemed to move at the speed of congealed porridge.

Voices were heard in the hall and Moth gave a series of sharp barks before racing to the dining-room door and then back to Hattie.

Kit put down his cup. 'Ah, here is Johnson, and Rupert as well. Their timing is impeccable. My stay was short, but most enjoyable, Mrs Wilkinson. Mrs Parteger, you will understand that I wish to get home as soon as possible. I do hope you will be at pains to point out that Mrs Wilkinson has behaved correctly in all circumstances.'

'Shall I see you out?'

'It is not necessary. I have everything in hand. Pray stay seated and visit with your sister. I can see my own way out.' He gave an approximation of his smile. 'Until next time, Mrs Wilkinson. Mrs Parteger.'

Hattie sat completely still until the voices had receded. He had gone just like that. No searing look or even a promise to call when he was better.

'I declare Sir Christopher is a gentleman—putting your reputation above his own comfort and consideration.' Stephanie reached for the coffee pot, a sure sign that she intended to stay a while. 'At last someone in this sorry affair thinks about reputations and the impact their actions may have on others. I declare you have no more sense than a gnat, Hattie. Livvy is due to make her début next season. The last thing you want is for your exploits to become common fodder for the gossips.'

'He certainly did that.' Hattie hated the way the butterflies in her stomach started. Surely he could not have forgotten about last night so quickly? They spoke at such length. It was impossible and if he had, how could she face him knowing that she had once divulged those secrets to him?

Stephanie dabbed her eyes with a lace handkerchief. 'Here I was a bit concerned about Mr Hook, but with an example such as his guardian, I know that he will behave with the upmost propriety.'

'You are resigned to Mr Hook now? Or do you think Livvy will do better in London?'

'Mr Hook's relations with Livvy are not something I entirely want to discuss. Rather I want to speak about your gloves.'

'Which gloves this time?' Hattie rapidly considered all her pairs of gloves. She knew where they were.

'It was so kind of you to buy Livvy that pair of but-ter-yellow gloves. They are far too expensive.'

'I bought Livvy a pair of gloves?'

'She tried to tell me that they were yours, but you never buy frivolous things like that. You are always so practical, Hattie. Charles always said that it was one of your more admirable qualities. I will confess that I failed to see it until after his death, but there you go. A sister is always the last to notice.'

'I am pleased she likes them.' Hattie made a men-tal note to speak to both Mr Hook and Livvy about lying. It was entirely possible that Stephanie had be-come muddled, but Livvy had to understand the conse-quences. A tiny prickle went down her back. Unless… 'Did you say they were butter-yellow?'

'They must have been tremendously expensive.'

'They were.' Hattie pressed her lips together, re-membering Kit's gesture to the stall keeper at the Hex-ham Tans stall. She should have intervened then. No matter what happened, she did not intend to accept gifts from him. It would make the relationship less equal.

'Is there any other news? Surely something else happened beside Livvy's mysterious pair of gloves?'

'Beyond Sir Christopher's injury?' Stephanie frowned. 'Mr Hook has agreed to give his lecture on newts. Apparently Mr Hook has decided that it would be best if they stay in the neighbourhood while Sir Christopher recuperates. That young man has a sound head on his shoulders. After you became separated from Livvy, he made certain that she was escorted back to me. I just pray he finds some confidence from somewhere or otherwise poor Livvy will be dreadfully disappointed.'

Hattie hid her smile behind her hand. It appeared that Livvy and Mr Hook were enjoying a romance, despite Stephanie's interference and she found that she wasn't inclined to stop it. It was no one's business and she had to trust that Livvy would be sensible. 'Is that so?'

'He is far too diffident. I doubt he has any idea about women.'

Hattie moved the conversation on to much safer topics. When she next saw Kit, she'd tackle him about the gloves. But whatever he had intended, the gloves now belonged to Livvy. Hattie quite looked forward to quizzing him about it.

The sickroom was immaculate. No sign beyond the tidily folded laundry that Kit had ever slept here. Hattie regarded it with distaste. She had come up immediately after Stephanie left, hoping for a little clue or perhaps a forgotten article which would enable her to visit him.

Hattie caught sight of her stricken reflection in the little mirror over the chest of drawers.

'What did you expect, my girl? You knew he had suffered from a concussion. He probably doesn't even remember.'

The irony did not escape her. How could she go to him and ask? What did one say—when you were suffering from a concussion, you promised to make love to me? Will you do so now? The mere thought made her feel sick to her stomach.

A great wave of tiredness came over her and she

stumbled to her bedroom. Everything would be clearer after a sleep.

She put her hand to her head as a wave of dizziness passed through her. Whatever happened, she was not going to humiliate herself again. She was going to retreat and lie down.

There, propped up on the middle of her bed, was a single red rose and a note. Hattie's tiredness melted away.

With trembling fingers, Hattie undid the sealing wax and opened to the note.

Summer house in your garden. Four p.m. Tomorrow. If you are still willing. Kit.

Hattie sank down on the soft bed. He'd left her a note where only she would find it.

She pressed the note to her lips, trying to think. He'd given her an option and had preserved her reputation in case she changed her mind.

Hattie tightened her grip on the paper. Retreating was the last thing she wanted to do.

She'd be naïve if she thought she was anything but a distraction. She knew the boundaries going in. This was not about love or finer feelings. She'd had all those words from Charles and had believed them. This was about proving her independence.

She could stop living the life that Charles had chosen for her now. She had a choice and she intended to take it.

She gulped twice. What did one wear to a seduction?

The garden was bathed in warm golden sun the next afternoon. Hattie had sent Mrs Hampstead to Highfield on the pretext of helping Livvy get ready for the dinner party the Dents were giving. She claimed tiredness and the wish to have some peace after the turmoil of the last few days. Mrs Hampstead had taken Moth with her so that Hattie could sleep properly and undisturbed.

A life of half-truths had begun, Hattie thought with a wry smile. Perhaps it said something about her that they sprang so easily to her lips. She had been certain that Mrs Hampstead guessed, but she accepted Hattie's rather garbled explanation.

At first, Hattie considered that no one was there, but then she saw movement in the shadows.

'Kit?' she called softly, wondering precisely how one went about this new life of sin.

When she had gone to the summer house with Charles, he had led the way, insisting that she could see the fireworks better from there. She had been far too young and in love with love to question him. It had seemed a dream that someone so handsome and at ease with society, not to mention brave, should be interested in her. She had never thought about it until far too late. Then, looking back with the benefit of hindsight, she had seen the signs—the unexplained absences, the moodiness, the perfunctory love-making. It was not going to happen again. This time, she wasn't going to give her heart.

He appeared in the doorway. He was simply dressed and bareheaded. The bruising on his face was starting to come out and gave him a decidedly roguish appearance.

'You made your decision.'

'It was painfully easy.' She held out her hands. 'I'm not certain about what happens next.'

He crossed the short distance between them. His fingers touched her jaw. 'We go slowly. It happens at the pace you want it to happen.'

'I sent Mrs Hampstead to Highfield. We have about two hours before she returns, I imagine.'

He cocked his head to one side. 'And that will be long enough?'

'More than ample. I want to do everything in my power to prevent Mrs Hampstead from guessing.'

'Mrs Hampstead is no fool.' His face sobered. 'You will need her as an ally rather than as an enemy. On another note, while we are together in public, we must not take chances.'

She refused to think about his words—*while we are together*. He had played this sort of game before, but she was a novice. The future was going to happen whether she wanted it to or not. She had stopped believing in for ever a long time ago.

'I know.' She moved closer to him. Her hand touched the broad cloth of his coat. 'But…' she stood on her tiptoes and brushed his lips '…I understand the rules, perfectly.'

He put his hands on her upper arms and held her from him. He searched her face. 'Why are you doing this? Is it because you want me or because you want to get back at some man who has been dead for seven years?'

'It is because I want you. What I might have felt for Charles vanished years ago. I am tired of living in fear. I want my life back.'

He lowered his mouth and drank from her lips. The kiss teased her senses and increased in urgency. Hattie twined her arms about his neck and pulled him closer. Her body arched towards his.

It was as if she had been encased in ice and his breath was setting her free. She mimicked his actions and slipped her tongue into his mouth, revelling in her new-found power.

His hands roamed down her body, arms, shoulders, sides. The light touch sent a series of tremors coursing through her body. He stilled when his hand reached her bottom.

'What are you wearing under that dress?' he rasped.

'Nothing. I came dressed for seduction.'

He gave a husky laugh and pulled her closer, leaving her in no doubt of his approval. 'Once you make up your mind, you are very determined.'

'I like to think it is a good trait.' She reached up and brought his head back down to her lips. 'I hope you think so, too.'

'Definitely.'

They stood there, kissing until Kit gently eased her back into the shadows of the summer house. She saw he'd brought a blanket and pillows. In the corner sat a basket full of food and wine.

'I also wanted to be prepared.' His breath caressed her ear. 'Food or passion first?'

'What do you think?' She brushed her lips against his. A liquid heat bubbled up within her. 'But why the pillows?'

'The hard ground does nothing except give one backache. This is about pleasure rather than discovering muscles you didn't know you had.'

She mutely nodded. A reminder, if she needed it, that he was used to trysts of this nature whereas she was a mere beginner. Above all things she didn't want to disappoint him.

'My ignorance is astonishing.'

'You are doing fine.' He kissed her temple. 'More than fine. Go with your instincts.'

'I feel awkward,' she admitted.

'May I?' he asked and gently took the hairpins out of her hair, allowing the mass of unruly curls to fall down about her shoulders. 'I have wanted to see it loose.'

'I normally wear it in braids because otherwise it goes wild.' Her voice sounded husky and thick.

'It is very passionate hair. It has a mind of its own.' He ran his hands through it, winding it about his hands. 'So many different colours.'

He pulled her to him and recaptured her mouth. His tongue played with hers, twisting and tangling. The fire in her belly grew more urgent. Her body moved against his, seeking his. She moaned in the back of her throat. Give in to your instinct, he'd said, and her entire being screamed that she wanted to touch his skin. Her fingers worked his neckcloth, revealing the strong column of his throat. She touched her lips to the base of his throat and felt his heart thrumming.

She pushed at his coat, wanting to see more and hoping that he'd understand. He gave a soft laugh and divested himself of his coat, waistcoat, shirt and trousers until he stood before her, naked. His skin gleamed golden in the afternoon light. A sprinkling of dark hair covered his chest with a line leading down to his erection. Firm. Rigid. Visible proof if she needed it that he wanted her. A primitive hunger surged through her.

She reached out and touched his warm chest, felt the nipples pucker beneath her fingertips.

'Can I see what lies underneath?' he asked, and at her wordless nod, quickly removed her dress.

She stood before him, dressed only in her stockings, garters and dancing slippers. She stepped out of the shoes and resisted the temptation to cover her nakedness. His appreciative gaze roamed over her. Slowly he reached forwards and undid one garter and then the other. With infinite patience he rolled the stockings down. She sank down to the blanket before her knees gave way. He removed the stockings, rubbing the base of her foot with his knuckle, sending ripples of pleasure cascading through her. Then he positioned himself between her legs, looming over.

He reached out his forefinger and traced a circle around the dusky rose of her nipple. 'Exquisite.'

Where his finger went, his mouth swiftly followed. He captured one nipple, suckled, released and took the other one in his mouth. Her back arched upwards. She dug her hands into his thick crisp hair, holding him there.

He moved his hands downwards, sliding them over her curves until they reached her nest of curls. There, he slipped a finger into her folds, seeking her innermost centre.

She gasped as his finger found the hardened nub. No one had ever touched her that intimately before. Always she had stayed rigid, afraid to move, but the liquid heat which filled her made that idea impossible. Her back arched upwards, inviting his fingers to probe deeper.

'Relax,' he breathed into her ear.

'I'm trying not to move,' she cried in desperation. 'It is the correct way to behave.'

He gave a husky laugh. 'I want you to move. I want you to enjoy this. Stop thinking. Listen to your body. Touch me. Here.'

She reached out her hand and ran it down the planes of his chest, following the line of hair until she encountered his arousal. Hot. Velvet smooth, but hard. Her hand closed around it as his fingers slid in a figure eight in her folds. Wave after wave of heat washed over her.

'Lie back. Enjoy.' His rich voice rippled through her.

Her hands grasped his shoulders, tugging, hoping he'd understand her wordless plea.

Slowly, slowly he wedged her thighs wide. The tip of him nudged her inner core. At her nod he drove himself forwards, impaling her willing flesh.

Her body opened and swallowed the entire length of him.

He lay there, joined and unmoving. He looked down at her and smoothed a tendril of hair from her forehead. He lowered his mouth to hers. His tongue penetrated, demanding a response as it teased and provoked. Her hips began to move, seeking relief from the increasing need that welled up in her. He responded, withdrawing and then driving deeper.

Then the world burst around her and he caught her cries in his mouth.

As she floated back down to earth, she stroked his cheek. 'Thank you.'

'My pleasure.'

She moved her hips slightly and felt him respond deep within her. No one had told her that being wicked could feel this good. She wanted it to continue. She wanted to make a memory and keep it with her for ever.

'Shall we try it again?' she whispered, ignoring the faint prickle of worry that this could not last.

Chapter Ten

A cold wet nose snuffled into Kit's shoulder, waking him from a sound sleep. He started, turned his head and saw Moth's brown eyes peering at him and Hattie. The summer house had sunk deep into twilight's shadow. Hattie's bottom curved into him and her hair spilled out across the both of them. Kit found it difficult to remember the last time he had felt this contented or relaxed.

Normally after a spot of bed-sport, he was full of energy and found the first excuse he could to leave. This time, he'd stayed, fallen asleep and now they had to face the possibility of discovery. And it was his responsibility.

'Harriet,' Kit murmured, his breath caressing her ear. The last thing he wanted was her to be startled and scream. 'Moth's here.'

Hattie mumbled slightly in her sleep, pushing him away. They had made love twice more after the first time. Her passion and inventiveness had surprised and delighted him. One time was not nearly enough. He wanted to explore her hidden depths. He wanted to catch her cry in his throat as she trembled on the brink of passion. And now she slept.

Moth sat down and gave a sharp bark before licking Kit's shoulder. There was an urgency to the little dog's movements.

'I understand, Moth. We have to move. Your mistress needs the veil of propriety.'

He shook Hattie's shoulder. Harder. 'Hattie. Time to wake up.'

Her eyes blinked open. He smiled down at her and she jumped. Startled. Kit clasped his hand over her mouth, stifling the cry.

'Quiet now.'

She gave a brief nod and he removed his hand.

'It wasn't a dream?'

'No dream. A much-desired reality.'

She sat up, moving away from the safety of his arms. Her blonde hair fell wildly about her shoulders, providing a soft veil over her chest. She wrapped her arms about her waist and turned her back towards him.

'It was wrong of me to fall asleep.'

'It happened.'

Moth immediately went to her and rubbed her head against Hattie. 'I didn't mean to sleep. I only intended to close my eyes for a moment.'

'Now Moth is here. Will anyone else be looking for you?' Kit pulled his trousers on and reached for his shirt, trying not to think about the consequences if they were caught. He would have to do the decent thing, but right now he prayed to anyone who might be listening that it would not happen.

'She wasn't supposed to be here. Not for a long while. Mrs Hampstead was going to stay at Stepha-

nie's for a couple of hours.' Hattie scooped the little
dog up and held her against her chest. Moth endured it
with a scrunched-up face before wriggling to escape.
'I only meant to close my eyes for a moment. I must
have drifted off. Goodness, how long were we there?'

'It happens after vigorous activity.'

'That is one explanation. How…how long did we
sleep?'

He gestured towards the garden where the shadows
were deep, but the darkness had not really begun. The
last rays of the sun remained red-orange. 'It remains
twilight. Barely any time.'

'Twilight comes much later in Northumberland.
At this time of year, it never gets properly dark.' She
stuffed her fist into her mouth. 'What are we going
to do?'

'It is up to you. Your house. Your rules. Panic never
solves anything. Keep a cool head.'

He reached down and retrieved the crumpled gown
from where he'd tossed it earlier and handed it to her.
She wrinkled her nose as she examined the now highly
creased gown.

'It looks precisely like what has happened to it.'

'It could be worse. It isn't grass-stained or torn,' he
said, trying to be encouraging. 'Will Mrs Hampstead
come out into the garden, looking for you?'

She clapped her hand over her mouth. 'I hadn't considered it. I told Mrs Hampstead that I might take a
turn about the garden before bed. It will have to do as
an excuse. Do you think she will accept the excuse?'

'It happened.' Kit caught Hattie's elbow and turned
her towards him. Her eyes were wide with fright and
panic. He gently lifted her chin so he was looking di-

rectly at her. 'I'm glad it did. It was delightful to wake up in your arms.'

She turned rosy in the dying sun. It pleased Kit that even after everything they had done, she remained innocent.

Her frantic hands tried to twist up her hair and singularly failed. 'Thankfully it was only Moth. I suspect Mrs Hampstead would have fainted. And it doesn't bear thinking about if it was Portia or Stephanie. I meant what I said, Kit. I have no plans to marry again. This must be a summer romance.'

Kit experienced an unexpected pang of regret that it was not either of them. It would have solved a problem. He knew with Hattie that he would do the honourable thing, if it came to it. It surprised and slightly unnerved him. He had never experienced regret like that before.

Kit pushed the thought away immediately.

He had no need of a wife, even one like Hattie. He had to keep perspective. Like him, she had no desire to stick her head in the parson's noose. Their affair would last for the summer, no longer.

He was in no hurry for autumn, but some day Hattie would get possessive and throw a tantrum as so many of his mistresses had done before he'd learnt. Time limits at the start saved heartache at the end.

Far better to cause a little hurt than to experience the great searing pain of one's heart breaking or having her discover that he was actually like his father—cruel and unlovable.

'Until the summer's end, then,' he remarked when he was certain he had his feelings under control. 'Unless you have regrets?'

'It is far too late for regrets. Far too late.'

He released his breath. 'You can only regret things you haven't done.'

She glanced at him over her shoulder, her hands pausing in their task. It was all Kit could do to keep from hauling her back into his arms. Instead he bent and picked up several of the scattered hairpins and held them out to her. She smiled her thanks.

'And I enjoyed myself far too much,' she said quietly. 'Whatever happens, thank you for that. I thought it was me, but it wasn't. I know now why people are so fond of the act.'

'The person matters more than the act.'

'Thank you for saying that.'

He reached out and straightened the folds of her gown. Once again she appeared prim and proper, reminding him of the night they had first encountered each other. He had what he wanted from her then, but it did not matter. This was not about teaching her a lesson in love. He desired her and her alone.

'You look well kissed,' he said, lightly touching her cheek.

She dipped her head. 'I shall take that as a compliment. But Mrs Hampstead will refrain from enquiring. I will tell her that I was gathering late roses and dropped off in the summer house.'

'Second thoughts? I thought you were determined to carve a new life for yourself.'

She worried her bottom lip. 'Because it is far too new and I have no wish for speculation. I've no wish to force you to do something you might regret.'

'Allow me to look after myself.'

'I knew I could count on you.' She gave a few final

twists to her hair and patted the side of her gown, signalling to Moth to follow. 'Until the next time, Kit.'

'I look forward to it.' Kit knew that any further meeting had to come from her. If he pursued, it would look like he cared. And he wasn't ready for that. 'And, Harriet...?'

'Yes, Kit?'

He smiled at her, enjoying the way her gown accentuated her curves. 'Make it soon.'

'I will try my level best.'

She clicked her fingers and Moth trotted along behind her. Kit watched until she had gone into the house and lit a lamp in the drawing room. He saw her speaking to Mrs Hampstead and laughing. She was safely back in her world without a stain on her character. He'd kept his word.

Kit leant against the doorway and closed his eyes.

'I wish you had come to dinner at the Dents. Doctor Hornby was there and everyone wanted to hear about your exploits. You are quite the heroine,' Stephanie said when Hattie stopped by Highfield the next morning.

In the depth of the night, Hattie had resolved to continue about her routine as if nothing had happened. She had determined that today would be making jam and doing things about the still room. She found making the preserves, flavoured vinegars and chutneys ultimately satisfying. She had discovered a real talent for the enterprise when she came up to Northumberland. Her elderflower cordial might be prone to exploding, but she knew her damson gin was some of the best in the county.

Above all, she wanted to avoid visiting, in particular seeing Mrs Reynaud. If anyone was going to guess about the affair, Mrs Reynaud was the most likely candidate. Her eyes were so sharp. She'd even guessed about the kiss at the Roman ruins. And everything was far too new and precious. Hattie needed to decide if she wanted anyone else to know, but for now she wanted to hug the news to her chest like some glorious secret.

'I take it that Sir Christopher and Mr Hook were absent?'

'Obviously.' Stephanie rolled her eyes heavenwards. 'A fight like that is not something you simply get up and walk away from. Mrs Dent agrees that you were reckless, but did what you did out of pure Christian spirit. If your reputation wasn't so spotless, questions might be asked, but you have been on the shelf for so long, there is little danger of anything untoward happening.'

'I don't very much care what Mrs Dent thinks.' Hattie crossed her arms. On the shelf, indeed! 'She has a mouth like the Tyne and speaks before she thinks.'

'Hattie, what has got into you today?' Stephanie frowned. 'You are not usually rude. Of course you care about what Mrs Dent thinks. She is our close neighbour and a powerful force in Tyne Valley society.'

'She is looking to marry off her eldest daughter.'

'Livvy is more than a match for her.' Stephanie tapped a forefinger against her mouth. 'Come to think of it, Mrs Dent was awfully curious about Mr Hook and his habits. She has heard about the proposed lecture.'

'I thought you were not interested in Mr Hook for Livvy. Livvy must have a title and all that.'

'Mr Hook has asked Mr Parteger if he will help

with the final preparation. Mr Parteger is reluctant. There is no good encouraging him, Mr Parteger says, as there is no title.'

Hattie leant forwards. She had been racking her brain all morning as she picked strawberries about how she could go about contacting Kit and the answer lay before her—the lecture preparations. 'But it was your scheme.'

Stephanie heaved a long drawn-out sigh. 'I swear my husband does not appreciate any of my schemes. I have had to ask the Colonel.'

Hattie glanced over to the firmly closed library door. 'I believe he likes a bit of peace, Stephanie. He doesn't see the same urgency as you and he has never been terribly social.'

'You know I was pregnant with Livvy when I was just a bit older than her. It scarcely seems possible.' Stephanie put her hand on her stomach. Her face crumpled. A single tear ran down her cheek.

'What is wrong, Stephanie? You are practically in tears.' Hattie covered Stephanie's hand with hers. 'Was Harold cruel? He doesn't mean to be cutting. He does want the best for Livvy.'

'I fear it might be happening again. I have been ill every morning for the last week. If it had not been for the fair, I'd have stayed in bed, but someone had to support dear Mr Parteger. He expects me to be there for him on that day of all days. Then you went and recklessly endangered your reputation with rescuing Sir Christopher after that dreadful fight where you needlessly exposed yourself. No one cares about my nerves.'

Hattie closed her eyes. Stephanie pregnant. Again.

She had half-hoped to suggest to Kit that they travel or arrange to meet abroad. And she'd even toyed with going down to London next spring for the entire Season…if their affair lasted that long. However, if Stephanie was pregnant, it would mean a baby in the late spring, and she knew how much Stephanie counted on her help.

'We shall cross that bridge when it comes.'

'But Livvy and her Season. It has been promised. Livvy is over the moon with excitement.' Stephanie dabbed the handkerchief to her eyes and gave a rather pathetic sniff. 'I will need you here. No one understands me and my babies like you do. But I dislike the thought of Livvy being without support and guidance.'

'I could go.'

'Of course you could go, Livvy respects your opinion, more than mine. But…how am I going to run the house? You are my sister and the only person that Harold truly tolerates.'

Hattie sighed. She knew that she had to stay, if only to ensure her brother-in-law's sanity. It did make things easier. If Kit asked, she'd explain. And if he didn't, she was safe in the knowledge that she could not have gone anyway. She curled her fists.

'Mrs Hampstead could stay with you. She is far more useful than I on such matters,' Hattie said more in hope than expectation. The colour drained from Stephanie's face. 'But Joyce should be willing to sponsor Livvy. Livvy and Joyce's eldest niece are close in age. It will give her someone to have as a friend. These affairs can be awfully daunting if you have to go alone.'

Instantly Stephanie's countenance cleared. 'You are right of course. It is about time our sister-in-law did something for this family. It is not as if they are troubled by us much.'

Hattie squeezed Stephanie's hand. Remorse washed over her. Stephanie always dreadfully suffered in the first few months of a pregnancy. What she was asking was not too difficult. It was simply that for once she wanted a little time to live her own life. She pushed the thought away.

'You must concentrate on the new life. I will make sure everything runs smoothly.'

'You are so good to me, Hattie. I couldn't ask for a better sister.'

'I try.' Hattie nodded towards where the baskets of strawberries stood. 'I have an appointment in the still room. It is that time of the year. Jams, jellies, tinctures and a wide variety of gins await preparation. It gives me an outlet for my energy.'

Stephanie put her handkerchief to her face. 'I can't bear the thought of the jam bubbling, particularly not now.'

'You always did prefer the eating of jam to the making of it.'

Stephanie had the grace to blush.

Kit rode his new stallion, Onyx, hard. He enjoyed the freedom and excercise after weeks of inactivity.

When he woke up this morning with the memory of Hattie's mouth moving under his, he resolved that he'd stay away for a little while. The last thing he wanted was to get involved in her life or for her to start to depend on him. He knew what women could be like. The rules of engagement were strict and developed after years of practice.

He reached the ridge above Pearl Cottage. He looked down at the little house with its curl of smoke. Something struck in the gut. His tenant, Mrs Reynaud, was down there in that cottage but her identity remained a mystery.

He had spent the majority of the day going through his uncle's papers while he tried not to think about Hattie and what she might be doing. As he suspected, the woman who had rented the cottage did not go by the name of Reynaud, but another name altogether: Smith. The tenancy agreement was odd to say the least and his uncle had ensured that Mrs Smith could never be thrown out of the cottage. According to his estate manager, the quarterly rent was always paid on time from a London bank. His Uncle John had overseen the details personally.

Kit bent down and patted Onyx's neck. The horse blew out his breath.

'Who is she, Onyx? And why did my uncle let the house to her in that fashion? What was she to him? A mistress? A former love?'

Onyx pawed the ground and tossed his head.

It would be easy to turn the horse's head towards the cottage and visit. He just couldn't shake the suspicion that this woman might be his mother—hidden away from her shame by his kindly uncle for all these years. He wasn't at all sure what he felt, but as he watched the door a bent figure came out. Nothing. She was too far away. He closed his eyes and tried to conjure his mother's features. They were a blur, an impression really. He recalled a scent of night jasmine, but nothing real and substantial.

A great part of him wanted to know the truth. He

deserved to know what his uncle wanted hidden. Had his uncle defied his father?

Silently he willed her to look up and acknowledge him. Take it out of his hands. He'd go down if she so much as waved.

The woman stretched and went back into the house without looking towards him.

Kit curled his hands about the reins. Did he truly want to know who the woman was? How would he cope if it really was his mother?

She knew where he was. He refused to beg. He was not going back to that little boy on the stairs, silently pleading with his mother to turn around and stay, not to leave him. He had left the past behind him.

To hell with his rules. He needed Hattie. He needed her to make the past vanish. His life was about the here and now and the past was kept in a little place marked Do Not Open.

Kit spurred his horse towards the Dower House and Hattie. Solace.

Hattie put her hands on her back and stretched. The scent of strawberries perfumed the still room. There was something supremely satisfying about making jams and preserves. And the entire process kept her mind off Kit and the fact that neither had arranged for the next meeting.

She carefully poured a bit of the bubbling liquid onto a cool plate.

'Mrs Hampstead said I would find you out here, but she neglected to say how delightful you'd look in your apron and mob cap.'

Hattie jumped and the plate crashed down on to the flagstones. 'Kit!'

She spun around and there he stood, dressed in riding gear. His highly polished black boots contrasted with the tight-fitting tan breeches. His top hat was rakishly tilted on his head. His grey eyes sparkled.

'I came to see if you'd like to go for a ride with me, but if you are busy…'

'I am making strawberry jam. It won't take long, but it has restored my mood. Stephanie was here earlier…' Hattie found she couldn't frame the words. To explain about her disappointment would mean having to explain why and that she had started to make castles in the clouds. She clenched her fist around the spoon. When she next saw him, she had wanted to be properly dressed, not in her oldest gown with a voluminous apron tied about her waist and the awful mob cap. How could he think she looked delightful? She looked a fright.

'I've never seen anyone make jam before.' He stepped into the small room, filling it. 'It is fascinating. You have a bit of jam on your cheek.'

Hattie gave a light laugh and scrubbed with her hand. 'All gone now. I'm a messy cook.'

'Is jam-making a messy occupation?'

He was exaggerating. How could anyone not have seen jam being made before? The preservation of food happened in all sorts of houses and it was the responsibility of the lady of the house. It was criminal to allow produce to go to waste. Stephanie might not enjoy the process, but she did lend a hand when called upon, particularly when it was the wines or other types of alcohol. 'You must have had a deprived childhood.'

His mouth turned down and the light faded from his eyes. 'An unusual one.'

'Surely your mother…'

'My mother was not part of my life after my fourth birthday.' His tone indicated the subject was closed.

'An aunt or another relative, then?' She gave a little shrug and moved the steaming pan off the stove to show she wasn't hurt by his refusal to talk about his childhood. Was his mother dead or had she just left? Hattie hastily bit back the question. Some day she'd question Mrs Reynaud, who knew of the family and their history if he never confided in her, as she was curious. But not now as that would be like spying. Silently she willed him to tell her.

'No, no one like that. My father's taste ran to other sorts of women.'

'A pity.'

With a practised eye, she began to pour the gleaming red liquid into the jars. Over the years she'd discovered Livvy and Portia were more likely to tell her secrets if she appeared to be doing something else.

'My father disliked having women in the house.'

That simple statement combined with the jumping-jack explained so much. Her heart bled for the little boy who was never scooped up or petted or given treats. 'How awkward.'

He gave a short laugh. 'My father enjoyed being awkward and contrary. It was his favourite sport. He liked it even better than the horses.'

'And you are nothing like that,' she teased. 'You never force anyone to anything they wish to avoid like waltzing.'

'Waltzing with you was an unexpected pleasure.'

The grey in his eyes deepened. 'I've discovered many pleasures with you.'

'Very charmingly put.'

'I try my best to be charming. I learnt from his example that it is easier to get your way when you are.'

'I shall remember that.' Hattie concentrated on the liquid. He hadn't liked his father and his mother had gone from the household by the time he was four. He would have used the word—dead. She wasn't sure why that was important, but she knew it was. She had to wonder if Mrs Reynaud knew anything or indeed if she would be willing to confide. All Hattie knew was she had to try. She wanted to unlock his secrets, but she also knew that if she pressed too hard, he'd turn away from her.

'Did it take you long to learn how to make jam?'

'Preserving is easy to do once you know how,' she said, allowing him to change the subject. 'There is something satisfying about seeing rows of jars and bottles. I can't cook, but I can preserve.'

'Why do you do it?'

'And not leave it to the servants?' Hattie leant back against the small wooden table. He appeared genuinely interested. 'I like to do it. I find it leaves me free to think as I work.'

'Are you finished?'

'For now.' She tilted her head to one side, assessing him.

His body was perfectly still, but coiled like a spring. She wanted to go to him and see if what they had experienced yesterday afternoon remained or if it had burnt out after one joining.

Her stomach knotted. She had imagined that he'd

stride over to her and kiss her as they were alone, but he just stood there. She balled her fist, wishing she knew more about how one actually conducted an affair. And there was no one she could ask! Stephanie would collapse in a fit of vapours even if she so much as hinted at having an affair.

To break the tension, she attempted a light laugh. 'You should have a taste. Dip your finger into the pot. It is one of the perks for knowing the cook.'

He stood watching her without moving. 'You do it. First.'

'Do what?'

'Stick your finger in the jam. Show me how it is done.'

'Don't tell you never have...' She rolled her eyes. 'Didn't you used to go and sneak biscuits from the cook?'

His face became shuttered. 'No, I never did. My father had simple tastes.'

Hattie ground her teeth. She hated to think of the lonely little boy he must have been. She stuck her finger in the cooling jam and held it out. 'There, see. It is simple.'

He captured her wrist and brought the finger to his mouth, suckling. The faint tugging at her finger made her insides skitter. He withdrew and wiped his hand over his mouth. 'I see what you mean. Thoroughly enjoyable.'

'That, Kit, was beneath you.' Her cheeks flamed. She was such a novice at things like flirting with one's lover. Even the thought felt wicked.

'But hugely enjoyable. Strawberry-flavoured Harriet. Definitely a good taste.'

She attempted to remain calm. They were alone and no one had seen. 'I'm pleased I have broadened your education, but you acted like you knew what you were doing.'

'Once you have the mechanics down, the rest falls into place.' He leant forwards so their foreheads touched. 'Your skin smells of strawberries.'

'That is hardly a revelation.' She tried for a sophisticated laugh. This meeting in the still room was not how their next encounter was supposed to go. 'Your charm is slipping, Kit.'

He softly kissed her temple. 'I have a confession. I was going to wait for you to contact me, but decided not to. Will you come out on a ride with me now?'

'You decided not to wait.' She leant back against his arms, staring up into his face. She wanted to believe that she was the only one he'd ever behaved like that with. That she was the only one he pursued.

She had been prepared not to hear from him again, except for a polite note and some little token of false esteem. The fact was he was here with such an eager expression, asking her to go horseback riding with him, looking like he desired her.

She was acutely aware that her hair curled in damp tendrils about her face and her apron was hopelessly stained. Not quite the picture of effortless perfection he required from his women. She gave a wry smile. 'A pleasant thought but…'

'You do ride?' he tilted his head and looked at her with his deep-grey eyes.

'I am a passable rider. I used to be better and take all the jumps, but someone needed to look after my nieces and so I feel my skills are rusty.'

'We shall have to make you a better one. All you are lacking is practice.'

'I suspect you are the sort of person who attempts the largest jumps and thinks about the consequences afterwards.'

His face became carved out of stone. 'I always think about the consequences. I know the price of failure.'

'Your father…'

'My father insisted I learn.' Kit frowned. 'He disliked it if I showed fear. The fear of his temper was far worse than my fear of heights. He left me up a tree once overnight until I developed the courage to climb down.'

'How old were you?

'Five.'

Righteous indignation filled Hattie. How could anyone have been that cruel and unfeeling? She wished the man was still alive so she could give him a piece of her mind. One simply did not do things like that. 'It was wrong of your father.'

'It helped me to learn. He worried that I would be weak, that I had bad blood like my mother.' He gave a self-deprecating smile. 'There are some who say that Eton is a hard place. When my uncle took me there, I found it a paradise beyond my wildest imaginings and never wanted to leave. That suited my father.'

Hattie shook her head in astonishment. When she had been sent to school as a young girl, she had been homesick for weeks, even though Stephanie had been in her final year there. She had lived for going home at the holidays. But Kit was right. He had been better off at school.

Hattie put her hand on his arm. He shrugged it off.

'What your father did was inexcusable, but it can't rule your life,' she whispered.

His face instantly fell and then he covered it up again with a bland mask and she knew she had over-stepped the mark. 'It doesn't. I live my life with style.'

'You are certainly proving a worthy mentor to Mr Hook.'

'I had little choice in the matter.' His mouth twisted with self-loathing.

Hattie reached out and covered his hand with hers. 'People die when they are meant to. You did not fire that bullet. And I suspect you would have taken it if you could have, but you didn't. You have no idea what attracted the marksman to your friend. You can't tor-ture yourself with "what ifs".'

'I will attempt to remember that when I wake up in a cold sweat, knowing that I begged him to change places with me.'

She stared at him for a long time, suddenly under-standing. He blamed himself. 'Do you expect me to turn away with loathing? Is that why you failed to say anything earlier? I won't. I do know something of war. My husband fell in battle.'

'It wasn't any of your business.'

'I'm pleased you lack any ounce of self-pity.'

'Irony is not one of your strong points, Harriet.' He gave a sardonic laugh.

'And you are doing a decent job with Mr Hook,' Hattie continued relentlessly onward, not allowing her-self to become discouraged. He had to see the good that he was doing and that he wasn't like his father. 'I'm impressed at how he has immersed himself in the study of newts. Even Portia is won over. He does know more than she does.'

He stared at her for a long moment. 'Shall we go for this ride or do I find another companion? Surely in the country, you can ride without a groom?'

'I would be delighted to go with you. Or rather to meet you. It is best if we happen to meet rather than ride out together. I have no wish to raise suspicions.'

'You can be overly correct at times, Harriet.'

'You don't have to contend with Stephanie.' Hattie wiped her hands on a towel. Her heat thumped loudly in her ears. She was going to go riding without a groom. She was going to escape from the Dower House and her responsibilities. One ride and that was all. She could stop any time she wanted to.

'Let me find my riding habit. And my horse is a bit slow, but she gets there in the end.'

He touched her cheek. 'That's all I can ask.'

Chapter Eleven

The horse auction was out near Yarridge and the Hexham race course hummed with activity. While Tatterstalls would have been Kit's first choice for purchasing a horse for Hattie, he doubted if she would consent to a journey down to London. He refused to think about how much time they could spend together away from the watchful eye of her sister and housekeeper if she had a mount of her own. Even getting her to come here had been a trial. Mrs Hampstead had shared her carriage, but thankfully had decided to stay at the refreshment tent, rather than look around at the horses. A groom trailed at a respectful distance.

Yarridge and its selection would have to suffice... for now.

Kit ran a practised eye over the stock available for auction, picking out several which might do for Hattie.

'Be careful where you step,' he said, catching Hattie's elbow and helping her around the pile of manure. A pulse of heat went through him.

'I am well aware of what a stockyard is like. Have you spotted which horse I should bid on? Or am I allowed the privilege of deciding that?'

'I am here in an advisory capacity only. Far be it from me to trample on your ideas.'

After their first ride, he had decided she needed something better so she could keep up with Onyx. He offered to get her a horse, but to his surprise and annoyance she refused, insisting that it was to be her horse. Gifts were not permitted. He wanted to spoil her, but she wouldn't let him. Normally he liked to keep the women he was seeing out of his daily life, but he found himself thinking about her at odd times of the day and storing up little stories so that he could relate them to her on their rides, particularly about Rupert's attempts to master newts and his sudden liking for the circulating library, a place Kit had never known him to visit before.

'There are more horses than I had considered there would be.' She clutched her reticule to her chest and skirted around a cart. 'I want a horse which can ride, looks good and has a reasonable temperament but where do I start? Who can I trust?'

'You can trust me.' Kit tucked her hand in his arm. 'Accept my verdict. Despite his many faults, my father did have good eye for horse flesh and he made sure I learnt. The patience he had with horses was amazing.'

Hattie merely raised an eyebrow at his words, but her face took on a fierce aspect. Kit shook his head. She looked like she wanted to do battle for the boy he'd once been.

'I'm far too independent now to allow someone free rein.' Her laugh sounded forced. 'You tell me what to look for and I will see if the horse has it. What is wrong with that bay?'

She pointed towards a showy bay which was prancing about, definitely changing the subject away from his past. Kit frowned. Normally it was his choice to keep his past separate. He had wanted to share, but she refused.

He always said that he preferred independent women, but Hattie carried her independence that bit too far.

'Can't you see me on that horse? We would practically fly over the walls.'

'You and how many other people? The owner means for that horse to be seen. It is the sort of horse that people buy for its beauty.'

'I like beautiful things.' Hattie developed a stubborn set to her jaw.

The horse reared up and pawed the air. All Kit could see was Hattie being crushed under the hooves. He shuddered and pushed the thought away. He turned, expecting to see Hattie cowering.

Hattie's eyes shone with admiration.

'That is a magnificent animal!'

'You like untamed animals.'

A mischievous smile lit her face. 'They have their uses. More than I thought.'

'You need a decent mount, Harriet,' he said, leading her away from the mayhem. 'Something reliable, but with a bit of spirit. The horse you have been riding plods, but that one would throw you as soon as look at you.'

'I'm amazed you can tell that with just one glance. High spirited, but I'm sure I can ride it with a bit of practice.'

Kit clenched his jaw. Not if he had anything to do with it. There was a balance to be struck—a horse who could keep up with Onyx, but not one which would harm Hattie.

'See how she throws her head about? She hasn't been schooled properly. Breaking your neck isn't part of this exercise. A novice rider and an unschooled horse are a disaster waiting to happen.'

'I doubt that will happen.'

In desperation Kit gestured towards the growing throng of people. 'See how many people are interested in her? Do you really want to compete against them?'

She withdrew her hand from his arm. 'I've no wish to pay over the odds for a horse. I want a horse with spirit, but not one that everyone else is competing for and therefore will cost me dearly.'

'Practicality in all things.'

'I learnt how to budget after my husband died.' She lifted her chin with a proud tilt. 'How can I tell the difference between a good horse and a bad one?'

'Look for the little clues—how they hold the bit, place their hooves or react to small noises—as well as the big items such as the way they move or their teeth.' He smiled down at her, preparing to be indulgent now that she'd agreed not to buy that horse.

She nodded seriously. 'Anything else?'

'My father used to say to look at the neck. You can tell a lot about a horse by the way it carries its head. It is probably an old wives' tale, but it has held me in good stead. There is something about a horse's neck.'

'Do you judge people in the same way?' She turned and Kit looked at her long swanlike neck. He wondered that he had ever thought her severe and lacking in beauty. Every time he saw her, he found something else to admire. Her charms might not be as on display as some, but he found himself thinking about her at odd times of the day, remembering different features.

'I like your neck.'

She laughed, a tinkling sound that filled the air with light. He could listen to it all day. 'I shall take that as a compliment.'

A horse crossed in front of them and he took the opportunity to move closer than strictly proper. 'I intend to show my appreciation later.'

'Is that a promise?'

'Of course and you know I never break my promises.'

He basked in her smile, but their current arrangement was unsatisfactory. Finding odd ways to meet and conducting their affair away from prying eyes was sensible, but he wanted to spend more time with her. He tried to tell himself that it was purely physical and, once they spent time together, he'd start to see her faults. He'd become bored or she'd become demanding. Right now the key to that was finding a suitable horse.

'We will find the proper horse for you today. Traipsing all over Northumberland is not going to happen. There will be more suitable horses over here.'

'Kit?' Hattie said, confused. Kit's mood had suddenly changed. He had to understand that the horse needed to be her choice, not his. He didn't answer, but continued to walk away from her.

She hurried after him. 'Where do you think you are going?'

A scrawny boy in rags leading a chestnut horse caused him to draw up and she caught up with him. His face appeared very serious.

'What is the problem?'

'I spied Mr Dent and wasn't sure if you wanted to be seen with me.'

She breathed a sigh of relief. He was considerate. 'Mrs Hampstead is sitting with a cup of tea and Harvey, my groom, is about ten paces behind. Everything is above board. I did think about that eventuality. Wherever you go in the Tyne Valley, you are sure to run into someone you know.'

'What about the grey?' He pointed towards where a large placid horse stood.

Hattie peered more closely at the ragged boy and then the chestnut horse shook her head and she knew. She knew precisely what Kit meant by looking for the little things. 'I want the chestnut unless you have an objection?'

'The chestnut? But that one is a bit more spirited than I would like.' He put his hand under her elbow. 'You might like to take another look at the grey. I think the chestnut may have been mistreated.'

Her eyes narrowed. 'Why do you say that?'

He nodded towards the boy who soothed the horse with his hand. The horse calmed instantly. 'Instinct.'

'But horses recover from ill treatment.'

'Some better than others.' He nodded. 'It takes time and patience. The boy has a way with horses that most people can only dream about. All you have to do is watch him and see how he moves.'

Hattie's heart constricted at the sight of the boy's pinched face and the way his ragged clothes hung off his frame. 'Oh, Kit. He looks half-starved. Can you do anything? We ought to buy him a pie.'

She fumbled in her reticule.

'I was willing to buy the horse for you. The boy is another matter.'

'Buy the boy?' She stared at him in astonishment. 'Is this Sir Christopher Foxton, the man who does not get involved, talking?'

'It will take more than a pie to cure him. He needs a chance.'

'I want the chestnut, Kit, and I am paying. Sometimes you just know deep within your gut that a horse is right.' She glanced up at him. 'A pie is better than nothing. And he will have made a sale.'

'Shall we put the horse through its paces then? First things first, Harriet. The horse, and then we'll see about the boy.'

Kit signalled to the boy, who brought the horse over. Kit ran his hands over the horse's legs, examining every inch and talking to it softly. The way he moved over the horse reminded Hattie of how his hands touched her when they were making love, never unhurried or rough, but gentle and firm. The boy answered all his questions, becoming more animated as he realised that Kit actually cared about the horses.

'She will do,' he said finally.

Hattie let out her breath. 'Thank you.'

Kit spoke quietly to the lad, who raced back to his master.

'What did you tell him?'

'That you were a lady and interested in buying the horse for a fair price, rather than haggling. I know you will pay the price, but for once, Hattie, let me do the speaking.'

A rather overbearing farmer approached with quick footsteps and a greedy eye, and the bargaining began.

Hattie was pleased that Kit took control and extracted a far better price than she thought possible. His eyes shone and she could tell that he was enjoying the process, whereas she would have been tempted to pay the first price.

'And now I will have the boy get us something to wet our whistles,' the farmer said, rubbing his hands together. 'You and your lady can surely spare the time to do that.'

'I am not his lady,' Hattie stiffly. 'We are merely...'

'Neighbours,' Kit supplied.

The farmer nodded as if he understood.

'Your boy?' Hattie asked as the lad ran off.

'The bastard son of my housemaid. His mam died when he were whelped and I have done my Christian duty by him.'

When the boy came back, he stumbled and spilled the tankard of ale. Hattie stifled a gasp as the man clouted him around the ear. Kit strode to the man and caught his wrist, preventing him from delivering the second blow.

'I don't think you want to do that.'

'Why not?'

'Mrs Wilkinson has just purchased that horse, but I want the boy. He has a way of gentling horses. It can't be taught, but it can be cultivated.'

The farmer frowned. 'He is mine, but good for nothing. Eats too much. Rarely minds.'

'Send him to Southview Lodge near Stagshaw. I will pay you twice the price of the horse.' Kit ignored Hattie's sudden indrawn breath. 'Better still, I will take him now. I can use a boy like that in my stables. It is an honest trade.'

The man held out a dirty hand. 'I ken a deal when I see it. John, you be a good lad to his lordship.'

Kit knelt down and looked the ragged boy square in the eyes. 'If you work hard, and are honest, I will promise not to beat you and to ensure you are taught an honest trade.'

The boy beamed back at him. Kit felt as if the world had lit up. 'Aye, that would be good, your lordship.'

'Take the horse, then. You see her back to this lady's house and get her settled, but you will be in my stables.'

'You will need the strap on him. He is a wilful lad.'

Kit turned towards the man and gave him an ice-cold stare. 'I sincerely doubt it.'

'You were magnificent, Kit,' Hattie breathed as they walked back to the carriage with Mrs Hampstead trailing behind, holding the boy's hand.

'Most women of my acquaintance are impressed with jewels or new gowns. Trust you to be different. Luckily I considered this when I made the offer.' Kit waggled his eyebrows in an exaggerated leer.

Hattie pressed her lips together. He was making light of what he'd done, dismissing it as nothing, just as he'd done about Waterloo. 'Giving that boy a chance. Do you normally do things like that?'

'Please don't make me out to be a saint. It was a whim, nothing more.' Kit pushed the brim of his hat down, shielding his eyes. 'I'm currently a stable boy short. It is just that I took a chance. He might run off or not work out. Selfish of me more than anything.'

She glanced at him under her lashes. Whatever his motivations, Kit had done it and it wasn't a whim or an impulse. He'd done it because of what had happened to him as a boy. It amazed her that she'd been so wrong about him when they first met. There was far more to him than superficial charm. 'I trust your judgement.'

'You should have allowed me to pay for the horse, then.'

'You did quite enough with the boy. More than enough. I suspect you saved his life.' Hattie looked over towards where the young boy stood quietly chatting with Kit's coachman as Mrs Hampstead got into the carriage. Less than an hour, and she could already see a change in the boy. He stood taller, his shoulders were less hunched. 'You did a great thing, Kit. Don't belittle what you did. Allow me to think you a hero.'

His face became stony. 'What you are going to call this new horse of yours?'

'Strawberry.' She allowed him to change the subject.

'Strawberry?'

'For obvious reasons. The horse's colour reminds me of strawberry jam.'

'And all that goes with it?'

Their shared laughter rang out over the stable yard. Several people turned around and looked at them as if they were mad. Hattie relaxed slightly. It didn't matter if people saw them together here as they were properly chaperoned. 'If you hadn't been so concerned about the boy, I'd never have noticed the horse. I might have gone for the obvious one and paid over the odds. This one had hidden talents. All it needed was a bit of encouragement.'

His eyes twinkled. 'It reminds me of someone I know. A tiny bit of encouragement and her full beauty was revealed.'

'I wonder who you might be thinking of?' Hattie

enjoyed the warm feeling rushing through her. It was the less obvious compliments which made her feel utterly beautiful. 'Now when we ride, you will be the one who needs to keep up.'

'You seem awfully sure about that. Would you care to wager?'

She glanced up at him. 'Are we at the point of wagering?'

He slid his hand slowly down her arm until his fingers curled about hers and squeezed tightly. 'Yes, definitely.'

Hattie leant forwards in her saddle and urged Strawberry up the slope. She'd had her horse only a few short weeks, but she already saw a huge difference in her riding ability. Over the past few weeks, even though it was never specifically planned, she and Kit seemed to meet most mornings on horseback for a gallop across the fells.

Keeping her independence was important. Whatever happened long term with Kit, she knew she'd treasure Strawberry. Kit had wanted to give her this horse and that was enough. She hated that she clung to every moment they were together, hoarding them like they were precious jewels. If she started to accept gifts, it would change their relationship. Hattie knew that she could never be a kept woman. She never wanted to become like Charles's mistress.

Kit was the perfect companion. They spoke about everything. She learnt how the renovations for the house were going and how John the stable boy was working out. Her concern appeared to amuse Kit. Kit predicted that with a little schooling, the boy could go far, but he never said when or where it would take place. In odd moments, when she was on her own, it bothered Hattie as it was another sign that this was a summer romance, rather than anything permanent. But wasn't that what she wanted, too? All she would allow herself?

Besides, being involved in a summer's romance was an exhilarating feeling. Even Stephanie's complaints about her pregnancy and her increasing demands failed to dampen Hattie's enthusiasm for riding and for the clandestine affair. She rejoiced in the knowledge that it belonged to her and Kit only.

She reined in Strawberry at the top of the hill. Kit came thundering up the hill, a few feet behind her. 'You see, Kit, I could do it. I was able to take the wall and land correctly.'

'You made it to the top of the hill first…for once.' His grey eyes twinkled as he dismounted. 'You are fast becoming an expert rider. Only a week ago, you'd have avoided that wall. Today, there was no hesitation.'

'It felt like flying.'

'You should take care. The last thing anyone wants is for you to get hurt.'

'What are my winnings?' She slid off Strawberry's back and looped the reins around a branch. A buoyant happiness filled her. She had done it. She had actually jumped the dry stone wall and flown over the stream, things she never dreamt possible. And she wasn't going to allow Kit's sudden concern to dampen her triumph.

A dimple shone in the corner of his mouth. 'What were you thinking?'

She glanced about her. The ridge was secluded and private. She stripped off her gloves and hat, and placed them on the ground. She lifted her face to his. 'A kiss. No one is here. No one will spy on us.'

'My lady is demanding. A kiss it shall be.' He lowered his mouth to hers and brushed her lips. She wrapped her arms about his neck and drank from his mouth.

'You call that a kiss? Your hat kept hitting my forehead.' Hattie knew her breath was coming a little too fast.

'A thousand pardons.' He took off his hat and tossed it neatly on top of hers before undoing his neckcloth.

'That's a bit better.' A deliciously wicked shiver went through her. There was something to be said for enjoying Kit's company. He was the perfect companion for playing and she had a hard time remembering when she'd last played so much.

He gave a husky laugh and pulled her body into his so that their pelvises touched. 'Perhaps I should allow you to win more often.'

'Only if I deserve it.'

'You definitely deserve to be kissed.' He pulled her more firmly into his arms. 'And for once no one is here.'

'I take it you wish to stay here for a while.'

'I might do…unless there is a call upon your time.'

'Do you think we dare?'

He placed his hands on her shoulders and looked down at her. His eyes crinkled in the corners. 'We can do what we want, but I suspect the grass will be itchy. And you will get seeds in your hair again.'

'Mrs Hampstead keeps her conversation to domestic trivialities these days and Stephanie is utterly absorbed in her family. She never asks about how I spend my time.' Hattie bit her lip. She'd been thinking about touching him all morning while she was listening to Stephanie's complaints about how Livvy had suddenly become a bluestocking and was constantly seeking to go to the circulating library. She'd wanted to feel his skin under her hands and had stopped herself from saying something just in time.

Sometimes, in her wilder moments, she did wonder what her sister would do if she confessed to her indiscretion.

'You're wearing your serious face.'

'Stephanie gets worse. She keeps dropping subtle hints about me moving in with her until the baby comes. And I can't. The walls would press down on me too much.' Hattie knew it was another half-truth. If she had to move back there, all these clandestine meetings with Kit would have to cease.

He brought her hand to his lips. His eyes turned deep grey. 'I'd prefer a soft bed with clean sheets and a roof over our head, and hour upon hour to enjoy you without your sister calling on you at all hours. Someone will have to give way.'

'That is impossible, here. This is not London where you can be anonymous.' She glanced over her shoulder. Thus far, the gossip had been muted, but she knew the limits. Discretion rather than full-blown flaunting of the relationship.

When they met at social occasions, it was never by design but by happenstance. Hattie was always careful not to spend too much time speaking to him. She loved hugging the secret to her bosom.

'We're far too well known,' she said firmly. 'I shudder to think what would happen if knowledge of this became common currency. It would ruin Livvy's chances. I couldn't do that.'

'Have you thought about taking a trip?' He moved closer. A faint breeze tousled his hair, giving him a rakish air. 'We could travel to the Continent. There is no trouble with travelling now that the war is truly over. You could see the places you always wanted to— Rome, Vienna, even Paris.'

Her heart turned over. He wanted to go travelling with her. A brief vision danced before her eyes. She could visit all those places that she had read about, but it would be better because he would by her side, sharing the experience. It would mean what was between them was more than a summer's romance.

He was fast becoming as necessary as breathing.

How had it happened? She cared about him. More than cared for him, she carried him in her heart. Loved him. That was not supposed to happen. Everything she'd done had been based on keeping her heart safe and enjoying the physical passion. She knew it was a summer's affair, nothing more, something that would fade when the autumn winds came, but somehow her heart had forgotten that important fact.

The feeling nearly took her breath away, only to be immediately replaced with despondency. He had never offered for ever. He'd been clear about that at the start. He was everything that she thought she'd despise—a man who used charm and who could not be counted on. He was not the sort of man to love.

She knew how destructive one-sided love had been to her once. She turned her face from his and attempted to control her emotions.

'Hattie, are you all right?' His voice penetrated

through her confusion. 'I'd expected you to smother my face with kisses. A trip to Europe this autumn. If you insist, we can take Mrs Hampstead as cover and pretend to accidentally meet.'

'Perfectly. I just remembered that Stephanie wanted help with the flowers this evening. She is giving a small dinner party before the Dents' musicale. I forgot to say no.'

'She makes too many demands of you,' he said flatly. 'You need to learn to refuse her sometimes.'

She shook her head. 'I could never do that. After my husband died, she was so good to me.'

'So good to you that you couldn't admit what had really happened to you.'

'It had nothing to do with her.' Hattie examined the grass. 'I promised her that I'd stay. She is expecting. She needs me. I don't know what I would have done without her after Charles died. I owe her this much. Perhaps it is best if we cut this ride short.'

She bent down to pick up her hat and gloves. Why when everything seemed fine, did he offer her something that she was scared about accepting? A trip with her to the Continent meant nothing to his ultimate future, but he was asking her to change her whole life, to give everything up and she wasn't ready for that.

He laced his fingers with hers, kept her there. 'You are saying that you don't want to travel. You fear it, just as you feared that stone wall. You cleared that wall without a problem, Harriet.'

'Some day I will…travel. I have it all planned out.' She took her hand from his. 'Like you, I don't go back on my promises.'

'That is because you are stubborn. The offer is

there, Harriet. I am going to the Continent this winter with or without you.'

A great hollow space developed inside her. He was asking her to choose and she couldn't. She wasn't ready. She needed time to think. 'I will let you know my decision. It needs careful consideration.'

'When?'

'Later.' She gave a shrug. 'How goes Mr Hook's preparation for the lecture? It is less than a week away now. Portia was asking this morning before she explained why the latest experiment with newts was doomed to failure. Livvy leapt to Mr Hook's defence. It made for a lively visit.'

'Stop trying to change the subject. You are unwilling to go away with me.'

'I can't go.' Hattie's heart tore into two pieces. He had to understand what he was asking. If she went, she would be even more in love with him. He wasn't offering marriage or for ever, but a trip, a way to pass the winter. When she returned, their affair would no longer be a secret—everyone would know who her travelling companion had been. She'd lose her entire way of life. 'But if you insist on an answer…no, not with Stephanie the way she is. Pregnancy doesn't agree with her. I'd never forgive myself if I wasn't there and you are wrong to press me. Arrangements would have to be put in place.'

'Some women would accept without a moment's hesitation.'

'I'm not those women!' Hattie's heart thudded. He had to understand how hard this was for her and how sudden.

'Then we know where we are. Forget I said anything.'

She hugged her arms about her waist, hating that the atmosphere had turned so suddenly. She'd been looking forward to making love in the late-summer sunshine and everything had gone wrong. It hurt all the worse because she knew she cared about him and wanted this enchanted time to go on for ever. She wanted to go to the Continent and see all those places she had dreamt about—to have him at her side would be heaven. But it would also be slipping further into an illusion that their relationship would last.

'I had best go. I've been neglecting my visiting and other duties.'

'Yes, you never hesitate to do your duty.' His mouth curled down.

'There is nothing wrong with doing your duty.' She put her hands on her hips.

'If you think that, we had best end it here as you will always find another duty to do.'

'You are putting words into my mouth. Did you only ask me so I'd refuse? So you have the excuse you were seeking to end our relationship?'

He caught her arms and dragged her against him. Her body collided with his. The fire which was never very far below the surface flared. 'I asked you because I want you with me. I'm not ready to end our affair. I'm not ready yet and neither are you. Shall I demonstrate?'

He ruthlessly lowered his head, plundering her mouth and feasting. It was a cold hard cynical kiss, one designed to punish her for refusing his invitation.

With only a token protest, she opened her mouth under his and allowed her body to tell him all the things she didn't dare. The kiss that started harshly became softer and more seductive, seeking rather than demanding.

She moaned in the back of her throat and squirmed against his body, seeking relief from the desire which was now raging out of control in her body.

'I want you,' he rasped in her ear. 'I want to enjoy you when I want to, not rushing around and hiding from prying eyes. That is the only reason I asked. Most of all I want you. Right here and right now.'

His lips trailed down her neck, making a fiery pathway. Pleasure rippled through her body as his hand roamed at will, sliding down her curves and caressing her over the heavy cloth. She silently wished that she hadn't taken such pains at dressing this morning.

As if he could read her mind, he reached down and bunched the skirt. His hand slipped under her skirts and parted her drawers, finding her moist core. His finger slipped in, stroked and played.

'I want you, too,' she said between gasps. A delicious vista opened before her. He'd always taken the lead in their love-making, but this time she wanted to be the one to be in control and in charge. 'I'm no longer a novice, but an expert. Allow me to ride you.'

Her hands slipped down his body and unbuttoned his trousers. His erection sprang free. She clasped it in her hand, feeling the velvet hardness. As he stroked her, she stroked him back, both of them using their hands to give each other pleasure.

'I don't know how much longer I can last.' He eased her down amongst the high grass. 'Ride me, Harriet. Ride me now.'

He lay back on the ground and she positioned herself above him, straddling his body. The moist tip of him nudged the apex of her thighs. She spread her leg wider.

Using her hand, she guided him to the very centre and slowly impaled herself. Rode him, controlling the movement. Up and down, going at her pace as he lay underneath her. She enjoyed the feeling of power, of bringing them to the brink and then slowing it down.

The weeks of riding had honed her muscles and she used them now to give him pleasure. Faster and faster until the wave crested, then crested again. Finally when she knew she could take no more, she clasped her arms around him and held him as he came to a shuddering climax deep within her, so deep it seemed like his seed was spilling directly into her womb. They were together, joined.

Chapter Twelve

Much later when they lay entwined in each other's arms, Kit smoothed her hair from her forehead. It amazed him that he once thought Harriet had no passion within her. His desire for her had grown rather than diminished. 'You are definitely an expert rider, now.'

'No longer in need of lessons? I think I have learnt lots about being wicked.' She stretched her arms above her head. 'It has been absolutely delicious.'

His heart gave an unexpected pang. Lessons in wickedness? Was that all she considered this? He knew they had agreed that it would be a summer's affair, but he had discovered that he wanted it to continue into the autumn and beyond. The thought shocked him. 'No more lessons. The pupil has outshone the master.'

'I shall take it as a compliment.' She moved her arm and Kit heard a faint tear. She wrinkled her nose. 'Oh, dear. More sewing.'

'I fear our exertions have ruined your dress.'

She pulled away slightly. 'It will mend and if Mrs Hampstead questions it, I will say that I acquired it riding. It is not less than the truth.'

A cold stab of fear went through Kit. 'Has she questioned you before?'

'No harm will come from today, I promise,' she said, pulling her sleeve a bit and rearranging the material so the tear didn't show as easily. 'Mrs Hampstead will not enquire too closely. She never does. Discretion rules all. We are safe.'

Safety. He rolled over onto his back, moving away from her. His body protested at the sudden space. He wanted to linger and relax in her arms. He wanted her to go away with him, but she had refused and it still hurt. Staying here was the worst of all possible worlds.

'There is always a chance of a slip. What then?' He forced his voice to be cold. 'A forced marriage? You know my feelings about marriage.'

'There won't be.' Her cheeks stained bright red. 'I've been careful.'

'Soon autumn will be here. It will be too cold for such things.'

'Are you really planning on travelling to the Continent so soon, then?' she asked quickly. 'I thought you might like to see Northumberland in the autumn. Stay a bit longer and stretch the summer out. Summer can sometimes last.'

He sighed and put his hands behind his head, staring up into the clear blue sky, rather than looking at her. Staying here with Harriet had its merits, but all it would do was to prolong the inevitable and increase the likelihood of discovery. Misery for all if he allowed it to continue.

'After Rupert gives his lecture, I have to go to London. It can no longer be avoided. I do have business interests that I have to look after. I've neglected them for far too long. Like you, I have responsibilities and people depending on me to make the right choices.'

The words caused his insides to twist. Normally when the time came for a parting, he looked forward to it. This time, he hated it. It was better now, though, while they remained friends. Rules were made to be kept.

Hattie smoothed her skirt down and hugged her knees to her chest. The silence grew deafening. He willed her to ask to come with him and give him some sign that she wanted to be with him.

'So soon?' she whispered. 'His lecture is tomorrow. Everyone is sure to want to fête him afterwards. He will be the toast of the Tyne for weeks to come. Surely you can stay to see your protégé shine?'

He stood absolutely still with a soft breeze blowing in his hair. Behind him, the swifts circled on the wind, getting ready to depart from Northumberland to go on their long journey back to Africa. Summer was drawing to a close as much as he might wish it to be otherwise. He'd ignored it for far too long.

'I have stayed longer than I intended.' His words sounded harsh, even to his own ears. 'I'd planned to ask you to come to London with me, but you are busy. You have made that abundantly clear today.'

Hattie bit her lip. 'But you will be back. The Lodge needs lots of work. Someone will have to supervise.'

He concentrated on doing up the buttons of his trousers and shrugging into his jacket. She wasn't even willing to make the smallest concession. It was the right thing to end it swiftly. He had lingered far too long as it was. He did have another life, even if it was less than appealing at the moment. 'Some day. It will depend on how my business goes, but we must stay in contact, Hattie.'

She picked a piece of grass from her skirt. 'You always call me Harriet.'

'Hattie, Harriet, does it really matter?' Kit slapped his hand against his forehead. She was splitting hairs. He'd offered to take her away and she'd refused. What did she expect?

'Yes, it does. It did.' Her chin was tilted upwards, not giving an inch. 'I will look forward to your return then, Sir Christopher.'

'As you wish, Mrs Wilkinson.' Kit mounted his horse and did not look back. It was always best in these circumstances not to. However, he could not stop a hollow opening up inside him.

Hattie made it to her drawing room without crying. The ride back, alone, was one that she wanted to forget. Each time Strawberry's hooves pounded the ground, she wanted to ask how long—how long had he planned this? He knew what her answer had to be.

'Hattie, what happened to your dress?' Stephanie's voice pierced through her misery. 'You look like you have gone through a hedge backwards. Hopefully no one saw you like that! People will talk, you know and it will reflect on the family. Everyone knows you are my sister.'

Hattie fumbled with the sleeve. Talk about bad luck. Why did Stephanie have to choose today to come over? And to be in such a terrible mood! Why didn't Mrs Hampstead warn her when she came through the kitchen? 'I tore it riding.'

'Riding? You tore it riding?' Stephanie came over and inspected the sleeve with a frown. 'It is the first time I have heard of riding causing such a thing.'

'I moved my arm far too quickly. The thread wasn't very stout.' Hattie shifted uneasily as Stephanie's gaze grew more piercing. 'It is the truth, Stephanie.'

'And with whom were you riding?'

'Sir Christopher,' Hattie said without thinking. 'We had a laugh about my ineptness.'

'Since when have you been riding with Sir Christopher?' Stephanie's voice rose an octave.

'We met accidentally.' Hattie kept her voice even. There was no need to panic. She'd had a slight slip of the tongue. It was not as if she'd actually confessed to the affair.

'I see…and how many times have you two met accidentally in recent weeks?'

'I fail to see why that is a concern of yours.'

'Often, I would wager. I can see it in your face.' Stephanie collapsed down on the damask sofa and buried her face in her hands. 'You are worse than Livvy, Hattie. Clandestine. You know what a man Sir Christopher is on about. How do you think you will force a marriage if you meet secretly?'

'Is there some trouble, Stephanie?' Hattie decided to ignore the remark about forcing a marriage. 'Surely it is not against the law to go out riding. One must be civil to those one encounters.'

'There is civility and then there is *civility*. Pray tell me that you have remained sensible in all things and that you have safeguarded your reputation.'

A cold sweat pricked at the back of Hattie's neck. *She knows*. But why now when everything had ended?

A sudden more horrific thought struck her. Had they been spotted? Was that why Kit had provoked the fight? 'Something is bothering you, Stephanie. You might as well come out and say it. What am I supposed to have done?'

'I heard you had gone to the Yarridge sale with Sir Christopher, but chose to overlook it.'

'To buy Strawberry. I explained about that.' Hattie leant forwards. 'Sir Christopher is an acknowledged expert in horse flesh. He wanted to thank me for assisting him during the fair. Mrs Hampstead and Harvey the groom were in attendance.'

'Hmmm, and now you just happen to be meeting him…accidentally.' Stephanie held out her hand. 'Think about what you are doing, the potential for scandal.'

'You are creating a difficulty where there is none. In any case, Sir Christopher will be departing for London soon. No more meetings.' Just saying the words out loud threatened to bring tears. Hattie blinked rapidly. 'You are worrying unnecessarily.'

Stephanie shook her head. 'You have been reckless, Hattie. I can see it in your eyes, your mouth and, yes, in your ripped jacket. Sir Christopher is an entirely different proposition to Charles Wilkinson.'

'What do you mean?'

'You have had clandestine meetings with him. Goodness knows what some farmhand or milk maid might have seen or who they might tell.' Stephanie's face became serious. 'You must not do anything that jeopardises Livvy's chances. We don't want a scandal.'

'There will be no scandal,' Hattie said tonelessly. Her entire body felt numb. Stephanie wasn't concerned about her or her reputation, but merely what it might to do to Livvy's prospects. She hadn't even asked Hattie how she was. Stephanie had to have seen that Hattie was upset. Instead she went on and on quizzing her about unimportant things.

Stephanie's gaze narrowed. 'You say this with a great deal of certainty.'

'Sir Christopher is returning to London. Directly after Mr Hook's lecture.'

'Will you continue to ride out once he is gone? Or will you start behaving normally?'

'I enjoy riding whether I encounter Sir Christopher or not. I had not really considered the proposition.' Hattie forced her voice to stay even. 'You are worse than a dog with a bone, Stephanie. What are you trying to tell me?'

'All I can say, Hattie, is that you are being selfish and extremely short-sighted.' Stephanie rose from the sofa in a huff. 'I need you now more than ever, Hattie. Stop being selfish. Livvy keeps making excuses about going to the circulating library. I can't have my eldest turning into a bluestocking. You will speak to her for me, won't you? She will never get a man that way.'

Hattie balled her fists. Stephanie wasn't really interested in her or her affair with Kit. She was simply inconvenienced. 'There is nothing wrong with the circulating library. I presume she takes Portia. Reading is a perfectly respectable occupation.'

'There is no need to be like that. They never meet anyone of import. Portia would tell me if they did.' Stephanie put her nose in the air. 'If Sir Christopher is departing, then it is all I have to say on the matter. I look forward to having the old Hattie back. You used to be so helpful, Hattie. What happened?'

'And what if I like the new Harriet?'

'That is your choice, obviously.' Stephanie sniffed. 'But don't come crying to me when you lose everything.'

Mrs Reynaud's face was a beacon of welcome as Hattie entered Pearl Cottage, carrying a basket of various jams, jellies and tinctures, the next morning. Moth immediately jumped out of the basket and ran over to Mrs Reynaud to demand a biscuit.

'I feared you had forgotten about me, Mrs Wilkinson.' Mrs Reynaud handed Moth her treat. 'Moth has been very bad not to insist on you coming here. And here I'd thought you and I had an arrangement, young Moth. Biscuits in return for your mistress's company.'

Moth gave a sharp bark.

'Your maid said that you have been under the weather.' Hattie kept the basket in front of her. All the way here she'd debated—did she confess to Mrs Reynaud about her relationship with Kit and ask her advice or not? Mrs Reynaud was the one person in the village who had experience with such things.

'Not so ill that I can't receive one of my favourite people. A slight chill, nothing more. My health is less robust than I might wish. The damp of this cottage does me no good. But going out is hard. I worry about people and the lecture series. How goes it this year? Still surviving, I take it.'

Hattie felt a tug of regret. Until Kit had told her this morning about his plans to leave, she'd been so wrapped up in him that she had quite forgotten her usual routine. Stephanie was right. Her behaviour was causing comment. No more. 'I've been busy. I've a new horse, the most lovely chestnut—Strawberry. Riding is a new passion of mine. I hadn't realised how enjoyable it was. The freedom it gives.'

She stopped, aware that her cheeks flamed.

'A gift from Sir Christopher, or so the gossip has it. A thank you for nursing him,' Mrs Reynaud said with a faint frown. 'His father always did have a good eye for horse flesh.'

'I bought her on favourable terms with Sir Christopher's assistance. He rescued a little stable boy.'

Mrs Reynaud waved an impatient hand. 'You meet him on this horse of yours? Don't lie to me, Mrs Wilkinson.'

'I've discovered that I enjoy the experience far more than I thought I would.' Hattie put down the basket. She clasped her hands together to stop them from trembling. She'd thought it over last night. She had to know more about Kit. Every time they had discussed about his childhood, he'd neatly turned the conversation away. She had to know what had gone wrong yesterday. 'You said you knew something of Sir Christopher's childhood. I understand it was very unhappy.'

'A bit.' Mrs Reynaud's eyes turned wary and her hand trembled as she lifted the coffee cup to her lips. 'Is it important?'

'It was something he said, or rather didn't say. It has been nagging at me.' Hattie drew a deep breath. She had come this far. Other than Kit, Mrs Reynaud was the only person who might know. 'I wondered what happened to his mother.'

'You ought to ask Sir Christopher.'

Hattie leant forwards. 'But you know.'

Mrs Reynaud gave a sad smile. 'Yes, my dear, I know.'

'Is it breaking a confidence?'

'I doubt that. There was a criminal conversation trial which was splashed all over the papers. It became the talk of England, Europe and, I believe, America. The cartoonists had a field day with the baronet spying on his wife and her lover in the bath.'

Hattie's heart clenched. Poor Kit. No wonder he didn't want to speak of it. She could vaguely remember her mother discussing it in hushed tones when a friend of hers had run away. 'I didn't know.'

'Now you do.'

'Unfortunately Kit's mother was less than discreet, that is what you are saying.' Hattie's heart constricted. It had to be awful to have one's parents involved in such a thing and it was never the man whose name was dragged through the mud, but the woman's. And Kit had been left with his father, the man who saw no use for toys. 'What a dreadful mess. The father always gets custody in those cases and Kit's father was horrible.'

'You call him Kit now, do you?' Mrs Reynaud gave a warm laugh. 'Behold the woman who will never have a flirtation, who is one of the walking dead because her husband died. Who disapproved of such things intensely.' Her gaze became piercing. 'I trust it remains only a flirtation. Sir Christopher has a certain reputation.'

'We are friends.' Hattie waved a vague hand before leaning forwards. She'd reached the crux of the matter and only Mrs Reynaud could assist. 'He helped me when I bought my new horse, but I am interested in his mother. Do you know what became of her? Is she dead?'

'Yes, his mother was silly and naïve. She sought romance in the wrong set of arms.' Mrs Reynaud's mouth twisted. 'A hopeless romantic who didn't realise what she had lost until too late. Pray do not concern yourself with a piece of flotsam like her.'

Hattie stared at Mrs Reynaud, remembering the stories she had told and the way she had described herself. Hattie narrowed her gaze, comparing. Her stomach tightened with excitement. It made sense now. She'd wondered that she had not seen it before. Mrs Reynaud's eyes were the exact same myriad shades of grey as Kit's. Then there was the shape of their jaws. 'You're Kit's mother, the scandalous woman.'

'I have no idea what you are talking about, my dear.' Mrs Reynaud raised her teacup, hiding her expression. 'Did I ever tell you about the sheikh and me? It is a wonderful story. It is sure to entertain you immensely.'

Hattie crossed the floor and knelt at Mrs Reynaud's feet and gathered Mrs Reynaud's hand between hers. 'I should like to think we are friends, Mrs Reynaud. Why didn't you tell me that Sir Christopher Foxton was your son when he first arrived here?'

Mrs Reynaud's body vibrated with emotion. A long drawn-out sigh emerged from her throat as she bowed her head. 'Does it really matter? I gave up the right to be anyone's mother years ago. All I did was to try to play matchmaker. You are the sort of woman he should have as a bride, rather than the women he has squired throughout the years. You are beautiful and intelligent, the sort of woman I always hoped he'd marry. I may not have seen him, but I have retained an interest.'

'I shall take that for a yes.' Hattie refused to think about Mrs Reynaud's attempt at matchmaking. Her stomach churned. She'd nearly confided about her affair to Kit's mother. 'He has your eyes and your jaw. I suspect your sense of humour as well.'

'I know about the eyes and jaw, but will have to take your word for the humour. I haven't spoken to Christopher for years.' Mrs Reynaud's cheeks flushed pink.

'And the other men? Did you really lead a scandalous life?'

Mrs Reynaud lifted her head defiantly. 'I had to survive after Christopher's father ruined me. Thanks to my marriage settlement, my late husband was able to lay claim to my inheritance and use it how he pleased. He refused to divorce me in the end and kept me on pin money. The criminal conversation was proved, but my lover only had to pay a meagre fivepence for destroying my reputation. He and I parted.' Mrs Reynaud spread her gnarled hands. 'I made sure my late husband knew about each and every one of my new lovers. It served my purposes to have him suffer.'

'Your late husband. Kit's father.' The words tasted like ash.

'Yes.' The word was barely audible. 'When I left, I thought it would be only for a few weeks before I could get Christopher to join me. Christopher's father had shown no interest in the boy. But I lived in a fool's paradise. The courts look ill on fallen women who leave their husbands.'

'But he's been dead for years. Why haven't you been in touch with Kit? He must long for his mother. He is your son. I know if my mother was alive, I'd want to see her.'

Mrs Reynaud touched her pockmarked face. 'You know what I look like. I fell ill just before Christopher's father died. Divine retribution. I changed my name by deed poll as soon as I could. I didn't want to shame him.'

'You're his mother.'

'I am the woman who left him. He was only four. At first I tried to justify it. He had his nurse. He had stability and John, my brother-in-law, promised to look after him as much as he could. John desired me once, you see. The brothers were like that—rivals.' She held up her hands and turned her face away. 'When John gave me this cottage, I agreed I would never contact Christopher. My late husband spent my inheritance. I had nothing. I had no choice.'

Hattie clenched her fists. Mrs Reynaud had had a choice. She had simply chosen not to take it. 'Go on.'

'The agreement was I would let him contact me. I have stuck by the agreement. John used to share his letters with me. He'd bring them over and read them. The highlight of my existence, those letters. I used to write to him. I have packets of letters which were never sent, just waiting for the day when he did contact me.'

'Does he know you are here?'

'John promised to leave him a letter. Once, a long time ago, I begged John for a chance to see Kit. He brought him to the Stagshaw fair. I made wild plans. John suggested we run away together and raise him. In the end I lacked the courage as I loved John like a brother, not a lover. It wouldn't be fair to him. I bought Christopher a jumping-jack and had John give it to him. Shortly afterwards, I left for the Continent.'

'Your former husband and brother-in-law are dead,'

Hattie whispered. She didn't dare tell Susan Reynaud about the jumping-jack and what it had meant to Kit. She also knew the longing she had seen in his face when he spoke about his mother. She and Kit might have ended, but she cared about him. He needed to know that his mother wanted him. He needed to read those letters that his mother had saved for him. The question was how to do it. She couldn't just show up at his house and demand.

'But I'm alive and I gave my word.' Mrs Reynaud shook her head. 'Some mistakes you never recover from, my dear. I learnt that the hard way. I would like to see him just once. Not to speak to, necessarily, but to see. There is nothing I could say to him which would explain why I did what I did. Could you help me?'

Hattie hated the way her stomach trembled. Kit was leaving. He might never be returning. It might be the only chance for Kit to learn the truth—that his mother did care about him. She hated to think about might-have-beens. She knew she'd regret it if she didn't do it. She wasn't going to think about giving him a reason to stay. They were finished. The summer was over.

'Kit's ward, Rupert Hook, is giving a lecture tomorrow,' she said, coming to a sudden decision. 'You could attend. You are one of the patrons of the lecture series. You can at least see what he looks like. You don't have to greet Kit, but you could see him.'

Mrs Reynaud's hands trembled and she set down her teacup. Her grey eyes swam. 'Yes, of course. No one would think it amiss. I just want to see what he looks like, to see if there is anything of me in him. I'm so frightened that...'

'You can sit next to me,' Hattie said.

'You are a good woman, Hattie Wilkinson.'

'I can't understand why you did what you did, Mrs Reynaud, but I do know you can only change the future. Take the first step.'

'It tore the life out of me to leave him, but my marriage was intolerable. I don't expect you to understand. I made some bad choices in my life and I have paid for them, but the one I never regretted was having Kit.' Mrs Reynaud straightened her back. 'You are right, my dear. It is time I faced my demons. I will take your suggestion and go to the lecture. You have given me strength.'

The Corbridge Village Hall was full to bursting for Rupert's lecture. Kit regarded the various personages—the great and the good going in to hear Rupert. He had handled things badly with Hattie. The break had been too abrupt, too final. Normally he was far more civilised about such things.

Rather than going to the front and taking his seat, he waited at the back to escort Hattie to hers. He'd make one last attempt and then they'd be through.

An elderly pockmarked lady half-stumbled on the step leading to the hall. Kit put out a hand and caught her before she tumbled completely.

'The steps up can be tricky,' he said.

She gave him an odd look. 'Yes, they can.'

'You must take better care on them.'

The woman gave a small smile. 'I will.'

'Mrs Reynaud—' Hattie stopped. The colour drained from her face.

Kit froze. He stared at Mrs Reynaud and knew. She was his mother. His stomach plummeted. He moved away from the woman, from his mother. This was most definitely not where he wanted to meet her and not in front of a crowd of people.

From Hattie's reaction, he knew that she knew the truth as well. Somehow Hattie was aware of who his mother was. For how long? Had she engineered this meeting?

Deep-seated anger filled him. He disliked being manipulated. If his mother wanted to meet him, she knew where he was. He had hardly kept his whereabouts secret, but she had. He struggled to control his temper. It was wrong of Hattie to do this, particularly after their quarrel. She had set him up. It seemed everyone in the entire lecture hall had turned to look at him and his mother. It was worse than a nightmare. His first impulse was to run away, but he rejected that idea. All that would show was cowardice. He was no coward.

Whatever happened, he refused to give anyone the satisfaction of seeing his emotions. Politeness and graciousness. Nothing to show that he was hurt beyond measure by both of their behaviours. He swallowed hard and regained control of his emotions. He knew what he had to do. Hattie with her superior expression would be held to account for her behaviour.

'I wish both of you the joy of the evening. You must forgive me, but I have a lecture to attend. I made a promise to my ward. Mrs Wilkinson, Mrs Reynaud, your servant.'

Hattie's hand flew to her mouth as she watched Kit stalk off. He had cut her and Mrs Reynaud with absolute aplomb.

She heard several shocked gasps and knew the encounter had not gone unremarked.

She had made a grave error. She had never considered Mrs Reynaud would actually encounter Kit face to face, as it were, in the lobby before everyone. The final look he gave her before he turned away had damned her for all eternity, but he seemed in control, greeting any number of people with perfect politeness as if the meeting meant nothing to him.

She went over to where Mrs Reynaud stood, clutching her reticule to her chest with a distressed look on her face. 'This is all my fault.'

'He knows?' Mrs Reynaud choked out.

'Yes, I believe he does…now.' She put an arm about Mrs Reynaud's shoulders. 'It will have been a shock for him and for you. If there is anything I can do for you…just ask.'

'I should go. It was wrong of me to come. I should have waited for him to contact me as John suggested. He looked so like his father then. It quite unnerved me.' She moved out of Hattie's embrace. 'You must allow me to depart, Mrs Wilkinson.'

'What, and miss this lecture? You can sit next to me and we shall hear this lecture. See, Livvy is signalling to us.'

Mrs Reynaud fumbled in her reticule and withdrew a battered lady jumping-jack. 'No, I won't enjoy it. Give Kit this jumping-jack from me. It is up to him then. You may tell him where to find me. Please do this for me, Mrs Wilkinson.'

Hattie closed her eyes. The last thing she wanted was to have a confrontation with Kit, but how could she refuse? She had to do something to make amends… to both of them.

Chapter Thirteen

Hattie walked into her darkened drawing room and struck a match so she could put the lamp on. She was far too keyed up to sleep. Somehow she had to find a way to deliver the jumping-jack to Kit in person. She had thought about it all during Mr Hook's lecture, but was no closer to an answer.

Despite the incident with Kit at the beginning, the lecture had been a huge success. Stephanie beamed afterwards, loudly declaring that she knew Rupert Hook had not been lying when he proclaimed he was an expert on newts. Hattie had answered vaguely, made her excuses and left.

'Don't bother to light the lamp.'

She nearly dropped the match in surprise. Kit stood in the middle of the drawing room, lit from the back by the small fire. Tall and forbidding. Her mouth went dry. 'Kit! What are you doing here?'

He indicated the French doors. 'It is easy to get into a house when you want, and your guard dog is a friend of mine.'

Moth turned on her back and wriggled.

Hattie put a hand to her head. 'Oh, Moth.'

'I have one question for you and then I will leave you in peace.' There was no mistaking the finality to his tone. 'Why did you do it, Harriet?'

'Why did I do what?' she asked cautiously. The last thing she wanted was a confrontation.

'When did you find out? How long have you known where my mother was? Why did you set me up like that?'

Hattie's heart thudded in her ears. She knew precisely what he was speaking about. The day of reckoning had arrived, much sooner than she thought it would.

'Earlier today.' Hattie blew out the match before it burnt her fingers. She struck another one, moved over to the small table and lit a candle. 'There wasn't time to tell you.'

'You convinced her to come to the lecture expressly to see me, without consulting my feelings on the subject. Don't deny it. My mother had all summer to contact me if she desired.' Kit gave a fierce scowl. 'What did you think would happen—a joyful reunion of two people long separated? Did you even consider how I might feel about the matter? About seeing my mother suddenly after so many years?'

Hattie gave a tiny shrug as Kit's scowl increased. When he put it like that, she could see there was no defence. She should have let him know, but if she had, the situation would have remained unresolved. She bit her lip. It wasn't exactly resolved now.

'Mrs Reynaud only wanted to see you.' Hattie held out her hands, palms upwards, willing him to understand. 'I didn't plan you two meeting like that. It was supposed to be different.'

He lifted a disbelieving eyebrow. 'Was she hard to convince?'

'It only took the slightest bit of encouragement. She wanted to go. She wanted to see you, but feared something bad would happen.' Hattie willed him to understand why she had done it. 'She is unwell, Kit. It might have been her last chance to make amends. She has a stack of letters which she wrote for you. She wants you to read them. She made a promise to your uncle not to contact you.'

'My uncle has been dead for over a year.' He slammed his fist down on the table making the china ornaments jump. 'Dead men don't know the difference between a kept promise and a broken one.'

'Like you, she believes a promise is a promise.' Hattie carefully put the china dog back in the centre of the table. Losing her temper was not going to accomplish anything.

Pure fury leapt from his eyes. 'And I was young, little more than a babe in arms. Do you think she thought about me when she turned her back on me? She never once sent me a letter. Ever.'

Hattie closed her eyes. It broke her heart. She wanted to gather him in her arms and tell him that it was not down to him that his mother had left, but she knew he'd refuse to believe it.

'I know,' she said miserably. 'Mrs Reynaud wrote you letters, but never posted them. She told me.'

'That woman…doesn't deserve to be called a mother.' His voice trembled.

'That woman gave birth to you,' Hattie said gently. She could never excuse what Mrs Reynaud had done, but she had heard Kit's stories about his father. She suspected the truth was complicated and complex and that

Mrs Reynaud knew precisely what she had lost. 'Your mother wanted to see you. She wanted to gaze upon you and see the sort of man you'd become. She was not seeking any sort of grand reunion watched by all and sundry. I thought… It doesn't matter what I thought.'

'You never even considered me or what I might think. You were utterly thoughtless, Harriet Wilkinson. You abused my trust. You want the world to be the way you want it and life isn't like that.'

Hattie put her hands into the small of her back. Her heart ached like the very devil. She refused to cry. She had known what could happen, where this was leading. Somehow a little piece of her had hoped that if he saw his mother, he might have a reason to stay. Instead he would use it as a reason to go. The last thing she wanted was to seem needy. She knew the bargain they had had—a summer romance, that was all.

'Very well then. We have reached that point. Summer is ended. We knew it was coming. I wish you godspeed, Sir Christopher. Forgive me if I don't bother to see you out, but you may go the same way that you came in. I do so hate confrontations.'

She died a little as she said the words.

His jaw dropped. 'No hysterics. No pleas for forgiveness or more time?'

'Should there be? We both knew what this was—a summer affair. Nothing more, nothing less.' Hattie kept her chin up. She refused to give him the satisfaction of collapsing. What did he expect—that she'd grab his ankles and beg or plead for forgiveness? Not her. She'd acted with the purest of motives. He'd warned her what he was capable of and she'd chosen to forget it.

'You are not going to complain about being used?'

'Why should I?' She crossed her arms. 'I was never one of your women, Kit. We both knew what this little piece of play-acting was all about.'

His nostrils flared. 'Play-acting?'

'You can't stand to have a woman leave you. You leave before your emotions are engaged because you are afraid that the woman might bolt like your mother. You set rules that dictate your actions. But you are wrong about me. I would have stayed the course. And you are wrong about your mother.' She fumbled in her reticule and drew out the little jumping-jack. 'Your mother asked me to give this to you. She lacked the courage at that long-ago fair. She has letters that she wants you to read. She is dying. To forgive is divine.'

She waited for Kit to relent and to show her that he was the man she'd fallen for. That the strong principled man was not some illusion her brain had conjured up.

'Will you do it for me? This one last thing?' she whispered. 'Visit your mother? Let her know that you care about her. I know you do.'

The only sound she heard was the tick-tock of the mantelpiece clock, ticking away the precious illusions of her life. She had told herself so many lies—that she was immune from him, that their relationship was purely physical, that she was not going to get hurt. Silently she willed him to take it and prove himself. His fingers stretched out, but then his gaze hardened. His hand fell to his side.

'I'm no longer a child, Mrs Wilkinson. I've grown beyond the need for toys. Thank you all the same. Perhaps one of your nieces will have a use for it.'

He wasn't going to do it. He was going to allow Mrs Reynaud to die without acknowledging her as his mother. A great hole opened within Hattie. She had to make one final attempt to reach the man she knew he could be.

'I did it because I cared about you and what happens in your future,' she whispered. 'Why don't you care enough about me to even try?'

His mouth twisted. 'I'm not the sort of man you should care about. I warned you of that before we began.'

Hattie balled her fists. The scene swam before her eyes and she desperately wished her heart had remembered that. Having him here, breaking all her illusions, was far worse than finding out about what Charles thought of her, but she refused to collapse in a heap. 'You are right. You did. We have nothing more to say to each other.'

'You are asking me to go.' He tilted his head to one side.

Hattie clung on to the remains of her self-control. 'I am demanding. I am sure you know the difference, Sir Christopher. Enjoy your life in London. I intend to enjoy mine here in Northumberland. Summer has ended. Irrevocably and completely.'

'Never let it be said that I don't do as a lady requests.' He gave an elaborate bow, but his expression might as well have been carved from marble. 'Your servant, Mrs Wilkinson.'

Hattie kept her body upright until she heard the front door slam. At the sound she crumpled down on the floor. Moth came over and nuzzled her shoulder. Hattie gathered the little dog to her breast and rocked back and forth.

'What have I done, Moth? Oh, what have I done?'

* * *

'I saw him,' Hattie said, coming to kneel beside Mrs Reynaud's bed early the next morning. She had called, but Mrs Reynaud's maid said that she didn't feel well enough to rise and she had refused to allow the doctor to be called. However, Hattie insisted on seeing Mrs Reynaud and was ushered up.

Mrs Reynaud's blue-veined hand grasped Hattie's as tears glimmered in her eyes. 'You saw him this morning? So early?'

'Last night. He was waiting for me when I returned from the lecture.' Hattie bit her lip, promising herself that she wouldn't burst into tears all over Mrs Reynaud. She had volunteered for this. She could hardly confess that she considered Kit to be a different sort of person. He had turned out to be made from the same cloth as her late husband—charming but unreliable, not someone to count on. 'I fulfilled your request and gave him the jumping-jack. He deserved to know that you regretted abandoning him. He reacted badly. He will be well on his way to London. He wasn't the man I thought him to be.'

'I'm sorry.' Mrs Reynaud gently placed her hand on Hattie's shoulder. 'I had such hopes. I wanted... It doesn't matter now.'

'This has nothing to do with you. I simply had a few misconceptions.' Hattie gave a careful shrug. There was little point in recounting the precise details of what had happened. 'The scales truly fell from my eyes. I realised that I was living a life full of illusions, thinking the best of people. From now on, I shall live a life full of practicality and strict cynicism.'

Mrs Reynaud's hand dropped from her shoulder. All

the vitality fell from her, leaving her an old and help-less woman. 'He isn't coming. Ever. You are trying to tell me gently. I hate gentle, Hattie. I always have.'

'I don't think he will.' Hattie forced the words from her throat.

'What sort of a child can forgive their mother for that? I was wrong to hope for understanding.' Mrs Reynaud's bottom lip quivered. Then she gave herself a shake and continued. 'There were so many things I wanted to tell him. I should have listened to John and stayed away. I ruined everything for you.'

'There was nothing to ruin,' Hattie admitted. 'You must get that idea out of your head. It was a summer flirtation and now summer is over. We both knew the rules.' Hattie forced a smile. 'Perhaps it will make for a cautionary tale to my nieces when I can bear to speak about it.'

'Last night I saw how he looked at you.'

'He has his life in London. He always did. He never made a secret of it, even if for a time I chose to forget it.' Hattie hated how the words stuck in her throat. She wasn't excusing Kit, but she had seen his unguarded expression when he realised who Mrs Reynaud was. Despite everything, her heart still bled for him and what he could be. Underneath his charm, part of him remained that little boy whose mother had rejected him. 'He has no interest in staying.'

'I understand.' Mrs Reynaud sat up straighter and tightened the shawl about her shoulders. 'He made his own fortune, you know. Far more than my unla-mented husband's. He can be very single minded. Over the years, I have followed every single scrap of news.'

'I wanted you to know and I will go now, leave you

to rest.' Hattie gripped her reticule. She wished she could offer Mrs Reynaud more comfort. She wanted to tell her that Kit was better than she thought and that he actually cared and would appear once his temper had cooled. 'It is not good to live a life of illusions. That lesson is now etched on my heart.'

'Mrs Wilkinson may know a lot of things, but she doesn't know everything,' a low voice said behind her. 'She remains far too quick in judging others.'

Hattie jumped. Half-afraid that somehow her fevered mind had conjured the voice, she could do nothing more than breathe. 'Kit.'

He stood in the doorway, wearing the same clothes that he'd worn last night. His eyes were sunken and his chin unshaved. Bits of bracken and twigs clung to his breeches. She had never seen him look that dishevelled or that dangerous before.

Hattie ruthlessly suppressed the leap in her pulse. After what she'd learnt about him, she refused to be attracted to him. She was not going to suffer any more lusting after someone who could never be the person she deserved. From now on, she took charge of her life. 'You should be on your way to London, Sir Christopher. You said you were going.'

'I am no apparition, Mrs Wilkinson. I am here and not on the road to London.'

'How? Why?'

Mrs Reynaud gave a little squeak and the colour drained from her face.

'Your maid let me in, Mother. I didn't mean to startle you.' Kit held out his hands. 'I am here as you requested.'

Tears flowed down Susan's face. 'You called me mother.'

'You did give birth to me.' Kit moved into the room, filling it. 'Until Mrs Wilkinson gave me the jumping-jack, I had no idea you were dying. You should have informed me. You knew where I was.'

'Would you have read the letter?'

Kit shrugged. 'As you didn't write it, it is a moot question. But I like to think I would have without prompting. But why did you involve Mrs Wilkinson in your scheme? That was unforgivable.'

Hattie pressed her fingers together, trying to take it in. Kit remained in Northumberland, rather than departing immediately for London. And he was calling Mrs Reynaud 'Mother' as if he had been saying such a thing every day of his life. She pushed her shoulders back and lifted her chin. 'I volunteered.'

Mrs Reynaud struggled to sit and a series of violent coughs racked her.

'Are you dying?' Kit asked when the coughs subsided. 'Or has Mrs Wilkinson been exaggerating in an attempt to appeal to my better nature?'

'Kit!' Hattie cried. 'One does not ask questions like that! Particularly not to one's mother.'

He raised an eyebrow. His sardonic glance raked her. 'You are going to tell me what to say as well as what to do now?'

The heat rose on Hattie's cheeks. 'I merely meant that you should not be so direct.'

'I appreciate direct,' Mrs Reynaud cackled. 'I'm not dead yet. I hope you appreciate that Mrs Wilkinson is a good person with a sterling reputation.'

'My reputation is my concern,' Hattie said proudly,

keeping her shoulders back. She was never going to ask him for anything.

'Is it really you, Kit?' The tears welled up in Mrs Reynaud's eyes. 'I've wanted to speak to you for so very long. I feared today would never come. Doctor Gormley has given me a little while yet, but my wicked past is catching up with me.'

'I have come, Mother.' He glanced about the small room. His gaze seemed to take in everything. Hattie was conscious of her old blue gown and the fact that the lace needed replacing. 'You should have let me know earlier that you were in trouble.'

'You see now why I did what I did,' Hattie said in an undertone. 'Your mother wanted to see you. It was important.'

He turned to her. His face was an imperious mask. 'I believe I have an adequate understanding of what is important.'

'I will take your word for it.'

'I'd appreciate it if you would allow me some time alone with my mother.' His face softened. 'Please, Hattie.'

Hattie gave a helpless glance at Mrs Reynaud. She hated leaving her alone with Kit, knowing how cold and cutting he could be. Mrs Reynaud nodded. 'I will be fine now, Hattie. You brought my son to me.'

'You don't allow him to bully you, Mrs Reynaud.'

'Such an opinion of me,' Kit said in a low tone.

'You deserve it.' Hattie did not pause as she walked through the door.

Kit sat with his mother quietly without saying anything. He had planned several speeches out on the moor, but no words were adequate to explain the depth of emotions which coursed through his body. This crumpled bit of humanity was his mother, the woman who had given birth to him. He tried to reconcile her with his memory of the beautiful, fascinating creature who had walked away from him all those years ago. But when he looked into her eyes, he knew and he saw something akin to love and regret.

'Don't leave me, Kit,' she murmured. 'Stay. I want you here.'

'I've no intentions of going anywhere,' Kit said, watching tears slide down her crumpled face. 'I am determined to stay. You are my only living relative in the world. I wanted to know you wanted me. You are my mother.'

'Good.' She frowned slightly. 'And your intentions towards Mrs Wilkinson?'

Kit crossed over to the door and shut it firmly. 'That is my business.'

'Do you love her?'

'We are here to speak about you,' Kit said, keeping his voice calm, but making sure that his mother knew that speaking about his relationship with Harriet was forbidden. He refused to discuss his feelings for her with anyone. 'First things first.'

'She is a good woman,' his mother persisted.

'I know that!'

'You hurt her deeply. Behaving in that fashion. Everyone saw you cut her.'

Kit crossed his arms. 'I warned her. Nothing happened that Harriet did not agree to.'

'You'd be a fool to allow her to slip through your fingers. You—'

'Are you going to keep telling me the obvious?' Kit made an annoyed sound in the back of his throat.

Susan Reynaud might be his mother, but it gave her no right to interfere in his life. His feelings for Harriet were private and very new. All he knew was that he'd never felt like this about any woman before. Harriet was more than a mistress, she was his friend. He knew he wanted her in his life.

The worst thing about last night had been the thought that he might never hold Harriet in his arms again. She had told him to go and it was as if his heart had been torn from his chest—a feeling which had only intensified throughout the night and he knew that he had thrown away something very precious.

The first step to winning back Hattie was to make peace with his mother. To see if Hattie was right and his mother did want him in her life. Out on the fell, he discovered that it was something he hardly dared hope for.

His mother gave a little laugh. 'I know that noise. It will work out. All you need to do is to go to her and explain. I believe she loves you despite your dreadful behaviour. You should marry her. I thought she might be right for you and I am never wrong in such matters.'

'And my father—was he right for you?'

'No, we should never have married,' his mother said firmly. 'My parents forced me into the marriage. I tried to run away, but they found me and dragged me to the altar. We fought worse than cats and dogs. You came along when the marriage was dead.' Her eyes filled with tears. 'I regretted many things about that time, but I never regretted having you. I naïvely thought they'd allow me to have you. The court does not look kindly on fallen women. And then later John extracted the promise in exchange for a roof over my head. All I could hope for was that, some day, you'd come and I could tell you of my love and my longing for us to be together. Today is that day.'

'You are a great believer in the power of love.'

'Sometimes, it has been all I have had to believe in.'

'I was waiting for you to come to me,' Kit explained. 'My uncle never left me any word. Until Harriet said your name at the Stagshaw fair, I had no idea what had happened to you. You vanished after my father died and that was all I knew. Then I was afraid that you'd see my father in me and would reject me.'

'Oh, Christopher.' A single tear ran down his mother's cheek.

Kit hung his head. 'I was rude to you last night. It was wrong of me. You gave me life and all I could do was to treat you badly.'

'We both made mistakes. Me more than most.' She raised her hand and stroked his cheek.

'Am I like my father?' The words slipped from his throat.

'In looks, maybe, but in temperament, no. He could never admit that he was wrong.' His mother held up her hand. 'Before you protest that I can't possibly know, John used to read me your letters and I have followed every scrap of news about you and your exploits.'

Kit regarded the woman who gave him life and knew that he wanted her in his life. He wanted her to play a part for the rest of her life. They both had wasted so many years.

'Where are those letters you wrote, Mother? I want to read them.'

* * *

Hattie sat in her drawing room, stroking Moth's head, trying to make sense of this morning. She had paused on the stairs, ready to sweep in if any pieces needed picking up, but all she had heard was the sound of silence and the click of a door.

Her heart squeezed. She should be pleased that he came back for his mother, but it caused problems. The desire she felt for him remained strong, but whatever happened, she was not going to go back to where they were before. That much had ended. She had more respect for herself.

'Sir Christopher Foxton for you, ma'am.' Mrs Hampstead gave a loud sniff.

Hattie stood up, determined to be gracious, rather than resentful. She held out her hand and ignored the way Moth ran immediately to him. 'Sir Christopher. How good of you to call.'

'Shall I stay, ma'am?' Mrs Hampstead asked, giving Kit a fierce glare.

'I believe I can handle Sir Christopher.'

'Very well, ma'am.' Mrs Hampstead picked Moth up and tucked her under her arm.

The silence when she left threatened to suffocate Hattie. She gulped a breath of air.

'Harriet.' Kit came forwards, his arms open wide as if he was going to enfold her in his embrace.

Hattie held up her hand and he stopped immediately. Standing close enough to touch if she reached out her hand. Hattie kept her arm rigidly at her side. 'You wished to see me, Sir Christopher?'

'You are angry with me. You need to know that I did not want it to be this way. I fought against it. This thing, this connection between us, was not supposed to happen. I conduct my affairs by strict rules. Always and without exception. But with you, I find myself breaking them.' He shook his head. 'Before you become angry, think about what this is doing to me. What agony it has been.'

'I have every right to be angry.' She swallowed hard and struggled to maintain control. The last thing she was going to do was to give him the satisfaction of seeing how deeply he affected her. She hated confrontations, but this time she had to do it. 'You were appalling. I never asked you to fight against anything.'

'I listened to you, Hattie.' He gave one of his smiles that had the power to turn her insides to mush. 'You see. I did as you asked. I met my mother. Surely that means something.'

She took a steadying breath. 'I'm supposed to be impressed with this sacrifice of yours?'

He tilted his head. 'You're not?'

'I am busily wondering what sort of game you are playing. You've suffered some minor inconveniences and now expect the world to bow down in gratitude.'

'I'm not playing any game. Your words reached me deep inside.' He thumped his fist against his chest. 'You made me realise the sort of man I wanted to be. Last night, I wandered the fells, unable to rest. I thought a lot about how my life was going and what I wanted from it. I most definitely didn't want my mother to die without me having taken the opportunity to meet her properly. I intend to do that. I am staying.'

'Good.' Hattie crossed her arms. What did he want—a medal for doing the right thing? 'I am sure your mother will be pleased to have you here.'

'Harriet, I'm staying. I want things to continue between us.' He put his hands on her shoulders.

Her heart thudded. He called her Harriet again.

'Are you seriously suggesting that everything is forgotten? That we go back to what we had before?' Hattie crossed her arms. 'Summer is over, Sir Christopher.'

Kit watched her much as a cat watched a mouse. 'And your objection is?'

'What we had was destroyed. I have no wish to go back to that.'

'What do you want from me, Harriet?' His voice was soft and insistent. 'Tell me and it shall be yours. I'll even marry you if it will make you happy.'

Hattie knew if he touched her again, she'd melt. And nothing would be solved. Kit might only want a physical relationship, but she wanted more. She deserved more.

'I don't want anything from you, Sir Christopher.' She hugged her arms about her waist. 'I explained why we must part. My reasoning has not changed. We agreed the rules when our affair began.'

'Rules are made to be broken.'

'Really?' She lifted an eyebrow. 'Rules should be broken only when it suits you. I don't live that way.'

Kit visibly winced.

'I was an ass. It was wrong of me. I know what is important.' He held out his hand. 'I didn't want to feel like this, Hattie. I fought against it, but it happened. I have accepted that now and stopped fighting. I want to do the right thing with your help.'

He didn't want it to happen. He accepted it. Hattie rolled her eyes. She was supposed to think this was an apology? Or, worse still, some sort of lily-livered offer? 'Fight harder and you will get over it. I promise.'

'What if I tell you that I am prepared to stay in Northumberland? For as long as you like?'

'And I am supposed to believe you? Just like that? The great Sir Christopher shows up at my house, gives a highly reluctant marriage proposal and I fall into his arms? Is that the way it works?'

A wicked glint appeared in his eyes. 'It sounds like a good scenario to me.'

'If that is all you wish to discuss, I shall bid you good day. You must leave, Sir Christopher. We have nothing further to say to each other. Ever.'

Chapter Fourteen

'What is going on here?' Kit asked when he arrived back at the Lodge and saw a stand off between Rupert and Johnson. Rupert physically blocked the door to his bedroom while Johnson glowered at him. Kit controlled his temper. The last thing he wanted to do was to have to deal with Rupert and Johnson. All he wanted was his bed and sleep. After he rested, he knew he'd come up with a viable plan to win Harriet.

'A slight misunderstanding, sir,' Johnson said. 'Mr Hook wishes to prevent me packing your things.'

'Returning to London would be a mistake, Kit. I beg you to reconsider.'

'Sir Christopher never reconsiders, Mr Hook. I have explained this to you several times,' Johnson said with a long-suffering sigh. 'I know my gentleman, begging your pardon. You should allow me to do my duty.'

'Unpack the bags, Johnson. I want the rose bedroom made ready as well.' Kit looked hard at his manservant. 'We are staying…for the foreseeable future.'

Both men's jaws dropped open. Johnson recovered himself first.

'Very good, sir. The rose bedroom will be made ready.' Johnson bustled off, shaking his head.

Kit fought hard not to laugh. He had never seen his manservant as flummoxed before. Seeing Johnson shaken out of his usual reserve was the sole moment of merriment he'd been able to derive from the catastrophe.

'We are not going to London?' Rupert squeaked.

'Are you deaf, Rupert? To repeat myself—we are staying.'

'Truly?' Rupert's voice cracked. 'We are staying. Here in Northumberland? I'm about to start believing in miracles.'

Kit raised an eyebrow. Miracles? Right now he needed one, but he would not allow himself to lose hope. He intended to prove to Harriet that he was worthy and worth taking a risk on.

'I simply saw the error of my ways,' Kit said in a tone that allowed for no further questions. 'I regret that I haven't been able to speak to you about the lecture before now. Perhaps going on about the mating habits of the newt while staring directly at Miss Parteger was not the best strategy. There was rather a shocked ripple which ran through the crowd. Next time, think about your audience's sensibilities.'

Rupert had the grace to flush. 'I adore her. The words came tumbling out.' He pressed his hand to his heart. 'Kit, do you think I have a chance? Her parents want a title and I have none.'

Kit pursed his lips. Once he would have told Rupert to forget Miss Parteger and move on, but now knowing Harriet, he knew that moving on was the wrong tack. There were times in a man's life when he had to dig in and fight.

'You are determined on this course?'

Rupert gave a slow nod.

'Titles are not everything, Rupert. It is more important that you two get on. Sometimes you have to hope.'

'Without a title I am nowhere.'

'Your great-uncle might die without an heir. You'd have a title then.'

Rupert looked dubious. 'He has just married a woman young enough to be my sister.'

'It remains a distant possibility, I grant you, but it might get you a hearing.'

'How will I convince her father and, more importantly, her mother of that? Mr Parteger only found the lecture of passing interest.'

'To a truly determined man, you should see this as an opportunity rather than a door closing in your face.' Kit repeated the words he'd told himself over and over on the way back to the Lodge.

'She is an angel, Kit. I swear. Every man jack will be after her when she has her Season.'

'Then you shall go to London when she goes, but for now, you can remain here.' Kit gritted his teeth. London right now held no attraction. He had to hope that Harriet would see sense before he had to take Rupert to London. 'I promise, Rupert.'

Rupert nodded, digesting the news. 'Who is going to use the rose bedroom?'

Kit noticed the distinct change in subject. A small prickle of concern went through him. What precisely was Rupert planning? 'My mother.'

'Your mother?'

'Even I have a mother, Rupert,' Kit said drily. 'She was lost and now she has been found again. I intend for her to live out the remainder of her days in comfort. And I shall be making my home here, for absence of doubt.'

'And Mrs Wilkinson? The way you cut her at the lecture was the talk of the village.'

'I never discuss ladies, Rupert, you know that. Now get on with your studies. You have a reputation to maintain.'

Rupert's face broke into a wide smile. 'You are right.'

Kit turned away. Rupert might have a reputation to maintain, but he had a reputation to change. Right now, he wasn't sure which was the harder task.

Late the next morning, Hattie discovered Stephanie in her drawing room, with a cloth over her eyes as she lay on the *chaise-longue*.

After Kit left, Hattie had been unable to summon the energy to do little more than sob. The sobbing had given way to steely determination late in the night. Going and unburdening herself to Mrs Reynaud was now impossible. She shuddered at the thought of explaining the situation to Kit's mother.

The only real option had been to go to Stephanie and hope she could bury herself again in trivial tasks, anything to keep from thinking and wishing that it could have been different, that Kit had really meant his proposal.

'You are bold coming here, Hattie,' Stephanie pronounced without removing the cloth when Hattie announced her presence. 'After what you did!'

'Is there some problem?'

'Yes, my nerves are torn to shreds.' Stephanie waved a hand. 'Yesterday, dear Mrs Hampstead informed me that Sir Christopher was at your house late on the night of Mr Hook's infamous lecture on the habits of newts. You entertained him. Goodness knows how many other people saw him go in. Your house can be seen from the road. Imagine what would happen if this news gets out! You can't claim that he was being heroic this time.'

'I'd rather not think about it.' A shiver went down Hattie's spine. Of all the times to be seen and remarked on. Right when she was finishing with Kit. She pinched her nose. It was, though, another explanation of why Kit felt the need to offer. 'It wasn't what you think, Stephanie.'

Stephanie tore the cloth from her eyes. 'You promised, Hattie. My sister! Think about what this will do to poor sweet Livvy!'

'You are not waiting to hear my side.'

'I have been comforting Mrs Hampstead, who is in floods of tears. She told me all about how you used to go out riding and return with grass stains. She thought she knew you!'

'Mrs Hampstead should have spoken to me. I would have explained.' Hattie removed her bonnet with a trembling hand. Never had she been so angry with herself. She had been foolish in the extreme to think the affair would remain undiscovered.

'Your *lover* reappeared yesterday morning and you entertained him alone.' Stephanie's lip curled. 'Not content with the other night, was he? He had to make doubly sure that everyone knew what sort of loose woman you are. My sister! You were a widow with a spotless reputation until that man came along. One come-hither glance and you forget your principles. Everything that is important to you.'

Hattie summoned all of her dignity. Stephanie had no right to speak to her like that. Ever. But screaming at her like a fishwife wasn't going to solve anything. 'Sir Christopher made an offer of marriage.'

'And you accepted?' Stephanie clapped her hands and her entire face changed. 'You might have said, Hattie, you sly puss. I have been worrying so. I couldn't eat all yesterday and my head pains me. You were really too bad not to think about my nerves.'

Hattie waited a heartbeat. 'I refused.'

'You...*what*?' Stephanie's shriek could be heard in two counties. 'Are you destined for a room in Bedlam?'

'It was an infamous offer, made in such a way that he knew I had to refuse.' Hattie tapped her foot, feeling her hard-won self-control starting to slip. 'What sort of woman did he think I was?'

'It was an offer, an offer that could have saved your life.'

'I know the difference between a genuine offer and a pastry crust, easily made and easily broken off, Stephanie. Sir Christopher's was one of the latter.' Hattie lifted her chin proudly. 'I told you after Charles died that I had no intention of marrying anyone and I meant it.'

'I declare, Harriet Wilkinson, you carry your devotion to your dead soldier too far. I know Charles was the love of your life, but you are facing ruin. Ruin of the most public kind. You couldn't afford to turn him down. Livvy can't afford to have you turn him down.'

Hattie stared at her sister, torn between laughing and crying. What she felt for Charles was a schoolgirl crush that had long since vanished. The Kit-shaped hole in her heart would take far longer to mend. Until the night of the lecture, she'd really believed in him. But there was little point in explaining this to Stephanie. Stephanie only heard what she wanted to hear.

'He made the offer with the expectation that I'd refuse,' she said carefully. 'He knew my feelings on marrying again.'

'Was your first marriage that idyllic?' Stephanie snapped. 'People get married for reasons of duty and then make the best of it. Will you ever marry again, Hattie? Do you truly require perfection?'

Hattie regarded her hands. The old Hattie would have simply allowed the assumption to stand, but it was time she stopped hiding behind a façade. 'You were always wrong about my marriage to Charles. It was a sham from start to finish and I only found out too late.'

'Sham?' Stephanie looked perplexed. 'You were so in love with him.'

Rapidly and with as few words as possible, Hattie explained about her discovery and what she had done about it. Stephanie listened in absolute silence. Telling her proved far easier than telling Kit.

'And now you see why I can't marry Kit,' Hattie finished.

'Oh, Hattie, you should have said something!' Stephanie held out her hand. 'You are my sister. You should have trusted me enough to explain. I want the best for you.'

'There was nothing you could do.' Hattie gave a

shrug. 'And I thought if I pretended that it had never happened that it would go away.'

Stephanie rolled her eyes. 'Perhaps you were right. If I had known, maybe I would have been more determined that you marry.'

Hattie glanced at Stephanie. A huge weight fell from her shoulders. Stephanie was behaving remarkably well. And she was right. She should have had enough courage to say the words years ago. 'I most definitely wouldn't have wanted more matchmaking. You've done enough as it is.'

Stephanie tapped a finger against her lips. 'Do you love Sir Christopher?'

'Yes...or rather I thought I did. I thought he was a different man.' Hattie pressed her hands together. Her feelings for Kit were all jumbled up. She wanted to hate him, but a tiny piece of her kept trying to convince her that he was the sort of man for her. 'Don't you see, Stephanie? I have done the same thing again—fallen in love with an illusion.'

'Sometimes, Hattie, you have to take a chance. You would have done everyone a favour. Think of the doors which would have opened for Livvy.'

Hattie shook her head. Trust Stephanie to be thinking of herself and her family's advancement. 'I refuse to marry simply to satisfy society, Stephanie.'

Stephanie pressed her lips together. 'This is the first time Sir Christopher has offered marriage?'

'To me? Yes.' Hattie pleated her skirt between her fingers. 'He only did it because of his mother, I am sure. He was adamant two days ago in his opposition to marriage. It is the only reason I can think of. Imagine being married because his mother forced the issue.'

'His mother?' Stephanie made a face. 'Surely Sir Christopher is old enough to decide what to do without his mother's input. Who is she that she commands such respect? If Sir Christopher is half the man he seems to be, he will have made the offer because he is worried about your reputation. This is typical of your excuses, Hattie. You see problems where there are none. You must trust me on this. I am your older sister.'

'Mrs Reynaud is his mother. They are no longer estranged.' Hattie clasped her hands together to stop them from trembling. Stephanie had to understand why she had refused the proposal. She was not some desperate young miss grateful for the smallest crumb to fall from his table. 'You should have heard the proposal—all about how he didn't want this and how he was breaking all his rules. It was ungracious. He expected me to refuse. It certainly deserved a refusal.'

Stephanie sat in silence. 'And where is Sir Christopher now?' she asked finally. 'I would like to speak to him.'

'Do not interfere, Stephanie. Allow me to run my life for once. I am a grown up and fully capable of doing so.'

Stephanie opened and closed her mouth several times. 'If that is what you desire, Hattie. I wash my hands of you. I will not interfere again, even if you go on bended knee to me.'

'I suppose Mr Hook will go to London,' Hattie said, trying to change the subject. 'Now that he has given his lecture, do you think he is suitable?'

'Livvy needs a successful Season before she thinks about marriage.' Stephanie shook her head. 'I fear Mr Hook is not for her. Did you hear what he said in his lecture? Poor Mr Parteger was beside himself with rage.'

'I thought it was laughter,' Hattie said, remembering the snort. 'Livvy will have to choose her husband carefully.'

'No, Livvy will marry who I tell her to. Honestly, I don't know what possesses that child these days. She keeps going outside to think. Portia says that she goes to the cedar of Lebanon and sits.'

'Do you want me to have a word with her…now that you are satisfied that I remain respectable in society's eyes?' Hattie asked. 'Put it in terms she might understand? Remember how you chafed when our parents forbade you meeting Mr Parteger?'

'I suppose a refused marriage offer is better than nothing.' Stephanie gave a loud sniff. 'As long as I have your word that nothing untoward like this will ever happen again, you may speak to Livvy and see if you can reason some sense into her.'

'I am through with romance and all other affairs.'

'Good to hear.' Stephanie fluffed out her skirts. 'Then we can discuss more interesting matters such as what will Livvy wear for her Season which now won't be ruined.'

Hattie's head throbbed so much by the time she left Stephanie's that she decided to walk straight home, rather than seeking out Livvy.

Later after the baby was born, Hattie decided that she would go abroad. Livvy could go with her. Between the excitement of a Season and going abroad, Mr Hook's charms didn't stand a chance. Hattie tucked her head down and started to increase her pace. She had a trip to plan.

'You need to watch where you are going, Harriet. You nearly walked straight past me without saying hello. Hopefully we are not that far out of civility.'

Hattie stumbled. Strong hands caught her. Instantly a pulse of heat coursed through her. Kit here and dressed in his day clothes with tan breeches and high-topped boots.

Her body wanted to melt against him. She kept herself perfectly rigid.

She stepped away from temptation. Kit might not have left, but things were finished between them. It bothered her that her headache melted away under the heat of his gaze.

'I thought you'd be well on your way to London,' she said around the sudden tightness in her throat.

'I told you that I was staying here, so why is it that you are so insistent on sending me to London?' Kit's mouth quirked upwards. 'One would almost consider that you wanted to be rid of me.'

Hattie clasped her hands together as the warmth of his voice flowed over her. This time, she'd be strong. She'd resist the lure of his voice.

'We have nothing more to say to each other.'

He inclined his head. 'And here I thought you were more neighbourly than that. We are close neighbours after all.'

Hattie regarded him suspiciously. Neighbourly? Was he really staying? 'You were serious before and intend on living in Northumberland? What about your urgent business in London?'

He snapped his fingers, dismissing the notion. 'My

mother is unable to travel. She enjoys the neighbour-hood. Then there is the Lodge, which needs fixing. Pressing matters. The business can wait.'

'Then I shall have to get used to seeing you at various functions.' She tilted her head upwards so that her bonnet shielded her eyes.

'I've no plans to be a hermit.'

'The entertainment around here is a bit more tame than you are used to.'

'I have found it adequate thus far.' He touched his hand to his hat. 'I trust it will continue.'

'Why are you out this way? And on foot?'

His body stilled. 'Rupert is about to meet Livvy in the woods. I came across a note from her this morning.'

Hattie's mouth dropped opened. She should have expected it. Livvy was headstrong, but she also was young. 'How long has this been going on?'

Kit carefully shrugged. His fingers itched to straighten Hattie's bonnet. He hadn't anticipated coming on her like this. Alone. He wanted to pull her into his arms and kiss her soundly, but he'd made a mess of things yesterday. Today was about proving that he was worthy. Discovering the note had been an answer to his prayers. It was his one chance to show to her that he cared about her and her family.

'I was occupied with other things and failed to pay attention. They have been communicating by leaving notes for each other in the circulating library,' he said and watched her cheeks colour. 'These clandestine liaisons need to stop.'

'As I have discovered, clandestine does little good to anyone.'

'Has something happened?' Kit asked, every nerve

on alert. She had to want him, rather than being forced into the marriage. He knew that now.

'Mrs Hampstead complained to Stephanie, but I explained your proposal and my reasons for refusal.' Her lips turned up in a mocking smile. 'All is well.'

Kit frowned. All was not well. Hattie was being utterly stubborn. She refused to hear what he had tried to say. He simply had to figure out another way. And the first piece was discovering what Rupert and Livvy were up to.

'In the note I saw, Livvy asked Rupert to meet her in the usual place. Do you have any idea where the usual place will be?'

Hattie frowned. 'What are you going to do?'

'Find out what is going on. The last thing I want to do is to panic them into taking drastic action.'

Harriet paled and he saw that she understood precisely what might be at stake. 'My sister and brother-in-law wish Livvy to marry a title. Mr Hook seems like a perfectly acceptable man, but Stephanie is immovable on this.'

'So Rupert informed me.' Kit stroked his chin. 'He might inherit a title if his great-uncle dies without an heir, but he has just married a young woman. He feels it wrong to make mention of something that might not happen.'

Harriet nodded. 'I understand the difficulty, but it might do for my brother-in-law. What is your solution?'

'A long engagement and Livvy doing a Season before the marriage,' Kit said, watching her like a hawk. He had to hope that she understood why he wanted to do this.

Harriet clapped her hands. 'Pure genius. It might work. I'm impressed.'

'I can be impressive, given the opportunity,' Kit said, making his voice become silk. 'The alternative is a quick elopement. Rupert appears very determined. You know what young lovers can be like when they feel thwarted.'

'Stephanie would never recover from the shame,' Harriet retorted decisively.

'Now are you going to tell me where they might meet?'

'By the cedar of Lebanon. It is where Livvy goes to think. Stephanie complained about it when I spoke to her today.'

'Now we know where they go.' He shook his head. 'I never thought Rupert had it in him.'

'It sounds like Livvy. She loves intrigue.' Her mouth twitched. 'You have to admit that it was a pretty good scheme. I suspect even Portia didn't guess. She can never keep a secret.'

'Is there a vantage point where we can see the tree?'

'Yes, up by the folly.' Harriet pointed towards a gentle hill. 'It is a bit far away.'

'I brought a spyglass.'

Her mouth dropped open. 'You are well prepared.'

'We observe and take action as necessary,' Kit explained. 'I've no wish to interrupt an innocent flirtation.'

'You seem to know all the tricks.'

'How do you think I learnt to avoid them?'

She laughed. The sound rushed through him and the tight place in his heart eased a little. The crisis had passed and he started to hope that he could triumph.

'I'm coming with you. If there is any confrontation to be done, I want to be there.'

'I shall be glad of the assistance.'

Hattie walked alongside Kit. Her entire being hummed with nerves. She couldn't tell if it was because she was apprehensive about discovering what Livvy was up to or because Kit was striding alongside her. She did trust Kit to put things right.

When he reached the crest of the hill, he withdrew his spyglass.

'Are they there?'

'Yes, holding hands and looking soulful.'

Her shoulders relaxed. She had feared the worst.

'Then something can be done. I blame myself for this. I had all the clues and did nothing about it. Livvy's sudden liking for the circulating library and your stories about the mountains of books that Mr Hook got out. I just don't understand why Portia kept silent.'

'What about her parents? What will they think?'

'But I'm her aunt.' Hattie hugged her waist. Panic started to claw at her stomach. A thousand what-ifs ran through her brain. 'How am I going to solve this?'

'Big gulp of air, Harriet. In and out.' Kit's calm voice penetrated through the fog.

'I am breathing.'

'Good, now trust me. You are not alone. Your niece won't be ruined. I promise you.'

Trust him? She had little choice.

'Stephanie will have a fit.'

'Better a fit now than a catastrophe later.' He jerked his head. 'Run and get her. I want her to see this while it remains innocent.'

Hattie nodded. 'You had better be right, Kit, or I will never forgive you.'

'I had better be right or I will never forgive myself.'

'What is wrong, Hattie?' Stephanie looked up from her sewing. 'I suppose you have come to apologise for your behaviour. Very well, I will listen.'

Hattie grasped the door frame and swallowed her quick retort. 'Apologies will have to wait. Come now, Stephanie. There is something you need to see. Livvy's happiness depends on it.'

Stephanie put down her embroidery. 'You are being awfully mysterious.'

'It has to do with Livvy and your forbidding of Mr Hook's courtship.'

Stephanie went white. 'She hasn't run away, has she? Mrs Smith's eldest did that. The shame of it. Mrs Smith had to hide her face for weeks.'

'Livvy remains at Highfield, but I hate to think what could happen. You need to come now. Simply sitting there and expecting other people to act for you won't wash this time, Stephanie.'

Stephanie opened and closed her mouth several times. 'Who alerted you to this?'

Hattie rubbed a hand across her face. 'Sir Christopher. He discovered Livvy's communication to Mr Hook. Hurry.'

'If what you say is true, then we shall be in his debt.' Stephanie grabbed her bonnet.

Kit breathed a sigh of relief when Harriet arrived back at the hill with Mrs Parteger in tow.

'They remain there.'

He silently handed the spyglass to Harriet, who took a look and passed it to her sister.

'Is all as it was?' Harriet asked. 'Hand-holding and gazing into each other's eyes?'

Kit pursed his lips. There was no need to describe the passionate embrace he'd witnessed. 'They are young and in love. And you know what can happen when love is thwarted. It is obvious that they are a resourceful pair. No one guessed until today about their little romance.'

Mrs Parteger gave a slight gasp and leant on Hattie's arm. Harriet put an arm about her. Kit suddenly understood why she had been reluctant to leave Northumberland. She had shouldered a vast amount of responsibility.

'Kit has a plan, Sister.'

Mrs Parteger wiped her eyes. 'I should like to hear it. I never considered my baby girl capable...capable of such things.'

Kit exchanged a glance with Harriet. Her eyes danced.

'A long engagement, but Miss Parteger should have her Season. I would suggest Mrs Wilkinson would be the best person to accompany her.'

'I couldn't possibly...' Mrs Parteger began.

Harriet cleared her throat and nodded towards where the couple stood.

'What I mean to say is that it is an excellent suggestion. I can't speak for my sister, but I would be honoured if she chose to serve as Livvy's chaperon.'

He watched Harriet's eyes widen. 'Of course I'd be delighted to go if the occasion arises.'

'Shall we break this embrace up?' Kit asked, giving a loud shout.

He started down the hill. Harriet's hand touched his sleeve. Kit fought against the urge to cover it with his hand.

'Do not think this means I have forgiven you, but thank you,' she said in an undertone. 'You appear to have saved the day.'

'Only appear? I have saved the day and allowed two people to have a chance to get to know each other before they are leg-shackled.'

'And, yes, I did want to go to London with Livvy before you ask.' Her eyes twinkled with mischief. 'I hope you are not going to be insufferably smug about the whole thing.'

'You are speaking to me and that is a start,' Kit answered. He inclined his head. His fight back had started. This time he intended to leave nothing to luck. He was going to do everything in his power to show Harriet that she should take a chance on him. 'Do remember to save me a dance at the Summerfields' ball. It is all the thanks I require.'

Chapter Fifteen

~⌘~

The ball to mark the end of summer hummed with activity when Hattie arrived at Summerfield three days later. She hated the bitter-sweetness of attending a ball here again. It shouldn't matter that the last time she had been here, she had met Kit, but somehow it did. That evening had changed her life in more ways than she had considered possible.

Now she was committed to dancing with him again. Over the past few days as the excitement of Livvy's engagement swirled around her, she had tried to think up an excuse, but none had come.

After he had engineered the engagement between Mr Hook and Livvy, her sister felt that Kit could do no wrong. And she kept going on about how Hattie had made a mistake in refusing him. Even now as they waited, Stephanie made several remarks about how useful Kit was. It was as if she had suddenly been re-infected with her matchmaking fever.

Hattie closed her ears.

A tingling went down her back. She glanced over her shoulder. A tall figure alighted from a carriage and then turned to help a woman down.

Kit.

As if she had spoken his name, he turned towards where she was standing, waiting to greet the hosts. A tiny smile briefly crossed his features. He nodded towards where she stood, waiting with Livvy, and then whispered something in his mother's ear.

Once she would have blushed. Now she forced herself to coolly nod, only to be greeted by an enthusiastic wave and a gesture to come over from Mrs Reynaud. To Hattie's astonishment, Mrs Reynaud was not veiled, but dressed in a   sumptuous gown with a necklace of diamonds sparking at her throat.

Briefly she contemplated pretending she had not seen the wave, but she knew that would go against the fibre of her being. She did want to see her.

'I will be back.' Hattie pressed Stephanie's hand. 'This queue is taking ages. Mrs Reynaud is here. I hadn't realised that she had recovered from her chill.'

Stephanie's gaze narrowed, taking in Hattie's reaction to the latest arrivals. 'You haven't been paying attention, Hattie. I called on Mrs Reynaud with Livvy two days ago when you were indisposed. Where is your head these days?'

'I'm going to greet my friend,' Hattie declared. 'Please don't read anything more into it.'

'As if you would allow me to!'

Hattie pulled back her shoulders, suddenly glad that she had given in to temptation and had worn a new garnet-red ball gown with cream-coloured lace around the neckline. She loved the way the skirt moved about her ankles and how the garnet-studded hairnet completed the look. She was not some widow content to stay on the shelf, but a woman determined to make the most of life. She might have agreed to dance with Kit, but it didn't mean he had to be the only man she danced with.

'You look lovely, my dear,' Mrs Reynaud said with a huge smile when she reached the pair. Close up, the family resemblance was so marked that Hattie wondered how she had missed it earlier. Whatever happened, the reconciliation had done wonders for Mrs Reynaud. 'Doesn't she look lovely, Christopher?'

Hattie forced herself not to move a muscle as Kit's gaze roamed over her.

'Mrs Wilkinson looks as she always does,' Kit said, inclining his head.

Hattie dropped the barest of curtsies. As far as compliments, she could have hardly thought of one which tasted more of ash. She searched his eyes for warmth, but found his expression guarded. 'I thank you for the compliment.'

'It was sincerely given.'

'I'm pleased you brought your mother here.'

'It took some doing. Up to the last moment she kept me guessing. Apparently she has not attended such events in years. I convinced her that no one would shun her because of past notoriety.'

Hattie lowered her voice. 'Mrs Reynaud has always been sensitive about her face, but the happiness now shines from her.'

'There is more to beauty than a face. I notice other things.'

'I agree.' Hattie shifted in her slippers, aware that the receiving line was finally moving. 'I should rejoin my party.'

'You promised me a dance.' He cleared his throat.

'As payment for arranging Rupert and Miss Parteger's engagement.'

'A promise is a promise.' Hattie knew her voice sounded too bright. 'A quadrille. It is the last ball of the summer after all. There is no harm in it.'

'I was hoping for a waltz, but a quadrille will have to do.'

Hattie's heart missed a beat as the image of them waltzing filled her brain. Her hand curled around her fan. She was not over him and was likely never to be over him. The knowledge thrummed through her. 'That would not be wise.'

'Sometimes it pays to be foolish.' He caught her hand and lifted it to his lips.

Hattie's mouth went dry. 'But not tonight.'

She hurried off before he could answer.

Kit forced himself to dance with his mother, Livvy Parteger and her mother before he approached the orchestra with his request. Every fibre of his being was aware precisely where Hattie was, but the thing had to be carefully down. He was not about to risk losing her again.

When the music stopped, he walked over to her and bowed, stepping in front of Dr Hornby. 'Our dance, I believe.'

At his look, Dr Hornby withdrew, muttering about his need to speak to someone. Kit waited.

'The master of ceremonies hasn't announced it. Shouldn't we wait and find out what the figure is?'

'Why don't we take a chance? Unless you are afraid?'

She tilted her chin upwards. 'I believe I am more than equal of dancing any dance with you.'

The master of ceremonies called out a Harlequin. Kit relaxed. There were a few opportunities about her waist. She would agree to listen by the end. She had to.

'Your sister approves of the choice of dance,' Kit remarked. 'See how she smiles?'

Harriet glanced over her shoulder and her body completely stiffened. 'I can't do this. Not with everyone watching me like I'm some backward child. I'm sorry, Kit. I just can't.'

She pulled away from him and raced from the ballroom.

Kit cursed and swiftly followed her. This time, she would hear him out.

Hattie didn't stop until she reached the small card room. With a distinct sense of irony, she went in and pulled the door shut. She thought she could dance with him until she saw Mrs Reynaud's and Stephanie's faces. It was as if everyone in the ballroom was watching her and Kit with a matchmaking gleam in their eye. The last thing she wanted was for Kit to feel forced to make another proposal.

'Harriet? Open the door.' Kit's voice allowed for no refusal. 'You can't hide for ever. Do you open it or do I knock it down?'

She went over and opened the door. Kit stood completely alone in the corridor. His hair was wild and his neckcloth askew. He had never looked handsomer. She took a step backwards.

'You promised a dance and left before it began.' He

gave a crooked smile. 'Are you ill? I can't know what is wrong if you refuse to tell me.'

'I'm sorry. In the circumstances…I thought it best. I saw Stephanie and your mother.' Hattie hated how ineffectual and weak it sounded. She curled her hand about her fan and straightened her shoulders. 'The music hadn't started. I felt faint.'

'It is a bad habit of yours, leaving before a promised dance has ended.' He gave a heart-stopping smile. 'We shall have to work on it. At our wedding breakfast, you will dance a full waltz with me.'

Wedding breakfast? Hattie gulped. A great black hole opened before her. She was not going back there. This time would be far worse.

'Kit…what happened back there. You don't have to feel that… I don't want you to think…'

'Hush. Listen to me. I tried being patient with you, but it hasn't worked.' He started to pull her into his arms, but she backed up against the card table. He let his hand drop to his side and came into the tiny room. 'Things need to be said between us.'

'What things?' She looked suspiciously up at him. 'We said everything we needed to that day. I refused your offer. You don't really want to marry me. You don't want to marry at all.'

'I was wrong about many things, Harriet.'

'But…' Her voice trailed away at his intense look.

'Have you examined this ring?' he asked, holding out a small gold ring with an inlaid garnet. 'Can you at least do that before you dismiss me out of hand?'

'Please…' Hattie knew her heart was breaking and she wasn't sure how long her composure would remain. She could not take another half-hearted proposal. 'Please, Kit, don't make this harder for the both of us. You made your feelings or lack of them quite clear when you asked me before. Nothing has changed.'

He ran a hand through his hair. 'I've gone about this all wrong. I did mean to finish the dance before I gave you the ring.'

She shrugged, but inside she died a little. She owed him an explanation of why they could never marry, even if she was utterly cast out from society and could no longer visit her family. 'I refuse to marry because society dictates, Kit. I won't have a loveless marriage. I made the mistake of enduring one once and I have no intention of ever entering such a thing again. What happened was not your fault. I take full responsibility for my folly. You are absolved of all blame. I've no idea what Stephanie has been saying, but you must ignore her.'

'I love you, Harriet.'

'What?' Her heart did odd little flips. She had to have heard wrong. This was Sir Christopher Foxton who was destined never to love.

'I love you with all my heart and soul.' He went down on one knee. 'Will you please make me the happiest man on earth and marry me? Please, Harriet, say yes. Say you find a small corner of your heart for me. Marry me and let me prove to you that my love is enough for the both of us. You won't have a loveless marriage with me, I promise.'

'You love me?' she asked, to control the hammering of her heart. She had never expected Kit to say those words. In her wildest imaginings she thought perhaps he might care for her, but declare his love in this fashion!

'With all my heart.' He took her hand. 'I did it all wrong when I made my first proposal. I should have started with the obvious facts.'

'What are the obvious facts?' Hattie braced herself for another onslaught of how he didn't want to love her and was fighting against it.

'I love you and I have no desire to live anywhere in the world without you. You make me glad that I am alive. You make me want to greet the world with a smile, instead of hiding away from it. It is why I want to marry you, so I can know that we will be together for the rest of our lives. And I want everyone else in the world to know that I have made that commitment to you.'

'And I am supposed to believe you were going say that?' Hattie hated the way she could not allow herself to believe, but a large part of her was afraid to believe. She had to know that this wasn't some great sacrifice on his part which he'd regret, not tomorrow or the next day but some day in the not-too-distant future.

'Look at the ring. I had it engraved. After what we have been through, I didn't want to take any chances of you failing to believe my sincerity. I intend to devote my life to you. It is why I arranged Rupert and Miss Parteger's engagement. I wanted to show you that I am capable and reliable.'

He placed the ring in the palm of her hand. She regarded the engraving on the inside. *H., the keeper of my heart, K.*

'You do love me,' she whispered finally.

'And you? You told me that you cared for me that night after the lecture, but when I proposed you refused. Tell me what I can do to make you care for me again.' He touched her cheek with gentle fingers. 'Have I truly destroyed all feelings you might have had for me? Tell me it isn't too late. I want to be the man you deserve to love. What are you afraid of? Tell me so I know how to reassure you.'

The naked longing in Kit's voice resounded throughout the small room. He stood there, not moving towards her, but she could sense how much he wanted to gather her in his arms.

She knew then that he'd stayed in Northumberland not for his mother, but to show her that he could try to be the man she deserved. It was the little things that counted—the way he'd shown responsibility over his mother, how he was restoring the Lodge and how he'd engineered a solution for Mr Hook and Livvy that allowed them the chance to grow up before making that ultimate commitment. And she loved him all the more for it. She had been utterly blind and she had nearly thrown away the single most-important person in her life.

'The trouble with truly loving someone is that even when your head tells you to stop, your heart keeps right on loving.' Hattie gave a smile and knew the time was right. She no longer had to hide her feelings or wish them away. The time had come to say them out loud. 'Yes, I love you, Kit, and suspect I always will.'

His smile could have lit a thousand lanterns.

'You won my heart a long time ago,' Hattie continued. 'I think it began when you fished my gloves out of the reticule, but I didn't really know how much I cared for you until that day when Strawberry and I jumped the stone wall. You taught me to face my fears. But there was one big hurdle I couldn't face—declar-

ing my love. You were right when you said that I had
to face my fear.'

'You were tardy in your love, but I shan't hold that
against you. You truly won my heart when you insisted
on giving me that blasted jumping-jack at the fair. You
knew what I wanted—no, what I needed. You made
me into a better man, even if I kicked and screamed a
bit, determined to prove you wrong.'

'You were always that man, Kit,' Hattie said gently.
'You had to believe in yourself.'

'A lesson you taught me. You showed me what loving and forgiveness was truly about.' He put his arms
about her and rested his forehead against hers. 'You
are willing to share the rest of your life with me, then?'

She threw her arms about his neck. 'Yes, oh, yes.
I will marry you.'

Kit whispered after they had soundly kissed, 'Shall
we tempt fate, Mrs Wilkinson, and return to the dance
floor? I've no wish to cause a scandal.'

Hattie laughed up at him. 'I will gladly dance with
you.'

When they arrived back at the ballroom, the dance
had finished. Hattie noticed that Kit gave a distinct
nod to the master of ceremonies. As he led her out
onto the floor, the man announced the next dance—
a German waltz.

Her eyes flew to his. 'You are incredibly lucky.'

'I took precautions, yes.' Kit rested his hand against
her waist. 'I wanted to hold you in my arms. I had anticipated moving straight on to the second dance after
the quadrille, but I prefer how things worked out.'

'You bribed the orchestra?'

'It will be worth every penny if you stay with me. Will you dance?'

She gave a decisive nod of her head. 'Yes, I'm feeling brave. I can risk being in your arms.'

The music swelled up around them and he began to move. Absolutely correctly and with great precision. Not even a Lady Patroness from Almack's or the most severe duenna could fault him. They slowly circled the room.

'As you can see, I am being utterly trustworthy,' he remarked.

'It makes a change.'

'Hopefully a welcome one.'

She moved closer. 'I am not sure what to make of it.'

'You don't have to make anything of it. Just dance. Let yourself be in the moment.'

'Are you attempting to teach me something?'

'I finished with lessons a long time ago.' Kit concentrated on moving his feet. With each passing step, the urge to crush her to him grew. 'I simply wanted to hold you in my arms.'

She started to pull away, but he tightened his grip, making their bodies collide.

With a whoosh, she fell against him. His body reacted instantly. He checked his movement and allowed her to find her feet.

'I had no plans to go.' Her voice was breathless.

'It is good to know. Shall we continue?' He started to move again. This time he held her closer, enjoying the way her skirts brushed against his legs as they moved around the ballroom. Looking down at her, he tried to make a memory. This was how, when they were old, he wanted to remember her—cheeks flushed, lips full and eyes sparkling, the most beautiful woman in his world.

'Kit,' she breathed, her lips parted slightly.

Giving in to impulse, he raised their hands to his mouth and touched her palm with his lips. A soft sigh emerged from her throat. She lifted her mouth and he bent his head. The briefest of touches.

The shocked exclamation poured ice water over Hattie, bringing her back from the enchanted bubble she had somehow existed in. The reality of where she was and what she had just done closed in around her, locking her in a prison.

'Everyone is looking at us,' Kit said in a low undertone.

'What are we going to do?'

Hattie froze. She had done the unthinkable. She had shown Kit affection in public, not just affection, but a full-blown meeting of the lips!

The growing chorus of shocked gasps resounded around the ballroom, drowning out the orchestra. All Hattie wanted to do was run and hide. Kissing on the dance floor when one was twenty-seven had to rank up there as one of the more foolish things she had done in her life.

'Leave this to me,' Kit rasped in her ear. 'Take off your glove.'

Hattie fumbled with the fingers. Her ring felt heavy and awkward on her hand. All the while she was conscious that everyone was watching. Even the orchestra had stopped playing. She knew that people could not see her ring. 'What do we do now?'

Kit went down on his knee, in front of everyone.

'Will you marry me, Mrs Wilkinson?' he asked in a loud voice.

Hattie nodded and answered so that everyone could hear as relief washed over her. 'Yes, of course. With all my heart.'

'Mrs Wilkinson has just done me the honour of agreeing to become my wife,' Kit announced. He held up her hand, with the ring clearly visible. 'I hope you will understand and forgive the indiscretion. In my joy I was unable to stop my baser instincts.'

A growing round of applause swelled around them. Hattie looked down at him, her heart filled to bursting. With Kit, she had found her match and she knew their life together would be filled with happiness.

* * * * *

An Ideal Husband?

For Katharine who asked, begged and otherwise pleaded.
Being an author's daughter can have its advantages...
even if you still die of embarrassment when I go
looking for my books in a bookshop.

Chapter One

Why was it that some men only understood the application of a frying pan to the head? And why was it that one often met such men at balls when all one could carry in one's reticule was a hair pin?

Sophie Ravel glared at Sir Vincent Putney and took a step backwards, narrowly avoiding his outstretched hand. Perhaps this contrived confrontation of Sir Vincent Putney in a deserted conservatory was not one of her better ideas, but Sophie knew it was the only way to help one of her oldest friends avoid a fate worse than death. Tonight was the final opportunity to carry out her scheme and prevent Cynthia from being sacrificed on the altar of her parents' ambition.

'Not one step further, Sir Vincent.' Sophie raised her reticule, ready to swat his hand away.

'I have no desire to see you fall, Miss Ravel.' The oily voice grated over her nerves. 'I know how precious you are to my dear Miss Johnson. She sang your praises for weeks before we journeyed to Newcastle. Will Miss

Johnson be joining us in the conservatory? Is that what she meant by a surprise?'

Sophie's eyes flew to the door. She'd been meticulous in her planning. Every eventuality covered, every solitary one except the one actually unfolding.

She should know the answer to the question, but her mind was a blank. She hated lying; avoiding the full truth was a necessity in certain circumstances.

'Miss Johnson has another matter to attend to before she can come to any conservatory.' Sophie straightened the skirt of her ball gown so that the cascades of blonde lace fell neatly once again. The tiny gesture restored her confidence. Precise planning would once again triumph and produce the perfect outcome. 'I'm sure she will appear when circumstances permit it.'

'Said with such a disdainful look.' Sir Vincent hooked his thumbs into his waistcoat. 'Despite your airs and graces, Miss Ravel, you have nothing to be proud about. I know all about your parentage and how your father acquired his considerable fortune.'

Sophie fought against the inclination to laugh. The man's accent was so entirely ridiculous, proclaiming about her parentage as if she was some brood mare.

She backed up so that her bottom touched one of the shelves. A particularly large fern nodded over her left shoulder.

'I suspect you have heard lies and half-truths.' She feinted to the left, only to be stopped when he placed his paw on the railing. 'Now, will you listen to what I have to say? Or are we going to have to play "Here we go round the mulberry bush" all night?'

He waggled his eyebrows, but did not remove his hand.

In the distance she could hear the faint strains of the orchestra as they struck up a polka. All she had to do was to calmly return to the ballroom after delivering her message. As long as she refused to panic, she was the mistress of the situation. Icy calm and a well-tilted chin. Poise.

'I regret to inform you, Sir Vincent, that Miss Johnson has other plans for this evening.' She ducked under his arm and wished she had chosen somewhere else besides the deserted conservatory to impart the news. Good ideas had a way of turning bad if not properly thought through. She should know that by now. 'Indeed, she has other plans for the rest of her life.'

'Other plans?' Sir Vincent cocked his head and Sophie could almost see the slow clogs of his brain moving. 'Miss Johnson arrived with her parents and me only a short while ago in my carriage. I know what her plans are. Her father has accepted my suit. They are watching her to ensure her reputation remains unsoiled. We are to be married come a week Saturday.'

'Her note. Miss Johnson asked me to give it to you once we were in the conservatory.'

He shook his ponderous head. 'Mr Johnson and I have come to an arrangement. He knows what is good for him. His wealth will go a long way towards restoring my family home. He saw sense in the match in the end.'

Sophie's stomach revolted. What she had considered Cynthia's fevered imaginings were utterly correct. Sir Vincent had used blackmail and threats to achieve his ends.

Since Cynthia's father had agreed to the marriage, Sir Vincent or her parents had hung about Cynthia like limpets. It was only at this ball that Cynthia stood any chance of escape. Sophie had brought the valise in her carriage. Hopefully Cynthia and her true love were now using the carriage to go straight to the railway station. The last train for Carlisle left in a half-hour. Then, at Carlisle, they would change trains and go to Liverpool, catching a boat to America leaving on tomorrow afternoon's tide. She'd left nothing to chance.

'Read the note, Sir Vincent, before you say anything we both might regret.'

He froze and his pig-like eyes narrowed, before snatching the note from her fingers. His lips formed the words as he read the note. The colour drained from his face.

'You're serious. Miss Johnson has jilted me.'

'She intends to marry someone else, someone far more congenial.'

He screwed up the note. 'We shall see about that! Her father has agreed to the match. He wants my name and status.'

Sophie rolled her eyes. What did he expect after the way he had behaved, cavorting with all manner of loose women, being insufferably rude to Cynthia and, worst of all, boasting about it to members of his club? 'I believe it is Miss Johnson's wishes that are paramount here. It is her life, rather than her father's or her mother's.'

She only hoped some day she'd meet a man who would make her want to forget her life and responsibility, but who would also be her friend. Why wasn't she deserving of a Great Romance? All of her friends had and all she'd discovered was alternative uses for hatpins and frying pans!

'You gambled and you have lost, Sir Vincent. Here is where I say goodbye.'

'We shall see about that!' He threw the crumpled note down on the ground.

'You are too late. Miss Johnson has eloped.'

'Scotland, it will be Scotland. Her father should never have come to Newcastle.'

'You will look like a fool if you go after her. Do you wish to be taken for a fool, Sir Vincent?'

Sir Vincent froze.

Sophie breathed easier. Nothing would happen to her now, but she could buy Cynthia a few more precious minutes.

'I'm no fool, Miss Ravel.'

'I'm glad to hear it.' Sophie cleared her throat. 'A notice will appear in *The Times* and a number of local papers in the morning, stating that your engagement is off. You will have to find another bride, Sir Vincent.' Sophie started towards the door. 'It is time I returned to the dance. I have a full dance card this evening.'

'This is all your fault!' He stepped in front of her, blocking her path. 'You will have to pay, Miss Ravel. You have done me out of a fortune. Nobody does that to me!'

'My fault? I'm merely the messenger.' An uneasy feeling crept down Sophie's spine. He still stood between her and the door to the ballroom. She needed to get away from this situation as quickly as possible before something untoward happened. Carefully she measured the distance to the outside door of the conservatory with her eyes. It was possible, but only as a last resort. She'd much prefer to walk back into the ballroom rather than going through the French doors. 'And having delivered my message, I shall get back to the ball. I doubt we need ever acknowledge each other again.'

'You are in it up to your pretty neck.' Sir Vincent turned a bright puce colour and shook his fist in her face. 'You will be sorry you ever crossed me, Miss Ravel. I will not rest until I've ruined your life.'

Sophie tapped her foot. 'Cease to threaten me this instant. You have no hold over me. Let me pass.'

His hand shot out, capturing her arm. 'I am not through with you.'

'Unhand me, sir. You overstep the mark!' Sophie struggled against his hold.

'Can you afford a scandal, Miss Ravel, despite your wealth? You may wear your ice-cold hauteur like armour, but do you truly think that will save you?' His vice-like hand tightened on her upper arm.

'I am well aware of what society requires. My reputation is spotless. You cannot touch me.' Sophie twisted her wrist first one way and then the next. She had been naïve in the extreme when she had consented to elope with Sebastian Cawburn several years ago. Luckily, her guardian Robert Montemorcy and the woman who became his wife had intervened and had the matter successfully suppressed. Every night she said an extra prayer of thanks that Henrietta Montemorcy had entered her life.

'Yet you allowed yourself to be alone with a man in a conservatory. Tsk, tsk, Miss Ravel.'

Thinking about Henri redoubled Sophie's determination. She brought her arm sharply downwards, broke free and pulled the French doors to the garden open. 'This is where we part.'

As she stepped down, she heard the distinct sound of ripping lace. One more reason to loathe Sir Vincent— she had really loved her new gown, particularly the blonde lace. She didn't stop to examine the extent of the tear, but picked up her skirts and scurried out into the garden. The cool evening air enveloped her and she moved away from the light and into the velvet darkness.

Sophie pressed her hands to her eyes and tried to think. What next? She'd circle around the house and go back into the house through the terrace. Easy enough. With a bit of luck, no one would notice. She could make her way to the ladies' withdrawing room, do the necessary repairs and then plead a headache and have a carriage called. Thankfully, her stepmother had been unwell tonight and so it would be all the explanation required.

Her foot squelched in a muddy pool and cold seeped through into her foot. Another pair of dancing slippers ruined and these ones were her favourite blue-satin ones.

Behind her, she heard footsteps. Sir Vincent called her name. He was closer to the house than she. He was going to head her off before the ballroom, Sophie realised, and a cold fist closed around her insides.

She could imagine the scandal if she suddenly appeared dishevelled and escorted by Sir Vincent. She knew precisely what happened in these sorts of situations and Sir Vincent was not in any mood to be a gentleman. The whispers would reverberate through Newcastle society before morning—*the proud Miss Ravel has slipped.*

It wouldn't stop there—the rumours would spread throughout society within a fortnight. She faced the very real prospect of ruin. Despite her earlier brave words, could she be sure of her stepmother's support? Being part of society meant everything to her stepmother. Unfortunately the Montemorcys were out of the country. She was truly on her own...this time.

She turned sharply and headed out into the dark of the garden. Two could play a waiting game.

'You can be a fool, Sophia Ravel,' she muttered to herself, stepping into another puddle. Her intricate hairstyle of small looped braids combined with curls tumbled down about her shoulders. 'Would Cynthia have done this for you? Or would she have found an excuse at the last moment? How could you have forgotten the pencil incident at school!'

Sophie gritted her teeth. It was too late to worry about what-might-have-been.

Behind her, she heard the sound of Sir Vincent's heavy breathing. 'I will find you. I know you are in the garden. I do so like games of hide and go seek, Miss Ravel.'

In the gloom of a May evening in Newcastle, she could see his black outline. She was going to lose, and lose badly.

She pivoted and ran blindly back towards the house and bumped straight into a well-muscled chest.

'Where are you going?' a deep rich baritone said as strong arms put her away from the unyielding chest.

'Are you running away from the ball? Has midnight struck already?'

Sophie's heart skipped a beat. All might not be lost. Silently she offered up a prayer that this man would be a friend rather than a foe.

'Please,' she whispered. 'You must help me. For the love of God, you must save me or else I shall be ruined.'

Richard Crawford, Viscount Bingfield, regarded the dishevelled blonde woman in his arms. The last thing he wanted or needed was to save some Cinderella-in-distress. But what choice did he have? He could hardly turn his back on her, not after he'd heard her ragged plea.

'If it is in my power, I will help.'

Her trembling stopped. 'Do you mean that?'

'I do. Are you some escaping Cinderella, fearful of missing her fairy godmother's deadline?'

'Hardly that.' Her hand tried to pin one of her braids up, but only succeeded in loosening more of the blonde curls. 'I'm not running away from the ball. I am running towards it.'

'Towards the ball? That dress?' Even in the gloom, Richard could see the rips and tears. A twig stuck to the top frill of her blouse. He pointed and hoped she was aware of the scandal which she was about to be engulfed in.

'I loved this dress.' Her hand brushed away the twig. 'Really loved and adored it. It is irreparable.'

Her lavender scent rose around him. All his instincts told him to crush her to him and hold her until her shaking stopped, but that would be less than wise. The last thing he needed was to be engulfed in a scandal and for his father to realise he was in Newcastle rather than in

London. His father, the Marquess of Hallington, was in ill health. In fact, he had only now begun to recover from the last fit at the end of April. With each passing week, his father seemed to slip more and more into a jealous rage against his mother and the scandal in which she had engulfed the family, even though those events had occurred many years ago.

Richard knew he shouldn't have come to Newcastle, but equally he knew he had to vet the man who had captured his half-sister's affections. His mother was untrustworthy on this matter and he had also taken the opportunity to once again sort out his mother's finances.

He forced his arms to let the young woman go and put her from him. 'Tell me quietly and quickly what you need and I will see what I can do about it.'

'I need to go back to the ball.'

'Looking like that? Brushing away one twig won't mend the ripped lace. You must know what will happen to you. Shall I call a carriage?'

Her hand instinctively tried to smooth her rumpled ball dress. 'Very well, then. I need to get back into the house and go to the ladies' withdrawing room where I can repair the damage. I do have my leaving arrangements in order.'

'It should be simple a matter to walk straight back.'

'Not so simple.' She lowered her voice. 'Someone is after me. He is determined to ruin me.'

Richard regarded the woman. The back of his neck pricked. He should walk away now. 'It is hard to ruin someone who does not wish to be ruined. Practically impossible.'

She gave a half-shrug. 'I was foolish and failed to

consider the possibility. I fear we have not been introduced, but you must accept my assurance that I am normally considered to be extremely reliable and sensible in such matters.'

'Viscount Bingfield.' He inclined his head. 'And I am most definitely received everywhere.'

'I will take your word for it.' Her voice dripped with ice cold.

'Miss Ravel. Miss Ravel. Where are you? I will find you. You can't hide for ever. And then you will see what happens to women who try to cross me!'

Richard's jaw clenched. There was no mistaking the grating voice of Putney! The man was a bounder and a cad of the first order. He'd detested the man ever since that first term at Eton where Putney had put his hand up the maid's skirt and lied about it, causing the poor girl to be dismissed. Richard had sneaked out to see if she was all right and then the newspaper stories started. Then there was Oxford and the tragedy of Mary. Again he could not prove Putney had a hand in it, but he had encountered Putney in the street the day before he'd been called in front of the Master. Even now he could remember the furtive smile Putney gave.

'Are you trying to hide from Sir Vincent Putney, Miss Ravel?'

She gave a quick nod of her head. 'I wish to return to the ball and avoid a scandal. I've done nothing wrong. That is all, Lord Bingfield. Once back under the chandeliers, all this will cease to be anything but a bad dream.'

'In that state? Scandal will reverberate throughout the land. Your name will be on everyone's lips as they attempt to work out how this happened and believe the worst.'

She glanced down and fluffed out her skirt. 'A few repairs need to be made. I slipped in the dark. Twice. I barely know the man. I was helping a friend out and matters failed to go as planned.'

'Indeed.'

'I was helping a friend elope.' She clasped her hands together. 'My friend was engaged to Sir Vincent, but desired to end the relationship against her father's wishes. She loved an American. I merely facilitated the elopement. It went like clockwork except…' She grabbed his arm. 'Quick, Sir Vincent is coming. I need to get away from him.'

Richard reacted instinctively. He swung her back into the shadows, up against the hedge and stood between Miss Ravel and the light.

'Follow my lead and keep silent,' he murmured against her lavender-scented hair. 'We don't have time.'

'Your lead?' she asked, attempting to peer around him. Her skirts brushed his leg. 'Should I trust you?'

'Do you have a choice?' He took a glimpse down at Miss Ravel, seeing her clearly for the first time.

Her lips hovered tantalisingly few inches beneath his. Her worried eyes looked up into his, trusting him to get this right and protect her. Truly Cinderella after the ball, missing a slipper and in need of a prince.

Richard resisted the urge to crush her to him. Another time and another place he would have given in to temptation, but this closeness was far from a prelude to seduction, it was instead a means to prevent Miss Ravel's ruin.

'With any luck Putney will walk on without even noticing anything beyond a man and a woman in the shadows. He will expect to find you alone. Foolproof.'

Footsteps resounded behind them. Every nerve went on alert. Silently he prayed this action would be enough.

Miss Ravel stiffened and shrank back further against the hedge. The heavy footsteps went on past. The nervous energy drained out of Richard's shoulders. They had done it! Miss Ravel would be safe. All that was needed was for him to step back.

His feet refused to move. Instead he lifted his hand and traced the outline of her jaw. Her skin quivered underneath the tips of his fingers and her lips parted, inviting him.

'Dear Richard, imagine! You should be in the ballroom, rather than in the garden,' a heart-sinkingly familiar woman's voice said. 'I shall have to tell your father that we met. He was asking after you at lunch last week. I had understood you were in London. Does he know you journeyed to Newcastle?'

Richard knew that things had suddenly become much worse. The most fearsome of his aunts had arrived.

He gave Miss Ravel an apologetic look and swung around.

'Aunt Parthenope, what an unexpected pleasure.' Richard made a slight bow. 'I would have called on you earlier today if I'd known you, too, were in Newcastle. I would have thought you'd be in London for the start of the Season.'

'The Season does not properly begin until after Queen Charlotte's ball. Plenty of time remains to sort out the hanger-ons and no hopers from the cream of this year's débutantes.' His aunt gave a loud sniff. 'You should have known that I always come to Newcastle at this time of year. I have done for years—to visit your grandmother's grave on the anniversary of her death. In any case, the train makes travel so convenient these days. It takes less than a day. Imagine—when I was a girl, it took more than a week by post carriage.'

'We truly do live in an age of miracles, Aunt,' Richard murmured, wondering if his mother was aware of his aunt's habit and why she hadn't warned him of the possibility.

'Why are you out in the garden, Richard?'

'Crowded ballrooms can cause claustrophobia. I wanted a breath of fresh air.' He moved towards his aunt and started to lead her away from where Miss Ravel stood, hidden in the shadows, touching his fingers to his lips before he turned away. Immediately Miss Ravel shrank back against the hedge.

'You know how it is, Aunt,' he said in an expansive tone. 'One minute, one is waltzing and the next, one needs to be away from the crowd. You have often remarked on how crowded these balls are, not like the days when you were a young girl.'

Sophie hardly dared to breathe. She could see what Lord Bingfield was about to do—lead his aunt and her party away and leave her to make her own way back to the house. It was far too late for regrets. She had to hope that Lord Bingfield's scheme would work.

'And this is why you were out in the garden, Nephew? A sudden and inexplicable need for fresh air? Do not seek to flannel me. Your father did explain about his ultimatum to you at luncheon. While I might not agree with it on principle, I should remind you, he is a man of his word.'

Sophie pursed her lips and wondered what ultimatum Lord Bingfield's father had issued. One of two things—women or gambling debts. Possibly both. Why would the man she begged for help have to turn out to be a dishonourable rake, rather than the honourable person she'd hoped? Her luck was truly out tonight.

'My father has no bearing on this matter, Aunt.' Lord Bingfield waved an impatient hand. 'I know what he said and he must do as he sees fit. I make my own way in the world.'

'You were always a reckless youth, Richard.'

'We should return to the ballroom, Aunt,' Lord Bingfield said, starting forwards and grasping his aunt's elbow so that she was turned away from Sophie. 'I find I am quite refreshed after a short turn. You must tell me all the news. How does my father fare? Does his latest pig show promise?'

Sophie flattened her back against the hedge. The prickles dug into her bodice. Silently she bid them to go.

'And your charming companion? Or do you wish to continue blathering fustian nonsense, thinking I would overlook her?' Lord Bingfield's aunt gave her nephew a rap on the sleeve with her fan. 'You do not fool me one little bit, Richard. I know how this game is played.'

'Charming companion?'

'You do know her name, I hope, Nephew. You were standing far too close to her to be complete strangers. However, with you, nothing surprises me.'

Sophie's heart sank as Lord Bingfield's aunt confirmed her growing fear. Lord Bingfield was not *safe in carriages* or indeed anywhere.

'Aunt, you wrong me dreadfully,' Lord Bingfield protested. 'Name one instance where I have behaved dishonourably.'

'I do declare it's Miss Ravel.' Sir Vincent loomed out of the darkness. In the gloom, Sophie could make out his smug grin. Her misery was complete. He intended to cause mischief, serious mischief, and she had inadvertently given him the opportunity, wrapped and tied up with a bow like a parcel. 'I am surprised that a woman such as yourself is out here in the night air, Miss Ravel, with a man such as the notorious Lord Bingfield. What will your guardian say?'

'My stepmother is aware of where I am and who I am with.' Sophie kept her chin up. It was the truth. Her stepmother knew Sophie was at the ball, not her precise location and she had approved of the company. Her stepmother trusted her. She refused to allow Sir Vincent to imply that something untoward had happened. But it was poor luck that Lord Bingfield seemed to have a less-than-illustrious reputation himself.

'You're Miss Ravel? Sophie Ravel? The heiress who came out over four years ago?' Lord Bingfield's aunt squawked. 'It would appear, Richard, that you have taken your father's words to heart after all. Impressive.'

'Everything, I assure you, is quite appropriate, Aunt,' Lord Bingfield said. 'It would be wrong of me to allow a lady such as Miss Ravel to wander about the garden on her own. Who knows the sort of ruffian she might encounter?'

He gave Sir Vincent a hard look. Sophie's heart did a

little flip. Unsuitable or not, Lord Bingfield shared her opinion of Sir Vincent. He was the only person standing between her and utter ruin.

'It was your chivalry coming to the fore, Nephew,' Lord Bingfield's aunt pronounced. 'All is now clear. I had feared you had decided to take after *your* mother's side of the family.'

A muscle jumped in Lord Bingfield's cheek and his hand clenched in a fist.

'I believe Miss Ravel wishes to return to the ball, now that this little misunderstanding has been cleared up,' he said in glacial tones.

'Has it?' Sir Vincent asked in a weasel-like tone. 'You were in a close embrace! Did you see it, Lady Parthenope? It was quite clear from where I stood. And I know what a stickler you are for propriety and how everyone at Almack's looks to your judgement.'

'You were standing rather close to my nephew, Miss Ravel,' Lord Bingfield's aunt pronounced. 'Young ladies need to be wary of their reputations at all times.'

'Your attire is a little more dishevelled than a simple turn about the garden would suggest. How did you manage to tear your dress?' Sir Vincent continued with a smirk.

Sophie winced. Lord Bingfield's aunt would be someone of importance. Seeds of doubt and suspicions, that was what Sir Vincent intended. Little by little until she had no reputation left.

Her stomach churned. There was no way she could explain the current state of her attire away. She gave Lord Bingfield a pleading look as she searched her brain for a good excuse.

'I do take offence at having Miss Ravel's attire discussed in such intimate terms, Putney,' Lord Bingfield said, stepping between her and Sir Vincent. His stance looked more like a pugilist preparing to enter the ring than a man at a ball.

Sophie released a breath. Despite her earlier fear, Lord Bingfield had kept his promise. He was protecting her.

'Why?' Sir Vincent stuck out his chest. 'I merely state what everyone will be thinking when they spot Miss Ravel.'

Lord Bingfield cleared his throat. 'Miss Ravel is doing me the honour of considering my proposal and, until she has time, discretion is the best option. You did not see anything untoward and I would refrain from mentioning something you might live to regret.'

Chapter Two

Lord Bingfield's words circled through her brain. A proposal! What sort of proposal did Lord Bingfield have in mind? Sophie's reticule slipped from her grasp and she made a last-second lunge to rescue it before it tumbled to the ground. At the same instant, Lord Bingfield reached down and caught it. Their fingers touched and a faint tremor went through her. He gave a slight nod and she remembered his earlier words—*whatever happens, follow my lead.*

She stood up and clutched the reticule to her chest. She had little choice. It was either go along with Lord Bingfield's scheme or face certain ruin at Sir Vincent's hands. She had to go against her hard-learnt habit and trust an acknowledged rake. All she had to do was ensure she refrained from making any rash promises to him. Easy if she maintained her poise and dignity.

'A proposal? Do tell, Nephew.' His formidable aunt rapped her fan against her hand. 'I am all ears.'

'It was the sort of proposal that I have longed to hear ever since I first encountered your nephew,' Sophie said in a loud voice. 'You do not know how happy it made me to hear his words. Perhaps it was a little rushed, but the location was so romantic. My heart simply soared.'

She glanced over at Lord Bingfield and saw that his eyes were dancing. They were as one on this plan. Her heart thudded.

'Are you going to give him your answer?'

'I think such a proposal merits careful consideration. Often a young woman has been led into folly by making too hasty a judgement one way or the other,' Sophie retorted. A sense of thrilling excitement swept through her. For the first time in a long time, she felt as though she was living rather than merely existing, trying to be good and attempting to maintain a poised cold dignity in all her dealings with men. The realisation shocked her.

'I am grateful that you are giving my proposal any consideration in light of my past,' Lord Bingfield said.

Sophie tilted her chin upwards. 'I have learnt that one's past is never a guarantee of one's future.'

'You appear to be a highly sensible young lady, Miss Ravel, despite being out in the garden alone with my nephew,' Lady Parthenope pronounced. 'A word to the wise—even if you are overcome with heat, it is always best to keep your chaperon in sight. To do otherwise is to invoke comment. However, on this happy occasion I must forgive the tiniest lapse of judgement.'

Relief swept through Sophie. Lady Parthenope was practically purring her approval. Her reputation might survive.

'I know your nephew has honourable intentions, your ladyship,' Sophie said firmly, fixing Lord Bingfield with her eye.

'I was unaware you were acquainted with my nephew. That is all, Miss Ravel. I must do more to further our acquaintance,' Lady Parthenope said.

'Come, come, Aunt.' Lord Bingfield put his hand on his aunt's sleeve. 'Do I need to send you a note every time I meet a suitable unmarried lady? Every time I wish to make a proposal of a sensitive nature to said lady? If that is to be the way of the world, I want no part of it.'

'It would be helpful, Richard.' The elderly woman gave a sniff. 'Your father was very tedious at our luncheon.'

'Nor was I aware that you shared a close friendship with Lord Bingfield, Miss Ravel,' Sir Vincent said. 'The things one learns at balls. It puts our earlier conversation in a very different light. I do hope you remember every word of our previous encounter.'

A faint prickle of alarm ran down Sophie's back, but she forced her lungs to fill with air. Sir Vincent's threat was hollow. She was safe. Lady Parthenope had pronounced judgement. Despite the slight hiccup of Lord Bingfield being notorious, he had behaved impeccably.

'Where did you think I was going to, Sir Vincent, after I delivered Miss Johnson's note? I do hate being late.' She made a curtsy which bordered on the discourteous. 'I did say that I had a prior engagement. I failed to mention Lord Bingfield before because, quite frankly, it is none of your business.'

Sir Vincent's mouth opened and closed several times.

Lady Parthenope suddenly developed a cough and Sophie struggled not to laugh after she caught Lord Bingfield's eye. Her heart suddenly seemed much lighter. Tonight's events were not going to be a catastrophe after all.

After tonight, she would not push her luck. She had to remember that adventures only became exciting in memory. During an adventure, one was often out of sorts and uncomfortable. Adventure should happen to other people, not to her if she wished to keep her reputation. Ice-cold calm and dignity while she waited to meet the man whom she could love. Friends first, but only after he'd proved himself worthy—it was the only way to have a great and lasting romance. She had seen the formula work with Robert and Henrietta and now Cynthia.

'Sir Vincent may escort me in,' Lady Parthenope said after she recovered from her coughing fit. 'His mother and I were at school together. And, dear Miss Ravel, you may take your time as long as you come to the right decision quickly. It is blindingly obvious to me that nothing untoward happened here. You must not presume the worst, Sir Vincent. There again, your mother possessed that unfortunate habit. It obviously runs in the family.'

Lady Parthenope swept towards the house with a bleating Sir Vincent on her arm and the rest of her party trailing in her wake. Sophie waited until the noise had abated, feeling the cool night air on her face. She had survived.

Lord Bingfield held out his arm. 'Shall we go, Miss Ravel? I take it you have had time to consider my proposal. My nerves shall be a-quiver until I hear your answer.'

'I doubt your nerves ever quiver, Lord Bingfield.'

'You wrong me.' He put his hand to his forehead. 'I may be the type to weep at dead daffodils.'

'Are you?'

He stood up straighter. 'Thankfully, no. I can't remember the last time I wept at anything. Shall we go in before we invoke more comment?'

Sophie placed her hand on his arm. Her body became instantly aware of him and his nearness. His proximity to her was doing strange things to her insides and her sensibilities. Had she learnt nothing in the past four years? Rakes oozed charm and women forgot propriety when they were near them. The best defence was to be calmly aloof.

A tiny prickle coursed down her spine. Even when she had considered an elopement in her youth, she had not felt as though she wanted Sebastian Cawburn to kiss her, not in the desperate deep-down way that she wanted Lord Bingfield to kiss her when they had stood so close earlier.

'Thank you for rescuing me,' she said, trying for the poised voice she'd perfected after the Sebastian débâcle. Failed miserably as it came out too breathless for her liking. 'Your idea of an unnamed proposal was particularly inspired. I hope… It doesn't matter what I thought. It is finished now and my reputation is safe. From what Sir Vincent said earlier, I believe Cynthia will be safely married soon to the man she has chosen. It is important to choose a congenial life's partner rather than have one chosen for you.'

'I agree entirely,' he said, helping her around a muddy puddle. 'A close call, but I feel it was easily accomplished in the end. There should be no repercussions. Who would dare gainsay Lady Parthenope's pronouncement of innocence?'

'Will your aunt be cross when she discovers we have no intention of marrying each other?' Sophie asked in an undertone. Her body was immediately aware of the way his gloved hand curled about hers. He frowned and let go of her hand.

'She will get over it. Being a disappointment to my aunt appeals. Someone has to be and my cousins have thus far all proved to be sterling examples of moral rectitude and sobriety.'

Sophie forced a smile, but her heart gave a little pang. Lord Bingfield was by far the most interesting man she had met in years and the most unsuitable. A poised demeanour had to be her armour. Never again would she return to that frightened girl, cowering behind a door. 'You were truly a shining knight.'

'I've no love for Putney and a soft spot for beautiful ladies in distress. It was no trouble. Think no more about it.'

They reached the doorway to the house and in the sudden light, she saw Lord Bingfield clearly for the first time. His dark-brown hair curled slightly at his temples, framing his burnished gold eyes. His mouth was a bit large, but hinted at passion. It was the sort of face to make a woman go weak at the knees and forget her solemn vows.

Sophie fought against an inclination to prolong the encounter. There was no future for her and Lord Bingfield. She had given up on notorious men years ago. The adventure had finished and she and her reputation were safe.

She stopped beside the ladies' withdrawing room. 'The adventure has ended.'

'Should you ever require a knight again, fair lady, let me know.' He raised her hand to his lips.

The light touch sent a throb of warmth coursing through her. It would be easy to believe in romance, rather than chemistry. Against her better judgement, she wanted to believe he could be a shining knight and protect her from harm, rather than destroy her utterly.

'You see, I did accept your proposal of protection from Sir Vincent. It was a truly honourable proposal.'

'My pleasure and you understood the proposal.' He gave a half-smile and inclined his head. 'You do know I have no intention of marrying despite what my aunt might believe or my father might dictate.'

'And you do know I have no intention of behaving badly,' Sophie said, clutching her reticule close to her chest. Her earlier instincts had been correct. Lord Bingfield was the sort of man who was *not safe in carriages*. He had saved her reputation, but she knew how that particular game was played. Some day she hoped she'd meet someone who would make her heart soar and fulfilled all the criteria she had agreed with Henri on that fateful day. A friend before a lover. Someone of honour and whom she could love with the right pedigree for her stepmother. Other people had found love—why shouldn't she?

A small dimple showed in the corner of his mouth. 'Have I asked you to?'

'No, but I suspect you entertain hopes. It falls to me to quash them.' She pinned him with her best I-am-a-formidable-person look. 'It is always best to be perfectly clear about such things.'

He threw back his head and laughed a deep rich laugh, utterly real and inviting rather than the arched one he'd used as he confronted Sir Vincent earlier. It warmed her all the way to her toes. Sophie started, surprised that the sound could affect her in that way. 'The day I lose hope is the day I die.'

She concentrated on the flickering light of the chandelier in the entrance hallway, rather than the dimple in the corner of his mouth. She had to keep her wits about her and not indulge in some flight of romantic fantasy. He had given her an explicit warning about his intention to avoid marriage.

Naïve women chose to ignore such words of warning, believing that they were special or unique. It was what a rake traded on. Soon without meaning to, the woman had crossed all manner of bridges and boundaries. That was when a rake struck, showing his true colours. Sophie had learnt this lesson the hard way. A rake meant what he said all the times, and most definitely when it was said in a light-hearted or jesting fashion. And when things didn't go as they wished...

'We are at an impasse,' she said, inclining her head. 'For my determination is every bit as strong as your hope.'

'Shall we risk a polka? Surely you can spare a dance for me?' He held out his hands and his smile became even more beguiling. 'I did save your reputation and I never ask a second time.'

Sophie swiftly shook her head, banishing the image of them swirling to the music together. It would be very easy to give in to the temptation and dance in his arms. And from there? Each little step would lead her further down a path she'd sworn never to go on again.

'Here we part. I shall bid you goodbye. We part as friends.' She held out her hand and allowed a frosty smile past her lips.

He ignored her hand. 'Until we meet again, Miss Ravel.'

He paused and his gaze travelled slowly down her, making Sophie aware of the way her hair tumbled about her shoulders and her torn dress. Perhaps not quite the ice-maiden look she had hoped to achieve. He gave a long slow smile. 'As we are no longer strangers.'

'How could you do it, Richard? You are insupportable. I declare you get that from your father!'

Richard shaded his eyes with his hand. His head throbbed slightly and he reluctantly bid the dream of Sophie Ravel, naked in his arms, goodbye.

After he'd left last night's ball, he'd spent time at the Northern Counties Club, playing cards and trying not to think about Miss Ravel and ways to meet her rather than returning to the house he rented for his mother and half-sister.

As his aunt had pointed out yesterday and the gossip in club confirmed, Sophie Ravel was a highly eligible heiress, rather than a young widow in need of money or the neglected wife of an aged and jaded aristocrat in search of an afternoon's amusement. But he also knew the gossip was wrong on one important point. Miss Ravel had the reputation of a fearsome ice maiden— beautiful to look at, but brimming with virtue and utterly lacking in passion. The woman he'd nearly kissed last night had simmered with passion under her frosty exterior.

Only if he wanted to stick his head in the parson's noose should he be having anything to do with her. Several of his dalliances had reached the scandal sheets in recent years—more for the women's indiscretions after they parted than his actions, but it was enough to make him wary. He refused to be the instrument of any woman's ruin.

The certain knowledge of his past notoriety had caused him to drink more than was good for him last night. How his father would laugh. He'd always predicted that his son would one day regret being in the gossip columnists' sights and the day of reckoning had arrived.

He winced. He might not have deserved the scandal sheet's attention when he was at Eton, but he'd certainly deserved it a few years ago when he'd attempted to forget his part in Mary's fall from grace, her forced marriage to a man she loathed and her untimely death. Then, after that, he'd run through a number of bored wives and widows, ending each affair on his terms and walking away without a backward glance. And he did make it a point of honour never to ask a woman twice for something.

It was only a chance encounter with his half-sister eighteen months ago which had led him from the path of self-destruction.

'Richard, are you going to speak to me? I know you are awake.' A tall woman stood silhouetted in the doorway. His man lurked behind her.

Richard shook his head. Myers had always been a soft touch where women were concerned. He focused on his mother instead of his valet. The sooner this contretemps in a teacup was sorted, the sooner he would get back to his dream.

'Mother, what are you doing waking me up so early?' Richard sat up and stretched. He glanced at the small ormolu clock on the bedside table. 'I thought you would find this time of day exceedingly early for civilised people.'

He waited for her to make her excuses and withdraw.

'I left you to sleep for as long as I dared,' his mother said, straightening her cap. 'Luckily your sister remains in ignorance of last night's events. I only pray we can keep it that way. Her head cold last night turned out to be a blessing in disguise after all. I dread to think what would have happened if Hannah had been at the ball.'

Richard's heart sank. His mother had obviously heard the wrong sort of gossip. Silently he bid goodbye to a morning's rest. He would have to sort out whichever mess.

'What promise have I broken?' Richard retained a leash on his temper. His mother enjoyed her dramatics. 'At least do me the courtesy of hearing the full accusation.'

'You obviously haven't seen the morning papers. It is in all of the local ones. It is sure to be in the London ones by nightfall. Your father will know you are here! He is far from stupid and he will know your reason for coming to Newcastle.'

'I'm a grown man, Mother. My father doesn't dictate or control my movements. There are numerous reasons why I might have travelled to Newcastle, none of which involved yourself or Hannah.'

'He will ruin any chance of Hannah's happiness out of sheer spite. You know what he is like when he is in one of his rages. How could you involve yourself in scandal at this juncture?'

Richard pressed his palms against his eyes. He did know what his father was capable of and how, each time, the fits of anger appeared to last longer. Most of all he feared the gentle father he loved would remain a raging mad man, incapable of coherent thought. The doctors told him that there was nothing they could do except lock him up, and Richard was not prepared for that to happen.

'Mother, as I went to bed in the not-so-early hours of the morning, I have not seen the papers. Whatever you are seeking to blame me for, I am innocent.' He held out his hand. 'Pinch me. See, I am here in my bed, alone.'

'At least tell me that the woman in question is an heiress, this redoubtable woman of yours. Your father might understand your need to chase her up here if she was eligible. Your being single must be a worry. I know how relieved he was when I produced you as the heir. All your father has ever cared about was having the line continue and those blasted pigs of his.'

He pressed his lips together, considering the first part of his mother's statement. He could explain away Newcastle on chasing an heiress. His father would accept that, rather than going into some apoplectic rage over the fact that his son had regular contact with the one woman he hated more than life itself. His father's mental state and health were far too fragile to risk that. He loved both parents and refused to bow to his father's insistence that he choose a side. Once his father's health improved, he would explain properly. For now, a small amount of subterfuge had to be used. Two parts of his life kept separate.

'What do the papers have to do with it?' he asked.

'Myers, the *Newcastle Courant* for your master, if you please.'

Richard nodded to his valet, who gave a bow.

His manservant brought the *Newcastle Courant* as well as one of the more popular scandal sheets, freshly ironed. He turned to the gossip page of the scandal sheet and pointed. Richard gave him a curious look.

'It has the best wording, my lord. The *Courant* used a bit more veiled language. I thought it best to take the precaution of examining all the papers. I like to be prepared for all mention of my gentlemen.'

Richard scanned the paper and winced. *Has the scandal-prone Lord B—been captured at last by the redoubtable Miss R—? Turtledoves were cooing last night. A wedding is devotedly hoped for but, given Lord B—'s form, not expected.*

Scandal-prone indeed! The last crim. con. trial had not been his fault at all. His name should never have been mentioned. The Duke of Blanchland admitted that later. He'd been the innocent party, attempting to assist a woman, driven to distraction by her errant husband. The Duchess had never been his mistress. He had already bedded her sister. He had his code.

He folded the offending paper in half and glared at his mother.

'Preposterous nonsense, Mother. You shouldn't believe things that you read in the papers. Surely you learnt that long ago!'

His mother slapped her gloves together. 'I won't have it, Richard. Not when Hannah is about to be married. They will drag up the whole contretemps between your father and myself…and the issue of Hannah's parentage. And if your father comes up here, there is no telling what he'd do. He swore revenge. I won't have my innocent child suffer!'

'And this has nothing to do with Hannah. In any case, your late husband adopted his daughter. It was all sorted in the end. My father did behave well on that.'

'He never paid back my dowry and he ensured I had to lead a life of economies.'

'It was your father who negotiated the settlement. The money was spent in part on refurbishments that you ordered.'

'Do you know this redoubtable Miss R?' His mother slapped her hand down on the paper. 'For the life of me I can't think of any acquaintances with the last name of R who would warrant the sobriquet of "redoubtable". There is Petronella Roberts, but she has spots, and Sarah Richards fills out her ball dress in all the wrong places.'

'Sophie Ravel—yes, I know her. I would have used the word ravishing rather than redoubtable.' Richard put his hands behind his head and conjured up Miss Ravel's delicate features. Her generous mouth had held the promise of passion, if a man could find a way to unlock it. 'Even Aunt Parthenope declared there was nothing scandalous in our behaviour.'

His mother went white. 'Parthenope was there?'

'My aunt attended the ball last night. Apparently my grandmother is buried in Jesmond. She visits the grave every year.' He glared at his mother. 'You never said.'

'She is sure to write to your father, giving a report. Even if he misses the papers, he will know you have been in Newcastle. Parthenope is like that—full of spite disguised as doing good. When she is at her most charming, she is also at her most deadly.'

'You overreact, Mother.'

'Richard, this is important. It is your sister's future. Hannah has an excellent chance to have a glittering marriage. Could you use this Miss Ravel as an excuse to stay, rather than dashing off to London this afternoon?'

Richard tapped his finger against the scandal sheet, the beginnings of an idea forming. Pursuing Miss Ravel without interference from either parent and seeing if there was passion underneath the ice she presented to the world was tempting, but...

Richard folded the paper in half again. 'What puzzles me is how quickly the papers have acquired the story.'

'Someone is always willing to sell a good story.' His mother gave an exaggerated sigh. 'Poor girl. It is the women I feel sorry for. The men can survive, but a woman, well, she always has the whiff of a scandal hanging about her skirts.'

'I will sort it out before it becomes an inferno, Mother.'

'I trust you to do the right thing, Richard.'

'I am surprised you even need to say that, Mother. I know my duty. The necessity of doing it has been beaten into me since childhood.'

* * *

'Did you have a pleasant time at the ball, Sophie? You said very little about it last night. You were back far earlier than I expected.'

Sophie's hand froze in the act of buttering her toast. It made no sense for her stepmother to be asking further questions about last night. She'd given an account when she came, an account in which Lord Bingfield did not feature as there was no point in alarming her. Her stepmother seemed well satisfied then, but now she regarded Sophie with razor-sharp eyes. Her stepmother waved a newspaper in Sophie's direction. 'I do read the papers. Every item.'

'The papers? Why should they say anything about me?' Sophie asked, genuinely perplexed. Lady Parthenope had declared that the little incident was entirely innocent. She'd left it to Lord Bingfield to explain to his aunt that they would…alas…not be marrying.

'It is what I want to know.' Tears shimmered in her stepmother's eyes. 'I trusted you, Sophie, last evening and allowed you to go to the ball without a chaperon. When you were younger, you used to be involved in harum-scarum affairs and I despaired. After Corbridge, you changed. Perhaps you became a bit too stand-off-ish, but I retained hopes of you fulfilling your father's dying wish and marrying into society.'

Sophie attempted to ignore the nasty prickle at the back of her neck. 'Do what? What have I done? I behaved perfectly properly all evening. You knew about Cynthia's elopement and approved.' Sophie carefully kept her mind away from how she'd nearly kissed Lord Bingfield in the dark. Wanting to kiss him and actually kissing him were two separate things. She had behaved properly and they would never encounter each other again. 'Show me the papers. I need to know what I have been accused of.'

Her stepmother held out one of the worst scandal sheets. Sophie's eyes widened. 'The redoubtable Miss R? Do I look redoubtable to you? I am the least formidable person I know. Really, Stepmother, I'm surprised you read such things! All they print are lies and tittle-tattle.'

'How else can I find out what is going on in Newcastle, let alone in the rest of the country?' Her stepmother dabbed her eyes. 'Who is this Lord B who has captured your attention? Were you too ashamed of me to introduce us? I know I used to be in service, but that was long ago before your father fell in love with me.'

'Ashamed of you?' Sophie stared at her stepmother in astonishment. 'I love you and whomever I marry had best love you as well or he will not be the man for me. Now that we have cleared that up, I want to know about your plans for your new bonnet.'

'Sophie, stop confusing the issue with bonnets. The item in the papers. I shall not be deterred.'

'You know it is a pack of lies, don't you?' She put her hand over her stepmother's. 'As if I would consider marrying without consulting you first. Honestly, Stepmother, sometimes you read too many penny-dreadfuls. When have I ever kept any of my friends from you? And I would never marry anyone who was not a friend first. I learnt a painful lesson three years ago.'

'But there is a kernel of truth.' Her stepmother's cap trembled. 'I know how to read your face, Sophie. You can never hide things from me, not things which truly matter. Who is this Lord B? Would Robert and Henri approve?'

'Lord Bingfield,' Sophie supplied. Her stepmother conveniently forgot the times when Sophie had kept things from her, including the precise truth about Sebastian. 'He assisted me after Cynthia's elopement. I doubt the entire proceedings would have gone as smoothly if not for his assistance. I was introduced to his aunt, Lady Parthenope, who is great friends with three of the Lady Patronesses at Almack's. However, that is as far as it went. Someone has an overblown imagination and is making mischief.'

Sophie waited for her stepmother to ask about Lady Parthenope's dress or what she had said.

'Almack's is far from the power it used to be and I won't be distracted.' Her stepmother frowned and Sophie's heart sank. Her stepmother was worse than a dog with a bone about this snippet of gossip. 'Why didn't you tell me about Lord Bingfield immediately?'

'Because you would have jumped to the wrong conclusion like you are doing now, and I was tired.' Sophie crumpled the toast between her fingers. The last thing she needed after her broken sleep was to be quizzed about Lord Bingfield. Every time she closed her eyes last night it seemed she remembered how his breath had fanned her cheek or how he had nearly kissed her. The encounter was nothing to him, but she couldn't forget it. About three o'clock, she had decided that she'd been foolish and arrogant to reject his offer of an innocent dance. She should have danced with him and been done with it. She never dreamt about any of the men she danced with. The knowledge did not make her any happier.

'You were thinking about me and my health.' The ribbons of her stepmother's cap swayed their indignation. 'Sophie! Do you think I was born yesterday?'

'Given how you are reacting now, is it any wonder? You are seeking a romance where there is none.' Sophie was unsure who she was trying to convince—her stepmother or that little place inside her which kept whispering about Lord Bingfield's fine eyes. 'Besides, I doubt Lord Bingfield's ultimate intentions towards me were honourable. He inhabits the scandal sheets, after all. Remember The Incident and why I had to hurry up to Corbridge? I've sworn off men like that.'

Her stepmother's eyes narrowed. 'You had better hope it is a proper proposal from Lord Bingfield. People have long memories, Sophie. Your name will now be tainted from the mere association with his. Did you think about that last night when you were so busy accepting his trifling assistance? You know what your father wanted for you—a marriage into the higher echelons of society—and you have jeopardised that.'

'You are talking fustian nonsense.' Sophie tapped her finger on the scandal sheet. 'How many papers?'

'I have sent the butler to check. I should think most of them. Lady Parthenope sent me a note. She has invited us to take tea with her.' Her stepmother's hand trembled with excitement as she reached for the letter. 'She wants to vet us. That's what this is. You know what they say about her door-keeping at Almack's. I shall need a new bonnet!'

Sophie bit her lip. 'You can always refuse.'

'One does not refuse Lady Parthenope, Sophie, and stay within the bounds of polite society.' Her stepmother folded her hands in her lap and gave a smug smile. 'I've been after an invitation for years. You will pass muster without a problem. My stepdaughter will become a member of the aristocracy, even if she will forget me.'

'Stop spinning fantasies and nothing is finalised.' Sophie slumped back against the chair. She would have to tell her stepmother the full unedifying story. It was the only option. 'But there are, and will be, no impending nuptials to Lord Bingfield. I'm quite decided on that point. It happened—'

'There is a gentleman to see you, Miss Ravel.' The footman came in, carrying a silver platter with a single card, interrupting Sophie's story.

With a trembling hand, Sophie picked it up. Richard Crawford, Viscount Bingfield.

She stood up and absurdly wished that she was dressed in something more up to the minute than her old blue gown. She ruthlessly quashed the notion. Lord Bingfield and last night's escapade needed to be consigned to the past. The papers this morning proved it. Scandal dogged his footsteps.

'I will see Lord Bingfield in the drawing room.'

'I shall come with you, my dear.' Her stepmother started to rise, but Sophie put a hand on her stepmother's shoulder.

'That is far from necessary, Stepmother. If I need assistance, I will shout. I have access to a poker and am not afraid to use it.'

'Sophie!'

'The truth, Stepmother.' Sophie narrowed her eyes.

'Allow me to do this or I shall write to Lady Parthenope, explaining that I have rejected her nephew's suit and therefore neither of us will be able to take tea with her.'

Her stepmother covered her eyes. 'I shudder to think what Robert—or Henri, for that matter—would say, but very well, my dear, you may see him on your own. On pain of death, do not close that door and I will be in earshot. Your father wanted the best for you and I am determined you shall have it, even if I have to beg Lady Parthenope on bended knee for a voucher to Almack's.'

'My father would expect me to sort out this mess. Despite what you or Henri or Robert might think, I am perfectly capable of sorting this tempest in a teacup out. I am an adult and, according to the papers, redoubtable.' Sophie raised her chin. 'I will simply tell him no.'

Chapter Three

Richard stood in the middle of the Ravels' overly ornamented and chintz-hung drawing room, trying not to knock over any of the porcelain shepherds, china ladies or vases filled with wax flowers of every hue imaginable. The entire drawing room was a riot of pink tassels, lace doilies and small tables strewn with knick-knacks, all in the most fashionable but horrendous taste. His frock-coat had narrowly missed one china pig and a precariously balanced bowl of waxen fruit already as he paced, waiting for Miss Ravel to put in an appearance.

What sort of woman was the redoubtable Miss Ravel? The woman he rescued last night had not seemed in any way formidable, but badly in need of protection. The gossip from the club said that she was aloof, an ice maiden, but he kept remembering the way her eyes had flashed when she rejected his offer of a polka.

His head pounded worse than ever. All the way here, he kept going over in his mind the possible scenarios and becoming angrier. Who else could have linked their names and informed the papers? He also knew that he had to make Miss Ravel understand that he had never made a proposal of that sort.

He had expected more from Miss Ravel. He regarded a particularly nauseating shepherdess who was more strangling a lamb than cuddling it. He knew next to nothing about her except that her ball gown had fetching sophistication and she had been in trouble. Hardly the stuff to build a relationship on. It was far better to get his painful interview over and get back to leading his life.

The lady in question strode into the drawing room. The simplicity of her blue dress contrasted sharply with the overly fussiness of the room. Richard drew in his breath sharply. His dreams had not done her features justice. A certain forthrightness about her jaw warred with the frankly sensuous curve of her bottom lip. Her waist appeared no bigger than his handspan.

Her quick backward glance at the door to ensure it remained wide open, rather than shut, was telling. She appeared determined to observe proprieties, even if no one else was in the room with them.

'Lord Bingfield,' she said, dropping a perfunctory curtsy and her lips curving up into a smile, but she failed to hold out her hand to be kissed. Truly redoubtable this morning. 'An unexpected development.'

'You have seen the papers?' he asked, surprised. 'I could hardly avoid calling on you after such item was printed. It would mean neglecting my duty. I may be many things, Miss Ravel, but I have never been a cad.'

'We both made our positions quite clear last evening.'

'I understand the item in question may have made some of the later London editions. My father—'

'This would be the father who doesn't know you are in Newcastle?' She gave a superior smile. 'I can remember what your aunt said. I'm far from stupid, Lord Bingfield. However, if your being in Newcastle was going to cause problems with your parent, you should have been open and honest about it.'

'My reasons for being in Newcastle are private.'

She raised a delicate eyebrow. 'I will allow you to keep your reasons private. I merely mentioned this as plans have a way of going awry.'

'Have you seen the item?'

'My stepmother informed me of it.' She gave a small cough. 'Apparently your aunt has written to her, inviting her to tea. My stepmother is transported with excitement at the thought of taking tea with the great Lady Parthenope.'

'How charming.'

Her eyes flashed blue fire. 'I won't have my stepmother mocked, Lord Bingfield.'

He inclined his head. 'I was referring to my aunt, rather than your stepmother. I had not anticipated this development.'

'Your aunt began it.'

'Aunts are a law unto themselves, Miss Ravel, particularly my aunts. They can be wildly unpredictable. It is part of their charm.' Aunts were a law unto themselves, but he'd never expect his aunt to take it this far, making contact with Miss Ravel's relations before any nuptials were publically announced. There again, his aunt prided herself on her ability to ferret out people's most discreet indiscretion and remembering snippets of gossips. It was why she proved such an effective gatekeeper for Almack's. Currently slow torture would be too good for her, in Richard's opinion. He'd suggest it to one of his cousins. 'I hope your stepmother will not be too disappointed when you explain why she must not accept this invitation.'

'My stepmother has longed for such an invitation ever since she first married my late father. She wishes to mingle with the truly genteel.' Her neat white teeth worried her bottom lip, turning it the colour of ripe cherries. There was something innocent about her. Despite her age and reputation of being formidable, she seemed soft and gentle and in definite need of protection. 'It was one of the reasons I was sent away to school for a time.'

'My aunt is haughty rather than genteel. Her rudeness and sense of entitlement can be shocking at times.'

'No matter how I explain that it doesn't matter, my stepmother persists.' Miss Ravel shrugged a shoulder. 'My stepmother must do as she pleases, but I have disabused her of any notion that we are considering an alliance. I leave it to you to inform your aunt.'

'Did you have anything to do with the item in papers? Are you responsible for it?'

'The appearance of the item is a mystery and most vexing.' Her eyes flared. 'Why on earth would I want to endanger my reputation by linking my name with yours? I am well aware of what happens to women who become entangled with men like you.'

'A simple yes or no to the original question will suffice.' Richard fought to control his temper. Miss Ravel made it sound as though he was some sort of affliction to be avoided at all costs. He had never knowingly ruined a woman. 'We shall go at it another way. Do you know your enemy, Miss Ravel?'

Her blue eyes met his. 'Then, no, if you must know, I did not contact the papers. And until today, I didn't consider that I had an enemy. Sir Vincent must be more persistent than I thought. He has ignored your aunt's pronouncement of total innocence. Why would he do such a thing, except that he knows the merest hint of your name will soil my reputation?'

The tension rushed out of Richard's shoulders. Her assessment was the same as his. 'Thank you. I believe you. Forgive me for doubting you, but I had to know.'

The fire went out of her eyes. 'You are apologising.'

'Sir Vincent and I have previous history. He is a formidable enemy.'

'Indeed.' She passed a hand over her eyes and sank down on to the pink-damask sofa. 'I have made an enemy who intends to use underhanded means to win.'

'He has succeeded before. I am determined to stop him. This time.' Without bidding, the image of Mary's face floated in front of his eyes. He would have done the decent thing and married Mary before he was sent down from Oxford, despite the pain it would have caused his father. If he'd done that, she'd never have been forced into that marriage; would have never run away and met her death in that canal accident. He forced his mind away. He had to concentrate on the now and saving Miss Ravel. He knew what she was up against. Miss Ravel was an innocent.

'Putney means to ruin you, Miss Ravel. I've seen him do it to other women years ago and this time I will stop him.'

'Ruin me? How?' she said with a hiccupping laugh. 'We have witnesses that you made an honourable proposal. Sir Vincent can't harm me.'

'There are several scandal-mongers lurking outside your house.' He gave an apologetic smile. 'When you have been notorious, you learn to know their type. I sent them on their way.'

'They are watching the house? Still?'

'It is entirely possible,' Richard admitted.

Miss Ravel walked over to the drawing-room window and closed the shutters with a bang.

'You should have told me about them before you started accusing me of informing the papers. My stepmother will be beside herself. My former guardian will have apoplexy. I would never have allowed you in if I'd known.'

'I went to my club after I left the ball. I hadn't seen the papers or I would have been here earlier…'

'But they will know you were here.' She put her hands to her head. Her face had gone pale. 'Don't you see? The scandal will be all the greater. The scandalous Lord B has called on the redoubtable Miss R…or possibly the not-so-fearsome Miss R…but wilful and headstrong.'

She clasped her hands together as if she was trying to keep them from trembling. Richard fought against the inclination to take her in his arms and hold her until the trembling stopped. She was right. His coming here had made matters worse, but he could not have just left her to face the coming storm alone. It was not in his nature.

'It had to be done. Your post could be watched. The gutter press is called that for a reason.'

'I shall have to quit society.' Miss Ravel began to pace the room. 'My stepmother will be displeased, but it will have to be done. She still harbours hopes of a glittering marriage for me. I'll leave for Corbridge in the morning.'

'The scandal hounds will follow you. Putney will ensure it. Running will only encourage them.'

She put a hand out to steady herself. 'This is positively the last time I assist in anyone's elopement. The consequences are far too grave.'

'Listen to me, Miss Ravel, before you panic utterly.'

'I never panic.' she shouted. 'This is my life you have ruined. All you have to do is leave this room. No one has any expectations of you.'

He raised an eyebrow and her cheeks infused with colour. He quickly calculated the odds and knew the risk was worth taking. He would have done everything possible and he could leave her with a clear conscience. He would also have fulfilled the vow that he made at Mary's graveside. Putney would never use him to ruin another woman. 'I have expectations of my behaviour. It is my expectations which are important here, not someone else's.'

'What do you suggest?' she whispered, clasping her hands together so tightly the knuckles shone white.

'It is nothing that either of us wanted, but I can see no other practical solution, one which allows us both some measure of honour.' He went down on one knee. 'Will you marry me, Sophie Ravel?'

Sophie stared at Lord Bingfield in astonishment. He had gone down on one knee with one hand clasped to his breast and was looking up at her with an intent expression.

Her mouth went dry. It was a proper proposal. He was truly proposing. Lord Bingfield, despite his scandalous reputation and his vowed intent never to marry, was doing the decent thing and properly proposing marriage. Her stepmother's drawing room filled with its waxen fruit, china dogs and vases full of wax flowers had a distinct air of unreality.

'You are silent for once, Miss Ravel. Have you been struck dumb?'

Her shoulders relaxed slightly. She refused to believe in fairy tales or instant love. He was doing this for his own purposes and not to save her.

She had learnt her lesson the hard way years ago. Some day she would find a man whom she could love and whom she wanted to share the remainder of her life with, but until then she kept her head. Bingfield expected her to refuse. Of course he did. Then he could say that he'd done the decent thing, but alas, the lady had been unwilling. She gave a small smile. She understood the game now. She fought against the temptation to whisper 'yes', simply because he must expect a 'no'.

'Am I supposed to give this serious consideration?' she asked, tilting her head to one side and allowing her lashes to sweep down. 'Or am I supposed to refuse outright, send you on your way with a clear conscience that you have behaved with propriety? It might solve your problem with your code of honour, but it will not solve mine.'

His eyes hardened to stones. 'That is not for me to say. I merely asked the question in the proper manner.

It is for you to answer when you have considered it. Simply know I will not ask the question twice. Being coy will get you nowhere.'

'You do not know me well enough to feel any finer feelings.'

'I never pretended any finer feelings, Miss Ravel. I asked you to marry me. You would hardly want me to be dishonest. The proposal suits my purposes for the moment. I will abide by your answer.'

The words served to puncture her entirely. Sophie frowned at the unexpected disappointment. It shouldn't matter what Lord Bingfield thought of her, but it did. A tiny piece of her had hoped that somehow she'd been wrong and he'd fallen instantly in love with her. She had thought that the romantic part of her had died in that inn on the road to Scotland along with the rest of her girlish dreams, but apparently it hadn't.

'Is this some sort of a joke, Lord Bingfield?'

He slowly rose to his full height. Sophie was aware of the power in his shoulders and the way they narrowed down to his slim hips. Her body remembered how close they had stood last night. Her cheeks grew hot. He might not have any finer feelings for her, but she knew she wanted him to kiss her and that was not going to happen.

'I would hardly go down on one knee unless I was serious.' His lips turned down and his eyes became shadowed. 'In light of today's papers, do you think Putney will stop?'

'He needs to be exposed.'

'Others have tried and failed. I refuse to be used as an instrument of your ruin by the likes of him. Equally

I refuse to be labelled a cad and have it whispered that I ruin eligible women for sport. Years ago, I made a vow that I would not be used by him to ruin any woman.' He gave her a resolute look. 'Marriage is the right and proper thing to do in these circumstances. If I had not asked, it would have weighed on my conscience. It is now up to you to make a decision. I will abide by your choice.'

Sophie stared at the ceiling. The proposal might be real, but he didn't expect her to accept it. Not truly, not given in such a manner and after last night's exchange. But did she need the protection of a marriage to save her reputation from Sir Vincent? All she needed was an engagement. Her heart thudded.

'You suggest a fake engagement until the newspapers lose interest and I can jilt you? Putney is sure to move on when he realises that I am no soft target.' She pursed her lips, considering. It made complete and utter sense. It would buy her time until the Montemorcys returned and she could get proper advice. She turned around and faced Lord Bingfield, adopting her best social smile. 'A false engagement should stop comment. Whoever is doing this expects you to run and to leave me ruined, but this way Sir Vincent Putney will be left exposed. Marriage is not the answer, an engagement is.'

His brows knitted together and he seemed genuinely perplexed. 'A false engagement? One is either engaged to be married or one is not, Miss Ravel. I don't deal in fakes and deceptions of that nature. Attempting to cozen society is fraught with difficulty.'

'It is in the novels my stepmother likes to read. They are all the rage.' Sophie gave him a breezy assurance, but her insides twisted. He made it seem as though she dealt in deception regularly. She didn't. Sometimes it was easier to give an impression of a certain behaviour for the greater good, that was all. 'We don't actually have to marry. Once the furore has died down and Putney is unmasked or quits the neighbourhood, we can part…amicably. Legitimate engagements are ended for all sorts of reasons.'

'I meant a marriage if it came to it. I knew the risks when I asked. And if you had refused, I would have told the various journalists that my heart was broken by the redoubtable Miss Ravel.' He inclined his head. 'I will not pretend instant undying love. I have seen enough of love to know it leads two people who are wholly unsuited to each other to do stupid things. Love has little place in marriage. We might have suited if you had desired it.'

'We obviously have different views on the subject. I would never have such a cold-blooded thing as an arranged marriage. A happy marriage needs a firm foundation of love.'

A half-smile flickered across his face. 'Despite your formidable reputation, Miss Ravel, you are a secret romantic. Love only complicates things and makes people profoundly unhappy in my experience.'

'I demand certain standards from any prospective bridegroom.' Sophie drew herself up to her full height. 'Standards which you sadly lack.'

'However, I will consider your wish of a fake engagement and evaluate the risks. We might be able to play Sir Vincent at his own game.'

His mouth twisted as he spat the word fake. Deep-seated anger at the injustice of the whole situation flooded through her. She was trapped in a situation not of her making and had found the perfect solution if only he'd agree. She was being honest and forthright, whereas if she'd accepted his offer he would have found a way to make her jilt him. And his idea of telling the press she'd rejected him would make them more interested in her, rather than less.

'Consider!' Sophie put her hands on her hips. 'It is the perfect solution. Surely you must see it. There will be no need for further scandal. We will quietly part at the end. There will be no hurt feelings or accusations as we both know from the outset that the marriage will never happen. Honesty on both our parts from the start.'

'You know nothing about me!'

Sophie crossed her arms. He was like any other rake, solely interested in himself. 'I know enough.'

'I had not considered a limited engagement, but it would serve the same purpose, I suppose.' He gave a long sigh. 'My father will be disappointed when the longed-for engagement ends, but he generally is with me these days.'

'You are a fortune hunter. It was why your aunt was so pleased to see you with me.'

Sophie backed away from the window. Her stomach knotted. She should have guessed. And she had handed him the perfect opportunity. Just once she wanted to be wanted for herself rather than for the fortune her father had amassed. The walls seemed to close in on her and she wished her corset wasn't as tight. Here when she walked into the drawing room, she'd been so pleased with the way the slenderness of her waist contrasted with her new crinoline. It was always the way—either look good or be able to breathe. Next time she'd remember that breathing was important when dealing with people like Lord Bingfield, particularly Lord Bingfield.

'Miss Ravel, jumping to conclusions is never good.' His ice-cold voice filled the room and cut through her panic. 'My fortune is quite secure. The estate is well funded thanks to my mother's dowry and eventually it will be mine. My father cannot change that. Do you wish to see the accounts? He merely wishes me to marry and provide an heir.'

Sophie pinched the top of her nose. She could hardly confess about her past mistake with Sebastian. Just thinking about that made her feel unclean. 'I have met fortune hunters in the past. They are a known hazard for heiresses. One has to be cautious. You can be left without any fortune at all.'

'So I understand.' His mouth twisted. 'There are ways to protect women if one acts before marriage. You must take your time and get the right settlement. It saves heartache, as my mother found out to her cost.'

'Your mother is still alive?'

'My parents are divorced. The settlement was not in her favour. They were in a unique situation, as I am sure you are aware. It was all in the papers at the time. My mother was for ever banished from polite society.'

Sophie hung her head. She had done it again—jumping to a conclusion when the truth was precisely the opposite. It made sense now why he had acted so quickly to protect her. 'I didn't know. I have no idea who your parents are.'

'Truly?' He raised an eyebrow and his features

seemed carved from stone. 'You surprise me, Miss Ravel. My parents' divorce was the subject of great scandal. The account of the crim. con. trial went into several editions. A best seller, or so Putney informed me when we were at Eton.'

'It happened a long time ago. The world moves on,' Sophie replied evenly. Her stomach clenched and she knew that she had to get this right. If she said the wrong words, he could decide not to help her. 'Scandal is not branded on people's foreheads. A person's true character is of far more relevance than any perceived scandal.'

'Other people may beg to differ. Ever since I was at Eton, the press have been interested in my doings. First because of my parents and then...'

She fixed him with her eye. It was obvious the sort of reputation he must have. He probably made Sebastian Cawburn look like an angelic choirboy. 'Because you decided to give them what they wanted.'

'I was determined to live my life as I pleased rather than looking over my shoulder for their approval. They have printed lies in the past and continue to twist my life so they can sell more papers. Once I had my head around that fact, I found it much easier to accept. Regardless of what the papers might say, there are certain lines I do not cross. Once I make a vow, I do my utmost to keep it. You must remember that, Miss Ravel.'

'I am not interested in other people's opinions and I am interested in how a person behaves.'

A light flared in his eyes. 'You are a unique individual, Miss Ravel.'

'I like to think so. Do you agree to my scheme?' Sophie held out her hand and willed him to take it, sealing their pact. 'Once I jilt you, you can nurse a broken heart for ages. The papers will be sympathetic. Your father will have to give you time to grieve. We are simply being honest with each other at the start, rather than playing games. Neither of us will get hurt. We have much to gain.'

He gathered her hands in his and she noticed how good it felt to touch him. Her body went rigid. She did not have to act on the attraction. Desire burnt itself out quickly. Desire was not the same as lasting love. 'We could have made a great team, Miss Ravel.'

'Sophie!' Her stepmother's outraged tones came from the open door. 'What is going on here? You are holding hands with a strange man! Where has your sense of propriety gone, my girl?'

Sophie slipped her hands from Lord Bingfield's. Her stepmother would have to choose this moment to come into the drawing room. Nothing had been settled. 'Going on, Stepmother? Everything is utterly innocent.'

'Hornswoggle! I have seen that look in your eye before, young lady. You had better not think to twist me around your little finger.'

'Allow me to introduce myself, Richard Crawford, Viscount Bingfield. My father is the Marquess of Hallington, Mrs Ravel.' Lord Bingfield recaptured her hand. Sophie gave a little tug, but he didn't let go. 'Your stepdaughter has done me the honour of becoming my fiancée in light of the news reported in today's papers.'

Sophie struggled to fill her lungs. He had done it, despite his misgivings. They were embarked on the deception.

'Sophie!' Her stepmother went white and then red.

'You had best sit down, Stepmother.' Sophie let go of Lord Bingfield's hand and led her stepmother to the pink-damask sofa. 'You have had a shock.'

'Then it is true, my dear child? Not some nonsense?' Her stepmother fumbled for her reticule and her smelling salts. 'You are going to marry this stranger? You could have told me that was the reason why you needed to meet him alone.'

'I had no idea he would offer, Stepmother.' Sophie took the reticule, retrieved the vial and waved it under her stepmother's nose. 'I didn't want to get your hopes up. An engagement is the best solution in the circumstances. The gutter press appear determined that we court.'

'I regret that subterfuge was necessary, but we didn't wish for the press to become interested with regards to your stepdaughter's innocence.' Lord Bingfield bowed his head. 'Alas…'

'I completely understand,' her stepmother said, her face alight with eagerness. 'The press must be such a bother for you, dogging your footsteps. You seem to be a great favourite of theirs.'

'Most of the stories they print about me have no bearing on reality, my dear Mrs Ravel. I do have my code of honour.'

Her stepmother gave a long sigh.

Sophie rolled her eyes. A few well-chosen words and her stepmother melted. She regretted the necessity of keeping her stepmother ignorant of the true arrangement, but her stepmother had never been able to keep a secret. And it was necessary to stop Sir Vincent once and for all time. But the sooner this deception was over, the better.

'I had never considered what the people in the scandal sheets must feel and how cautious they have to be.'

'You read the scandal sheets?'

Her stepmother put her hand to the side of her mouth and leant forwards. 'Sophie disapproves.'

'Does she?'

'What a truly noble thing you have done. They were all wrong about you and how you break women's hearts. I never believed the story about you, that Russian countess and her husband, the one who committed suicide rather than compete with you.'

'I am grateful.' Lord Bingfield inclined his head. 'The situation was not how the press portrayed it. I met the countess after her husband died, and introduced her to her new husband. We remain friends.'

Sophie stared at him. Precisely how much of a favourite with the gutter press was he?

'Lord Bingfield, you must partake of some tea or perhaps something stronger.' Her stepmother straightened her cap. 'I know how fond you gentlemen are of something a little more potent. I am dying to learn the truth behind some of the latest scandals.'

Sophie attempted to signal over her stepmother's head, but Lord Bingfield simply gave a superior smile. 'I would be delighted to spend time with you, Mrs Ravel, but I never discuss the latest tittle-tattle for obvious reasons.'

'I shall leave you two now,' her stepmother said at the end of a very long cup of tea. 'Sophie has been glowering at me ever since the teapot arrived. I, too, remember what it is like to be young. I am so pleased you decided to do the decent thing, Lord Bingfield. I do worry about Sophie. Her future happiness has been a source of sleepless nights and now it is all settled. The late Mr Ravel must be beaming down from heaven. His Sophie will be a marchioness. He'd never thought his daughter would climb so high, but I knew she would.'

'I am sure he is, Mrs Ravel.'

Her stepmother turned a bright pink and hurried off. Lord Bingfield closed the door firmly behind her. He loomed larger than ever. Sophie retreated a step.

'The die is cast and the deception has begun,' she said, adopting an ice-cold tone. 'There was no need to close the door. We can take our leave in full view of any passing servant.'

'There is every need.' The gold in his eyes deepened. 'I want to know why you believe you have only your fortune to offer in a marriage.'

'What I have to offer is none of your business!' Sophie crossed her arms. Her stomach tightened. In suggesting the false engagement, she'd just given Lord Bingfield an iron-clad opportunity for a seduction! She'd simply have to insist that certain boundaries weren't crossed. 'I was merely seeking to understand why you were insistent we have a real engagement. You have no regard for me.'

He took a step closer. 'Are you saying that you are indifferent to me?'

'Yes.' Sophie stuck her chin in the air. 'Yes, definitely.'

'Liar.'

She went still. Her heart raced and her mouth became parched. She wet her lips. 'I do not make a habit of lying, Lord Bingfield.'

'Richard.' He reached her and put his hands on her shoulders. 'I am your fiancé now. You need to think of me as your true betrothed or Putney will create an even bigger scandal. Remember that. This might help you. Think of it as an *aide-mémoire*.'

She was aware of him in the same heart-thumping way she'd been aware of him the night before. She concentrated on the chintz curtains behind his left shoulder, rather than on his mouth. 'What are you intending on doing?'

'Demonstrating…Sophie.'

Her name sounded like a soft caress, sliding over her jangled nerves and soothing her. A warm pulse went down her spine. No one had ever used her name in quite that fashion before.

His hand tilted her chin so she looked into his eyes of pure gold.

She had only time to blink before his mouth descended, slowly, like a tiny fluttering of a breeze and then increasing intensity. Sophie told herself that she should keep her body still or scream. She should do something besides enjoying the kiss, but she discovered she was powerless to do anything else.

She closed her eyes, savoured the sensation and swayed towards him.

He let her go and stepped back. 'Point proved…Sophie.'

This time her name was anything but a caress. Her cheeks grew hot and she rubbed her aching lips furiously. 'It proves nothing except you, like any self-respecting rake, know how to kiss.'

He picked up his hat. 'I will pick you up tonight.'

'What is happening tonight?' Sophie asked, her hand freezing in mid-air. The hard part of this engagement was not going to be pretending to be attracted to him, but keeping the attraction at bay. After insisting on the fake engagement, she could hardly back down now. When it was all over, she wanted to walk away with her head held high, knowing she had withstood the cynical seduction of a rake.

'You and I will go to the Assembly Rooms tonight. You will demonstrate your waltzing skills to me. We want people to talk.'

'Are we announcing the engagement?'

'Not yet.' He leant forwards and his breath caressed her cheek. 'Everyone needs to see how besotted we are with each other. You can do besotted, Sophie, can't you?'

Chapter Four

Sometimes it was better to know than not to know, Sophie decided as she fastened her earrings, the final detail in tonight's dress. In the grand scheme of things she would have liked to ask Richard Crawford more about himself and to have set the precise boundaries for their relationship, but she didn't have time.

She glanced at her stepmother, who was already dressed in her evening finery and hovering behind her, making comments. 'You will tell me what you know about Lord Bingfield from the scandal sheets.'

'You should ask your intended about what the scandal sheets have printed over the years, if you want to know. If you had read them before now, you wouldn't have to ask me. You must do the decent thing and wait for Lord Bingfield to tell you.'

'Stepmother!' Sophie turned on the stool and motioned for her maid to leave the room. 'You may tell me what is bothering you.'

'It is difficult to understand why you have kept your cards so close to your chest. How well do you know this Lord Bingfield? He does have a reputation for sweeping married women off their feet. There was that Russian countess with the dead husband and a duchess more recently. Possibly there have been more.'

Sophie stood up and fluffed out the upper tier of her skirt. Married women. Women of experience. Not unmarried heiresses. He had not lied about that. He had his code. 'It is what an engagement is for. A chance to get to know the gentleman in question. I have not married him...yet. If I decide we will not suit, then I have the chance of changing my mind. The item in the newspaper left me few alternatives, Stepmother. Once the gutter press get hold of you, they keep hold. You can remember what Robert said after The Incident.'

'Sometimes I feel like you are keeping secrets from me. We used to share everything, Sophie, when I first married your father.'

'You are the one keeping secrets now, Stepmother. You love gossip. Generally I have to block my ears. Tell me something about Lord Bingfield and his family, please. Help me to understand why the press are so interested in him.'

Sophie waited as a variety of emotions warred on her stepmother's face. If her stepmother would not supply the information, she would go to the Lit and the Phil and spend time looking at old papers to see if she could discover the scandal.

'Very well, I shall tell you about his parents,' her stepmother said when Sophie had given up hope. 'Lord Bingfield's parents were involved in a massive scandal about twenty years ago. The marchioness ran away with her lover and there was a huge crim. con. case. It was absolutely fascinating and a best seller. Of course they say the marquess never recovered from it. And the marchioness…well…she was never received in polite society again. When Lord Bingfield entered society, everyone was naturally curious, and he didn't disappoint.'

'It must have been awful for Lord Bingfield,' Sophie said. 'He was a child, the innocent victim of two people's complicated lives.'

'He certainly hasn't been shy about courting scandal in his adult life,' her stepmother remarked tartly. 'He must have a list of mistresses as long as your arm. Women seem to forget the sense they were born with around him. There are things which have to come from the other person, my dear, rather than from reading a newspaper.'

'You know the newspapers do print lies. Robert has told you enough times.' Sophie tilted her chin upwards. Her stepmother's revelations were proof enough that she needed to be cautious.

'Sophie, are you sure you want to marry this man?' her stepmother asked in a rush. 'With Robert and Henri out of the country, I feel I must say something. Refuse to be rushed. You can have a long engagement. You don't need a special licence, an ordinary one will do.'

'I thought you always wanted me to marry by special licence.'

'Only if the man is suitable for you.' Her stepmother gave a long sigh. 'I don't know what is wrong with me. This morning when Lord Bingfield was here, I was transported with happiness for you, but I have spent all afternoon staring at Mr Ravel's portrait and wondering—is this the sort of man your father would have approved of? Is being in the aristocracy worth your ultimate happiness?'

Sophie concentrated on her bare hands, rather than looking at her stepmother's face. Her stepmother only ever spent time talking to her father's portrait when she felt overwhelmed. It was tempting to confide in her, but the arrangement would only make her more agitated. And could she trust her stepmother to keep it a secret? Her stepmother had the habit of gossiping with friends. It was far more important to catch Sir Vincent and destroy him. She'd confess later. Her stepmother would understand. Far better to beg forgiveness, than request permission in this case.

Sophie glanced at her stepmother's kindly face and swallowed. Or at least she hoped her stepmother would understand.

'I know what I am doing. And it was in all the papers, Stepmother. You know what happened to the Neville girl. She was banned from court and that was fifteen years ago. Once the gutter press get hold of you, they do not let go.'

'Do you know about his finances? Such men can be dreadfully let in the pockets. You remember Lord Cawburn. He tried to rush you and it was only through Henri's intervention that your reputation emerged unscathed. Now, this business with the newspapers... Could he...? That is to say, Lord Bingfield has much to gain.'

'Lord Bingfield is not trying to rush me. We are engaged because the gutter press demanded a robust response. There is little point in denying the rumour as Lord Bingfield was prepared to do the honourable thing.

I refused to do anything irrevocable without a proper settlement.' Sophie patted her stepmother's hand.

Everything would work out if her scheme was allowed to happen. There had to be a simple way of trapping Sir Vincent and then saying goodbye to Richard Crawford before she started liking him too much. They were allies only because they faced a common enemy, not because they shared a mutual understanding or finer feelings.

'You have eased my mind.' Her stepmother took her mother's single pearl and undid the clasp before fastening it around Sophie's neck. 'I hope you are not doing this just to please me. All I have ever wanted for you is to be happy.'

A tiny prickle of fear went through Sophie. What if they didn't succeed in trapping Sir Vincent? She pushed it away. They had to win. 'And if I can't do that within society?'

'Your father worked his entire life to ensure his daughter would be gentry. You won't dishonour your father's memory.'

'Trust me, please. I am all grown up. I've survived three seasons since Lord Cawburn without incident.'

'It is what makes this situation so strange. I don't understand how you could have met a man such as Lord Bingfield without me knowing.' Her stepmother stepped back. 'There, pretty as a picture. I do wish your father had lived to see you triumphant and in love.'

Sophie straightened her blouse. With her favourite pair of earrings, and the cream ball gown with cascades of lace, she was armed for battle.

Sir Vincent was not going to get away with his

scheme and he wasn't going to be allowed to wreck anyone else's life. She simply had to figure out how to feed him information which would incriminate him before she did truly become besotted with Richard Crawford. She had to remember that above all things she had to keep her heart safe. Men who were *not safe in carriages* were best handled at arm's length, rather than offering up her lips at the earliest opportunity. Boundaries were required and it was up to her to set them.

She reached for her tortoise-shell fan and ignored the way her lips ached in memory of that kiss. Kissing complicated matters. They might be posing as an engaged couple, but it did not mean he had any finer feelings or regard for her. She was a means to an end.

One last glance in the mirror told her everything she needed to know. The dress was passable, but she looked far too excited. And she was excited, excited about the possibility of beating Sir Vincent, rather than seeing Richard Crawford.

'Shall we go? I feel capable of achieving great things tonight.'

Richard drew in his breath as Sophie walked down the stairs. Tonight she was the perfect epitome of a redoubtable ice princess rather than a woman in distress. Her blonde hair was immaculate and the bodice of her ball dress skimmed the tops of her breasts. A single pearl nestled in the hollow of her throat. But for all her finery, he could see the nerves underneath—the slight hesitation on the last step, the pinched way she held her mouth and the way she clutched her gloves until her knuckles shone white. Sophie was less certain about tonight's piece of play-acting than she wanted to be.

He had a great longing to throw her over his shoulder, and take her somewhere where he could protect her. But tonight was necessary for more than one reason. Not only would he demonstrate to Putney that seeking revenge on Sophie in this manner was doomed to failure, but he would also provide the perfect excuse for any visit to Newcastle. His father would understand the need to pursue an heiress far better than Richard's need to be part of his mother and sister's life.

'You look exquisite,' he said when Sophie reached the bottom of the stairs.

'It is last Season's dress and the sleeves didn't alter as well I wanted them to, but I like the shape of the skirt too much.'

'You sew your own clothes?' Richard struggled to think of a woman of his acquaintance who would admit it. The last one was probably Mary. His mind moved firmly away from that memory. He was not going to start liking Sophie Ravel. He only became friends with women after he no longer desired them. To allow a woman into his heart and his whole life was to invite her to abandon him. It was not going to happen to him as it had happened to his father. He was the one who left first, before his heart became involved.

'Only alterations. I want perfection and my stepmother ensured my accomplishments included both fine sewing and the making of clothes.' Her smile lit the hallway. 'One has to be practical. A dress can easily be made over into the latest fashion. I never want to disappoint.'

'You won't do that.' He reached into the pocket of his evening coat. 'But you are missing one thing.'

She glanced down. 'I believe I have everything. Slippers, reticule, fan and gloves.'

'A ring.'

Her cheeks flamed. 'I…I hadn't considered it necessary. Not for tonight.'

His heart gave an odd wrench. It was ironic. Normally he was the one who put limits on his relationships with women, but this time it was Sophie. He'd seen the ring at the jewellers and knew it would be the one thing to give her confidence. 'How else will people know we are engaged?'

'A notice in the papers?' Her laugh rang hollow.

Richard held on to his temper. He wanted to murder the man who had made her so distrustful. She should try trusting him. He wanted to prove to her that he could solve their difficulty.

'Hold out your finger and stop being awkward. It will remind you that you belong to me if you are tempted to waltz with any divine dancer. No flirting with any other man.'

She held out her hand and he slipped on the ring, a pearl flanked by two sapphires. She twisted her hand back and forth. 'It is very pretty and it fits. I never flirt, Lord Bingfield. It goes against my nature.'

He allowed the remark to pass. He had seen a glimpse of the passionate woman underneath her frosty exterior and wanted to see her again. 'I saw it in a jeweller's window this afternoon and guessed your size. Sapphires for your eyes. It suits your hand.'

'It is elegant rather than showy.' Sophie tilted her

chin upwards. 'It is the sort of ring I would have cho-sen...if asked.'

'I will remember for the future.'

'You mean you don't intend for her to have the fam-ily jewels?' Mrs Ravel asked with a suspicious glance at the ring as she came to stand guard over Sophie. 'I would have thought the fiancée of a viscount deserved something better.'

Richard gave a quick glance at Sophie, who shrugged. She had obviously failed to confide in her stepmother about the false engagement as he'd expected her to do after he left. Intriguing.

'Engagement rings have an unfortunate past in my family. With your stepdaughter, I thought it best to break with tradition.' Richard made a bow. 'Should So-phie wish it, she may of course exchange it for another.'

'And the family jewels? I presume there are some. There again, the family jewels are always the first to go. Several women I know were palmed off with paste.' She tapped the side of her nose. 'You can always tell.'

'Honestly, Stepmother! I explained that Lord Bing-field is not let in the pockets.'

Richard controlled his temper. The pair had obvi-ously dealt with a fortune hunter before. Could he be the one responsible for Sophie's caution? A stab of jeal-ousy went through him. He wished... Richard pushed the thought away. He never speculated on a woman's past. Ever.

'Kept in a vault at Hallington, awaiting the next mar-chioness. After we are married, the jewels can be reset to her taste. My father has always been clear on that.'

'Admit it, Stepmother, you simply wanted to boast

that I was wearing a family heirloom. Personally, I am pleased Richard has shown some restraint and taste.' Sophie flashed a smile. 'How perfect to be able to wear it tonight. I believe I shall keep my gloves on to start with. It will make the revelation of our engagement all that more sensational if the need arises.'

'My thinking entirely.' Richard's shoulders relaxed as they shared a conspiratorial smile. Tonight was about laying the foundation of the trap for Putney and ensuring Sophie remembered whom she belonged to at the moment, rather than proclaiming the engagement to everyone. Patience was required. He could risk liking Sophie as he knew what the outcome would be. He could stop this before it went too far.

'I'm pleased we are as one on this.'

Her level blue eyes met his. 'We are.'

The Assembly Rooms blazed with light and sound when Sophie arrived with Richard and her stepmother.

With each turn of the carriage wheel, the ring grew heavier on Sophie's finger. It became harder and harder to keep up a light conversation. There were so many things she wanted to say to Richard about the necessity of boundaries, but her stepmother was there. And her stepmother was sure to pick up any attempt at subterfuge. Her head pained her and she wished she'd found an excuse not to attend, rather than trying for this pretence.

'The first dance must be mine,' Richard murmured as he handed her down from the carriage. The simple touch of his gloved hand on her elbow did nothing to calm her nerves. If anything, it heightened her awareness of him and the way her body reacted when he was near. 'We must begin as we mean to go on. Besotted, Sophie, not looking like a death sentence hangs over your head. You were the one to suggest this. For it to succeed, people need to believe in the romance. We met and fell instantly and irrevocably in love. Right now you appear more ready for a funeral.'

'I thought you liked my dress,' she said in dismay. Besotted indeed! There was no possibility of allowing her heart to rule her head. What she was feeling was attraction and desire towards a distinctly unsuitable man. She didn't have to act on that attraction. This engagement was about saving her reputation, not destroying it for ever.

'I do, but it is your expression I worry about and I was sure you would break your fan in the carriage. You clutched it far too tightly and you chose to sit as far away from me as possible, practically hugging the door.'

Sophie pressed her lips together, hating that he had noticed her discomfort. She could hardly confess to being wary of him. It would only mean making it easier for him to seduce her. 'It is difficult to fit two dresses in the same carriage.'

He laughed. 'If that is what you want to believe you may, but I prefer to trust my instincts.'

Sophie forced her features to relax. Her stomach was in more knots than the first time she had attended a dance. It amazed her that Richard had noticed anything and had thought to ask. Her stepmother had sailed on, seemingly oblivious as her earlier misgivings proved groundless.

There were so many pitfalls to this current plan. She

wished she had actually thought it through thoroughly before she suggested it. But it was this or ruin. *Or accepting his offer for real.* She ruthlessly quashed that little voice.

'We need to speak. Urgently,' Sophie whispered back. 'There is so much which is unsettled between us. Ways other people, particularly Sir Vincent, can expose us.'

'It must be a waltz. Waltzing is more convenient for speaking than a polka.'

She refused to consider how he knew such things. If they waltzed, she'd be in his arms, Sophie realised with a gulp. 'I thought you never asked a woman twice. I refused you last night.'

'Last night I asked. Tonight I am telling you. I trust you know the difference.'

'A quadrille won't do?' she squeaked.

'Not for a prolonged conversation.' A faint dimple shone in the corner of his mouth. 'There is always bound to be a quiet card room where we will not be disturbed.'

She didn't want to think about going to a card room with him. She could remember all too clearly what had happened when she went into that deserted card room with Sebastian. Never again would she be like that!

'I have had enough of card rooms, thank you. In any case my stepmother will think it odd if we simply disappear at the first opportunity. She knows about the promises I gave my guardian years ago and how I have endeavoured to keep those promises.'

'A waltz or the card room, Sophie.'

'The first waltz, it is. I believe it will go a long way towards the besotted impression.'

His entire being stiffened and didn't appear to hear her last teasing remark.

'Is there a problem?' she asked, peering at the young lady and stylishly dressed older woman who seemed to have caught Crawford's eye. The young lady was beautiful in that dark sort of way that Sophie knew she could never be. There was a faint exoticism about her features. The older woman was clearly her mother.

He shook his head and cupped his hand under her elbow, definitely turning her away from the pair. Her body reverberated from the touch. 'It was simply someone I thought I recognised. A mistake.'

'Another one of your conquests?' She laughed and tried to concentrate on the poster advertising the visit of Charles Dickens that coming August. She should have expected it, but it still hurt. Once a rake, always a rake. She had no right to expect anything from him. This entire engagement was spun-sugar pretence and artifice, rather than truly solid and secure love. 'I don't mind. There is no finer feeling between us. Indeed, I have no interest in you beyond securing my reputation.'

Her heart thudded that it was a lie. She was certainly aware of him. And he had been perceptive enough to realise that she was nervous. She simply didn't want to start liking him. There had to be reasons to keep her heart safe. Soon enough, he would revert to type. She had to keep remembering that he was the worst sort of rake, the sort of man whom the gutter press loved. It was only because he wanted to conduct a private war against Sir Vincent that her reputation stood any chance of survival. He had not done this because he cared about her or her prospects.

'Most definitely not one of my conquests. Nor ever likely to be.' The light in his eyes flared gold. 'And, Sophie, when we are together, I will not look at any other woman. I promise. It is not the way I was made or brought up.'

'It can happen.'

'And it causes tremendous heartache for other people.' He stared down at her. 'I have witnessed the consequences firsthand. Many times. And I have never knowingly caused a woman to break her vows, but it has always been a matter for her, rather than for me.'

Sophie swallowed hard. She could hardly confess she had asked her stepmother about the scandals he had been involved in. 'But you do know the women.'

'After a fashion.' His brows knitted. 'I had not expected them to be here tonight. It changes nothing. Until our association ends, I am yours.'

'Once the first waltz starts, you can come and find me if you wish to speak to them now,' Sophie said brightly, forcing her mind away from the way her heart wanted to believe his words. Underneath he would be the same as any other rake—selfish and solely concerned with his own pleasure. 'There is no need to introduce me. There are a number of other people I need to speak to.'

Sophie silently prayed the waltz would be soon. Otherwise it was going to be torture waiting to speak to him and hoping that they had their story correct. But staying close to him was another sort of torture, undermining her resolve to keep aloof from his seductive technique.

A smile transformed his features. 'Our luck appears to be holding. I believe I can hear the first strains now. There is no need to greet distant acquaintances.'

She allowed him to lead her into the middle of the dance floor. While some of the other rooms had gas lighting, the main ballroom still had its magnificent chandelier lighting system.

He placed his hand on her waist, holding her a bit more tightly than strictly necessary. She pointedly twisted her waist to gain a little space.

'I have been civilised, Miss Ravel. You will come to no harm.'

'Everyone is watching us.' She swallowed hard and attempted to ignore the fluttering in her stomach.

'Everyone will have read the papers. They want to see what happens. Abject devotion.'

'From you or me?' Sophie gave a pointed smile. She was on firmer ground here. 'Abject devotion fails to agree with me, Lord Bingfield. Never has done and I have no plans to start. Remember, I am redoubtable.'

'I never believe anything I read in the press.'

'You should believe that. I have spent years ensuring I do not have pointless flirtations.'

'What a pity.' He clasped his hand over hers. 'I shall take comfort in the fact that you are far from indifferent to me. Your body must remember what happened the last time I held you in my arms.'

Sophie ground her teeth. 'A gentleman would refrain from mentioning that kiss.'

'It was utterly delightful.' He gave an unrepentant smile. 'That is better. Your cheeks have colour. Far better for giving the impression of being besotted.'

Besotted indeed! The one thing this engagement was not going to become was a way for him to seduce her. She knew the boundaries. The kiss would not be repeated. She refused to slip slowly but inexorably along that path again towards an illicit room in a rundown inn.

She cleared her throat. 'The dance has begun.'

He began to move and she discovered that he was an expert dancer. She had danced with some very good dancers before, but Richard moved differently. It was more like floating on a cloud or having her body move as one with his. It would be easy to forget everything and simply enjoy the sensation of being in his arms.

'We need to come up with a story,' she said and ignored how his hand had moved to fit her waist far more snugly. 'Something to test Sir Vincent.'

'I doubt that will be necessary.'

'We need to prove that he is our mutual enemy.'

'Proving is nothing. What we need to do is ensure that he will not continue with his scheme. And he needs to learn that he should not try that sort of behaviour with anyone else.'

'I take it you have a plan.'

'I promised to protect you.' His hand moved around to her back. 'Trust me to do so and not abandon you to the winds of fate. You are far from alone, Miss Ravel. Relax and enjoy the dance. Look me in the eyes as if you never want to look anywhere else.'

'And if someone asks how we met? I can hardly tell them the truth.'

He missed his step, but recovered. 'I had not considered it. Have you been away from Newcastle recently?'

'Carlisle,' Sophie answered with a faint smile. 'I trust you know where that is.'

He cleared his throat. 'I meant somewhere in the south.'

'We went to Liverpool in late March as a new design of tea clipper was being launched and I wanted to see the hull. I know everyone says that steam will replace the sail, but there is something so glorious about the way the sails fill.'

'I shall take your word for it. I had never considered the design of a hull before. All I want to know is that a ship will get me from one port to another, safely, if I am forced to take it.'

'Much of my fortune comes from shipbuilding, Lord Bingfield.' Sophie breathed easier. Speaking of shipbuilding kept her mind from the way he moved or the shape of his lips. Feigning being besotted was one thing, actually being so was another problem altogether. 'I was brought up to have a keen interest. The board of directors may run the day-to-day business, but it is the lifeblood which brings all the good things in my life. It is important not to take such things for granted, but to understand and to be able to question.'

His smile became genuine. 'I knew you were more than a pretty face.'

'Do you like ships?' Sophie asked quickly.

'I am invariably seasick. It doesn't matter if it is a rowing boat or a tea clipper—once I am on the water, my stomach heaves. Always has done. I suspect it always will.'

'You do get used to the sea in time. Lots of people get over it and are never troubled again. A long sea voyage would do the trick. It did with me when I was seven. We went to the West Indies and I was so sick to begin with, but then I recovered. My father told me even Admiral Lord Nelson was seasick on occasion. Somehow it made it easier to bear.'

'I shall take your word for it since you argue so passionately. Some day maybe I will test your theory.' His eyes crinkled at the corners. A bubbly sense of excitement filled her. 'But for now Liverpool with its shipbuilding will have to do. The timing is reasonable and plausible. I do hope you did attend some sort of gala or a ball while you were there and your trip wasn't entirely business.'

'Do for what?' Sophie frowned, trying to remember precisely what she had done. It was disappointing that Lord Bingfield wasn't interested in ships and more than slightly disconcerting that she had hoped he would be. She shouldn't want any connection with him, but she did. She trod down heavier than she should have and narrowly missed his foot. It was only Richard's skill as a dancer which kept them upright. The heat in Sophie's cheeks increased.

'We went to the theatre. It was an amusing comedy that my stepmother was desperate to see. I cried off the launch ball because I had twisted my ankle at the shipyard. Is it important?'

'For where we met? Yes.' His eyes crinkled at the corners. Sophie hurriedly glanced away. 'I'd have hardly liked to have met you in a shipyard or on a railway platform. The theatre is a splendid choice. Plenty of time to spy people from a box and arrange a meeting. I take it you are adept at fan language despite your pretensions towards formidability?'

He was going to imply she had arranged a meeting with her fan. Typically arrogant. Sophie started to pull away, but his hand tightened on her waist, holding her against his body.

'Why is this necessary?' she asked.

'I must have had a reason to come to Newcastle to see you and see if the spark we both felt was something more. And your stepmother most blatantly had not met me before.' He gave her hand a squeeze. 'Our meeting yesterday was hardly a chance one. You were enchanted by my persistence and overcome with desire. I had completely rearranged my life to be with you and you were utterly captivated. The press always do love a romance.'

Sophie concentrated on taking the next few steps, rather than considering the desire part of his statement. She hated that a tiny part of her wanted to believe in the tale which he had spun. She wanted to believe that he would rearrange his life for her. 'It does make sense. As a personal rule, I dislike being enchanted about anything. I have learnt, Lord Bingfield, that it is best to examine faults thoroughly.'

He gave a bark of laughter. Several people turned to stare at them. 'You might wish to pretend you are practical, but you possess the soul of a romantic, Miss Ravel. I see straight through you. You long to be swept off your feet. Otherwise why assist in an elopement?'

'I much prefer being practical to starry-eyed. I gave up endangering my heart years ago.'

'You are unlike any woman I have met.'

'I hope that is a good thing. I like the idea of being an individual.'

'Never doubt that! You, Sophie Ravel, are a one-off. You have even given me a hankering to test your theory about seasickness with a voyage to the West Indies, but only if you were with me.'

'That won't happen.'

'A pity. A sea voyage with you could have been intriguing.' A dimple played in the corner of his mouth. 'You won't even consider a trip across the Channel? You and I together? You could hold my hand.'

Sophie glanced down. It would be so easy to allow herself to slip a bit more under his spell. She gave her head a shake and tried to remember all the reasons why he was not a good prospect for marriage. 'Liverpool and the theatre in late March is where we met. Stop trying to cloud the issue with talks of voyages which will never happen. I want to save my reputation, not throw it away by giving in to the determined seduction of a man like you.'

'Relax.' His breath caressed her ear. 'You see, everything is sorted. You don't have to worry about a thing. All you have to do is to enjoy the waltz. Nothing will happen on a dance floor. I gave you my promise.'

His hand firmly pressed against her back and she became more aware than ever of the way he moved.

It was only a dance, but Sophie could feel her self-control ebbing away. With each step, she seemed to be more encased in a dream bubble of romance which she wanted desperately to believe in.

It wasn't real. She had made a mistake like this before, confusing the excitement of being noticed by someone who was older and more experienced than she was with real romance. She knew she wanted her romance real and true, like Robert and Henri shared, something which had grown over time rather than hitting her suddenly. What she felt for Richard Crawford was far too sudden to be real and substantial. It was another illusion and this time she refused to be taken in.

Sophie concentrated on taking another step, rather than looking him in the face. She had to hope that his scheme worked quickly, otherwise Sophie knew all of her resolutions would be for nothing—she'd start believing in the romance. And she knew precisely where that led—straight to her barricading herself in a room at some rundown coaching inn.

What was worse, this time, this time there would be no expectation of marriage. It would only be an affair as she had refused his proper offer of marriage and he would never ask her again. On that point, she knew he'd keep his word.

Chapter Five

The cool night air bathed Sophie's flushed face as she stood out on one of the little balconies which fronted the Assembly Rooms' first floor. After the waltz finished, Richard had abandoned her in search of refreshment, but Sophie knew everyone had seen their little display of being besotted with each other.

The trouble was she knew that she could not keep it up. It would be far too easy to slip into the habit of dancing with him and being held far too closely. Her body still thrummed with awareness of how he'd placed his hand on the small of her back and how his fingers had curled about hers.

Richard Crawford was precisely the sort of man she could easily lose her heart to, but he had one fatal flaw—he was *unsafe in carriages* and she'd be wrong to forget that. She recited the vows she had made in that inn bedroom; only they seemed to be of little substance.

Sophie pressed her hand to her forehead. When he left her, Richard whispered in her ear that they would dance a polka later. And every fibre of her being looked forward to it. It was wrong of her. This was a temporary arrangement, not something that was going to last the rest of her life.

A marriage needed to be more than physical desire. Sophie firmed her mouth. She'd been right to refuse his reluctant proposal. She wanted a steady love borne of friendship, rather than will-o'-the-wisp desire masquerading as something more.

'Enjoying making a spectacle of yourself?' The overly oily voice grated over her nerves and the stench of Madagascar hair oil washed over her. Sir Vincent had discovered her refuge.

Sophie counted to ten and composed her features before she turned. She wished Richard had confided his plan to expose Sir Vincent, but he hadn't. The next few minutes were up to her. Richard would simply have to go along with whatever happened. 'Sir Vincent. Imagine encountering you here. I had not thought to see you again so soon.'

'Lord Bingfield won't marry you. You are simply making my job easier. I wonder where your recklessness will next take you. It is amazing that you have enjoyed such a spotless reputation until now.'

Sophie deliberately widened her eyes and adopted her best naïve débutante voice. 'Why wouldn't Lord Bingfield marry me? He has offered to protect me.'

'He is not the marrying sort.' Sir Vincent shook his ponderous head. 'Other ladies have deluded themselves in the past and been terribly disappointed. Can you risk being more exposed in the press? They are already highly intrigued by you. I do hope you have no secrets in your past.'

'Did you supply today's item of tittle-tattle?'

He gave a slight cough and adopted a pious expression. 'People will speculate and I was unable to resist confirming what I knew. Unlike some, the press trust me.'

Sophie rolled her eyes heavenwards and struggled to keep her temper. 'Will the press speculate? That does surprise me no end. Gossip is endemic in Newcastle and always has been, Sir Vincent. It is such a shame when it proves to be false or people spread malicious rumours. It is amazing how quickly the gutter press can turn on one of their trusted sources.'

'Your friend's parents inform me that their daughter was caught on the road to Edinburgh and they hope hourly for her safe return.' He blew on his nails. 'But I have gone against the idea. Who wants an unwilling bride? Perhaps one of their other daughters will suit.'

Sophie gulped hard. 'You mean to have one of Cynthia's sisters?'

'Yes, one of them might be suitable as Lady Putney. There again, they all might bear the taint of their eldest sister's conduct. What a pity you assisted in ruining another person's life. Possibly several young persons' lives. You must seriously reflect on your behaviour, Miss Ravel. Someone must stop you before you ruin anyone else's life.'

Sophie's stomach clenched. It was a deliberate lie. She had received Cynthia's postcard in the second post. The couple had made it to Carlisle without mishap. She would not put it past Mr Johnson to offer one of his other daughters, but she doubted that he would enforce it, not after Cynthia had made her dramatic bid for freedom. Mr and Mrs Johnson did love their children.

'Do you enjoy theatricals, Sir Vincent?' Sophie asked, making sure her voice flowed like honey. Her insides churned, but she refused to give way to panic. Somewhere in that crowded ballroom was Richard Crawford and he had behaved perfectly correctly. He refused to be used by this man. The thought gave her confidence. 'Plays and the like?'

'Not overly.' He gave a smug smile. 'Sometimes the actresses are worth watching, but I only go to the theatre to be seen. The true spectacle happens in the stalls.'

'A pity. You would have made the exact prototype of a pantomime villain.' Sophie clenched her fan tighter and sought to control her temper. This time she would walk away and not lose her head or panic. She would find Richard and demand they carry their engagement a step further—only an announcement in the papers would end the speculation.

Even Sir Vincent in his arrogance must know where that particular line of polite society was drawn. Sophie's head spun. That was it. She had to find a way of getting him to cross that line in full view of everyone. Expose him and his pathetic attempts at blackmail. And she had to do it now.

Behind Sir Vincent, she could see the crowds of people standing on the edge of the ballroom.

A few steps into the room and this conversation would be overheard. Sophie's stomach clenched. She didn't have time to wait for Richard to appear. Long ago, she'd given up on any errant knights coming to her rescue. She would have to execute the entire operation herself.

Sophie judged the distance. Too much in the open

and he'd never react. Too far into the balcony and no one would hear or react. It had to be just right. Without giving herself time to think, she edged towards the ballroom.

'You dare to insult me!' Sir Vincent took a step towards her, blocking her exit and obviously intent on forcing her more fully on to the balcony.

'Why would I do that?' Sophie's mind raced and she attempted to remember the way he had lost his temper last night. She ducked under his arm. 'Could it be because you are a pompous fool? Why would anyone in their right mind wish to be married to someone like you? I know Cynthia's younger sisters and they feel exactly the same way about you. They think you a pompous braying fool.'

She was out from behind the curtain now. The ballroom teemed with people and music. Everyone had their back to her and her personal duel with Sir Vincent.

Richard was nowhere to be seen. She was truly on her own. Silently she prayed that she had done enough. Her heart thudded in her ears.

'No one calls me that!' Sir Vincent parted the curtain and emerged red-faced and spitting with anger.

'I just have! Now I must bid you adieu, Sir Vincent.' She made a curtsy which bordered on the insulting. 'Pray remember I am not some snivelling scullery maid or a naïve débutante. I do have friends, so stay out of my way. Do not attempt to blacken my name again!'

He reached out and grabbed her arm. 'We are finished when I say we are.'

'Unhand me!'

'Not until we have finished our discussion.' He started to drag her back towards the balcony.

'Someone help me. Please.'

A fist connected with Sir Vincent's jaw and he staggered backwards against the heavy curtain and fell down. The curtain tumbled with a loud thud and rip which resounded through the room.

'You have insulted Miss Ravel for the last time, Putney.' Richard's voice held none of its usual warmth.

He had arrived! Precisely at the right moment. Sophie's heart did a little flip.

Richard towered over Sir Vincent. 'When a lady asks you to let go, you do so. I demand an apology!'

'What right do you have to intervene?' Sir Vincent rose to his feet and adopted a pugilist's stance. 'Hit me again and see if I am slow to respond. Fight like a gentleman, Bingfield.'

Richard's voice held a note of barely controlled fury. 'I claim the right of any gentleman to act when a lady is accosted.'

'We were merely conversing. I demand satisfaction. You have impugned my character for the last time, Bingfield.'

'I can see the marks of your hand on her elbow, Putney. I heard Miss Ravel beg for help. I suspect the vast majority of the gathering heard her plea. What man among you would fail to assist a woman in need? Are you a molester of women, Putney? Is that the reputation you seek to defend?'

Sir Vincent went a violent colour of puce and foam speckled his mouth.

Sophie saw a crowd had gathered around them and

the orchestra had stopped playing. In the silence, she made sure her voice could carry. 'Sir Vincent threatened me and grabbed hold of my arm. He refused to let go. I feared for my person and my reputation. Lord Bingfield rescued me.'

'I couldn't help overhearing the conversation,' an elderly lady piped up. 'That gentleman grabbed hold of the lady in a most unbecoming manner.'

'That's precisely right,' said a well-upholstered man. 'This gentleman acted bravely in rescuing the lady.'

Various other people in the crowd murmured their agreement. Sir Vincent stood there with an increasingly panic-stricken look on his face.

Sophie pointed towards the large double doors on the other side of the ballroom. 'Depart, Sir Vincent, and reflect on your behaviour. It falls far short of what civilised society requires.'

A small round of applause rippled throughout the room.

Sir Vincent glanced over his shoulder and slowly lowered his fists. 'I will remember this, Bingfield.'

Sophie held out her hand to Richard. She started towards the dance floor. 'Shall we go, Lord Bingfield? I fear the incident has quite spoilt my evening and here I was having such an enchanting time. Perhaps another dance with you will restore my mood.'

'Putney's behaviour was not what I would have wished for, not tonight of all nights, but I could hardly allow your plea for help to go unanswered.' A faint smile touched his lips. 'Another waltz will suit admirably, Miss Ravel.'

'He won't marry you, Miss Ravel. You will have only

yourself to blame when it ends in tears,' Sir Vincent called out, halting their progress. 'You should look to your own reputation before you start smearing others. Do you know how many women he has cozened and fooled? How many women he has ruined?'

Richard's entire being stiffened as his hand became a clenched fist. Sophie knew what she had to do to prevent a brawl breaking out. Richard might want to beat him into the ground, but she had a better means of destroying him once and for all.

The moment had come. Silently she thanked his foresight of getting her a ring. Her stomach clenched slightly. Finally the time had come to triumph. She peeled off her glove and raised her hand so the two sapphires twinkled in the candlelight.

'If he has no intention of marrying me, why did Lord Bingfield give me this ring?' Sophie asked, twisting her hand to and fro so everyone could see it. 'And my behaviour this very evening? You must forgive the extravagant display earlier, but how often does a woman accept a proposal from the man of her dreams?'

Sir Vincent spluttered, but no sound came from his throat. The gathered crowd, however, gave a long collective sigh.

She put her hand on Richard's arm and forced her feet to move away from the scene where Sir Vincent was now surrounded by various people intent on getting their penny's worth in before he was hustled out of the ballroom. It would appear he was not as well liked or thought of as he'd boasted.

A great crowd of people surrounded them, blocking Sophie's view. The men wrung Richard's hand, offering congratulations, while the women all wanted to admire the ring. Everyone said how delighted they were with the outcome. One or two of the ladies confessed that it was the most romantic thing they had ever seen and wasn't Lord Bingfield the epitome of a hero. Sophie found it harder and harder to mouth the words about how much in love they were and how sudden and totally thrilling it was.

Her head started to spin and she gave a helpless look at Richard. He appeared to understand instantly and ushered her away to a small antechamber, the very model of a solicitous fiancé. Her heart did a queer leap as her body instantly responded to his touch and she knew her cheeks flamed worse than before.

Once they were away from the crowds, he removed his hand. Sophie sank down on a chair and waved her fan frantically, hoping Richard would think it was speaking to all the well-wishers, rather than his touch, which had caused her high colour. The cool breeze did much to restore her equilibrium.

'My knees threatened to give way out there. The number of people who wanted to congratulate us was simply astonishing. I didn't anticipate there would have been so many interested in my ring. The news of our betrothal seems to have spread like wildfire. The re-doubtable Miss Ravel has captured the Rake.'

He stood with his back to her, making it impossible for her to tell his true feelings. 'Interesting and dramatic tittle-tattle has a way of doing that. Particularly when you announced things in the way you did.'

'I've recovered from my faint,' Sophie said firmly. She refused to apologise for her actions. Surely Richard had to see they were positively inspirational. 'The crush overwhelmed me. So many people demanded to see my ring that I struggled to breathe.'

'Your timing was impeccable both in leaving the crowd and earlier when we left Putney,' he said, turning around to look at her. His eyes glowed with a sort of admiration. 'Well played, Miss Ravel. Very well played indeed.'

'Yes, I was rather proud of the way I handled Sir Vincent, particularly the final flourish.' Sophie leant forwards. 'I simply had not accounted for how many people were listening in.'

A smile tugged at the corner of his mouth. 'I quite like the thought of being someone's dream, although it gives me a lot to live up to.'

Sophie primly folded her hands in her lap. Perhaps her word choice had been extravagant, but it had utterly crushed Sir Vincent.

'A figure of speech, that is all,' she said, meeting his gaze full on. 'I never thought you would hit Sir Vincent.'

'I saw the opportunity and seized it. The punch was long overdue.'

Sophie pressed her lips together. She had to remember that Richard had his own reasons for wanting to hit Sir Vincent. It had nothing to do with her and her troubles, but what had passed between the pair years ago. He had no finer feelings for her. She was simply the means to the end of exacting revenge on Sir Vincent. Because he had made a vow. She was a duty rather than a pleasure.

Drawing a steadying breath, she stood. It was imperative to keep her wits about her and not to start believing in the romantic fantasy she had spun for various female acquaintances in the crowd of well-wishers. She knew precisely the sort of man Richard Crawford was and she'd be a fool to forget it.

'My father used to say that opportunities are to be used, rather than lamented about later. You make your luck. Thankfully everything went the way I hoped. Sir Vincent is utterly destroyed.'

'With a little assistance from me.'

She smiled up at him. 'Some very welcome assistance. I couldn't have done it without you. Cynthia's parents will hear of tonight's events. They may not be so quick to offer one of their daughters up as Sir Vincent predicted. A fantastic victory.'

'Do you play croquet?'

'On occasion.' She tilted her head and regarded his features. 'It is the latest craze. We brought a set back from the Great Exhibition. I spent last summer in Corbridge perfecting my technique. I used to play cricket and was quite handy with the bat. It felt good to be hitting a ball again.'

'I suspect you give no mercy to your opponents.'

'I enjoy winning, but I don't grind my opponents in the ground like some.'

'We must play some time.'

'It might be a pleasant way to pass the time.' Sophie hesitated. The time had come to end their fake engagement and put temptation beyond reach. 'I must warn you, Lord Bingfield, that what I said last night remains true. I have no intention of giving up my reputation, even for a man like yourself who did save me. I fear we must soon part.'

His finely chiselled features frowned. 'Do you wish to go home?'

'Now that tonight's performance has ended?' Sophie stopped and replaced her glove, covering up her ring. She had only worn the ring for a short while, but she would be sorry to give it back.

'I am at your disposal.' He inclined his head. 'Most women would be overwhelmed by what just occurred. No one will remark when we leave.'

Sophie froze, considering. Did he mean that he wanted her to stay or that he thought a woman of delicate sensibilities would have to leave the ball immediately? Her backbone was made of far sterner stuff, but she could see how leaving would make matters easier. 'Before you hit him, Sir Vincent as good as admitted to me that it was he who had informed the papers. I doubt he will try that again. Should he attempt to ruin me, I can point to tonight's events as a reason why his poison should not be believed. Our engagement is finished. I can leave on my own if you wish to stay.'

She waited for his agreement. His frown increased.

'Your actions do mean we are tied to each other for a while longer.' A tiny smile played on his lips. 'Becoming engaged to your dream man meant you forgot your sensibilities. Your words, not mine. Consider what will happen if you jilt me tomorrow. Consider what the press will say then. Will you be known as a flighty heiress?'

Sophie gulped. She could see the headline now. 'They were a figure of speech, an added flourish.'

'Added little flourishes can have grave consequences, Miss Ravel. Perhaps you should think before you act.'

She bowed her head, acknowledging the truth in his

words. 'I can hardly jilt you tonight or any time soon. I shall have to wait until the furore dies down.'

'It may take weeks or even months.' His eyes glittered amber. 'The episode has ensured that the engagement will be on everyone's lips tomorrow morning. Various members of the gutter press were in the crowd. Our engagement will be the lead item in the gossip columns throughout the land. "The Redoubtable captures the Rake" has a certain resonance. Prior to your intervention, I had thought "Lord exposes caddish behaviour" or, better still, "blackmailer".'

Sophie winced. He had exposed a fatal flaw in her actions and had stated very clearly that he could not wait to be rid of her. Only now they were shackled together. Her doing, not his. All of his actions had been designed to take revenge on Putney and he had nearly succeeded in provoking a duel. Now, she had inadvertently prolonged the time they had to spend together.

'It was the killing blow. I could not be certain your scheme would work,' she argued.

'You failed to think. Emotion carried you.' He looked down at her. 'It carries you still. Luckily, I still possess my faculties. We will have to spend more time in each other's company, pretending that our engagement is one of the great love stories, or we shall be exposed as cheats.'

Sophie put her hand on her stomach and tried to stop her insides roiling. She would have to dance with him again. She would have to pretend to be besotted. And there would be no expectation of marriage if she gave in to his charm. 'I would like to return home now. Will you please find my stepmother and make the necessary arrangements? We can discuss how long our engagement must continue at a later date. My head pains me too much to think straight.'

Richard struggled to control his temper as the carriage stopped outside Miss Ravel's house. There were things which needed to be said between Sophie and him, but Mrs Ravel sat squarely between them. Mrs Ravel kept up a steady stream of conversation, seemingly oblivious to the stony silence from Sophie.

It was far from his fault that the engagement had been announced in the way it was. That was entirely her doing. There again, it had prevented him from beating Putney into a bloody pulp.

The sight of Putney's hand restraining Sophie had filled him with a primitive anger. He had wanted to murder him for daring to even look at Sophie, let alone touch her in that fashion. His actions had nothing to do with the past and everything to do with Sophie.

'There is no need to see us in, Lord Bingfield,' Sophie said, alighting from the carriage before he had a chance to hold out his hand and help her down.

'There is every need,' Richard retorted silkily, managing to swallow his annoyance. Despite her public declaration, in private, Sophie made it all too clear how she felt about him. 'I could hardly allow my fiancée or her stepmother to make their way home without being there to ensure their safety.'

What made it worse was that he had to accept all the congratulations, knowing that the woman beside him could not wait to be rid of him.

He had never considered that he was like his father

and would lose his reason over a woman, but now it seemed he had. His feelings tonight made a mockery of his proposal. No finer feelings. He definitely wanted to hold Sophie in his arms again and feel her lips tremble under his. He wanted to unlock the passion he glimpsed again tonight when they had waltzed.

Sophie pointed. 'We can easily make it to our door, Lord Bingfield. You can see the door from where you are standing.'

'Sophie!' Mrs Ravel exclaimed. 'Where are your manners tonight? First you insist on leaving before I finish my hand at whist and now you seek to dismiss your fiancé like a lackey.'

'The upset at the Assembly Rooms has quite turned my brain.' Sophie inclined her head. 'I merely meant Lord Bingfield did not need to feel obliged. He has done so much for us tonight. It would be wrong for us to presume further. I didn't want to put him to any trouble.'

'I am sure it is no trouble, Sophie. Is it, Lord Bingfield?'

Richard silently blessed Mrs Ravel. Sophie's earlier caution in confiding in her stepmother had resulted in him gaining a valuable ally, one which he intended to exploit fully. Everything was fair in this battle between him and Sophie's fears. He intended to win and unlock her passion. He wanted to see what she'd be like when she forgot herself.

He could not remember when a woman had intrigued him as much. She made him forget about his family and his reasons for being in Newcastle.

'It is not an obligation, but a pleasure,' Richard added smoothly.

Mrs Ravel shook her head. 'I do wonder about young people these days. Not an ounce of romance in their soul. You two may say your goodnights in the drawing room. I am quite weary and will take myself off to bed. I do trust you, Sophie. Lord Bingfield, if Sophie failed to inform you—tomorrow and every Thursday is our At Home.'

'I am grateful for the intelligence, Mrs Ravel.' Richard gave Sophie a hard look. If she thought she'd get rid of him that easily, she had another think coming. He intended to exploit the situation to his advantage and see what the woman Sophie tried to hide was like. 'Sophie and I obviously have had other things on our minds. I'll make a note of it, but I can't make any promises.'

Sophie marched ahead of him into the drawing room, her skirt slightly swaying to reveal her slender ankles. She stopped to turn up the gas lamps, bathing the room in a soft light before facing him with her arms crossed and blue eyes glowing like star sapphires.

'What was that little demonstration with my stepmother in aid of? A goodnight in the carriage would have sufficed.'

Richard assessed her with half-closed eyes. She was attracted to him and he would get her to admit it. Tonight. 'You haven't informed your stepmother of our arrangement. I would hardly wish for her to think ill of me. It would be impolite to miss an At Home simply for lack of knowledge. It might cause speculation. I believe there has been more than enough speculation and gossip recently. If you are not careful, people will begin to look at your waistline.'

She flushed scarlet. 'That…that is an impossibility.'

'You were the one who uttered the words about our impulsive marriage, not I. Women who have found their dream man often forget their sensibilities.'

She gave a decisive nod and removed her gloves. 'My stepmother has gone upstairs. There is no need for you to linger. Or indeed for you to appear at the At Home at all. We can slowly drift away. It will provide an excuse for me jilting you. Ultimately you can forget some important function. Isn't that what men like you do? Selfishly put their own needs above others?'

Her words stung. Women had flung the words at him before, but generally when he ended the association.

He recalled the gossip of the Northern Counties Club about her icy behaviour. Was it him or all men? He clenched his fist and wanted to murder whichever man had sown the seeds of distrust.

'There is every need,' he said smoothly, plucking a stray thread from her shoulder. 'Your stepmother said your next At Home was tomorrow. For your sake, I need to be there.'

Sophie slapped her gloves against her hand. 'What is your prediction for my stepmother's At Home? They are not very well attended. The great and the good often have other calls to make.'

'It will be full to bursting with well-wishers, people who have grudges and simply the curious, all wanting to know about the great romance and when our next appearance as a couple will be. The polite ones will only stay fifteen minutes, hoping to see us together in their allotted time, but the curious will find an excuse to linger and see if your unknown bridegroom-to-be puts in an appearance or if it was all fustian nonsense.'

A faint line appeared between Sophie's perfect brows and the tapping stopped as she considered his words. 'I sincerely doubt it. True, people will speculate of course. I will concede your point—in light of tonight's events the At Home will be more crowded than usual. I will have the footmen put out extra chairs. But no one will want to meet you or send invitations for the both of us.'

'I shall rearrange my plans.' He paused, watching her digest the news. 'My friends will understand why I have decided to linger in Newcastle for an indefinite period. There was an expectation I would attend a house party in Hampshire next week.'

There was no need to tell Sophie that he had written declining the invitation, before he went to see her this morning and proposed marriage. The woman who had invited him had expected him to continue to grace her bed. After meeting Sophie, such sport with another woman held no attraction.

He simply refused to allow Sophie to have a hold over him. This wasn't about love or romance, but satisfying his curiosity. When it was over, he'd walk away with his heart intact and the knowledge that he'd solved the puzzle of Sophie.

'I've no wish to interrupt your plans and be a bother,' she said, turning towards the fire. 'You were right earlier when you said I didn't think. You must go if that is what you wish to do. If invitations do come, the disappointment of you not attending will make it easier to explain the breach when it comes.'

'If we have a breach too quickly, Putney's words will be remembered,' he reminded her. 'I did make a vow that I would not be used as an instrument of your downfall. With each new scheme you propose, you make it easier for him. I am the one with experience. You are a novice.'

She covered her mouth. 'I hadn't considered…'

'Next time do. It is not just your reputation at stake here, but mine—'

'Won't the woman mind?'

He shrugged. 'I was looking for an excuse to end it. The affair was pleasant while it lasted, but she had begun to bore me. I dislike being bored.'

Her cheeks coloured at the remark. 'I…I hadn't thought. I know very little about such matters.'

His shoulders relaxed. Sophie was truly innocent and unlike his normal sort of woman. In her company, he'd been exasperated, amused, bemused, but never bored.

'I gave you my word that I would not pursue another woman while we are together,' he said. 'When I am interested in a woman, my interest stays on her. When it is finished, it is done, with no regrets or backward glances on my part. But I always inform the woman first.'

He clamped his mouth shut. He never allowed regrets. Leaving was far better than being left. And he knew while there might be a few tears, it was always hurt pride, rather than actual feelings. Since Mary, he'd never permitted himself to fall for an inexperienced woman.

She dipped her head and did not meet his eyes. 'Other people have. The woman can be the last to know.'

Silently he once more cursed the man who had made her so wary. He wanted to run him through for causing Sophie to doubt her charms and power. And an unexpected surge of jealousy went through him. She should not be comparing him to such a cad.

He went over to her and raised her chin so that she was staring directly into his face. She did not pull away.

'I am not other men, Sophie Ravel,' he said in a soft voice. 'Why should I want to pursue other women when the world thinks I am engaged to you?'

'Because…' Her tongue flicked out, moistening her lips and turning them to the colour of ripe cherries. 'Because we are not truly engaged.'

'I would hardly dishonour any fiancée in that way, particularly not one I'd sworn to protect. Whatever you might think of me, know I keep my promises.'

Giving in to temptation, he bent his head and tasted her lips.

This time, they trembled under his and parted slightly, inviting him to prolong the kiss. Before deepening the kiss, he brought his arms about her, pulling her close so that her body collided with his, just as he had longed to do ever since they had waltzed together. It fitted perfectly—her curves meeting his hard planes in exactly the right places. She melted further, opening her mouth wide so that he delved his tongue in. He tasted. There was something so right about her taste, something that had been missing from his life. He hadn't known he needed it until that instant and the longing frightened him.

With the last vestige of self-control, he raised his head and put her from him. He drew a ragged breath and resisted the overwhelming urge to take one more taste.

She looked up at him with uncomprehending eyes as her chest heaved. And he knew what he was destined to dream about tonight—Sophie naked in his arms. This was desire and nothing more. His shoulders relaxed. He understood desire.

Once he'd solved the puzzle of her, it would fade. He touched her cheek, enjoying its petal softness.

She looped a strand of hair about one shell-like ear, making a pretence of icy fortitude. 'What…what was that about?'

'There, that is how I say goodnight to my fiancée.' He inclined his head. 'Remember that the next time you wish to make an accusation about my habits, or believe yourself unworthy. You are my fiancée and I refuse to expose you to ridicule.'

Chapter Six

The last place Sophie wanted to be was at her step-mother's At Home. Crowded At Homes generally made her feel as though she was some exotic beast on show for the masses and this week was worse than usual.

She had lost track of the number of people who just happened to call, most with congratulations about the engagement. And those who had not bothered to read today's editions were soon apprised of the fact by others in the room. As she had predicted, 'The Redoubtable captures the Rake' was the lead item.

Everyone wanted to meet the prospective bridegroom and hear the thrilling tale of a whirlwind romance which had turned into the engagement of the Season, if not the year!

Richard had been right. Their engagement was now an established fact. She couldn't cancel it without seeming flighty or, worse still, a liar. She was well and truly trapped in a scheme of her own making. Worse, he had not put in an appearance.

She found herself watching the door and the clock,

but the minutes were slipping by. The At Home would end without an appearance from him.

She wanted to run and hide and not face the humiliation of his non-show, but she felt guilty for even thinking of the idea. A Ravel always met her social obligations. The fact had been drilled into her at a young age when she'd hidden behind a curtain rather than meet one of her father's business associates. So she smiled and asked after various children and elderly relatives and hoped no one else noticed that Richard wasn't there and she had declined to give a time or date for the engagement party which her stepmother loudly proclaimed would be happening soon.

Sophie forcibly turned her gaze from the front door, tilted her head and graciously enquired after a neighbour's son who was cutting his first tooth. If she concentrated on other people, then maybe she'd forget the deepening hole inside and all the doubts and what ifs.

'Lady Parthenope will be arriving momentarily,' her stepmother's latest butler declared in an overly theatrical fashion. 'Her carriage has been spotted.'

Her stepmother went red with pleasure. Sophie excused herself and hurried over to her stepmother, putting her hand on her stepmother's sleeve. 'Is there some reason that Lady Parthenope has come to call? I wasn't aware you are intimates.'

'I sent her a note, dear, after you refused to allow me to go to her tea,' her stepmother explained with the sort of smile which could light up a thousand ballrooms. 'It seemed the right thing to do. She is dear Bingfield's only female relation in the neighbourhood. I wanted her advice on the engagement party. I do hope she gives me a moment to compose myself before she finally appears. I declared I'm all at sixes and sevens. It is worse than waiting for the Queen.'

'Her advice on the engagement party?' Sophie put her hand on her stepmother's sleeve. Composing herself for Lady Parthenope would have to wait. She needed to know precisely the full horror of what her stepmother had done.

'It needs to be an event of glittering magnitude. There again, perhaps the aristocracy do things differently. I do want to be guided, my dear, and Henri is away in Europe. People have expectations.'

'You have written to Henri!' Sophie's heart sank. She had hoped to present the entire episode as an amusing anecdote when Henri and Robert returned with their two young children, but her stepmother had closed that door.

'I thought she'd want to know.' Mrs Ravel peered around her and motioned to the footman to move several tables and chairs. 'I do think it bad of Lord Bingfield not to call. I had wanted a chance to quiz him about it as well. After all, it will be his engagement party, too.'

'You sent Lord Bingfield a note about the party?' The complete horror of what her stepmother had done penetrated Sophie's brain. Any engagement party would make things worse. They would have to be there as a couple in love. She might even start depending on him to be there. But she had no idea of how to stop it. Her stepmother's juggernaut would flatten everything in its path.

'First thing this morning while you were showing your new maid your clothes. Is there any reason

I shouldn't? Sophie, have you entirely forgotten your manners?' Her stepmother waved a hand. 'And invitations have been arriving all morning along with an unsigned postcard from Liverpool. You and Lord Bingfield will be much in demand, I am happy to say, but where is he? It is most vexing.'

'Lord Bingfield will call when he has the time.' Sophie concentrated on the teacup. Cynthia arriving in Liverpool was the best news she had had all day. She had to remember that Cynthia's love was true. She and her intended had known each other for months before they eloped. Sophie knew she had to hang on to the thought, rather than dreaming about Richard and his goodnight kiss. Desire did not make a love match. Desire did not mean she actually liked him. *It didn't mean she disliked him, either*, a little voice whispered.

She narrowed her eyes. 'How many others did you happen to ask for advice about this engagement party?'

Her stepmother counted on her fingers. 'Fourteen, maybe seventeen. It depends on who you count. Miss Smith and her sister were visiting Mrs Butterworth when I happened to mention the engagement yesterday. They were the ones who suggested a party. It is not as if I am spreading lies, Sophie. You are going to marry Viscount Bingfield and will eventually be a marchioness.'

'An engagement has been agreed,' Sophie corrected. 'There is a difference. You know how many engagements were broken last year.'

'Hornswoggle. Last night anyone with half an eye could see how entranced you were with each other when you waltzed. And then your declaration after Lord Bingfield punched that dreadful toad Sir Vincent Putney. It made my heart thrill. Romance truly does live. Your father would be fit to burst.'

'You shouldn't have done it, Stepmother, without consulting me.'

'Mrs Butterworth was overly proud last year when her eldest daughter married a baronet. You being married to a viscount will be just the sort of setdown she needs. You will take precedence. My stepdaughter, one of the higher-ranking peers, just as your father always dreamt.'

'But I would have preferred to have been consulted about this party first. You have no idea whether Lord Bingfield wants a party or not.'

'It is why I want to speak to him.' Her stepmother patted Sophie's hand. 'People always speculate. In any case, most of the people here I didn't mention the party to, but everyone is asking about it.'

'I wonder why that is.'

'It will have to be a glittering affair. Your father did love a good party. Imagine if Lord Hallington attended. A living marquess in this house!'

'We haven't agreed on the settlement yet.' Sophie lifted her cup to her lips. This entire affair seemed to have taken a life of its own. She had to begin to sow seeds of doubt or her stepmother would take to her bed for weeks when Richard and she broke it off. And what better place with all these people attending the At Home? Sophie raised her voice slightly. 'I shouldn't have even shown my ring last night. It was wrong of me. Premature. My father would be appalled at my lack of prudence. Perhaps Robert Montemorcy, my former guardian, should be consulted before this goes further.'

Sophie glanced about the room which was now filled with an expectant hush, awaiting Lady Parthenope's arrival. Seed sown, her job was done.

Her stepmother gave a little frown. 'I suppose you are right. I will put the party off until later in the year.'

'Once it has been announced officially, then we can plan the party, properly with Henri. You know what an expert she is with such things.' Sophie nodded towards the door. 'You must go greet Lady Parthenope. It would not do to keep her ladyship waiting.'

Her stepmother's ribbons trembled. 'What shall I say to her?'

'Hello?' Sophie offered with a faint laugh, but her stepmother's agitation only increased.

Lady Parthenope swept into the room and nearly knocked over a table of china pugs as the entire room fell silent and teacups were poised halfway to the lips. Sophie watched fascinated as her stepmother warred with two emotions—the desire to protect her china collection and the pride that so illustrious a personage should visit her house. In the end, pride won out. She hurriedly waved towards the china-dog table, which the butler moved without saying a word, and the background of a busy At Home recommenced.

'I shan't beat about the bush,' Lady Parthenope said after she had greeted her stepmother. 'Is it true you intend to give a party to celebrate your engagement to my nephew? I would have thought informing a family circle would be the first order of business before you announced to all and sundry, but what do I know about young people these days? The manners are all so different from when I was young after the war. Then things were done in a certain fashion or not at all.'

'It is something you will need to consult with your nephew about—why he asked before getting your permission to marry,' Sophie replied and was pleased the words came out far more assured than she felt inside. 'I would hardly like to break a confidence. You must understand that, Lady Parthenope, and these matters, much as we hope otherwise, are often fraught with inner peril. My stepmother is perhaps over-eager with the plans for a party, but they are far from well advanced.'

'Humph,' Lady Parthenope said with a glacial frown. She turned and began to greet the other women, asking after various relations or mutual acquaintances.

Sophie noted with no small amount of admiration that the woman appeared to know how to greet everyone graciously. She had to wonder if Lady Parthenope had always been like this or if she had ever hidden behind a curtain. No, she decided, Lady Parthenope belonged to that special breed of woman who was always sure in any social situation.

'I see you wasted no time, Aunt, in making your acquaintance with my intended's family,' Lord Bingfield said as he came into the room. His frock-coat was immaculate and he seemed to fill the drawing room. She noticed the way his hair curled about his temple and how the cut of his coat showed off his hips. Their eyes locked and a slow smile spread over his face.

Realising she was staring, Sophie hurriedly set down her teacup, managing to slosh the liquid on to her hand. Painfully obvious. The sudden heat jolted her back to reality. She winced, knowing her cheeks must be flushed. She was behaving worse than some débutante who was only a few weeks into her first Season. She was a veteran of four and knew better than to respond to men like Lord Bingfield. She had made so many mistakes in their short acquaintance.

'Someone had to, dear boy. Your father is hardly likely to travel to the north. And the less said about your mother's side of the family, the better, in my opinion,' Lady Parthenope pronounced.

'Finally you appear, Lord Bingfield. Sophie has been counting the minutes,' her stepmother cooed, much to Sophie's surprise and annoyance.

Her stepmother made it sound as though she had nothing better to do than to moon over him. Things were problematic enough with Lord Bingfield getting ideas about how she might feel about him. Her stepmother's triumphant look did nothing to calm Sophie's nerves.

'My pleasure, Mrs Ravel.' He bowed low over her stepmother's hand. 'I regret the slight delay, but what does that matter as I am here now? I am at your disposal, Mrs Ravel. Who would you like me to meet first? Your friends all appear charming and I don't want to get the order of precedence wrong.'

His smile spread over the entire gathering. Her normally poised stepmother turned a shade of red, highly akin to beetroot, while a gaggle of her stepmother's friends gave barely concealed sighs. His voice was the sort that warmed your toes, oozing superficial charm.

Sophie frowned and concentrated on the alabaster vase containing a bouquet of wax flowers. She'd be wrong to forget that it was superficial, pretty to look at but having no real substances, and the fact that this was all an act. She knew precisely what happened when the charm faded and the rake in question was turned down.

Her temple throbbed slightly. She refused to go back to that inn. She had ceased to be that carefree girl years ago. Real and honest love took months, if not years, to develop and he had been quite honest about not having finer feelings for her. She was not going to believe in the romance of it all. She had to be the practical one and search for other opportunities to sow seeds of doubt, so that when the end came, it would not cause her step-mother to take to her bed for weeks.

Richard accepted a cup of tea from her stepmother and came over to her. Her nerves pulsed with warmth. She found it impossible to forget the way his mouth had tasted when he'd kissed her last night.

She concentrated on the spill and tried to think of something else beside him and the way his shoulders filled out his frock-coat.

'Do you need a handkerchief, Miss Ravel?'

His heady scent of balsam mixed with a subtle spice wafted over her, tickling her nose. And she inhaled deeply, savouring it, but then recollected where she was, sat up straighter and fixed him with her eye.

'Everything is under control. I knocked the cup a little. I am fully capable of cleaning up my own messes.'

'I would hate to think anything untoward happened to your delicate flesh.' He came over and took her hand. His brow furrowed as his palm brushed her ring finger before releasing it. A subtle caress. 'You are wearing the ring.'

Sophie fought against the temptation to flee. He knew precisely what he was doing. He had played this sort of *double entendre* game with countless other females. It would be wrong of her to think otherwise. 'I felt it best. Everyone wanted to see it. Even if it is tempting fate to wear it.'

'Fate?' A dimple played in the corner of his mouth, reminding her that her dreams had been full of that mouth and the way it tasted.

'Nothing has been settled until certain agreements have been reached,' she said decisively, banishing the thought.

He raised her hand to his lips. The tiniest touch, but enough to make her stomach flutter and the heat rise on her cheeks. She tried to tell herself that every woman had that sort of reaction to him, but it didn't make it any easier.

'It will be settled to our mutual benefit,' he said, releasing her hand. 'You have my word on that. From now on wear it with pride and stop worrying.'

The room chose that moment to fall silent. Sophie winced and knew the colour in her cheeks flamed higher.

'You see, Sophie,' her stepmother crowed. 'What did I say! Settlements can be easily achieved when a couple is in love.'

'I apologise.' Sophie gestured about the room. 'It was quite unnecessary of you to call.'

'We must disagree. It was completely necessary. I gave my word.' He inclined his head. 'If you would manipulate public opinion, Miss Ravel, the public do have to have something to talk about. It is far better that they discuss our engagement, rather than anything else about either of us.'

'You make it sound like you are an expert.'

His eyes glinted like hard glass. 'I had to learn. You were the one who increased the stakes.'

'I will remember it for the next time and bow to your expertise.'

'You may run along, then,' he said, touching her sleeve. 'I still have to greet a variety of other ladies, but my duties here must be short.'

'And do what?' Sophie put her hand on her hip. How dare he order her about! 'The At Home is in its dying throes. I suspect once this lot have finished, we will not get any more callers. My stepmother has the tea and coffee under control.'

'Grab your hat and cloak, of course. Unless you wish to have more gossip in the papers. I have a new pair of horses and a carriage up from Tattersalls. I want to put them through their paces in the northern air.'

'Do you drive?'

'I leave that to others but I do know the difference between a good carriage horse and an unsuitable one.' A dimple played in the corner of his mouth. 'Unless you are frightened to be seen with me?'

'I welcome it.'

Richard stood in the hallway. He struggled to remember when he'd last enjoyed himself so much. Gently tweaking Sophie Ravel's pretence of cold hauteur so that she was forced to reveal her inner passion was his new favourite sport. He wanted to explore her layers and find out more. He looked forward to it. He could not be sorry that circumstances forced them to spend time with each other.

'Have you written to your father, Richard, informing him of your proposed alliance?' his aunt said, coming into the hallway.

'You are departing so soon, Aunt Parthenope?'

'One stays precisely fifteen minutes. Always. I know the timing exactly. One should never be seen to regard a clock.' His aunt sniffed. 'You are leaving too soon.'

'I will bear that in mind.' Richard pointed towards the drawing room. 'The crush was overly heavy. I'm waiting for Sophie.'

'The girl is perfectly acceptable if one's taste is for icy blondes, but the stepmother...' His aunt lowered her voice. 'Have you seen the décor? Your father would turn puce. Far too much china. Far too much chintz. Her manner is far too fine.'

'Mrs Ravel is a perfectly charming lady. Sophie knows her own mind about decoration and fashion, just as she knows her own mind about me.' Richard forced a smile over a tremor of horror. He did not want to think about his father travelling to Newcastle and the complications that it would bring.

His relationship with Sophie had nothing to do with his family. She belonged to another part of his life, separate and distinct from his duty towards his family.

He had taken the time to move into a well-appointed set of rooms on Granger Street this morning. Luckily, for once, his mother had agreed with his caution, although her reasoning differed from his.

'My father will adore Sophie once he meets her. Does he have plans to travel here?'

'Who knows what your father will do?' His aunt made a disapproving noise. 'He is a law unto himself, but I have every reason to think that he will not set foot in Newcastle. I, myself, have tried to persuade him for years to visit our mother's grave, but he has always refused. His pigs must come before everything. I swear he uses them as an excuse to avoid doing his duty.'

'My father is a man of steadfast devotion to his pigs.'

His aunt fixed him with a stare and he had to wonder if she had guessed his true reason for being up in Newcastle. 'I shall have to write to your father about this fiancée of yours. You understand why it is necessary, I hope. The best that can be said for her stepmother is that she is no conversationalist.'

'You do that. It will not change the outcome, Aunt.' Richard nodded towards the stairs. 'Here comes my intended, Aunt. I would hate to think you had caused her one moment of distress.'

His aunt put her hand over his. 'Any wife of yours should be a credit to our family and its standing. You must not allow love to cloud your judgement.'

'We are agreed on that. Love will never do that.'

Richard went towards Sophie, who looked absolutely fetching in her dark-blue leghorn bonnet and matching cloak, truly a breath of fresh air and peace in his turbulent life.

She did not have any side in his parents' war. He'd learnt a long time ago that explaining about his family only made him feel uncomfortable and awkward rather than contributing anything meaningful. He saw no reason to break the habit with Sophie.

'Where are these horses?' Sophie asked with a pretty smile after his aunt departed.

'Waiting outside. Will you be bringing your maid?' he enquired, wondering how much further he'd push her today. She would melt.

Sophie hesitated, understanding what he was asking. It would be prudent to have someone else there to prevent things getting out of hand, but it would also mean speaking in front of her. She could hardly explain about the party débâcle with someone listening in.

'We are an acknowledged couple.'

He tucked her hand into his arm. 'So I am given to understand. I promise to be on my best behaviour.'

'My maid hasn't been with us very long and she has a pile of mending to do.'

'I understand entirely now. Do you go through servants easily? I only ask because your butler appeared quite new.'

He made it seem as though she was careless. 'My stepmother does demand the best, but normally I keep my maids unless they marry. My last one ran away with the underfootman from two houses down. Jane has only been with us for two weeks.'

'And you have no idea if she is reliable,' he said, handing her into the smart carriage.

'Precisely.' Sophie turned towards him. 'I have no idea if she can be tempted to tell her story to the papers. Such things have been known to happen.'

'With great regularity.' The dimple showed in the corner of his mouth. He stretched slightly and his arm came around the back of the seat. Sophie sat straighter.

He gestured to the coachman, who started off

abruptly and she was jolted back against the seat and his arm, which instantly tightened about her. She gave him a sideways glance, certain he had arranged the incident. His hand squeezed her shoulder, sending a warm pulse through her before he removed it.

'I'm pleased with your foresight,' he said. 'What did you want to speak to me about? What has agitated you? You were positively clinging to that teacup with a death grip.'

Sophie gulped. He had noticed! It made it worse that he'd noticed. She could almost think he cared. She pulled her bonnet forwards so that it covered her face. 'Was I that obvious?'

'Only to me. My aunt takes unholy glee in making people agitated and upset. It provides her chief amusement.' He put his hand over hers and squeezed it. 'You appeared perfectly in control to everyone else, I am sure.'

Sophie swallowed hard and withdrew her hand from his. She concentrated on looking out the carriage window. Every time they met, she found a reason to like him more. He said precisely the right thing to reassure her, but how hard was that? Men like him did these things for one purpose only—seduction.

'I need to apologise for my stepmother and her engagement-party scheme,' she said before she lost her nerve or he developed the wrong idea about why she'd agreed to come without a chaperon. 'She had the idea fixated in her brain. I had no idea she entertained the notion…until it was too late.'

'And you haven't told her the truth.'

'How could I!' Sophie turned slightly and faced him.

He had to understand about her stepmother and her kind heart. 'I planned to say something this morning, but my stepmother was preoccupied with the At Home arrangements. I want to let her down gently, Richard. My stepmother means well. She made this promise to my father on his deathbed…and she sees this as a gold opportunity to fulfil it. My father…my father made his own fortune. He wanted his daughter to live like a princess.'

Richard said nothing for a while and Sophie listened to the wheels of the carriage turning, hating that she'd confessed about her father's naked ambition.

'My aunt has obviously written to my father,' he said when her nerves were at breaking point. 'We will have to instruct our various men of business to begin drawing up the settlement.'

Sophie blinked hard. 'Excuse me?'

'During the At Home, you made some remarks about settlements.'

Sophie fiddled with the lace edge of her glove, rather than meet his eyes. Her posturing at the At Home seemed ill conceived now that he was here, questioning her on it. 'I thought it a kinder way of sowing doubt. I don't want my stepmother to be too disappointed… when it ends.'

He raised an eyebrow and Sophie knew what he had tactfully not said. The only way she could keep her stepmother from being disappointed now was to actually marry him. She wished she had considered her stepmother's reaction before embarking on this adventure.

'You are reluctant to tell your stepmother the truth, particularly in light of her extreme reaction.'

She gave a hesitant nod.

'Then there is only one course of action. You must instruct your man of business straight away. The matter of settlement must be seen to be being addressed. I shall instruct my solicitors.' He named a very well-known London firm. 'My father always uses them. He would think something amiss if I didn't. I will trust you to make the appropriate outrageous demands.'

She stared at him in wonderment. He actually had the perfect solution to the problem, one she'd never ask, assuming he'd reject it out of hand. She swallowed hard and attempted to puzzle out the implications. 'You intend to keep your father in ignorance as well?'

'You would hardly want him replying to your stepmother when she writes to him.' He paused and gave her a hard look. 'And you know your stepmother will… if the letter isn't already in the post. My father is not a man to mince words, Sophie. Neither will he see any reason to lie.'

Sophie closed her eyes. She could readily picture the scene when her stepmother received a terse reply from Richard's father. The blow would destroy her. Utterly and completely. 'It is very kind of you. Unexpectedly kind.'

He raised her hand to his lips. 'I told you that I'd protect you. Why do you harbour so many doubts about my intentions?'

'Because I do.'

Sophie sat up straighter and tried to ignore the way the warmth crept up her arm. Somehow it felt right to have his hand holding hers. And that was very wrong.

No good could come of this carriage ride if she allowed liberties.

'I will instruct my solicitor.' She concentrated on taking steadying breaths as the warm tingling feeling increased. It was in moments like these that a woman was most in danger. If she kept her wits about her, she'd survive. She gave her hand a slight tug, but only succeeded in dislodging her bonnet. 'My old guardian is out of the country with his family and will need to look it over before it is approved, of course. My stepmother will understand the delay. It will buy us time.'

'Who was it?' he enquired softly, not letting her hand go. Instead he put his other arm along the back of the seat, almost as if he held her in his arms.

'Who was who?' Sophie edged towards the carriage door.

He released her and leant forwards to straighten her bonnet. 'Who made you so wary of men? Of me?'

Chapter Seven

'You are talking nonsense. Absolute and complete nonsense.' Sophie searched for her reticule and wished she had thought to bring more than a hatpin with her as Richard's question echoed round and round in her brain. He wanted to know why she was terrified of men. It wasn't all men. It was men who were unsafe in carriages.

The carriage suddenly seemed claustrophobic and tiny, and a complete mistake. How could she have thought for one instant she'd be safe with someone like Richard?

Sophie struggled to breathe. The last thing she wanted was to confess about that dreadful night, particularly here in Richard's carriage. The consequences to her reputation could be dreadful if he realised the sort of person she truly was. All the vile words Sebastian called her on that night echoed in her mind.

What if she was truly like those words? What if it wasn't the man, but her? What if she caused men to be unsafe in carriages?

'I have no idea why you said this! I am not wary of men.'

Richard said nothing in reply. He simply looked at her with a steady expression in his eyes. 'Why, Sophie?'

Suddenly it came to her—the logical answer, the perfect answer. Air rushed into her lungs. There was no need for a confession. He need never know what sort of person she was underneath her cold exterior. Bluster and outrage had always served before. She could turn the conversation to his failings.

'Why shouldn't I exercise caution? Everyone knows about men who are *not safe in carriages* and the untold damage they can wreak on a woman's reputation. She might never recover while the man simply moves on to the next unsuspecting soul.' Sophie stabbed a finger at his chest. 'You, Richard, are most definitely *not safe in carriages*. Had the desire to protect my stepmother's feelings not preyed on my mind, I would have refused. I should have refused. We have settled very little and now I wish to return to my home. Immediately.'

Sophie hated the tremor in her voice and that she wanted him to do something to prove once and for all that he was the sort of man she knew he must be.

'You want to believe the worst in me.' Richard's golden gaze peered into her soul, but he kept completely still. 'What have I done? How have I behaved improperly towards you? All I have done is to try to preserve your reputation, rather than seek to destroy it or entice you into bad behaviour.'

Sophie straightened her shoulders and forced an uneasy laugh. 'You have a certain well-deserved reputation. Your exploits are favourite fodder for the scandal-mongers. There is little smoke without fire, as my father used to say. Oh, you might say it is lies, but how much is half the truth?'

'I have never denied my less-than-angelic past, but it is more than that.' He ticked the points off on his fingers. 'You are skittish. You maintain this façade of icy hauteur because you are terrified of any man paying you attention. When you forget, you are full of feisty wit. Someone made you that way. What was his name? You owe it to me for saving your reputation.'

Sophie's mouth went dry. He had guessed. Richard had seen her for what she was—petrified of becoming what Sebastian Cawburn predicted she was. She should have thought. Crawford had a vast amount of experience with women. He had saved her from Sir Vincent's machinations. She owed him the truth.

'Sebastian Cawburn. Lord Cawburn,' she whispered, staring straight ahead, rather than looking him in the eye.

'That old lecher! You are comparing me to him?'

At the exclamation, Sophie rapidly glanced at him. An expression of extreme hurt flickered across his face so quickly that Sophie wondered if she had imagined it.

'Sophie. We are nothing alike. I can't stand the man.'

'Not comparing, exactly,' Sophie admitted. Her grip on her reticule caused her hand to hurt. She should have guessed Richard Crawford would be acquainted with Sebastian. They travelled in similar circles. 'You both enjoy a certain reputation, to put it bluntly. It terrifies me that I might be attracted to someone like him again. That I am destined to repeat my mistakes.'

She closed her eyes and tried to control the trembling

in her stomach. There, she had finally said the words out loud. Finally admitted her attraction to him and the impossibility of it going any further.

'Sophie, you wound me. I am nothing like that man.' Richard leant forwards and raised his hands in supplication before her. It hurt more than he liked to admit that Sophie equated him with Sebastian Cawburn. He wanted her to see him for who he was, not who she thought he was.

She simply sat there with her eyes closed.

'He cheats at cards,' Richard continued. 'He maintains two mistresses. He had to flee to the Continent to escape his creditors three months ago. I've done none of those things. Nor will I ever do such things. Believe me, please!'

She cautiously opened her eyes.

'I'm sorry. I can't help it. I refuse to repeat my mistakes. I made a solemn vow.'

'When…when did it happen to you? When did you encounter Cawburn? Tell me that much.' He swallowed hard and tried to control his frustration. Shouting at her would make matters worse, but he wanted to know how she'd become mixed up with Cawburn and what he'd done to her. A primitive urge to do violence to the man filled Richard. Somehow, he'd harmed Sophie. 'Help me to understand why you might be comparing us.'

'It was my first Season. I was naïve.' Sophie raised her chin and he could see tears shimmering in her eyes. She clenched her fists before continuing. 'Lord Cawburn can be very charming when he wants to be, but when he doesn't get his own way, he is…he becomes a violent monster.'

Sophie pressed her hands to her eyes, making a sudden decision. She had to tell him everything, then he'd see why their relationship was doomed and why she refused to act on her attraction to him. He was sure to turn away from her in disgust. It would hurt a little, but better to be hurt now than to be led inexorably towards another room in a seedy inn.

'Go on.' He put his hand on hers. His voice was soothing as if he were speaking to a nervous horse. 'Whatever happens, know I won't be angry with you. I want to understand. It was during your first Season you had the misfortune to encounter Cawburn…'

'I believed his promises. The ones I wanted to, rather than the ones I thought he said as a joke. I should have paid more attention to those ones.' Sophie slowly withdrew her hand from his. He made no attempt to recapture it. He simply looked at her with burning gold eyes that bored deep into her soul.

'It was very flattering,' Sophie said when the silence became too great to bear. 'I was his angel put on the earth. It was exciting to have someone that experienced interested in me. Before that I was Sophie, the one with the awkward hair who could never remember to start on the correct foot during the quadrille. It all went to my head. He kept arranging for us to meet at various balls and entertainments. When my stepmother discovered us in a deserted card room, holding hands, my guardian objected to the match and brought me away, but that only increased my desire for Lord Cawburn. He bribed my maid and sent clandestine letters, declaring his undying devotion. He followed me north. We eloped together at his insistence.'

'But you didn't marry.'

'My guardian and Sebastian's cousin, Henrietta, caught up with us the next day.' Sophie gave a hollow laugh. 'We hadn't even reached Scotland. The carriage had broken down. Trust me to pick someone who couldn't even organise a proper elopement.'

She waited to hear his sarcastic laughter at her youthful folly. Her heart thudded as the only sounds were the turning of the carriage wheels.

'There has never been a whiff of scandal,' he said finally. 'I have never heard that Cawburn eloped with anyone. Not that I don't believe you, but I am at a loss to explain how such a thing was kept out of the papers. Cawburn has never breathed a word of it, either, not even when he was completely pie-eyed after a Derby win. And he is the sort of repellent individual who regularly boasts about his conquests to anyone who might listen. How did you manage it?'

Sophie's shoulders sagged slightly. He believed her story, rather than accusing her of lying. Or worse.

'That was Henri's doing,' she said, leaning forwards. Richard had to understand how grateful she was to Henri Montemorcy. 'She is marvellous at arranging things like that. I shall never know what she said to Lord Cawburn. We've never spoken about it. Henri married my guardian soon after. That part was very romantic. It made me realise the importance of true love versus flattery.'

A primitive surge of anger swept through Richard. Sophie had gone through hell and she'd had to rely on Cawburn's cousin. 'You spent the night with Cawburn.

It is an intriguing little fact. I am surprised your guardian didn't insist on a marriage.'

'Henri sorted it out. In the excitement of her marriage to my guardian, my indiscretion was overlooked, just as Henri predicted. Henri is marvellous. She has been so helpful in showing me how to behave correctly.'

'Your guardian's wife must be very good at arranging things.' Richard struggled to contain his anger and frustration. Cawburn had not suffered at all for his part in this. 'Most things like that appear within the first months, if not days. How long has it been since it happened?'

'Nearly four years.'

'Four years! My God, she is better than good. I'd never have thought Cawburn would keep quiet that long. Of course, if he said anything now, who would believe it?' His eyes narrowed. 'Why is it that your guardian did not force the marriage? Even if his brain was love-addled, he had to have appreciated the risks to your reputation.'

Sophie winced. And Richard knew his words had come out too harshly.

'I spent the night barricaded in an inn's upstairs room. I hit Lord Cawburn with a frying pan when he decided to take liberties and, once he left, I pulled a chest of drawers, a trunk and the bed against the door. I sat up all night with the frying pan in my hand. Lord Cawburn came up twice to shout at me through the keyhole, but I refused to open the door until Henri appeared.'

The muscles in Richard's shoulders relaxed. Sophie remained an innocent. He had thought he'd have to go and make sure that Cawburn suffered a slow and painful death, but he'd allow him to live. He would simply use his influence to ensure Cawburn had a frosty welcome when he next turned up in London.

Silently he vowed he'd demonstrate that she was wrong in her assessment of him. He wanted to show beyond a shadow of a doubt that he could never do what Cawburn had done to her. He put all thoughts of seduction from him. Sophie needed a friend, not a lover.

'You hit Cawburn with a frying pan. Thoroughly deserved.' Richard banged his hand on his knee and barely stopped himself from hugging Sophie. Trust her to sort out Cawburn. 'What did he do after you hit him once? Did he take the hint that you were no fragile flower and run?'

'It took three goes, but he went. It is lucky that I know how to play cricket and how to hit the ball hard.'

He laughed out loud.

Sophie smiled back at him. Relief flooded through her. Somehow it made it easier to talk about it. Henri and Robert had never wanted to discuss that night. After they left the inn, Henri told her it was unnecessary as nothing had happened. But it had and Sophie couldn't forget it. Sometimes she woke up with a pounding heart, reaching for the frying pan, trying to get it from her bag and finding her bag empty. 'Three times, but I succeeded in the end.'

He instantly sobered and the fury returned to his face. 'It should have taken him one, but it should never have to come to that. He should have accepted your no. You did say no, Sophie, before you started swinging your frying pan?'

'I screamed it!'

'Good girl. That's what I like to hear.' He patted her shoulder. The tiny gesture of approval sent a pulse of warmth throbbing through her. Richard agreed with her actions. 'But why did you have a frying pan? It is not the usual sort of equipment one carries on an elopement. Are you a keen cook?'

'When we first met, Henri had warned me that her cousin might have difficulties in understanding no. She thought a hatpin wouldn't do, but he might need a frying pan applied to his head. I think she was joking when she said it, but I couldn't be sure. When Sebastian insisted on eloping, I took the frying pan as precaution. I might have been a naïve débutante and inclined to believe flattery, Richard, but I am far from stupid.'

'And what happened afterwards? Once you were rescued? Did no one tell you that it was Cawburn to blame, not you? Did your friends explain that you were young and unused to the ways of rogues and cads?'

Sophie looked at her hands. All sorts of things had been said, but she knew they were easy words. The shame at what she'd done and how she'd behaved rose in her throat. 'Henri told me that I was to forget that it had ever happened. My life was supposed to go on as before. No one would ever know, but I knew. And I have made sure that I am never in situations like that again…until the other night. I thought I was safe. All I was doing was delivering a note from Cynthia. It was the work of a moment. I had no interest in Sir Vincent as a man. Sir Vincent seemed so…so…'

'Infused with gentlemanly virtue?' Richard supplied with a bitter twist to his mouth.

'Exactly, but he wasn't. He...he called me the same sorts of names and threaten—'

A shudder went through her. Her throat worked up and down, but she knew if she continued, she'd break down in tears. She refused to cry, particularly not in front of Richard.

Without a word, he gathered her into his arms and rested his head on top of hers. Unlike the other times he had held her, this time had a quality of caring and comfort to it. The gentleness of his touch made her feel secure. Safe in a way that she had not felt for years, not since the inn. She laid her head on his chest and listened to the steady beat of his heart.

'What did he say to you?' he asked, gently stroking her back. 'Cawburn, I mean. I can guess, but I need to know, Sophie. Can you tell me, please?'

'He turned very nasty and called me all sorts of names. A hell-cat, a she-devil. He said that I had led him on. It was all my fault and that he'd never behave like that around a true lady. I had shown my true breeding—a common whore.'

A single tear trickled down her cheek. She sat up and wiped it away with furious fingers. He silently passed her a handkerchief. She dabbed her eyes and regained control.

'I have made a mess of your shirt front. You must realise that—'

'Hush. They were all lies.' He tilted her face so he looked her directly in the eyes. 'All wicked lies, Sophie, from a cowardly scoundrel. You are the epitome of a lady. You were young. He took advantage of you. Cawburn bears all the blame. You were and remain the innocent victim who used all the means at your disposal and some brilliant ingenuity. Did he say anything else? Threaten you?'

She gave a brief nod. He might believe that, but she had to wonder, particularly given how much she'd enjoyed Richard's kisses yesterday—was she truly a bad woman who simply played at being good? 'Finally he said that we would have to marry and he'd spend all my money. He'd enjoy seeing me reduced to poverty and dressed in the meanest rags.'

'You can see what a liar he was.' He ticked off the points on his fingers. 'You didn't have to marry. And he most definitely has not spent all your money. You have a sterling reputation and are admired by many people, while he was forced to flee to France to escape his creditors…and I know of at least one incident where he cheated at cards. He was caught red handed and denied it with very great bleats, accusing everyone else, until I drew the card from his boot.'

'You did?'

'A man who will cheat at cards will cheat and lie at anything, and most particularly in love. Think of that the next time you are tempted to believe anything else he said. The reason you enjoy such a good reputation is because you are a good person, Sophie. Everyone is allowed one mistake.'

'It was because of Henri… It was all her doing.'

He shook his head. 'I have never met this Henri, but I know you. No one wields that much power. She might have kept it quiet for a little while, but your subsequent actions ensured silence. You haven't hidden or stopped doing what you pleased. You simply stopped some of the lies he told you. It is time you stopped believing the rest of the filth.'

'I still have nightmares,' Sophie confessed.

'Always with him. Never with me starring in his role.' He pinned her with his gaze. 'You are not frightened of me, are you, Sophie?'

Sophie bit her lip. She could hardly confess to the sort of dreams she was having about him! And how for the past two nights, she had woken with his name on her lips and a deep longing to have his lips against hers. It was trying to make those sorts of dreams real which led to her utter destruction.

'Only with him,' she managed. 'I haven't known you very long.'

'I will never give you a reason to have a nightmare.'

'Thank you.'

'Is there any dream you have given up because of him and his lies?' he asked into the silence which had filled the carriage. 'Something you could do to prove to yourself that he no longer has power over you?'

'I used to enjoy drawing. I was going to be a great painter. He had promised to take me to the Alps so I could paint.' Sophie tried to swallow the hard lump which had formed in her throat. 'I…I had always dreamt of going there on my honeymoon. I wanted to paint the mountains. I read somewhere that the light was good. People used to say that I was quite accomplished. Afterwards, I found it difficult to hold my brush or pen without the feelings of shame and remorse washing over me. Drawing became torture, something I did before. It was like my life was divided into two parts.'

Her limbs started to shake as she struggled to keep control and not allow those feelings to swamp her.

He pulled her back into his arms. 'Hush, now. Your friend didn't put a frying pan to Cawburn's head. You did. And you are safe now. You can go to the Alps and paint if you want to. You don't have to wait for a wedding trip. You can travel, Sophie. It is easy. All you have to do is buy a ticket and go. You mustn't allow a creature like that and his self-serving lies to rule your existence. You allow him to win by doing that. And that is nothing you want.'

She breathed deeply and allowed the crisp masculine scent to fill her nostrils. She'd shed all the tears she needed to over that man and what he'd done to her innocence. Richard was right. She had to start living again. She breathed deeply one more time, made a memory and then sat up.

'Thank you. I will get some new paints when I next go to the shops.' She looped a strand of hair behind her ear. 'The trip might have to wait a while. Perhaps after our engagement is done, I might need to get away to recover. My stepmother might agree. She has always wanted to take the waters.'

A half-smile touched his lips. 'There, better already.'

'Much better.'

'Good.'

His hand stroked her cheek. A warm tingle pulsed through her. He was going to kiss her again. She closed her eyes, parted her lips and hoped.

Rather than kissing her, he gave a great sigh before rapping the carriage roof. The carriage turned around almost immediately.

'Where are we going?' Sophie asked, her eyes flying open as a pang of disappointment went through her. No kisses today. Despite his easy words, he felt she was tainted in some way.

'Back to your home, but I want you to do something for me, Sophie.'

'What is that?' she whispered.

'Give me a chance to prove that I am as far removed from the sort of creature that Cawburn is. I do understand the word no and that when a lady says it, she means it.' He raised her hand to his lips. 'Will you do that for me, Sophie? Judge me for me, rather than considering me to be like Cawburn?'

'I...I will try.'

The box of paints with its bright colours neatly arrayed stared up at her. She fingered the aquamarine and then the crimson red. Gorgeous rich colours which made her soul ache to use them. She pulled her hand away before the temptation overwhelmed her.

'You have given me oil paints?'

'They seemed more appropriate than watercolours. You are not some milk-sop miss content with a pastel-coloured life, but a vibrant being who requires true colour to match her view of the world,' Richard replied. 'Or that was my thought.'

'I know how to paint with oils. I used to prefer them, but watercolours seem more ladylike.' Sophie gently closed the wooden box, before she gave in to the urge to start painting there and then. Oil paints were for people who led reckless and chaotic lives, rather than ordered ones.

'Sophie, you are a lady whether you paint in oil or water. It is how you act. Your stepmother will confirm it.' He tilted his head. 'Where is Mrs Ravel? I have a present of wax fruit for her.'

'She has a dress fitting.' Sophie gestured to the piles of old magazines, penny-dreadfuls and fashion plates. 'I'm sorting through these and trying to decide which to keep and which to throw away. I hadn't thought you would call. There is no At Home on a Friday.'

Rather than living in hope of Richard calling, she had chosen to wear a faded rose-coloured gown with a high-necked collar and her loosest corset. Her hair was drawn back in a simple knot, rather than being artfully done. Sophie absurdly wished she was in the dark-blue gown which set off her eyes and that she had used curling tongs to make sure her ringlets framed her face.

She squashed the thought. It did not matter what he thought of her looks. They were thrown together by circumstance. She was not going to act on any feelings of attraction towards him. He might have been the perfect gentleman yesterday, but could she trust him today?

'Is there something wrong with a man calling on his fiancée?' He glanced about the small sitting room which her stepmother and she used in the evenings when they were not entertaining. 'This room is far more pleasant than the drawing room. Cosy and more you.'

'No, nothing is wrong. And I like this room better with fewer china ornaments to knock.' Sophie picked up a brush and toyed with it, twisting it about her fingers. 'I will make sure my stepmother gets the fruit. It is good of you to remember her.'

'I have brought some paper as well as a variety of

pencils,' Richard said, holding out another parcel. 'In case you didn't have any. I wasn't sure about the size of canvas you might require, but the man at the shop will drop off a selection later today.'

Sophie tilted her head to one side, eyeing the parcel with suspicion. 'I don't understand. Why are you giving me these things?'

'Have you forgotten what we spoke about yesterday? You promised to try drawing again. As you said you stopped four years ago, I reckoned you would not have paints, pencils or drawing paper.' His eyes glinted gold. 'Finding excuses is a terrible thing.'

'Spoken like someone who knows.'

'There are things I avoided until I was forced to,' he admitted with a studied shrug.

Sophie caught her breath and waited.

'I am not here to speak about my failings,' he said finally. 'Know I have many. Are you going to draw?'

'And I do intend to after I have finished with the magazines. But these are far too much, Richard.' Sophie gave the paintbox a wistful stroke. The tubes were new and unclotted. When she had looked this morning at her old oil paints, she couldn't even squeeze the tube, the paint was so old and cracked. Her brushes were matted and glued. The thought of going and buying more had been beyond her and she'd put it off for another day.

'What is the harm in spoiling you? Do you like them?'

'Very much,' Sophie admitted. 'I am puzzled why you have given me all this.'

'Can't a man give his fiancée a present?'

'It is nothing that others will see,' she explained. 'I'm hardly likely to bring it up in conversation, either.'

'And what of it? You will know I gave it to you. Sometimes it is not about creating an impression, Sophie, but doing the right thing.' He shrugged. 'After our conversation yesterday, I wanted to encourage you. To paint.'

She knew he was talking about more than that. He wanted her to stop allowing The Incident to rule her life. Rather than fearing it, a sort of reckless excitement filled her. It was an unexpected challenge. 'You are very kind.'

'Some day you might get to the Alps and want to paint, but you won't have practised for a long time. You need to practise now, so you are ready. The wax fruit are in case you need a subject. But I thought your stepmother was more the wax-fruit type.'

'I will definitely go...one of these days.' Privately Sophie vowed that she would go once they had ended. And she would paint meadows filled with flowers with snow-capped mountains towering over them. It would be a way to ease the pain in her heart. She froze and buried the thought. She liked Richard and enjoyed his company, but nothing more. They could never be real friends. There was far too much between them. After this false engagement ended, she'd never see him again. They would be strangers. The thought depressed her. 'Yes, I will definitely go.'

'Then you will accept the gift? I give it to you as a friend. I do consider you a friend, Sophie. I hope you will come to consider me as a friend.'

A friend. Sophie's heart thudded.

'Can a man and a woman ever be friends?' she asked lightly.

'I like to think you are. We share a secret.'

Friends for now, strangers in a few weeks. She'd miss him. 'How could I refuse when it was given in the interests of friendship?'

He stood there without moving and she wondered if he expected a kiss. She carefully placed the box down on the table with the drawing paper and pencils next to them, making a show of straightening them, but all the time watching him out of the corner of her eye.

'I shall start a painting today to show you I'm serious,' she said to cover the awkward silence. 'You can see it tomorrow…I mean, whenever you next come to call.'

'Tomorrow will be fine. There is a concert of Handel's *Water Music* on at the Royal Theatre. I thought you and your stepmother might enjoy going. You did enjoy the theatre so much in Liverpool last March.'

'I promise not to flirt with any strange men with my fan. I gave that up after I met you. Lesson learnt.'

A tiny smile touched his lips. 'You have our story down.'

'It is important not to make a mistake.' Sophie turned back to the paints. 'I've no wish to come undone over it. I've told the story so many times now that I almost believe it myself.'

'Do you have a subject in mind for this painting of yours or shall I pose for you?'

Sophie examined the carpet of the small sitting room. If he posed for her, he'd have to stay. A large chunk of her wanted him here, but the more prudent side knew he should go. She had given up being reckless years ago. And while Richard might say he was different, she had no desire to put him to the test. Once bitten, twice shy as her nurse used to say.

'It normally takes me an age to decide on the subject,' she said. 'I like to spend time arranging things and doing preliminary sketches. Paintings don't happen like that. They need to be prepared.'

'Do you draw people?'

'I used to.' Sophie gestured towards the pen-and-ink portrait of her stepmother that stood on a side table. 'I did that one the spring before I made my début. My stepmother was a poor sitter. She kept moving her hands and changing expressions. Most aggravating—the drawing took twice as long as it should have done.'

'You are very talented.'

'You're being kind.'

'Kindness has nothing to do with it. I merely appreciated your talent.' He nodded towards the paints. 'Another time, then. When you are more confident at drawing people. I promise to sit very still and not move a muscle…no matter how much my nose itches.'

'Perhaps.'

'No perhaps. I shall look forward to sitting with anticipation.'

Sophie's mouth went dry. And she privately decided the time would never come. The risk to her resolve was far too great. There would be too many opportunities for seduction. Richard might proclaim to be different from Sebastian, but she didn't want to tempt fate.

She hugged the paintbox to her chest. 'I will think about it, but your suggestion to paint the wax fruit is a good one. My stepmother has a silver bowl which will work admirably. Nothing too complicated to begin with.'

'I am counting the hours...' His mouth quirked upwards at her expression. Her cheeks burnt. 'Until the theatre. It is your decision if you need a model. Know that I am a willing volunteer, if required.'

'And I will let you know if you are ever required.'

'We understand each other.' He took the box from her nerveless fingers and placed it on the table. 'Don't worry, I shall show myself out. You get on with your painting.'

Sophie stood in the middle of the sitting room, staring at the paints for a long time. Why did Richard Crawford have to turn out to be kind? He was right. He wasn't like Sebastian at all. He was infinitely more dangerous.

Chapter Eight

'There you see, all done.' Sophie held up the still life of wax fruit in a silver bowl for Richard's inspection a few days later. Her eager expression lit the room with its glow.

He'd done the right thing coming here, instead of going to the club or sitting and fuming about his mother's spending habits. Somehow being with Sophie made all of this morning's annoyances fade into insignificance.

He took the painting from her and their fingertips brushed. A warm pulse shot up his arm. Demonstrating to Sophie that he was far removed from Cawburn was getting harder and harder when all he wanted to do was to take her into his arms and kiss her.

Rather than having his desire for her diminish through seeing her, it had grown. But more than that he looked forward to pitting his wits against her and talking to her about things which had nothing to do with his family or the other demands on his time. When he was with her, everything faded into insignificance.

'You are very talented.' Richard concentrated on the

painting and regained control of his body. Sophie was not the sort of woman one seduced; she was the sort of woman one married. 'That painting is more than a simple bowl of fruit. It looks good enough to eat. And I love how the shapes complement each other.'

'It is fine, but the apple gave me trouble. The red proved harder to get right than I thought it would.'

Sophie moved closer to him and their shoulders accidentally touched. Richard kept his body rigid.

'I could never do something like that. I wouldn't even know where to begin.'

'I had a strict drawing mistress. Do you know how many different colours a simple shadow can be? They are not dabs of black paint.'

He shook his head. Even now, Sophie wanted to belittle her accomplishments. 'It is more than simple-rote, schoolgirl painting. There is something indefinable here. You must learn how to take a compliment, Sophie, or I shall be forced to pay you them until you do.'

Her eyes danced. 'How do you take a compliment?'

'You say thank you and don't attempt to deflect it or apologise for it or make it seem less than it is. All it takes is a thank you and nothing more.'

He put the painting down. Sophie needed to have her confidence grow. He could only keep making excuses to his mother about the need to ensure Hannah's engagement for so long, before awkward questions would be asked, and Richard knew he wasn't ready to share Sophie with his family. His relationship with Sophie had no bearing on his relationship with his mother or sister.

'I shall try to remember that.' Sophie gave a mocking curtsy. 'Thank you for the compliment about the painting.'

'Shall we practise to make sure you understand the concept? Your blue dress looks exceptionally charming today, Miss Ravel.'

'This is hardly necessary. I do know how to take a compliment.'

'I used to think your eyes were the colour of sapphires, like your ring, but now I see the colour depends on your mood. Midnight blue when you are angry right through the blue of a summer's day when you are happy.'

'You are being foolish. Cease this blather immediately.'

He took a step closer. 'I intend to keep paying you compliments until you show me that you know how to take them. I prefer your hair like this when it makes little ringlets of its own accord.'

Sophie wet her suddenly aching lips. Her entire being trembled. Where did he intend taking this game? Her dreams had been full of him lately but ever since the carriage ride, he had made no attempt to kiss her.

'Thank you,' she gasped out as he took another step closer, so close her skirt brushed his leg. Another step, and she'd be in his arms. What was worse, she wanted to be in his arms. She wanted to taste his lips again and see if they matched her memory of them.

'At last my fiancée shows some sense.' His eyes danced with a thousand different lights. 'Shall I continue?'

'No.'

He inclined his head and stepped backwards. 'I bow to your no and stop immediately.'

A tiny bubble of amazement burst through her. He'd obeyed her no. She hated that she wished she'd urged him to continue. She put her hand to her mouth, exploring the way it faintly tingled as if he had indeed kissed her. The trouble with Richard was that she liked him far too much.

To cover her confusion, she grabbed the painting and held it out.

'You may have the painting if you like it. I painted it with you in mind.'

He tilted his head and she caught a sudden flaring in his eyes. 'It is kind of you. I will treasure it. I don't think anyone has ever done something like that for me before.'

'A thank you for the paints and for getting me started on painting again.' Sophie clasped her hands together and hoped he'd think the redness of her cheeks was from the fire, rather than the awkwardness she suddenly felt. 'I hope you don't consider it too forward.'

'Forward?' His eyes widened. 'Perish the thought. I'm very touched and honoured.'

'It is funny how you don't realise you missed something until it comes back into your life and suddenly your life takes on a new meaning.'

He stilled. 'Have you decided to start painting people again?'

Sophie put a hand on her stomach to stop the butterflies. Somehow she knew she had to get the answer right. Because if she got it wrong, he'd go and she wasn't ready for that yet.

'I have only ever done pen-and-ink drawings, but

some day, I will start using oils for painting portraits. I promise.'

'I live in hope, then.'

Sophie let out a breath. She had passed the test.

He reached for the painting and his fingers brushed hers, almost a caress. A little touch which could have been accidental, but she chose to consider it deliberate. 'You will go with me tomorrow to the cricket? The match is an important one.'

'I look forward to it.' Sophie held her body utterly still.

'Out with it, Sophie. What is wrong?'

'How could you tell that something was wrong?'

'You always develop a little frown between your brows. And you have glanced at the desk ten times since I arrived. What is on that desk?'

He had noticed that! Sophie forced her features to relax. She walked over to the little desk she used for correspondence and withdrew the letter which had arrived in this morning's post.

'I have had a letter from my solicitors. You agreed to my terms for the settlement. No quibbling!'

'Your terms were the same as I wish for any bride.' He lifted an eyebrow as if daring her to say differently. 'I thought you would have made them much more onerous and demanded a massive allowance or something outrageous. Having complete control over your own money makes common sense.'

'My stepmother would have questioned it, particularly after I made the claim of undying devotion at the Assembly Rooms. She did look over the request I sent to the solicitors to make sure my interests were well looked after.'

He lowered his voice. 'When do you plan to tell her about it?'

Sophie chose to assume he meant the letter about the settlement, rather than the bigger question of their false engagement. Her stepmother simply would not understand. And she would not understand why Sophie had to keep on seeing Richard and how precious these moments were becoming to her. She'd start on about a blossoming romance and what a shame it was that Sophie had not agreed to a true engagement when she was asked, instead of being mealy-mouthed.

'About the settlement being agreed?' Sophie tapped the letter against her hand. 'I had to show her the letter.'

'And is she insisting on that engagement party now the settlement is finalised?'

'She has agreed to wait until Robert and Henri return. Robert should look over the settlement first was my excuse. My stepmother thinks I'm overly cautious. You know how she adores you and the fact you agreed so readily to the settlement has only enhanced your standing. She refuses to hear a word against you.'

'Why did you tell her you wanted to wait?'

Sophie turned away from his burning eyes. If she looked at him, she'd be tempted to blurt out the truth. She enjoyed his company and wanted to prolong the time they spent together, but she knew it had to end. There wasn't a future for them. They were strangers, not friends and certainly not lovers.

She wasn't going back to the romantic fool who faced utter ruin. And she was determined to marry for love, real and lasting love rather than a fleeting illusion of romance. Lasting love happened quietly, not this sudden bolt of lightning longing she'd experienced in connection with Richard. It reminded her too much of how she'd felt with Sebastian—unsettled and unbalanced. Surely if it was love, she'd feel complete and whole?

She put the letter back on the desk. Her hand trembled. It was far too soon to think about love in connection with Richard.

'I had to tell her something, otherwise she'd have been penning invitations this morning rather than going out visiting. Needing Robert's and Henri's blessing seemed like a sensible excuse.'

He tapped his fingers together and his lips pursed. 'When are the Montemorcys expected to return?'

'In the early part of June, no later than the eighteenth. Lady Forbisher always has a ball to celebrate Wellington's victory at Waterloo and then there is the Stagshaw Fair on the fourth of July. Henri helps with the planning of that. We had a letter from Henri yesterday.' She kept her head up. 'The timing should be perfect. All the commotion will have died down. Our parting will go unremarked.'

'We shall have to hope that Montemorcy sees some reason to object, then,' he murmured.

'I'm sure he will,' Sophie assured him. 'Robert is quite protective. He was the one who saw through Sebastian straight away. And Henri is brilliant at matchmaking. She is sure to find a reason why we wouldn't suit if Robert doesn't.'

The words tasted like ash in Sophie's mouth. She wanted Richard to deny it was a good idea and that he intended to remain in Newcastle for the summer with her—in fact, that against all expectation he wanted to marry her.

'It is good to know how long we have left. Early June after Montemorcy arrives back and sees the terms. After he has withheld his consent, we part. Amicably.' His lips became a thin white line. 'It is what happens in these cases.'

A pang went through Sophie. He was right. 'It is the most sensible thing. And it has happened to other people. Our parting will hardly be remarked on. I promise you.'

'And if it is? How will you weather the storm?'

'I'll go to Corbridge with Henri and Robert to ride out any lingering tittle-tattle. I won't be judged there.' Sophie kept her head up. It would be the perfect place to recover from the ache she felt now that the date had been decided.

His eyes became inscrutable. 'Early June, then. It is good to know so I can make plans...for my return to London.'

Sophie brushed away the great empty hollow which opened inside of her at the thought of never seeing him again. 'But we have until then.'

The dimple in the corner of his mouth deepened. 'Yes, we have until then. Best not waste any time, Sophie.'

Richard stood on the pavement and looked back at the brown-brick house. The day which had seemed bright and cheerful when he went in had become gloomy and overcast, matching his mood. The first few splashes of rain fell on his hat and frock-coat. Richard ignored them.

He had an ending date for his friendship with Sophie. Early June. Somewhere deep inside him, he had known that this was going to have to end. Only he wasn't ready. The very prospect of not being able to spend time with Sophie filled him with horror.

He had no wish to be judged unworthy by some former guardian. The man could not even take care of Sophie properly. Richard wanted to know Sophie would be looked after as she deserved to be. Her so-called friends had not even seen that she did much better when she was painting.

There was no hope for it. In order to keep Sophie safe, he'd have to marry her.

He groaned as he remembered what she had said when she refused his earlier proposal. Sophie wanted to marry for love and love was the one thing he couldn't offer. Love only led to heartache.

'I will find a way to marry you, Sophie Ravel, but I will not mouth lies.'

Was she truly ready to say goodbye for ever to Richard?

Sophie bit the top of her thumb and tried to concentrate on the cricket match unfolding in front of her. Richard was batting and doing a sterling job of knocking the ball all over the ground after their team had had a disastrous start. The cricketing whites suited his figure. She noticed many admiring glances from the other ladies as he strode out to occupy the crease.

Today was far worse than yesterday. Yesterday,

she'd known it would happen some day in the future. Today was the start of the march towards when Robert returned and she parted from Richard for ever. Each moment with Richard seemed to take on an added intensity. It was as if some secret part of her wanted to store every second she had with him so she could remember them later.

Perhaps today, after the match when he dropped her off, she would risk lifting her face up to him and seeing if his kisses were as exciting as her memory of them. She'd use the excuse of him winning the match. With the number of runs he'd scored, he was today's hero and heroes did deserve their rewards.

'Are you enjoying the match, miss?' a well-dressed woman about her age asked, bringing Sophie back to the game which was unfolding in front of her. Richard had just hit the ball for four more runs.

Sophie frowned. There was something vaguely familiar about the woman's exotic features, but Sophie felt certain they had never met before. She rarely forgot the shape of a face or the eyes. It would come to her in a little while where she knew the woman from.

'Yes, very much. And it is Miss Ravel, Sophie Ravel.'

The woman regarded the cricket bat which lay at Sophie's feet. 'Are you going to play?'

'My fiancé is batting now and I go in after if necessary. I haven't played since my school days so I hope I can bat well if I have to go in. It would be dreadful to make a mess of it as our team stands a chance of winning. But there is every chance I won't have to go in. Only ten more runs. Lord Bingfield did promise he'd arrange things so that I would not have to go in. And it appears he has.'

'I am Hannah Grayson.' The woman said the name like she should know it. 'My fiancé is playing for the other team. He is the bowler for this over. You know, the bowler who took all those wickets in the first few overs. Sir Ronald Ferguson. We became officially engaged last night.'

'Congratulations.' A pang went through Sophie. Miss Grayson seemed so happy and in love. She could well imagine how that engagement went. Nothing like her own pretend one. 'Have you known each other long?'

'For a year or so, but I never expected things to go so quickly. I thought we were simply friends, even though Mama had hopes.' Miss Grayson held out her hand where a diamond surrounded by garnets sparkled. 'Sir Ronald gave me the ring last night. It is completely perfect. I am ever so grateful to my brother. I owe everything to him. I had feared that this day would never come to pass.'

'Your brother?'

Miss Grayson bent her head and picked at her glove. 'He came up from London and sorted everything out. At first I thought he wouldn't be able to stay beyond a day and a night, but he has. It turns out that Sir Ronald was the year below him at Eton and that made everything easier. And yesterday evening, everything fell into place. The settlement, everything. I feel so happy that I could embrace the whole world. Isn't it marvellous how things work out sometimes? Love is a truly wonderful thing.'

'Yes, it is. I am very pleased for you.' Sophie composed her face. Somehow Miss Grayson's unbridled joy only served to underline the hypocrisy of her own position. Getting married should be because you were in love with someone, deeply and irrevocably. It should not be because society dictates you must marry a stranger in order to save your reputation after an item has appeared in a newspaper. And it should not be because you want that stranger to kiss you. There ought to be more.

'Do you have a brother, Miss Ravel?' Miss Grayson asked as the bowler started his run up.

'I'm an only child. I've often wished for a sister, but never a brother. Alas, it was not to be.'

'I agree it would be pleasant to have a sister, but I shall make do with my brother…for now.' Miss Grayson's brow knitted. 'It is most vexing that he remains unmarried. He truly is the most perfect of brothers. I pray he finds a woman who deserves him.'

'Maybe he will marry and you will get a sister,' Sophie said. Miss Grayson did seem overly keen about her paragon of a brother. She had to hope the mysterious Mr Grayson was worthy of such praise.

Miss Grayson's lips parted as if she wanted to say something more, but a great shout went up and the bowler appealed to the umpire, who nodded and raised a finger, signalling out.

'I fear, Miss Ravel, my fiancé has taken your fiancé's middle stump. You'll have to go in after all. A pity.' Miss Grayson gave a little clap of her hands. 'There is only one more wicket to go and then Ronald will have won the match. It is terribly exciting. I had never considered cricket to be anything but dull, but it isn't. Good luck, Miss Ravel.'

Sophie stood up and grabbed her bat. She swung it lightly to test her arm. She could do this. There were only five more runs required.

On the way out to the middle, she met Richard, who looked furious at making the mistake.

'Never mind, it was a difficult ball to hit,' she said. 'You played marvellously to get us so close to the number of runs required. Before you went in, I feared our side would lose by a huge amount. Now we are nearly level and poised to win, if I can avoid getting out.'

'Who were you speaking with?' he asked, his brows knitting together. 'Just now? Another recruit to the game of cricket?'

'A Miss Grayson.' Sophie swung her bat slightly, testing its weight. She was surprised that Richard had even noticed where she was sitting or whom she was conversing with. She had thought he would be totally focused on the game. Her heart gave a leap at the intelligence. Despite everything he had noticed her!

'Are you acquainted with Miss Grayson?'

'She has very recently become engaged and wanted to sing her brother's praises as he apparently enabled it to happen. I was the nearest person to hand,' Sophie explained. 'I suppose love will do that—make people overly inclined to speak to strangers.'

'I regret my mistake interrupted your conversation.' He stopped her bat swinging and adjusted the grip. 'You were marvellous to volunteer when Charlton failed to show. It has allowed the entire match to proceed. I never thought you'd actually have to bat.'

Sophie's heart did a little skip as she basked in his praise, but it put more pressure on her to do well. The last thing she wanted was to let him down. And she had known that taking part in the match was the only way she could spend time with him. If it had been called off, she wouldn't have an excuse to stay. She would have had to go visiting with her stepmother. The prospect had held little appeal, particularly as it would have meant less time to be with him.

'It is perfectly fine,' she said, tightening her grip on the cricket bat. 'I hope I don't make a mess of things. I would hate to think we will lose because of me.'

'You won't.' He put a hand on her shoulder and his eyes turned serious. 'Keep the bat straight and swing if you have to. Keep the bat low and the ball will fall harmless to the ground. There is only one more ball left in the over. Let Armstrong do the rest.'

'Thank you for the advice.'

'My pleasure. You will do wonderfully, Sophie.'

Richard allowed Sophie to walk out to the crease and then went towards where his sister sat, shading her face with a parasol.

'Hannah!' Richard glowered at his sister. He had known Ferguson was on the other side, but he had thought Hannah would stay at home with their mother, discussing plans for the wedding. He had given his approval last night and had simply assumed Hannah would be too busy to attend today's match. The last thing he had wanted was Hannah here when he was attempting to manoeuvre Sophie towards marriage. It was a delicate operation, but it was for Sophie's own good. The last thing he needed was his sister causing mischief.

'It is not like you to miss a shot,' his sister said with a faintly smug smile. 'Ronald clean bowled you. Took out your middle stump. When was the last time that happened? At Eton? Or before that? You see, he is the better cricket player after all. You shouldn't boast so much, Richard. It doesn't become you.'

Richard tightened his jaw. He had missed the shot when he saw his sister speaking to Sophie, against his direct orders.

'I thought you were not to speak to Miss Ravel until I told you that you could.'

Hannah pouted slightly. 'I wanted to see what she was like. I'd only had a glimpse of her at the Assembly Rooms the night she announced the engagement to everyone. I thought her wonderfully brave, no matter what Mama said.'

'And you should have told me that you intended on defying me over this cricket match. I would have found an excuse not to bring Miss Ravel.'

'But I'm pleased you did.' Hannah clapped her hands together. 'She is extremely beautiful, Richard. It is the sort of beauty which lasts rather than coming from a paint pot or cleverly dressed hair. And she was sitting on her own. I thought it couldn't hurt.' Hannah's teeth worried her bottom lip. 'It seemed opportune. I wanted to meet the woman who has made my happiness possible. I wanted to see if she was worthy of my brother!'

'Did you have to go on about your brother? We had agreed to keep everything separate for our mother's sake. Sophie needs to remain in ignorance. It is far too risky.'

Richard closed his eyes. Sophie provided a bright spot in his life, untainted by his parents' warfare.

Would she understand why he loved them both and

wanted to maintain cordial relations with both of them, rather than choosing a side? They were both part of him. He did not want to upset the delicate balance that he now enjoyed. Neither did he want her used as a pawn in that war. He could not stand to see Sophie hurt by either of them.

He could be married to Sophie and protect her from the taint of his past. It was possible.

'Are you going to marry her, Richard, for real? She wants a sister.' Hannah gave a small sigh. 'I think we could be friends. It would be so romantic to have a double wedding.'

'A double wedding is an impossibility. Stop this foolish behaviour and think of our mother. You know my father will insist on being at any marriage of mine.'

'Then you mean to marry her. Mama was wrong. I knew you must love her.'

Richard watched Sophie face the first ball. Her blouse tightened, revealing her curves as she batted the ball away to safety.

She was secure now and should not have to face another ball if Armstrong did his job. Sophie seemed so eager to play her part in the match and he knew he didn't want her to be the one to make the team lose.

'Stop putting words in my mouth, Hannah! Simply because you are love-addled, it doesn't mean you need to see romance with the rest of the world. I explained about Miss Ravel's necessity. Nothing has altered my view.'

The last thing he needed was marriage advice from his baby sister. He wanted Sophie in his life. He wanted Sophie happy. Love made people unhappy and foolish.

'Stop being foolish!' Hannah whispered in a furious tone and put her hand on her hip. 'You wrong me and Miss Ravel. I was curious. You have been spending an inordinate amount of time with her. Far more than Mama or I expected when you told us of the plan. Every day seems to bring something more that you must do. No wonder it took so long to negotiate my settlement with Ronald. Both he and I despaired of you.'

'Allow me to conduct my relations with Miss Ravel in my own fashion. Please.'

Hannah's marriage arrangements had given him the excuse to linger without family interference. But Sophie had changed the rules and he no longer had time. He had made sure that Hannah's interests were looked after, now he intended to look after his own. Everything had taken on a new urgency because of his father's note which he'd received this morning. Against all expectation his father had decided to travel and inspect his son's choice of bride. He declined to give a date, but Richard knew he had a week, ten days at most, before his father appeared.

If Sophie truly did not want to marry him, he needed to break it off for her sake, but he did have hope his plan would succeed. Silently he damned Cawburn for all eternity for making her wary of men.

It wasn't love, not the sort of love that he'd seen his parents experience, but he wanted to protect her and keep her safe from harm. He did have feelings for her and they frightened him to death.

Now his sister had nearly ruined his delicate plans. Sophie needed to be cajoled into this or she'd bolt and he'd lose her for ever. He didn't want to give her the additional excuse of his family. He tolerated them because he was related to them, but he was under no illusion—they were an acquired taste.

'Go away, Hannah. Keep your nose out of my business.'

'I shall go back to my seat now if you are going to be horrid,' his sister said, sticking her nose in the air. 'You failed to pay me the slightest bit of attention.'

'Do! And next time, keep your solemn promise.'

Hannah stalked off without replying.

Richard sank down in the chair and contemplated the scene in front of him. Sophie stood at the non-bowling end, her straw hat pushed back on her forehead, poised to run if the occasion called for it while Armstrong faced the new bowler.

A smattering of applause rippled through the ground as Armstrong ran one run. At a moment's hesitation, Sophie ran the other way. Silently he willed Armstrong to take another, but Armstrong motioned for Sophie to stay where she was.

Sophie nodded and banged the bat on the ground, signalling she was ready for the next ball.

The bowler's run took an inordinately long time. Richard clenched his fists. All Sophie had to do was hit a single run and then allow Armstrong to face the next four balls.

She swung and missed, but the ball carried on harmlessly to the wicket keeper. Richard silently vowed that the next time she offered to play cricket, he'd refuse. His nerves couldn't stand it. She glanced over to him and he gave an encouraging smile. Sophie had done a good thing with volunteering, but should he have allowed it? What moment of madness had he experienced?

He had never considered that she'd actually have to bat. A humiliated Sophie would hardly be conducive to seduction.

The bowler lifted his arm.

The ball came in at a slow curve and looked like it, too, would miss her stumps.

'Leave it alone, Sophie,' Richard muttered under his breath. 'Just survive.'

Sophie lifted her bat and swung.

The crack of the bat hitting the ball echoed around the ground.

Richard watched in amazement as the ball arched out over the field, finally landing some feet on the other side of the boundary.

A huge cheer went up from the crowd. Richard leapt to his feet.

Sophie had done it! She had hit a six and scored the winning runs.

He ran out to the crease along with the rest of the team.

'We won!' Sophie shrieked happily. 'And I can't believe it. We really won!'

'Thanks to you.'

He took the bat from her and tucked it under his arm before catching her hands. She circled around him, her face lit with happiness. It was all he could do not to kiss her thoroughly in front of everyone. His Sophie had won the match. She'd stepped up and played the game, beautifully.

'The bowler thought I was a helpless female and sent

me an easy ball.' Sophie gave an infectious laugh. 'But I was determined not to let the side down, particularly not after you had done so much to get us in the winning position.'

'Where did you learn to swing like that?'

'At school. That ball reminded me of the sort of delivery Miss Denton used to give the new girls. I knew I could do it and I did!' Sophie gave a happy sigh. 'I really did.'

'You should have told me that you were a crack shot.'

'I told you that I used to play at school. It is why I knew how to use the frying pan.' A mischievous smile lit her face. 'The third time I hit Sebastian was just like I hit that ball. Thwack!'

'Makes perfect sense why he retreated,' Richard said with mock gravity.

She laughed, a happy unaffected laugh, her face glowing with pride at her accomplishment. He wanted to swing her up in his arms in front of everyone and kiss her soundly. She had come so far in the past few weeks. Cawburn hadn't destroyed her. He fought to keep his arms at his sides.

She ducked her head and spoke to the ground. 'You have no idea how competitive girls can be at sport.'

'I can well imagine.'

Before she replied, the team came up and surrounded her, blocking his view of her face. Their cheers rang out throughout the ground, but Richard wanted to murder each and every one of them. Sophie should be his and his alone. And he would do everything in his power to claim her.

Chapter Nine

Sophie sighed happily, leaned back against the horse-hair seat in Richard's carriage and closed her eyes as the carriage started off from the cricket ground in Jesmond.

The day had gone perfectly from start to finish. She knew it wasn't strictly proper, but she had adored having the rest of the team crowd around her, congratulating her on her skill at batting. Mr Armstrong had asked her to play the next time. Sophie declined with a laugh, but it felt good to be asked. Richard had been very silent while this was happening, glowering in particular at Mr Armstrong as if in truth he were a jealous fiancé, instead of a pretend one.

She gave a sideways glance at Richard. Was it possible to fall in love with someone after only a few short weeks? Or was it simply the heady romance of the moment? Finally, after so many years, to be free of the guilt and the shame of that one night?

It would be easy to start to depend on Richard, but it also would be a huge mistake. Once Robert and Henri returned, Richard would go out of her life for ever. All this pleasantness would be mere memories.

'I was sorry not to say goodbye to Miss Grayson,' she said, putting the thought from her mind. 'I looked for her after the match, but she had gone.'

'Who?' Richard sat bolt upright next to her, suddenly alert.

Sophie shivered and made a show of straightening her gloves.

'The lady I told you about when I met you on the way out to the crease. She was pleasant and bubbly. She had just become engaged to the bowler who took your wicket, the one I hit for six.'

'Ah, the one with the brother. You told me about her when you went to the crease.' There was a new note to his voice, something she couldn't quite put her finger on. 'Was there some reason you brought her up again?'

'Yes.' She turned towards him and leant forwards. His eyes watched her much as a cat might watch a mouse. Her hand toyed with the collar of her blouse and his eyes followed her hand as if he wanted to touch her there. An awareness of him filled her.

A sudden recklessness filled her. The fearful Sophie would have ignored it, but the new Sophie, the one who dared play cricket with gentlemen and win, wanted to test her theory. He was not indifferent to her. He had been jealous earlier.

'I wondered if her brother was at the match. Do you think anyone could be as good as Miss Grayson painted this man? Such a paragon of virtue and apparently extremely handsome,' she added for good measure, embellishing the story.

'Does it matter what he looks like?' Richard's face

became very stern. 'Speculation does no one any favours. You of all people should know that by now.'

'You never know.' Sophie toyed with her gloves, straightening the seams, rather than looking at him. Every fibre of her being was aware of him and the way he glowered. He was jealous, she realised with a start. 'They live in Newcastle. We must travel in the same social circles. I wish I could figure out why I thought at first I must know her from somewhere. I felt we could be friends. It is all most peculiar.'

'Leave it, Sophie. You are unlikely to encounter this lady again...if you haven't encountered her before.' His voice held a certain finality. Sophie twisted her engagement ring. It was amazing how it felt part of her now. She had become accustomed to wearing it. She gave a soft sigh. But she had no right to it, not like Miss Grayson and her ring. Hers was a lie from start to finish, doomed to end in three weeks at the outside.

After today, she must refuse his invitations or else her heart would be seriously involved. And he wouldn't be jealous. Jealousy only happened if feelings were involved.

'I suppose you are right,' she said as a pang ran through her. No more conversations. No more gentle teasing. No more cricket matches. 'I was simply curious. It intrigued me, that's all. To have a sister that devoted. She swore that the only reason she was engaged was down to him.'

Richard's voice became even colder. 'I am sure he is not worth wondering about.'

She turned towards him, surprised. Normally he encouraged her to talk about people and make observations. 'Is there some problem? You were quiet during the celebrations afterwards.'

'I don't like the thought of you wondering about men when you are engaged to me.'

He regarded her with a fierce expression. Sophie's heart thumped and her lips tingled. He was jealous! Truly jealous of an unknown man, simply because she'd expressed an interest in that man. Her earlier instincts were correct. A heady sense of power coursed through her veins. He did feel something for her. Maybe they would not have to part for ever. Maybe it could blossom into something more. Maybe the romance was real, instead of pretend.

She wanted him to kiss her. Thoroughly and completely. Here in the carriage where no one could see. She wanted to see if his kisses were different when feelings were involved. And he would if she pushed him a bit further. The knowledge thudded through her, making her limbs feel weak.

She felt as if she was playing with fire, but that only served to make her feel more reckless. She could do anything she set her mind to. She had hit that six and won the game!

One single kiss to end a perfect day. She was safe with Richard. She trusted him to stop when she said so and she did know the boundaries.

The knowledge thrummed through her. She loved him and she wanted to pretend that she was worthy of experiencing romance in the same way Miss Grayson had. She wanted to prove once and for all time that she wasn't like those names Sebastian had called her. She wanted to believe for a little while that this romance was real. She could risk one kiss without endangering her reputation.

She tilted her chin in the air and lowered her lashes.

'Strictly speaking we are not engaged nor are we ever likely to be. We are merely using it as a convenience to stop untoward comment. Therefore I can speculate all I like. My heart belongs to no man.'

The blood raced through her veins and she hoped that he would not see her blatant lie. But she knew she had to provoke him.

He gave a soft curse and pulled her firmly into his arms. His lips lowered and captured hers.

Where his other kisses had been gentle and coaxing, this one was possessive and demanding. It seemed as though he wanted to brand her. A warm thrill went through her and she yielded up her mouth to his, opening under his onslaught, tasting the interior of his mouth. Their tongues tangled, retreated and then met again.

The warmth became a wildfire and she knew she wanted more than this one kiss. Her body desired his touch. She arched forwards, bringing her arm about his neck and holding his head against hers as their mouths continued to do battle.

His arms pulled her tight, knocking her straw hat down to the floor. He rained little kisses on her face, nibbling and caressing her as if that one touch had unlocked the floodgates of passion. With each new touch, her heart beat faster and she knew she had to have more. She had been wrong to think that one kiss would satisfy her.

Sophie dug her hands in his hair and felt its silky

smoothness against her fingers and brought his mouth
back to hers. She opened her mouth and took him fully
inside, and suckled, allowing her instinct to guide her.

Her breasts grew full and strained against her corset,
causing her blouse to choke her. She tugged impatiently
at it, seeking relief from its constriction, squirming
against Richard's chest. He clasped her to him, preventing her from moving.

'Please,' she whispered. 'My blouse, it's choking me.
Far too tight.'

'Allow me to help.'

'Yes.'

His hand roamed down her back, stopping on the
tiny buttons and then skimming upwards. Her body
arched forwards.

'Please,' he growled in her ear. 'Let me.'

All she could do was nod. His hands started to undo
the blouse. Her blouse immediately loosened and he
slipped his hand under the fabric, sending little licks of
fire coursing through her body as he stroked her skin
and his mouth tugged at her earlobe. Her body arched
forwards. This was what she had been longing for—his
touch. It felt so right and necessary.

His fingers moved ever lower, reaching her breast.
One finger brushed her nipple, turning it to a hardened point. With the other hand, he pushed the material down on to her arms so that the tops of her breasts
were exposed.

Slowly he lowered his mouth, placing tiny kisses
on her throat until he reached her breast. He tilted the
breast so that the dark-rose nipple just peaked out and

captured it, running his tongue over it. Again and again he circled until it hardened to a tight point.

She moaned in the back of her throat as stars exploded around her. Her body surged upwards and she knew she had to have more. She wanted to feel his skin beneath her fingers. She wanted to see if her dreams were real.

She reached out and stroked his chest. Her hands went to his neckcloth and started to undo it. She wanted to see if the strong column of his throat was as soft as his face.

Instantly he froze. His hands went to hers and stilled them. He lifted his head and looked at her with dark passion-filled eyes.

'No,' he said in a ragged voice. 'Say it, Sophie.'

'No?' she whispered. Surely he couldn't mean to stop. Her body wanted—no, needed his touch. She wanted to touch him like he had touched her. 'Why not?'

'Just say it. Like you mean it. You must, Sophie!'

'No! Richard—'

He put two fingers against her aching lips and shook his head, before flopping back against the cushion. 'Because I refuse to have your first time be a frantic coupling in a carriage.'

Sophie looked down at her naked breasts. They puckered slightly in the cold air now that his mouth wasn't on them. Exposed. Lewd and wanton. All the words she'd been called before.

She quickly crossed her arms over them. The delicate fabric of the blouse tore, a loud ripping sound which seemed to signal her reputation was equally torn and shredded.

She struggled to get the words out. 'My first time?'

His eyes were heavy-lidded with passion.

'You do know what passes between a man and a woman, Sophie.'

'Yes, of course.' Her cheeks burnt. It was all the worse for the gentleness of his tone. He thought her completely ignorant in the ways of men. Another man would have taken advantage of her, but not Richard. She straightened her shoulders. 'We whispered about it at school, and one of the girls had *Aristotle's Compleat Masterpiece.*'

'How did she get it?'

'She had borrowed it from her father's library and sneaked it back after the Christmas break. We passed it from girl to girl until Miss Denton found it and destroyed it. She would have expelled the girl, but her grandfather was an earl.' Sophie gave an uneasy laugh. Talking made it easier to forget what she had nearly done, how she was truly wicked rather than good. Her last few years of keeping herself aloof had been for nothing. She forced a soft laugh which sounded far too throaty. 'You would not have believed the uproar.'

'But you read it first. You were not the sort of girl to allow an opportunity like that to slip between her fingers.'

Sophie gave a reluctant nod. He seemed to know her young self so well. 'It was full of astonishing information. I wanted to know. Thinking back, it probably was one of the reasons why I was such easy prey.'

'You have a good instinct, Sophie. It is better to know

than to be frightened.' He reached out and pulled her over to him so that her head lay against his chest. The racing thud of his heart resounded in her ear. 'You did the right thing. Cawburn took advantage of you and your good nature. Never stop believing that. You are delightful, innocent and very much a lady.'

She started to sit up, but he gently held her there with one hand, while the other moved her blouse up over her shoulders, straightening her costume with almost impersonal expertise.

'Shush now, let me put you right. Nothing happened here that can't be fixed. I am to blame, not you.'

His fingers neatly did up her back. He was probably used to playing the ladies' maid, Sophie thought miserably.

He knew how this game was played and she had only heard rumours and read the book. She knew the theory and none of the practicalities. She should feel better that he accepted the blame, but all she felt was hollow and depressed. Her inexperience had stopped him, not her virtue.

She'd hate herself later, but right now, even the impersonal touch of his putting her clothing to rights made her thrum with desire. She'd spent years denying what she was and now she knew.

When he had finished, he set her from him. His face was very serious, far more serious than she had ever seen it before.

'If we continued on,' he said in a low voice, 'I would have been unable to stop. I was barely able to control myself as it was. You do understand how hard it can be to stop when two people desire each other, don't you?'

'I suppose you say it was all my fault. I should never have goaded you.' The words tasted bitter in her mouth. He was going to behave precisely like Sebastian Cawburn. She had been wrong to think any differently. It was all her fault for allowing the romance to go to her head. She couldn't be trusted. 'And I should be grateful for your restraint. My behaviour must disgust you. It falls so far short of what is socially acceptable.'

He placed two fingers over her mouth and shook his head.

'I want you, Sophie,' he said slowly and patiently. 'I have wanted you since the first time I held you in my arms. I want you more than I have ever wanted a woman. But not here and not like this. I want it done right. There is far too much at stake.'

'You want me?' she whispered. Her heart gave a little leap. She didn't disgust him. He desired her. But desiring her didn't mean he wanted to marry her or even that he cared about her.

'Desperately.' He took her hand and placed it on the front of his trousers. He was rigid beneath her palm. Her traitorous fingers itched to linger and trace the line of him.

Sophie jerked her hand back as if it had burnt her. She was all the words Sebastian had snarled at her— wanton, a cock-tease and worse. She had the soul of a loose woman. She had fought for years, trying to deny it, but she'd proved it in this carriage. She'd allowed her heart to overrule her common sense. She would have to take steps. They would have to end today.

'I suppose you want me to thank you for your forbearance then, for resisting your baser instincts,' she

said, tears brimming in her eyes. 'It was an act of sin-
gular virtue. It won't happen again. I have learnt my
lesson.'

'Thank me for what?' Richard asked, remorse and
regret swamping his senses. Sophie made it sound as
though he was a saint. He was far from that.

He had gone further than he wanted, but the result
would be the same. There could be no objections to their
marriage...from anyone. He could make sure that she
stayed in his life. He had wanted her to have a choice,
but now she had none. He had to keep her off balance
and use the desire she felt for him to achieve his goal.
He knew the power of seduction and had sworn not to
use it against Sophie, but he saw no other way of securing her agreement in marriage.

'For saving me and reminding me of what could
have happened here.' Sophie made a helpless gesture
with her hand. 'I will hate myself enough as it is later.
I thought I was better than that, but obviously I was
wrong. I overestimated my own virtue. We will have
to end after today, never be alone again. I thought you
should know I do appreciate the way you have protected
me, even from myself.'

'I think you want me as well.' He forced his voice
to continue on as if she hadn't spoken. Her virtue did
not stand a chance against his seduction. He'd known
that since the first time they kissed. Now, he'd broken
his promise. He was seducing her, but seducing her
into a marriage, a marriage which was not the sort she
wanted. He could not promise love. He didn't believe in
it. The very thought of it scared him to death. To love
someone was to be abandoned when you needed them

the most. When given a choice, those he'd loved had chosen someone else.

His heart thudded so loudly he thought she must hear. Sophie had no choice if she wanted to remain within society—she had to marry him. Just now he'd taken every other option from her.

Because of her desire to appear virtuous, she wouldn't abandon him, even if she found out what he was truly like. Even if she found out that his mother had not wanted him and his father wasn't interested in him beyond what was required of his duty.

It bothered him that a small piece of him wanted her to have a choice. For once he wanted someone to choose him, but he also knew he wasn't prepared to take the risk. He'd deal with the consequences later. He'd trust Sophie's desire to appear virtuous would outweigh any need to escape from the marriage.

'There are two people in this carriage, Sophie. You kissed me back, more than dutifully kissed me. There was passion in your kiss and I heard your cry when I suckled your breasts. You enjoyed it. But you deserve better than this for your first time. You deserve white sheets and a closed door. You deserve time, rather than frenzy. It needs to be done properly, Sophie.'

'It was wrong of me. It won't happen again.' Sophie stared straight ahead, not meeting his eye. 'No one has to know.'

'You are wrong there. You and I both know and I have little desire to forget.'

Tears brimmed in her eyes. It took all of his self-control not to pull her into his arms. But he had gone too far already. He had to make certain she would be his.

He refused to risk losing her. Once her former guardian returned, the objections to his suit would overwhelm her desire for him. He had to act now. He had to be ruthless about it.

'But we can be strong,' she whispered.

'This thing between us is growing. It is not diminishing.' He lifted her hand to his lips. 'Say you feel it as well and it is not just me who is waking every night in a hot sweat with your name on my lips and the dream of you in my arms.'

Sophie knew he was right. The ache in her middle had grown and she knew she craved his touch. For the past ten days, she'd woken with her hand between her legs, a nameless ache in her middle and Richard's name ringing in her ears. Every night she promised herself that this time she'd dream of something else and she never did.

During the day, she found herself hoping that he would call unexpectedly and reliving each one of his accidental touches when he was not there. She had taken to sketching the shape of his eyes, the way his hands looked when they held his cane and the curve of his mouth, most especially the curve of his mouth.

She wanted to feel ashamed about what she had done in the carriage, but she found it was impossible. He made her feel womanly and desirable. He was right. She might be wicked, but he was totally different from Sebastian. He had stopped it before she was utterly ruined. It had been him to pull back, not her, and she'd know that to her dying day.

She shook her head and tried to get control of her wayward thoughts. There were so many reasons why they needed to end it today, before the unthinkable happened and she was utterly ruined. But she could not bear the thought of never seeing him again, never hearing his voice or having his lips against hers. But he had said nothing of marriage.

'I suppose it is best that no one discovered us.' She waited for his agreement.

'And if I say that I want you in my bed? I want to spend hours exploring your body? I want to see your golden hair spread out against white-linen sheets. I want to see what moonlight does to your skin. I want to wake up in the morning and have your face be the first thing I see.'

'It can't happen.' She forced her shoulders to relax. The picture he painted was doing strange things to her insides. He had only mentioned desire, she reminded her rebellious heart. And she knew where that led. She refused to go back to that room where she felt unclean and sordid, even for Richard. Silently she bid the picture goodbye. A deep empty well opened within her. Richard Crawford was precisely like Sebastian Cawburn and she'd be wrong to forget that. She'd refused his first offer, had insisted on this sham and why would he ask her again, particularly now when he knew what she was like? 'You are wrong to ask me.'

'It can happen.' He leant forwards and smoothed a tendril of hair from her forehead. 'It can, Sophie.'

'How?' she whispered from aching lips. 'How can it? If I do that I will be outside society and I refuse to behave that way, even for you, Richard. How can you ask this of me, knowing all that, knowing my background?'

'You wrong me.' He gathered her in his arms and

pressed his mouth to her hair. 'There is only one remedy, Sophie. We must marry.'

She leant back against his arms and tried to ignore the sudden leaping of her heart. He wanted to marry her! He was asking her again. She quashed the thought. Men like him dealt in some day, not in reality. They were back to where they had started. 'You mean in due course. Some day. Easy words, but you are asking me to take an unacceptable risk.'

He laced his fingers through her hand. 'No, I mean as soon as possible. A special licence. I take full responsibility for what happened here and I would never insult you by making you my mistress. My honour gives me no alternative but to make you my wife…if you will have me.'

'A special licence?' Her heart thudded. Richard was utterly serious. And despite her actions, he was prepared to behave honourably. She'd wronged him in thinking he wasn't safe in carriages. It was she who wasn't, but this time it had worked out.

'Neither of us is made of steel. The next time, we might not be so lucky and we might be discovered. The choice would be taken out of your hands. Either marriage to me, or confess to your stepmother on your own and you know she will look at your state of undress and make the logical conclusion.'

'But…but…' Sophie tried to think of a logical reason while her heart soared. Richard was right. They could be married by a special licence. Given Richard's family background, there would be no problem in getting a licence. He wanted to truly marry her. He felt the same way about her. He had to. She put her hand to her head.

Against the odds, he had proposed a second time. If she refused, there would be no third time.

He placed a gentle kiss on the corner of her mouth. The touch was filled with possibility. 'Say yes, Sophie. Put me out of my agony. Or let me go, but don't keep torturing me in this way. Say yes, Sophie, and come into my bed. Be my wife, please.'

She knew in that instant she couldn't allow him to go, even though he had not mentioned finer feelings or love. He made her feel alive. If he went, the world would be a miserable place. She had to take the greatest risk of her life. She had to believe in the romance. She had to do it or face a lifetime of wondering what might have been. He might not have said anything about his finer feelings, but she had to believe in them. She wanted to believe in this improbable romance.

'Yes,' she whispered back. 'We will marry as soon as possible.'

'Sophie! What on earth has happened to you?' Her stepmother's outraged voice greeted Sophie the instant she walked in the door. And she knew Richard's ministrations as a lady's maid had failed.

As she caught sight of her hair, her ripped blouse and her overly kissed mouth in the hall mirror confirmed her hunch. There was no hiding what she had done. She was only thankful that Richard had immediately ordered the carriage to start moving again and that he had simply held her hand all the way back home.

'Congratulate me, Stepmother.' A huge bubble of excitement coursed through Sophie's veins. She cleared her throat and straightened her shoulders. 'I'm proud to announce I am getting married to Lord Bingfield.'

'I know you are getting married. When Robert and Henri return from the Continent. It is all decided.' Her stepmother clasped her hands together. 'You told me this not three days ago when the news that the settlement had been reached. I'm so grateful that Henri will be able to help with planning the engagement party. It should be the pinnacle of the summer's entertainment. An autumn wedding will do.' Her stepmother walked around Sophie. 'I want to know what has happened to you! If anyone saw you…well, they'd think the worst. Did the carriage turn over? You look as if you have been through a hedge backwards.'

Sophie was grateful for Richard's hand in the middle of her back. He was there, supporting her. They had discussed in the carriage about the best way to tell her stepmother. While Sophie had wanted to tell her on her own, Richard refused to hear of it. They were doing it together or not at all.

'We are marrying as soon as practicable, Mrs Ravel,' Richard said in a tone which allowed for no opposition. 'I will see the Bishop after I leave here. There will be no problem with obtaining a licence.'

'But the settlement, the party after Robert and Henri arrive, the society wedding. The wedding breakfast.' Her stepmother started to fan herself. 'I want it to be special…for Sophie. Everyone is sure to want to be there.'

Sophie's insides twisted. All of her white lies to placate her stepmother were coming back to haunt her. *But would it have been any better if she'd known the truth?* a little voice inside her nagged.

'Sophie! Are you going to answer me?'

'Sophie and I—' Richard began, but her stepmother turned towards him, fury contorting her face.

'Pardon me, Lord Bingfield, but I want to hear my stepdaughter's answer. It seems from the look of her that she has been up to mischief and I want to know how deep this mischief runs! Sophie, what have you done? Did you go to the cricket match? Or did you go to an inn? Are you breeding?'

'Mrs Ravel!' Richard thundered.

Sophie gave Richard's hand a squeeze. She'd have to play this out. To confess to her stepmother what she had just done and why a marriage was now imperative, particularly as the engagement had been a false one, was impossible. Her stepmother's hysterics was the last thing she wanted to face.

'The settlement is more than adequate and stop using Robert's approval as an excuse.' Sophie fixed her step-mother with her eye. 'Richard's solicitor agreed to all my demands and you know they were designed to pro-tect mine and Father's fortune. I showed you the letter from the solicitors. Robert and Henri will understand. We don't truly know the date they intended to return. Everything else like the wedding breakfast and a large wedding is mere frippery.'

Her stepmother opened her mouth several times, but no sound came out.

'Even if they did intend to come back in early June, they might be delayed for all sorts of reasons,' Sophie argued. 'I don't see any reason to wait any longer. Sometimes you just know when the time is right. And Richard agrees with me.'

'But the party? I wanted everything to be special for you. You are to be a society bride. This sudden headlong dash towards marriage sounds like a very hole-in-the-corner affair. People will talk. They will look at your waist and count.'

'Let them.' Sophie tilted her chin in the air. 'I've nothing to hide. Let them whisper and titter if they must, but I haven't done *anything* to be ashamed of.'

Richard's hand tightened over hers. She was grateful for the touch. She'd been foolish to worry that they weren't well acquainted. They would be spending the rest of their lives together and Richard appeared to understand her so well.

'We shall have to have a ball to celebrate the wedding when we return from the wedding trip. Problem solved. Right, Richard?'

'I feel certain my father would approve of such a measure, Mrs Ravel,' Richard said in a smooth voice. 'We should have two. One in Newcastle and one at Hallington to introduce Sophie to the neighbourhood. After all, she will be the Marchioness of Hallington one day.'

Her stepmother beamed with pleasure and Sophie knew Richard had promised precisely the right thing.

'And London, let there be a ball in London.' Her stepmother clapped her hands. 'It will be the talk of the autumn season.'

Richard squeezed Sophie's hand tighter. It amazed her that he seemed to instinctively know the prospect of a ball unnerved her. 'That will be for Sophie to decide. But before any of that happens, Sophie and I will marry. We see no point in waiting. I expect you to attend the wedding.'

Her stepmother's ribbons trembled. 'You are eloping?'

'We will be married by special licence as soon as possible. I intend to see the Bishop of Durham this evening. If he is unwilling, I will travel down to Canterbury tomorrow and get permission from the Archbishop himself. At the very worst we will be married in two days' time.'

'What I don't understand is the sudden need for haste!' Her stepmother's eyes narrowed and she examined Sophie's waist.

Now it was Sophie's turn to be outraged by what her stepmother was thinking. She crossed her arms and glared. 'Stepmother.'

'I want Sophie for my bride; I am hardly likely to take her for my mistress. I value her too highly.'

Value. The word thudded a warning through Sophie. She dismissed it. Value was close enough to love.

'Your stepdaughter has not been dishonoured, Mrs Ravel. You have my word on it.'

Sophie could hear the unspoken 'yet' in Richard's voice. She swallowed hard, knowing how close they had come in the carriage and whose fault it had been. It could so easily have been a forced marriage. As it was she had had a choice and she had chosen Richard. She loved how she had felt alive in his arms. Her entire body thrummed with the memory.

Sophie held out her arms and willed her stepmother to give in. 'Please say you will be there. Help me make my wedding a joyous occasion. Give me your blessing.'

Her stepmother threw up her hands in capitulation. The tension flowed out of Sophie. She had won. 'But the wedding breakfast. Sophie's wedding dress?'

'You had best start preparing it.' Richard's eyes twinkled. 'There is not a moment to lose. Once I have the licence, I will marry Sophie in whatever dress she happens to be wearing.'

'And I am more than happy to wear my white ball gown. We can easily fashion a veil. There is a mountain of tulle lace left from my latest ball gown. I will look like a fashionable bride, Stepmother.' Sophie gave her stepmother a hard stare. 'I will not disgrace you or my late father, but I will be married as soon as Richard can arrange it. The alternative is unthinkable.'

Her stepmother turned bright red and hurried from the hall.

Richard's laugh boomed out. He caught her in his arms and hugged her to him. 'That went well. Better than you feared. Your stepmother will be at the wedding.'

'Thank you,' Sophie said, letting out a breath. He seemed to understand her so well. 'You made it easy. I didn't know what I was going to say to her and how to confess about what nearly happened in the carriage.'

'There is nothing to confess. We were engaged and now we are getting married. It is the natural order of things.' He placed a soft kiss on her lips. Her entire being tingled with anticipation. She looped her arms about his neck, inviting him to deepen the kiss, but he gave a slight shake of his head. 'The next time I see you I will have the licence and we can be together, properly.'

A quiet thrill filled Sophie. She had left this morning thinking that she should end their acquaintance and she'd come back a nearly bride. The quickness of it made her head spin.

They were right not to wait. The alternative was far too dangerous. This way they could say that there was no dishonour and that they chose to marry, rather than being forced into it.

She leant back against his arms, memorising the planes of his face and the way a lock of hair flopped over his forehead. Later she intended to draw him from memory so she could have a memento of today.

'Is everything all right, Sophie?'

Her smile widened. She could tease him now. 'Then you had best get the licence and I will see about this wedding breakfast you require. Send me a note when you know.'

He nipped her chin. 'The only thing I require is you in my bed as soon as possible. As my lawful bride.'

Chapter Ten

'Richard, what is going on? Hannah returned practically in tears because of your cruelty this afternoon.
How dare you!' His mother's voice assaulted Richard
when he walked into his rooms later that evening.

Myers gave him an apologetic look, but Richard
merely smiled at his valet. He patted his coat pocket
which held the special licence. Nothing was going to
disrupt his happiness, not even his mother and her accusations. Sophie would be properly his tomorrow. He
had done it. Sophie would belong to him. His refuge
from the world would be secure.

As he had suspected, the Bishop of Durham had been
more than happy to oblige the son of the Marquess of
Hallington and had even offered to perform the ceremony tomorrow morning at eleven. Before he left the
Bishop, Richard penned a note to Sophie to be ready and
sent his coachman off to Sophie's house to deliver it.

Tension flowed from his shoulders. Sophie would
know now what tomorrow would bring. Things had
worked out better than he'd hoped this morning. He

had succeeded—even his mother and her accusations of cruelty towards his sister could not change his future.

He looked forward to initiating Sophie tomorrow afternoon in the art of bedsport, but first he had to deal with his mother.

'Congratulate me, Mother, I am going to marry.'

His mother's face pursed like she had just swallowed a sour plum. 'To the common chit whom you have used as a decoy when you were negotiating Hannah's marriage? But how? Why? You have barely spent any time with her beyond your duty.'

'To Sophie, yes.' Richard frowned. His mother had no right to speak of Sophie in that fashion. And he had kept his visits with Sophie private. Sometimes his mother was a worse snob than his aunt. 'You will like her when you meet her. You will find her an admirable daughter-in-law. There is nothing common about Sophie at all. You will see why I married her once you are acquainted with her.'

His mother raised an eyebrow. 'I have heard from your sister that Miss Ravel is a classic Beauty with a friendly unaffected manner. However, Hannah is no judge of character. I thought we had agreed—there is no need to actually marry the girl. If a woman wishes to ruin herself, allow her. You did the honourable thing. You proposed, she refused. You have squired her to a few amusements, but you were well chaperoned.'

'She has accepted my offer. My second offer.'

'This woman was merely the excuse you were going to give your father if he required an answer.'

'You chose to believe that, Mother. I saw no need to correct your assumption.'

'Are you telling me that there was more to it?' His mother paled visibly. 'What have you done, Richard? How did she trap you?'

'Mother, my relationship with Sophie is none of your business.' Richard breathed deeply. His mother had never met Sophie. She could not possibly understand why he needed to be certain that she would remain in his life. He wasn't even sure he understood. He only knew that he had to have her. 'Why did you allow Hannah to go to the match today? I asked you to prevent it.'

'She wanted to. Ronald wanted her there.' His mother ran a finger along the oak table. 'I don't see why you had to take rooms here in Granger Street. Your man does not clean properly. You could have stayed with us. It would have been good to have you there when you were needed, rather than me having to seek you out.'

Richard gave a faint shudder at the thought of staying any length of time with either of his parents. With his father, they were at least able to be in separate wings. His mother's house on Charlotte Square was a reasonable size, but not overly large. And given his impending marriage, these rooms would have to do as a bridal suite. He withdrew the licence from his coat pocket.

'I will be married tomorrow, Mother, and that is the end of it. Remember, Sophie is *my* chosen bride and address her civilly. Otherwise don't bother.'

'May I come to the wedding or am I to be forbidden as unfit for society? My father was a baronet. And now every door is shut to me.' His mother slammed her fists together. 'Why? Because of your father and his vindictive nature.'

'I haven't told Sophie about you and Hannah yet,'

Richard admitted between clenched teeth. Trust his mother to hit on the nub of the problem. His plans had moved at a breathtaking rate after Sophie melted in his arms. He had to trust Sophie would understand why he hadn't told her before the wedding. 'Events rather overtook us. If there was any trapping to be done, it was me who pushed. I want her for my bride. You who followed your heart and abandoned your family surely must understand this?'

His mother digested the news with difficulty. 'Do you love her?'

'What does love have to do with it?' He refused to discuss his feelings for Sophie with his mother of all people! They were far too new and raw. He had never felt like this about anyone before. All he knew was that he wanted her in his arms for always. He also knew he'd forced the marriage, rather than trusting Sophie to make the right decision.

'I know what it is like to be in a loveless marriage, Richard. I suffered dreadfully. You have no idea how it can suffocate you. I thought I'd go mad if your father mentioned his pigs again.'

He crossed over to the desk. 'My father has written. The letter arrived this morning. He is coming to Newcastle. I have no idea when he will arrive. I thought you should know. He is apparently prepared to leave his pigs to meet Sophie.'

His mother went white and she staggered over to the sofa. 'You swore this wouldn't happen. He never travels up here. He knows I am here. Whatever am I to do? Do you suppose he knows about Hannah's impending marriage? Could Parthenope have heard a whisper?

That woman is a menace! She has always aided and abetted your father.'

'He wants to meet Sophie. He makes no mention of you or my sister.' Richard's mouth twisted and he clenched his fist. He'd been the one to taunt his aunt at the At Home. Now, he potentially had both his parents thinking Sophie was beneath him. 'I suspect my aunt did not send a favourable report. And I do not intend to have any of his interference in my marriage.'

His mother nodded as she withdrew a handkerchief and dabbed her eyes. She gave a shuddering sigh before she continued. 'Perhaps you are wise. It is best your bride meets your father without knowing about your sister or me.'

'Why? I would have thought Hannah would want to go to my wedding.'

'Your bride-to-be is the one who was supposed to be keeping your engagement quiet, but before twenty-four hours were up, she announced it to the packed Assembly Rooms in a very dramatic fashion. If she meets your father, she might suddenly take it into her head to blurt out about Hannah and her engagement.'

'There were circumstances beyond her control.'

His mother gave a faint shudder. 'Can you trust this Sophie with the secret? With your father in the same city as me? After all these years? Don't you care about your sister and her happiness?'

'Mother! You are speaking about the woman who will be my wife. If I didn't trust her, I would hardly marry her.'

His mother raised her hands in supplication. 'Let me get your sister properly married first. After that, your father can't touch her. Please, for Hannah's sake. I've told you how vengeful your father is. How he hounded me and wouldn't rest. How he refused to hand over any of my dowry. He will destroy Hannah out of sheer spite, if he realises the true reason why you travelled up here. I know he will. Is this such a little request to ask of you?'

Richard pressed his lips together. The excuse would serve. The last thing he wanted was Sophie having to deal with his mother's unwarranted snobbery on her wedding day.

On the way back from the Bishop's, he had stopped at John Ormston shipping agents on the quayside and booked two first-class tickets to Hamburg, reserving the best cabin. Sophie and he could spend the summer touring Germany and Austria, taking the waters in various fashionable resorts. For Sophie, he'd brave the crossing. The agent promised as-smooth-as-glass sailing at this time of the year. They could return in the autumn, in time for Hannah's wedding. It would give his mother enough time to realise Sophie was his wife, rather than a woman who could be snubbed.

'I agree, Mother. I will tell Sophie everything eventually…when the time is right, but she will dance at my sister's wedding.' He glared at his mother. 'It will mean you and Hannah will not be able to come to my wedding.'

Tears glimmered in his mother's eyes. 'I knew I could count on you to understand, Richard. It means I fulfil my final promise to my beloved and see our daughter properly settled. It has been a worry and a bother for many years. Hannah's future must come first. You will explain that to this bride of yours. You have a title and an inheritance. Dear Grayson's daughter has nothing but her beauty and sweet nature. She must make this match.'

Richard nodded, knowing his mother had made a choice, the same choice she had made years ago when she had chosen bringing up Hannah over maintaining any contact with him. Her excuse was that he was his father's heir and his father would never have allowed him to go. His mother could never understand why he kept in contact with his father after knowing the truth about how she was treated. But his father was his father and he loved him for his eccentricities and for the way he had been there when Richard needed him as a boy.

'Happy to oblige.'

Sophie stood next to Richard before the high altar in St Nicholas's church, waiting for the ceremony to begin. She grasped the tiny nosegay of baby's breath and rosebuds, which her stepmother had managed to procure in time from the florist, tightly to her bosom and drew a quick breath. Yesterday at this time, she had just agreed to play in the cricket match, and today she was a properly attired bride.

Everything seemed to happen at such a speed, once she received Richard's note that the wedding was set for eleven this morning because of the Bishop's commitments.

Jane, her lady's maid, had been up until the early hours making sure the ball dress was properly altered and the veil securely attached to her newest straw bonnet. When she looked at herself in the full-length mirror just before going downstairs, she had to agree with

Jane's assessment that she was fashion-plate perfect. It might be a rushed wedding, but the bride would not disappoint the crowd.

Sophie wrinkled her nose. Not that there were many gathered when she arrived in her stepmother's carriage.

The large Gothic interior of St Nicholas's church loomed around her. Cold and silent. Her footsteps had echoed when she walked to the altar. Besides her stepmother, Jane and Richard's valet, the church was empty of witnesses.

'Are you all right?' Richard asked in an undertone. 'You appear pale.'

'I think my corset is one notch too tight, but I won't lock my knees and faint. I've no desire to collapse at my wedding like my friend Judith did.'

'I will catch you if you faint.'

'I believe you would.' Sophie pasted a smile on her face. Richard was here and that was all that mattered.

The Bishop began to intone the words of the service and Sophie turned to look at her bridegroom and make a memory.

Richard stood upright with a very serious expression on his face. He answered the Bishop in a loud ringing voice, whereas Sophie found it difficult to utter the words above a whisper.

'Those whom God hath joined together let no man put asunder.'

The Bishop's words as he concluded the ceremony sent a shiver down Sophie's back. And the enormity of what she had just done hit her. For better or for worse, she had married Richard Crawford and was now Lady Bingfield.

Until a few weeks ago, they had been strangers. Not like Henri, who had known Robert for years before they married, or even Cynthia, who had known her new husband for a year before they eloped. All she knew was that she had to do it or face ruin. She couldn't bear the thought of not seeing Richard again and she couldn't trust herself to stop the next time. She was so glad that Richard had given her a choice.

She would make it for better, she decided. She would be a good wife.

Richard raised her veil and placed a chaste kiss on her lips. The gentle touch did much to settle her nerves. He did want her as his wife.

'It is done,' she said, looking into his burning-gold eyes.

'Let no man put asunder,' Richard replied with a determined set of his jaw. 'We are properly married, Sophie. No one can remark now. Shall we go and have the wedding breakfast your stepmother prepared, even though I'd prefer to get straight to the wedding night?'

Sophie's cheeks heated as his warm voice did things to her insides. 'You mustn't say such things, even in jest.'

He lowered his voice as his hand squeezed her waist. 'But I am thinking them. Know that I am counting the minutes until I get you alone and in my bed.'

'Hush! My stepmother will hear and she was up nearly all night making the wedding breakfast. She even made her famous seed cake.'

'I am honoured. I will eat a slice and then we shall make our excuses. Your stepmother will understand.'

He started to escort her down the aisle. 'Neither of us is hungry for food.'

'What is going on here?' a loud overbearing masculine voice thundered at the back of the church. 'Richard, I went to your rooms and they said you were at church. Is this harum-scarum affair your wedding? And this woman—is she the common chit your aunt wrote me about?'

Sophie halted. She looked up at Richard, whose face had gone thunderous before becoming a mask of urbanity.

'The Bishop finished not a moment too soon,' Richard murmured. His hand tightened on Sophie's elbow. 'My father has arrived and is his usual charming self. Shall we go and greet him before he bellows the church down?'

'Did you know he was coming to Newcastle?' Sophie whispered, an uneasy feeling creeping up the back of her neck. Richard had known his father wouldn't approve of the match.

'I knew he had plans to travel to Newcastle. I didn't know when he'd arrive.'

Sophie stared at her new husband. He had deliberately kept his father's imminent arrival from her. What else had he hidden from her? 'You should have said.'

'What, and risk giving you or your stepmother a chance to delay the proceedings?' He gave a short laugh. 'Not likely. You are hard won, Sophie. I want my prize. I want you in my bed and this is the only way I could get you there.'

Hard won. Her heart did a little leap, but a niggling doubt filled her. Did he think his father would object to her, was that why he'd rushed the marriage? He had given her a choice, hadn't he? 'But your father...'

He pulled her closer and whispered in her ear, 'Remember you are my wife, Sophie. There is nothing my father or anyone else can do about it. You are Lady Bingfield now. You are my chosen bride. It matters not a jot what my aunt or indeed my father thinks of you. It only matters what I think.'

Sophie bit her lip. Richard made it sound as though she was somehow likely to be found wanting by Lord Hallington. Her pedigree might not be top drawer, but she was hardly a pauper. Her father had wanted her to marry into the aristocracy. She had had the right sort of education. She wasn't some governess or vicar's daughter, but... All the memories of feeling inadequate and that people were whispering behind their hands at her during her first Season came flooding back.

She regarded the red-faced Lord Hallington. Despite his high colour, she could see the family resemblance. She would have known that he was Richard's father anywhere. They shared the same facial structure and their eyes were the same colour. She tried to breathe. This was not how she had envisioned spending her first few moments of married life, confronting an irate father-in-law and trying to convince him that she was the proper person to marry his son, when she knew she had behaved very improperly. She knew the true reason for the haste.

'Meet your new daughter, Father,' Richard said, putting his hand about Sophie's waist as his gaze warred with his father's. Lord Hallington was the first to look away, defeated.

'You have married the chit!' he growled. 'Do you know what your aunt wrote about her and her family? Parthenope did not mince her words. Do you know how her father made his money? How he got his start?'

'Hardly a chit, Father, Sophie is my bride. Be civil,' Richard said, giving his father a hard look. He could happily murder his aunt. 'I have no idea what sort of report my aunt wrote, but I assure you that Sophie is *my* choice. I am the one who married her. My aunt had nothing to do with it. The sort of woman she approves of leaves me cold. As Sophie's father died years ago and I never met him, I can offer no opinion on his manners, but I've been increasingly impressed with Sophie's gentility and civility. Her stepmother is one of the kindest souls I have ever met.'

His father's frown increased. 'You would say that!'

'Sophie is now Lady Bingfield and my wife. She shares my status. I married her because I wanted to. I was determined to have her.'

'Just as you were determined to have that other chit, the one who died, the one who had you sent down from Oxford. Marry in haste, repent at leisure as my dear mother used to say.'

Sophie went cold. She'd known Richard had been sent down from Oxford, but he'd never said about wanting to marry anyone. How many other things had Richard kept from her? How well did she really know her husband?

'I see little point in bringing up ancient history, Father, and as I only received your letter after I made the appointment with the Bishop, your assumption is incorrect.'

His father spluttered something incoherent.

'If you wish to cause mischief, you may leave,' Richard continued. 'Now, you may begin again and give my bride proper congratulations or you turn around and go. I do not care which.'

He waited, barely clinging on to his temper. His father should know better. The last thing he wanted was to have a fight with his father on his wedding day, but he would protect Sophie.

His father's shoulders sagged and he appeared to age, but his face remained an unnaturally red colour. Richard braced himself for the next onslaught. Silently he thanked his guardian angel that his mother and sister were not here. When his father was in these moods, there was no reasoning with him. It was only after the colour receded that some semblance of normality returned. His father always regretted his actions, but that was not the point.

'Welcome to the family, Sophie,' his father said, holding out his hand. 'You must forgive my rough speaking. Lately I have been spending much of my time in the company of pig keepers.'

'My father's passion is pig-breeding,' Richard explained between gritted teeth. His father's bad grace was clearly evident with the way his mouth curled. He had to hope that neither Sophie nor her stepmother had noticed the rudeness. 'It is why he rarely travels far from Hallington. It rules him.'

'That is not true, Richard,' his father protested. 'I went to the Great Exhibition last year in London. I wanted to see the improvements in pig farming that the Americans had. Excellent farmers, those Americans. They truly know their pigs.'

'Did you see anything else?' Richard enquired. 'Be honest, Father.'

His father puffed up his chest. 'There wasn't time. I had to get back to my pigs. Your aunts wanted me to attend some ball. I hate balls.'

'I am not personally acquainted with any pigs,' Sophie said slowly. 'Therefore, I have much to learn. Hopefully we can have a good conversation about pigs later. I am sure they are very fascinating creatures. And sometimes I am sure they are better and more honest company than some in society.'

The red receded from his father's face and Richard knew Sophie had said precisely the right thing. His father always calmed down when he spoke of his pigs. To him, the pigs were the most important thing in the world.

'My dear, they are completely fascinating. Far more intelligent than most people.'

'You must come to the wedding breakfast, Lord Hallington,' Sophie said with a very pretty curtsy. Richard silently blessed her for being understanding. He was hard pressed to think of anyone else who could handle the situation so well.

His father raised an imperious eyebrow and looked at Richard with a disdainful expression. 'Am I invited to my only son's wedding breakfast?'

Richard's fist balled and he fought against the urge to deny the request and tell him to leave immediately. It would only end badly with both of them shouting. He refused to air his dirty linen in public. It was the last way he wanted Sophie to remember the moments after their wedding.

He struggled to find the right words which would tell his father that he was unwelcome if he persisted in this behaviour, but held the thinnest veneer of politeness. His only hope now was that Sophie remained unaware of how incredibly rude his father was being.

'Of course you are invited,' Sophie said with a perplexed frown. 'You are Richard's father and his nearest relation. Now you are mine. Had we known that you were expected today, we would have waited the ceremony for you.'

Unexpected tears came into his father's eyes. 'Truly? You would have waited for me?'

'You failed to give a time or date of your arrival, Father. You have no one to blame but yourself,' Richard said, silently blessing the fact that Sophie had not known about his father's intended arrival. He could not have taken another night without her in his arms. 'You must become more modern and consult a train timetable before you write your letters.'

His father gave an incommunicative grunt.

Richard barely restrained himself from shaking him.

'Lord Hallington, I'm Dorothy Ravel, Sophie's stepmother.' Mrs Ravel bustled up and did an extravagant curtsy. Her many ribbons and flounces quivered.

His father looked taken back at the vision of ribbons, flounces and violent clashing colours which was Mrs Ravel.

Richard wanted to shake him for not seeing the good heart which beat underneath. He was going to react like his aunt and mother—condemning the Ravels for having too fine of a manner for their station before actually knowing them.

Mrs Ravel's voice might not be cut-glass, but she was Sophie's stepmother and now his mother-in-law. She deserved more respect than a curled lip. Surely his father had to see that there was no point in making matters worse and saying the words out loud where other people could hear?

'You must come back for the wedding breakfast,' Mrs Ravel said from where she remained in the curtsy. 'I'm sure dear Bingfield had no idea of your arrival. You must be famished. I have made my famous seed cake. I found it wonderful for restoring the late Mr Ravel after travelling.'

His father's eyes gleamed for an instant before his mouth turned down. 'Seed cake? I am partial to seed cake, if it is properly made. You can't get the sort I had as a child these days. More is the pity.'

There was a defiant tilt to Sophie's head and her eyes flashed dangerously. 'My stepmother's seed cake is famous throughout Northumberland. She has won a number of competitions with it, including the blue riband at Stagshaw Fair last year. You should try it before you dismiss it out of hand, Lord Hallington.'

Richard glowed with pride. His father had not succeeded in cowing Sophie, despite his fearsome rage. His father's mouth opened and closed several times, but no sound emerged.

'I find any sort of shock is better dealt with a drop of Marsala and piece of seed cake,' Mrs Ravel said in a soothing voice. 'It is what my late husband, Sophie's father, used to swear by.'

'With an invitation like that, how can I refuse?' His father inclined his head and his eyes began to twinkle. 'Particularly when it is given by two such charming ladies.'

Richard's neck muscles relaxed. Crisis averted. He silently bid farewell to his plan of taking Sophie away to the Alps for their wedding trip straight away. A few days' delay while his father remained in Newcastle. He could not risk having his parents meet and not being there to deal with the fallout. His father was unpredictable at the best of times, and his mother might give way to hysterics. It would be wrong to expect Hannah to cope on her own.

He kicked himself for having given the promise to his mother to delay telling Sophie the full truth. But a promise was a promise, even if it was an unwise one. He could not break it without informing his mother first.

'You must ride back in my carriage, Lord Hallington. The newlyweds need a bit of privacy. Now, you will advise me… What sort of clothes will dear Sophie need in her new position? I have not had time to sort out the trousseau. And a future marchioness needs to be a leader in fashion, rather than a follower. I am sure you understand, Lord Hallington, the necessity.'

Mrs Ravel hustled his astonished father away, leaving him alone with a white-faced Sophie. Her hand clutched her nosegay as if she were drowning and it was the only thing which could save her. His father had badly shaken her. He struggled to control his anger at his father and recapture that feeling of pride and anticipation he had had when they finished their vows.

'Shall we go to this wedding breakfast?'

Chapter Eleven

Sophie bit back her questions about Richard's past until they were in Richard's carriage. Safely out of earshot of anyone else. The last thing she wanted was the humiliation of having to ask for explanations for things her new husband should have told her about *before* they married. She had her pride.

When they had come out of the church, a light rain had started to fall, but a small crowd had gathered, waiting for them. She thought she'd seen Hannah Grayson hurrying away with a heavily veiled woman and somehow it made things worse.

Yesterday, Miss Grayson had been so happy about her upcoming wedding and all the plans. It was sure to be a big society affair with lots of friends and relations, much as Robert and Henri's had been.

There could not be a greater contrast with her hurried hole-in-the-corner affair with barely anyone attending. She had never considered her wedding would be like this, particularly not with her bridegroom's father demanding an explanation as to why Richard had married so quickly.

There could be only one conclusion. Lord Hallington had intended to stop this marriage, just as he had stopped another marriage. If he had arrived sooner, would Richard have even married her? Would she even have been in that carriage with him?

A small knot of misery formed in the pit of her stomach. Moments before she'd been so happy and excited to be married to Richard. Now she realised that she knew very little about him. She knew small things like how passionate he was about cricket and what a brilliant dancer he was, that he took his tea black, but she didn't know any of the truly big things, particularly how he'd conducted his previous relationships. She'd waited and waited for him to talk about the scandals in his past, or indeed anything significant about his childhood, but he hadn't. He hadn't even given her a subtle opportunity. And now they were married. Rather than marrying a friend, she'd married a stranger.

'When were you going to tell me about your father's imminent arrival in Newcastle? Before or after the wedding trip?' she asked in a deadly calm voice, the sort she only used when she was very upset. The taste of unshed tears slid down the back of her throat. She looked up at the roof and blinked rapidly. She absolutely refused to cry on her wedding day. Her wedding day! She was supposed to be happy, not feel as though she had been kicked in the stomach by a horse.

'My father sent a note saying he intended to travel to Newcastle. He failed to give a date or time, merely that I should expect him.' He put an arm about her shoulders, but she shrugged it off. 'I am a grown man. I refuse to wait attendance on him.'

'People don't travel like that, not these days,' Sophie protested as her mind reeled. What was it that Richard wasn't telling her? She had always hated it when her father was alive and he had kept things from her. She'd always vowed it would not happen to her again. She didn't need protecting from anything, particularly not his family. 'There are timetables and schedules. People send letters. The post takes a matter of hours.'

'My father is remarkably old-fashioned about such things, as you will discover. This is possibly the first time he has ever taken a train.' He covered her hand with his, but she withdrew it. 'In the past he called trains the devil's creation and stoutly refused to consider boarding one.'

The back of Sophie's neck prickled. Old-fashioned. Was he also old-fashioned about the sort of woman he wanted his son to marry? She wanted to be a credit to Richard, not drive a wedge between him and his father. 'You know your father best.'

'You must believe me, Sophie.' He put his hands on her shoulders and turned her to face him. His face bore a pleading expression. 'I truly didn't expect him to arrive today. There have been times in my life that he has promised to arrive, but some crisis with his pigs has prevented him. I have given up expecting him to do things because I want him to be there. And I did want to marry you as soon as possible, rather than waiting for my father who might not appear. My aunts always came to Montem Day at Eton with a picnic for my cousins, but my father never managed, despite saying he would. Do you know how hard it is to wait for someone to appear and then for them not to show up because their prized sow has given birth to piglets?'

Sophie's heart bled for the younger Richard who had wanted his father and had been overlooked for a load of pigs. Her father might have been busy, but he'd always been there when she had needed him. She couldn't imagine the pain and humiliation Richard must have felt.

'I didn't know. My father always made time for me… after my mother died.'

'My father has said on numerous occasions that he will never go to Newcastle. You heard my aunt at your stepmother's At Home. I refused to wait any longer for you in my bed and in my life.' He raised her hand to his lips. 'I refused to give you an opportunity for delay and you wanted this marriage to happen quickly as well. You agreed to it.'

'I suppose.'

'I'm selfish, Sophie.' He put his hand to his heart. 'One of my worst faults. I admit it, but can you blame me? You are too great a prize to risk.'

Sophie gripped her flowers tighter. She had spent her entire life trying to be genteel and refined, and Richard's family didn't think she was. Any more than Sebastian had or indeed some of the truly refined girls at school. 'But you were going to tell me about your aunt's verdict.'

'Any report my aunt made to my father matters not a jot to me. I told her so at the At Home.' He gave a heart-melting smile which sent a shot of warmth coursing through her. Sophie struggled to ignore it.

His aunt's verdict might not have mattered to him

then, back when the engagement was false, but would it matter one day? His aunt's report had mattered to his father.

'I have the wedding trip all planned,' Richard said, seemingly oblivious to her concerns. 'We are going to Hamburg and then we will travel to the Alps. For you and your dreams, I will travel on the sea. You would not believe how efficient shipping agents can be when you explain it is for a wedding trip and are willing to pay. It is where you said you always wanted to go. I shall pose for you in an Alpine meadow. You can paint and then we shall see where it leads.'

Sophie's heart did a little leap. He did remember the dream she had abandoned after the Sebastian incident. It was more than the painting. She bit her lip, torn between her desire to see the Alps and the knowledge that her father-in-law had indeed travelled all the way up from Hampshire to Newcastle. And if Richard was to be believed, taking a train for the first time in order to meet her and see if his aunt's judgement was correct.

She drew a shuddering breath and felt stronger. There was little point in crying over what might have been. 'We may have to postpone the wedding trip. Your father is here now. It seems churlish to leave. Can you work up your courage again to brave the sea? I promise to hold your hand all the way.'

'You have a very sweet nature, Lady Bingfield.' He raised her hand to his lips. 'Very sweet indeed. My father was a foul-tempered brute today, but he is my father. He can be very charming when he makes the effort. It will mean a lot to him if we stay.'

'We can go later in the year. It will be all the more

pleasant.' Silently Sophie resolved to win Lord Hallington over. She would prove to him that she was a worthy daughter-in-law, rather than the sort of woman he thought her to be.

'You are sitting far, far too far away from me, Lady Bingfield.'

Sophie sat up straighter and concentrated on her nosegay. If she allowed it, he would change the subject and she might never learn anything more about him. It was important that she know. The true extent of her ignorance frightened her and the knot of misery seemed to be growing larger.

'Was it true what your father said about you marrying someone else?' she asked around the hard lump in her throat.

'I hardly intend to spend my wedding day discussing other people, but I made my vow never to be the knowing instrument of Putney after I learnt of Mary's tragic death in an accident.' He made a cutting motion with his hand. 'I was young and had been just sent down. Mary's family decided not to wait and married her off before I had a chance to return. Mary had been resisting the match before. He was a friend of Putney's. Mary decided to escape the marriage and died in a canal-boat accident. Her sister said that she was on her way to me. How much of that was true I didn't know. I resolved never again to knowingly let that happen.'

'I'm sorry.' Sophie closed her eyes. His insistence that his first proposal was a real one now made sense.

'Whether or not I'd have married her is pure speculation. It didn't happen. I can truly say that of all the women I have met, you are the only one who has tempted me to put my head in the parson's noose.'

'My friend Henri lost her first husband shortly after they married. For years she refused to even look at another man.'

'The state of my heart had nothing to do with my reasons for not marrying.' Richard's features appeared carved out of stone. 'I have seen the problems firsthand when your heart rules your head. I had not met anyone I wanted to marry until I met you. All of the women I became involved with did not tempt me, Sophie. Several of them tried.'

Sophie looked at her nosegay where the tiny pink roses stared up at her in mute rebuke. He had not claimed any finer feeling. She had simply assumed. She had wanted to marry a friend for love and she'd married a stranger for desire. And the stranger was highly experienced, whereas she had no experience in these matters.

'Your father didn't approve of me. It is why he came up.' Sophie tightened her grip on the nosegay and hoped he'd understand and give her some measure of reassurance. 'Your father seemed so angry at the wedding. I have never seen anyone go red like that before.'

'Once he gets to know you properly, he will approve wholeheartedly. Trust me on this. I know my father and what he wants for me. You are precisely what I require in a wife and that is what is important.' He leant over and kissed her forehead.

Sophie tried to hang on to his words and use them to quieten the hard knot in her stomach. What he required in a wife. They were not precisely words of love, but it would have to do. For now. But he seemed to be holding something back, something vital, and it niggled at her insides. 'I will attempt to remember that.'

'Now, are we going to enjoy the day, our wedding day, or are we going to spend the time discussing people and events that have no bearing on our future?'

'That went better than I had hoped,' Sophie said as they left the wedding breakfast in Richard's carriage. She had changed from her wedding dress into a smart bottle-green dress with a matching tailored jacket. Her tiny pillbox hat with its dyed green feather and the beaded gloves completed the outfit. She thought it set off her blonde hair admirably. The warmth she had seen in Richard's eyes when she came down the stairs with her crinoline imported directly from Paris slightly swinging to reveal her ankles encased in half-boots made the time she'd spent getting ready worth it.

The tiny hard knot in the pit of her stomach faded.

Contrary to her earlier fears, Lord Hallington had proved remarkably charming at the wedding breakfast and had gone out of his way to be kind to her stepmother, even going so far as to compliment her on using wax flowers rather than the real thing. Apparently Lord Hallington had recently developed a passion for collecting china pugs, but her stepmother had a number which he had not seen before.

'Did my father say how long he was staying in Newcastle? He merely told me that he was staying as long as necessary. I want to start the wedding trip as soon as possible. I have promised you the Alps and you shall have them.'

Sophie laughed at Richard's expression. It had been obvious to her at the wedding breakfast that Lord Hallington adored his only child. He had simply been upset at the suddenness of the marriage and hungry. Once he had eaten a bit, she could see where Richard had acquired his charm from.

'He has taken rooms at the Neville Hotel on my stepmother's advice. He said nothing to me, but from what I understood from my stepmother when I changed into my going-away dress, it will be a week or two, possibly three.'

'As long as that?'

'He plans to visit his mother's grave. My stepmother has undertaken to be his guide as he is now family.' Sophie tapped her finger to her chin. She should have remembered what Lady Parthenope had said on the first night about visiting her mother's grave. It provided the perfect explanation as to why Lord Hallington was uncomfortable in Newcastle. 'That must be the reason he never visits here. The memory is far too painful for him.'

'I am thankful that he had enough sense to realise that he would not be a welcome addition to our rooms.' Richard wrapped his arms about her and pulled her close. 'I am postponing the wedding trip on his account. I'm not postponing anything else.'

'You shall have to take me to your grandmother's grave so I can pay my respects.'

He loosened his arms and a surprised expression crossed his face. 'I will find out from my father where it is.'

'Don't you know?' Sophie asked in dismay.

'Until my aunt said something the other day, I had forgotten—if I had ever known. My grandmother died before I was born. I know its general location.'

'It would be a good thing for me to visit it.' Sophie forced a smile. 'Something to discuss with your aunt when I next meet her.'

'I do refuse to discuss the dead, departed and most particularly my aunts on my wedding day, Sophie.'

The tiny hard knot returned with a vengeance. Her husband was a stranger. She had thought she'd known, but could she count on him in a crisis?

She reached up and brushed her lips against his. 'I'm sorry.'

'That's better.' He gathered her to him again and returned the kiss, nibbling her bottom lip. 'I have wanted to do this all day.'

'Do you think it is too early? The sun hasn't set. What will the servants think?'

He put his hands on either side of her face. 'Promise me never to be shy with me, Sophie. You are beautiful and I want to unwrap all the layers of your clothes and feast on your magnificent body.'

'My stepmother sent Jane on ahead, so that she'd be there with my things, waiting to help me get ready. We have everything planned.'

'Your stepmother and your maid have no place in our marriage bed.' He put his forehead against hers. 'It is well that I told Myers that the entire staff were to have the afternoon and the evening off. He will ensure your things have been safely put away, but no one remains. You will have to allow me to be your maid for tonight.'

Sophie gulped. 'We will be entirely alone.'

'What passes between us, Sophie, is strictly private. No audience needed.'

Rather than glancing at his face, Sophie toyed with the beaded portion of her glove. She wasn't sure if she should feel pleased or distinctly shocked. He made it seem as though it was an everyday occurrence. And for him perhaps it was. She didn't want to think about all the other women he must have known. She had to wonder if Myers was used to disappearing when Richard brought his new mistress back to his rooms. Not mistress, she corrected her thoughts. She was his wife. 'Is it normal for married people to behave this way?'

'Normal people be damned! It is how I want to behave.'

Sophie folded her hands together primly. 'I merely asked. I didn't want to provoke comment. I know how servants talk and gossip. I was brought up to respect convention.'

'There won't be, not about that.' He took her hand and slowly removed her glove, finger by finger. The gold band gleamed against her naked flesh. 'People do not pry into the bedroom of married people, Sophie. Our marriage will be on everyone's lips for a few weeks. Can your conventional soul withstand that?'

'Yes.' She put her hand on Richard's cheek and felt the soft bristles against her palm. 'I have never done this before.'

'We are both new at marriage.' He turned his face to her palm and kissed it. 'We shall grow in it together.'

His words sent a soothing balm over her jangled nerves. He might be infinitely more experienced in the ways of love than she, but he had never been married before, either. This was the start of a new life for the both of them. It was something they could share together.

'It is a good thought.'

Sophie started to lean towards him. The carriage jolted to a halt and the coachman opened the door. Instantly she sat bolt upright. Richard got out first and turned back to her with his hands outstretched.

'Are you ready?'

'Ready?'

'I intend to carry you over the threshold.'

'You don't have to. I must weigh a ton. I ate far too much of the seed cake.'

'You will be as light as a feather. I want this to be perfect.'

'Very well. You may carry me.'

He put his arms about her and she looped her hands about his neck. Sophie noticed the servants filed out after the door had been opened. Richard had arranged everything to perfection.

Richard carried Sophie into the bedroom. Myers and Jane had done their work well. The severe masculinity of the room had been transformed with vases of flowers, flickering candles and Sophie's nightdress, prettily arranged with ribbons. A cold repast of cheese, apples and bread sat on a small table beside the small coal fire. Everything ripe for seduction.

He could not have planned it better.

'Shall I put you on the bed?' he whispered in Sophie's ear.

'I'd prefer to stand.'

'Would you mind telling me why?' he asked, slowly

lowering her to the floor. He had to hope that Sophie's stepmother hadn't filled her head with silly notions about propriety. When Sophie had insisted on changing and her stepmother followed her up, Richard had known what was coming—the talk about doing your duty and allowing a man to take his pleasure. Always have the light off and other nonsensical rules. It was little wonder she had seemed distant in the carriage, bringing up all manner of topics for discussion. Her stepmother had probably scared her half to death.

'Why, Sophie, is it necessary for you to stand?' he enquired softly when she bowed her head.

'You have to be careful when you sit in a crinoline. They have tendency to fly up and expose everything.' Sophie gave a feeble laugh. 'It took me ages of practising before my stepmother would allow me out of the house. And you have to know where your skirts are. Fanny Hubert suffered terrible burns to her legs when her skirt caught fire. Luckily, I remembered to shout roll like Henri had taught me or it could have been far worse.'

'Why wear it if it is so dangerous?'

'Because it weighs so much less than six petticoats.' She laughed and placed her finger against his lips. 'And here I thought you were more than adequate as a maid.'

'I'm obviously out of practise.'

'Then we must hope you do a good job of it tonight.' Her hands went to her tiny hat. 'I expect you to be neat and tidy or Jane will grumble.'

'I will be what I am,' Richard growled, reaching for her. 'And your maid will mind her manners about you or she will have to find another situation. But since you asked so prettily, I will do my best to keep your clothes neat.'

Sophie's heart gave a little leap as he quickly divested her of the jacket and undid the back buttons of the dress. The cool air licked her shoulders as she stood in the centre of the room dressed only in her crinoline, corset and combination.

He walked all around her.

'It is a cage.'

'It hooks at the back.' Somehow the knowledge he had not encountered a crinoline before made everything easier. The enormity of what was about to happen hit her as he carried her into the bedroom. She wanted to please him and all she could think about was that awful night four years ago.

The last thing she wanted was Richard getting angry with her. She wanted to be perfection and drive all thoughts of other women out of his mind. She wanted to match the picture he had painted in her mind yesterday, but she'd never done anything like this before.

'Step,' he commanded, releasing the crinoline and pushing it down over her hips. His hands caressed her hips, sending tiny licks of fire throughout her body, driving all thoughts of the other time away. This was different. This was Richard and she desired his touch.

He undid the hooks of her corset and sent that tumbling to the ground as well. Without giving her time to think, he lifted her up again and gently laid her on the bed.

'I prefer slippers to boots, Sophie,' he said, undoing the laces of her half-boots and easing them off.

'And I don't care about fashion, I want you to be able to breathe.'

'I like to look fashionable.' Sophie lifted her hands and removed the pins from her hair, allowing it to tumble about her shoulders.

'You look utterly delectable.' He moved her hair and kissed her neck. 'Even better when you are undressed.'

He undid his neckcloth and quickly took off his shoes, coat and shirt but left on his trousers.

Sophie realised with a start that he wasn't wearing anything underneath. His skin gleamed golden in the candlelight.

The bed sagged when he sat down next to her. His hand stroked her hair, sending a tingle down her spine.

The hard knot of misery had vanished to be replaced by something new and exciting.

She reached up a hand and stroked his cheek. 'Hello, husband.'

Instantly he rolled over on top of her and she felt the full hard length of him.

He bent his head and kissed her. Their tongues met and parted. The wildfire which had spread through her yesterday, reignited, blazing hotter and more out of control because she knew what was coming. Her nipples tightened and her back arched, demanding more of him.

His mouth left hers and trailed down her throat, lower and lower until he reached her breasts. Rather than moving the material away, his tongue drew lazy circles, turning it translucent, so that her nipples showed a dusky pink.

She squirmed and her drawers rubbed against the

apex of her thighs, sending a fresh wave of pleasure throughout her body.

Her head thrashed backwards and forwards on the pillow, but still he continued to suckle through the cloth. Her breasts grew full and ached.

'Please,' she gasped out, tugging at his shoulders. 'Please.'

He lifted his head. 'Allow me to pleasure you, Sophie. It makes me happy. I have dreamt about this. We are man and wife. Nothing is forbidden.'

'I know,' she said in a small voice. 'I want to do it right.'

'Relax.' He ran his hand down her flank, before placing his fingers at the apex of her thighs. The new sensation sent pulses of warmth through her. Her body bucked and she knew she wanted more. She wanted to feel all of him.

'We are overdressed,' she whispered.

He started to undo her combination, but the buttons stuck and he ripped it.

'I will buy you a new one,' he murmured, nuzzling her ear as his hands slipped off his trousers. 'You are more beautiful than I dreamt. Allow me to explore you.'

She gave a nod.

His hand returned to the apex of her thighs and slipped in between her nest of curls, parting her folds. The action sent fresh waves of pleasure throughout her body.

His silken warmth covered her. She ran her hand down his hard muscular back, marvelling. She cupped his buttocks and held his against her, lifting her hips to meet his.

The tip of him nudged her.

'I'm sorry,' he breathed in her ear. 'This will hurt. There is no way around it.'

He positioned himself and drove deeply between her thighs.

The pain and burning instantly blotted out all the earlier pleasure.

Sophie froze, shocked. She'd expected a pinprick of pain, not this burning sensation. A tiny cry of 'no' emerged from her throat. She tried to close her legs and her body bucked upwards, driving him deeper, making it worse. She beat her fists against the mattress in frustration. She had wanted this to be perfect. She wanted it to be like her dreams.

'Shush, it will be fine. Trust me. It was necessary, but now I will make it better.' His voice came through the pain and the panic subsided.

She forced her body to lie still and concentrated on the bed hanging and trying to breathe slowly.

He was deep within her, unmoving. She noticed the small things—how his chest felt against hers, how the candlelight highlighted the planes of his face and the way his fists were clenched as if he was under some nearly overpowering urge. She ran an experimental hand down his back, but he still didn't move.

His lips brushed her temple. 'There, it wasn't too bad. I had to break your maidenhead.'

'Is that all there is?'

He raised himself up on his elbows and his mouth curved up in a sensuous smile. 'Do you want more?'

She wrinkled her nose, considering. 'Yes, please.

I liked the first bit very much, but not what just happened.'

He began to slowly move within her. 'We shall have to see if we can get you to enjoy this bit as well. Relax and open your legs wider.'

She tried to and he moved his hips slowly, going deeper, then retreating as his mouth returned to hers. The gentle movement reignited the fire within her. Her hips lifted in time with his, matching him.

The movement became faster and more intense, but she was swept along on a wave of intense pleasure.

Finally he drove hard and cried out before collapsing on her.

She put her arms about him and held him, glorying in being one with him, her body alive with new sensations. Richard was right. It would have been foolish to wait any longer. She was pleased he'd insisted on their marriage.

'Thank you,' he said, placing a kiss on her temple.

'For what?'

'For being you.'

'How can I be anyone else?'

He rolled off her and started to move away.

'Where are you going?' She held out her hand. Her entire body seemed to be remade and he wanted to leave her.

He returned with a damp cloth. 'We need to clean you up.'

She looked down and saw the blood on her thighs. Her hands went to hide it. 'I'm no longer a virgin.'

'You are truly my wife.' He nipped her chin. 'And well worth waiting for.'

He moved her hands and wiped her thighs. The cool cloth contrasted with the burning, soothing her. Her hips moved upwards, seeking the relief. He slowed the movement of the cloth and stroked her gently. The heady longing returned and she knew she wanted his hands on her. She wanted him inside her again.

When he had finished, he gathered her in his arms and held her. She felt him grow hard and knew he wanted her again. The thought gave her a heady sense of power.

'All gone.'

'Do you intend to do it again?' She hesitated. 'Please?'

He gave a brief laugh. 'Unfortunately you are too sore. We have the rest of our lives and I intend to teach you all the ways it is possible to have pleasure.'

She wriggled. 'I believe I shall like that very much.'

Much later, Richard lay with Sophie in his arms. It had taken more self-control than he thought possible to avoid taking her again.

He had done the right thing in marrying her. He was not going to become like his father, overly possessive and jealous, driving her away. He wasn't going to fall in love with her at all. He was going to look after her and protect her. The way he felt about her and having her in his life frightened him.

Richard stiffened. His father. With mental apologies to Sophie, he released her and rolled away from her warm body.

He needed to tell his mother about his father's arrival and plans such as he knew them. It was not something which he could put in a letter. He had to see his mother and suffer the hysterics, but then he'd be done.

He ran his fingers through Sophie's hair. It was better to keep Sophie out of any fireworks. She didn't understand the problems and the way both parents had used him when he was little. The last thing he wanted was for her to be hurt. He'd promised to keep her safe. He could not ask her to take on this burden.

'When we are in the Alps, Sophie, and we know each other better,' he murmured. 'Then I will explain. I'm sure you will understand.'

She murmured softly in her sleep. He took it for a 'yes'.

Chapter Twelve

Sophie awoke, naked and alone in the large bed. The sunlight flooded on to her face. Her only ornaments were her engagement ring and the thin band of gold Richard had placed on her finger yesterday. It took her an instant to think where she was and why. Her body ached with muscles she didn't know she had. She reached out a hand to touch Richard. Even though she could see the imprint of his head on the pillow, the space beside her was cold.

She glanced about the bedroom. Someone had cleaned up the candle wax and the uneaten meal. Her dress and underthings no longer lay on the floor and her robe was neatly folded at the foot of the bed. A small fire blazed in the grate. But Richard was nowhere to be seen.

Something inside her shrivelled. She reached for the robe and slipped it on. What had she expected—that Richard would watch over her while she slept, transfixed by her beauty? That he'd be so enamoured of her charms that he wouldn't bear being separated from her?

Her mouth twisted. All of her doubts and fears from

yesterday came crowding back in. Had she done the right thing by marrying this quickly? Did she truly know the man she had married? The man who promised passion, but never mentioned his finer feelings?

Marry in haste, repent at leisure.

She had certainly married in haste. She hadn't even given herself time to think. And Richard had never claimed anything more than desiring her. Was desire enough to build a marriage?

And she was stuck here until Richard returned, unable to dress herself without assistance. Silently she cursed the twenty-four hooks of her corset and the fifteen back buttons of her going-away dress. The other dresses she'd packed were just as bad. Without assistance, she was as helpless as a babe in arms.

Sophie swung her feet on the floor. 'Hello? Is anyone there? Richard! I'm awake.'

Jane hurried in. 'Oh, I hope I didn't wake your ladyship with my tidying earlier.'

Sophie's throat closed. Jane, not Richard, had tidied the room.

'You are back.'

'Mr Myers and I arrived back from the hotel early this morning. I could hardly allow my lady to be on her own on the morning after the wedding.' Jane's plain face broke in a wreath of smiles. 'I need to have my lady looking her best for her new husband.'

'You tidied everything up?' Sophie's face flamed.

'There wasn't much. Your clothes hadn't been properly hung and the fire needed cleaning and restarting. The master said that I wasn't to disturb you, that you needed your sleep.' Jane bit her lip. 'I dropped the shovel as I went out, but you slept for another hour.'

'You have done nothing wrong,' Sophie assured her, trying to peer around Jane, hoping to see if Richard would suddenly appear, having heard the murmur of voices.

Her maid's shoulders sagged. 'I am so glad. I want to be a good maid, your ladyship. I want to serve you well, particularly now you are a viscountess and will some day be a marchioness. I never thought I'd be a maid to such quality when I first entered service.'

'Is his lordship here?'

Jane shook her head quickly. 'His lordship went out over an hour ago. He didn't tell me or Mr Myers where he'd be going.'

'Did he say when he'd return?'

'I doubt he will be long. He thought you'd sleep as you had such a big day yesterday with the wedding and all the preparations. You were such a picture, my lady. A fairy princess bride could not have looked finer.'

Sophie silently blessed Jane for not remarking how odd it was that a man should leave his bride on the morning after their wedding night.

'I suspect he has gone to see his father.'

'I shouldn't like to speculate.'

'We are not going on our wedding trip until his father departs from Newcastle.'

'Do you know where you are going?'

'The Alps, I believe.'

'Mr Myers and I are to go on the trip.' Jane clapped her hands. 'I have always wanted to go abroad. The delay will give us time to get you a proper wardrobe. One fit for a peeress!'

Even her maid didn't consider her a fit person to be Richard's wife.

Jane began detailing the sort of costumes Sophie needed, from walking dresses to ball gowns and parasols for keeping the sun off. Sophie listened with half an ear and tried to ignore the tiny hard knot in her stomach.

If Richard had not returned by the time she finished breakfast, she would go to her stepmother's rather than sitting around here, waiting. She'd use the pretext of sorting through the wardrobe she'd left and seeing if any of it was suitable. She wouldn't go and see Lord Hallington until Richard was with her—that would be prying. She didn't want Richard to think she was checking up on him or becoming a shrewish wife, but if she remained here, waiting, she'd go mad.

'There you are, my dear,' her stepmother called out from the sitting room.

'I...I came back for some of my things,' Sophie called back.

'Is dear Richard with you?'

'No, I believe he went to see his father.'

'His father is here, dear, taking tea with me in the small sitting room. Neither of us expected to see you today. But I am ever so pleased you called. We have something to ask you. Can you spare a moment?'

Sophie's stomach knotted. Richard wasn't with his father. He had gone somewhere else. The knowledge thrummed her. 'I...I...'

'No doubt Richard will be along as soon as he discovers where his father is. You will have time for a cup of tea.'

Sophie breathed more easily. Her stepmother thought that they had just parted. The last thing she wanted to explain was how she'd woken up alone, without even a note. And Richard was sure to come here once he had finished whatever he was doing. Staying in those empty rooms would have given her time to panic. This way she could begin her acquaintance with her father-in-law properly.

'I am sure he will be,' Sophie said, going into the small sitting room.

Her stepmother and father-in-law were sitting in front of a fire. A variety of china pigs were placed in front of her father-in-law and it was obvious they had been discussing their respective collections. Her stepmother probably wanted to know where one of the china pigs was. Sophie attempted to remember if any had broken lately.

'What is it that you wanted to ask me?' Sophie asked, opting for a bright voice as her stepmother passed her a cup of tea.

'Where did you say you and dear Richard met?'

The back of Sophie's neck prickled. The story was foolproof, but somehow it didn't seem right to lie any more to her stepmother or her father-in-law. They deserved the truth, but Richard might want to be there when she explained fully.

Sophie mentally sighed. She had to play for time. She placed the cup down with a clank. 'We met in Liverpool last spring. I was there for the ship launch. You remember, Stepmother, the ship launch. It was such a big occasion.'

'That's what I thought. We were there on the nineteenth of March.' Her stepmother gave a smug smile. 'I consulted my diary. You enjoyed the play very much.'

'Yes, it was…it was that evening when we went to the theatre that I first encountered Richard.'

'Impossible!' Lord Hallington thundered, banging his fist down.

'Impossible?' Sophie clasped her hands together and looked to the door, hoping Richard would appear. 'No, no, I assure you it was then. Richard could not get me out of his mind. It was why he journeyed up to Newcastle and we became engaged. Things progressed more quickly than either of us imagined, but why wait?'

Sophie included her father-in-law in her smile. She was proud of her explanation.

'The nineteenth of March is my birthday, my dear. Richard was at Hallington for the entire week. In fact, he stayed ten days,' her father-in-law said in a firm voice. 'Perhaps you are remembering the date incorrectly.'

'Hornswoggle! The nineteenth was when we were in Liverpool,' her stepmother declared stoutly. 'It was the only time we were away from Newcastle, except to go to Corbridge for Christmas and the New Year. And the one short excursion to Carlisle Sophie made when I had a cold. I have shown you the diary.'

'Do you have an explanation, Sophie?' Lord Hallington asked. His brows lowered. 'How could my son be in two places at once?'

'Yes, I want to hear it.' Her stepmother pinned her

with her gaze. 'We have been arguing over this for more than an hour.'

Sophie sank back against the sofa, suddenly sick. She had to tell the truth without Richard being there. She had no choice.

'We didn't meet in Liverpool,' she whispered.

Lord Hallington gave her stepmother a triumphant glance.

'Where did you meet if it wasn't Liverpool?' her stepmother asked in a deadly quiet voice. Even her cap radiated disappointment. 'I think I deserve that much, Sophie.'

'We met the night Cynthia Johnson eloped,' Sophie said in a rush.

'But that… But you said…' Her stepmother's face crumpled and she fumbled for her handkerchief. 'How could you, Sophie?'

'I know what I said.' Sophie handed her stepmother her handkerchief. 'I am ever so sorry, Stepmother. It wasn't supposed to come to this. We…we never planned to marry. The engagement was false, but the marriage isn't.'

'You had best explain from the beginning, young lady,' her father-in-law thundered as her stepmother wept. 'You have caused your stepmother considerable distress.'

'I will be happy to.' Sophie glanced over her shoulder and prayed that Richard would arrive to rescue her. 'Shall we wait for Richard's arrival? It will be better if we are both here.'

'No, I don't think we shall,' Lord Hallington said with a severe frown. 'I take it that you are truly married? Your marriage was not some sort of attempt to trick everyone again for your own purpose?'

'Of course they are married.' Her stepmother pointed towards the door. 'If you are going to make outrageous allegations, Lord Hallington, you may leave. Dear Richard is my son now. Sophie is properly wed and there isn't anything you can do about it. Anyone with half a brain can see how much in love they are!'

'We are truly married.' Sophie winced. She wanted to kiss her stepmother for being such a romantic and so loyal. She was going to have to hope her stepmother would understand. But love didn't come into it, not on Richard's part. And some day, when she'd shown him that she was worthy to be a marchioness, it would be different. She had to believe that. Out of unpromising starts, happiness could be found.

'Sophie, start from the beginning. Start with the night you met. Lord Hallington and I need to hear the truth.'

Lord Hallington started to say something, but her stepmother hushed him.

'Sophie will tell us everything, Lord Hallington. I find it best in these situations to allow Sophie to explain in her own time. My stepdaughter is normally a truthful person. I am sure there is a logical explanation. After all, they are married and the settlement agreed to everyone's satisfaction.'

Seeing no other option, Sophie began to explain, starting with the ball and how Richard had saved her. She skated over the kisses they had shared and the incident in the carriage where Richard had acted honourably.

'In any case, what does it matter now?' Sophie finished. 'Richard and I are married and everyone is happy. All is well that ends well.'

Sophie choked back the 'in love' part. She loved Richard or rather the Richard she thought she knew, but she had no idea about his feelings for her. He had only married her to satisfy his notion of honour. Was he starting to regret his actions already? She wished he was there and then her doubts might vanish.

'Do you know why Richard was in Newcastle to begin with?' Lord Hallington asked, drawing his brows together.

'What does it matter why Richard was here? He stayed to help out Sophie and they fell in love.' Her stepmother gave a happy sigh. 'Harum-scarum to begin with, Sophie, but ultimately one of the most romantic things I have heard in years.'

Richard's father looked less convinced.

'Do you know, young lady? Until I had his letter, I was unaware that he had ever visited this city. He was supposed to be in London.'

Sophie kept her head up. Richard had never said why he was at the ball that night. It hadn't seemed important. 'He was undoubtedly visiting friends. There are several men he was at Eton with on the cricket team.'

'But why keep it from his father?' Her stepmother rapped her finger against the diary.

'Richard is a grown man. He doesn't live in his father's pocket and have to explain where he is going and who he is seeing. Perhaps the invitation was sudden,' Sophie replied evenly. 'I know he stayed only to help me out. The events at the Assembly Rooms meant he could not just disappear. He was quite clear on that point. He had a score to settle with Sir Vincent. That was the only reason he stayed. Then there seemed to be no reason to wait after the settlement was agreed.'

'I wonder why my son failed to mention his journey? He went out of his way to make me think he was in London.'

'Perhaps he knew that mention of the city upsets you.' Sophie took a deep breath. 'Your son loves you, Lord Hallington. He knows your mother is buried here and that is why you don't visit it. Surely after all this time, you can visit her grave.'

Lord Hallington frowned. 'That is not why. Newcastle is where my former wife lives, or rather lived.'

Sophie's mind reeled. Richard's mother. The woman who had caused a huge scandal. If his mother was in Newcastle, surely she would have attended the wedding? 'Richard's mother? He never mentioned her. Does he know?'

'The divorce was a bad business. I had Marguerite agree never to speak to him as a condition of the divorce. I couldn't risk my son being hurt the way I was. The woman is a she-devil.'

'Funny, Richard has never mentioned his mother,' her stepmother said. 'Did he mention his mother to you, Sophie?'

'Only in passing,' Sophie answered truthfully as her stomach knotted. Richard would have said something about his mother. He had no reason to hide his mother from her and he didn't know his father would appear at the wedding, unless... Sophie refused to allow her mind to go there. Despite what his aunt thought about her lack of suitability, he had married her.

'I am sure he would have done, Sophie, if his mother was the reason for being in Newcastle,' her stepmother said soothingly, handing Lord Hallington another piece of seed cake. 'You have upset Sophie by implying differently, Lord Hallington. Do you know if your son and your former wife are in contact with each other? Do you even know for certain that she resides in Newcastle now? People do move about so these days, not like when I was young.'

'I have no idea.' The colour in Lord Hallington's face subsided. 'I don't want him being hurt. I can forgive most things, but I can't forgive what that woman did to my boy. How could a mother treat her child like that? Even now it makes my blood boil and the doctor has told me it does nothing for my heart.'

'Did you ever tell him why you didn't want him in Newcastle?' Sophie asked, curious.

'Of course not!'

'Well, then, you are making mountains out of molehills,' Sophie argued. Her stepmother was right. Richard would have confided in her something so important as his mother living in Newcastle. 'Think about the consequences if you had accused Richard of it.'

Privately she decided that when they returned from their wedding trip, she'd make an effort to find the woman and see if she wanted her son in her life. She knew that if either of her parents were alive, she'd want to see them. She loved her stepmother dearly, but it wasn't the same. Her mother might have died when she was just a little girl, but she still had memories of her gentle hand on her brow and the way her rose scent hung about her. It would be a good thing to do, she decided, feeling virtuous. But until she discovered where his mother lived, she wouldn't say.

'You are right, my dear. It is no wonder that Richard decided to act so quickly. He knew a good thing when he saw it.' Lord Hallington mopped his brow with a spotted handkerchief. His high colour had receded, but a sheen of sweat shone on his forehead. 'What a blessing it is to have you in my family. I hope we can become good friends. I have longed for a daughter for… for a long time.'

'I hope so as well.' Sophie took a cautious sip of her tea while she glowed internally. She'd won Lord Hallington's approval and her stepmother understood. Everything was going to be wonderful once Richard arrived. She put a hand to her throbbing head…if he arrived.

'What is going on here?' Richard asked from the doorway. Her heart did a crazy leap and she remembered how he'd kissed her so thoroughly last night. 'Did no one think to invite me to the family party?'

Sophie gulped. Richard had arrived at precisely the wrong moment. 'I was just explaining how we met.'

'In Liverpool?' His face seemed to be carved from stone, but his eyes flickered between her and his father.

Sophie stood up and linked her arm with his. 'The true circumstances.'

The colour drained from Richard's face. 'Did you volunteer the information, Sophie?'

'The nineteenth of March is your father's birthday.'

'I know when my father's birthday is.'

'The ship was launched on the nineteenth,' Sophie explained evenly, willing him to understand the problem. 'My stepmother noted it in her diary.'

'But you said late March.'

'In my world, the nineteenth is late March.'

Richard put a hand to his throbbing head. His quick visit to his mother and sister had turned into a disaster of epic proportions. His mother had flown into hysterics, making all sorts of wild accusations about his father and what he'd do to her and how Sophie was sure to be a she-devil. In the end, he had gone for the doctor, who sedated her with laudanum. Richard waited with a terrified Hannah until his mother slept and then had left for home.

All he had wanted to do was to sink deep inside Sophie and forget the trauma. He wanted to enjoy further awakening Sophie's passionate nature and making her truly his own.

He had hopes that Sophie would have remained asleep while he was away, but she was nowhere to be seen and neither was there a note. The rooms were devoid of life. The pit of his stomach roiled. Abandoned again. Always. It hurt that he cared when she cared so little.

Luckily Myers had returned from shopping for the ingredients for his black boot polish and volunteered the information that Sophie and her maid had gone to her stepmother's to get more clothes. Richard had not stopped to change his neckcloth, but had hurried off.

Now, rather than collecting Sophie and departing with all speed, he had to cope with more trauma—his father and Sophie's confession. There had been no need to check the date of the Liverpool launch before. It hadn't been important.

'I hadn't realised the launch was on the nineteenth,' he admitted as evenly as he could. 'The nineteenth is my father's birthday. I always spend that day with my father.'

'So Lord Hallington informed my stepmother. They were in midst of an argument about it when I arrived.' Sophie held out her hands. Her blue eyes were wide and pleading. 'You can see why I had to tell them. My stepmother thinks it very romantic what you did. Apparently it is just like in one of her novels.'

He was suddenly glad that Sophie knew nothing about his mother or Hannah. She would have been unable to resist telling his father and then all hell would have broken loose and Sophie would have been hurt, used as a pawn or worse. His parents were his burden, not Sophie's. He had made her marry him. She had not asked for the craziness of his family.

He ran his hand through his hair and peered more closely at his father, searching for signs of his temper. One hysterical parent on the day after his wedding was enough, two were unthinkable. Against the odds, his father appeared happy with the situation, far happier than he'd seen his father in a long time.

'You did admirably, my boy,' his father said. 'I can see why you decided to remain in the north, and why you married Sophie so quickly. You were always headstrong, but a good woman is hard to find.'

'You approve?'

'Yes, I approve!' His father clapped his hands together. 'I'm utterly impressed and astonished. Despite the unorthodox meeting and courtship, you managed to find the sort of woman I have always wanted for you. Your aunt as usual wrote a load of blathering nonsense. I should have guessed. No sense about pigs, none whatsoever about people!'

'Then you won't mind if I take my bride away now?' Richard put a hand on Sophie's shoulder and felt her flesh quiver under his fingers. Today could be redeemed. 'We did only marry yesterday.'

'We entirely understand,' Mrs Ravel said with a beatific smile. 'I was surprised to see Sophie here. I would have thought you'd depart on your wedding trip today. Sophie's father took me to Paris and then to Venice.'

'When do you leave for your wedding trip, Richard?' his father asked.

Richard froze. This was his chance to get his father to leave without causing a scene or alarming Sophie.

'Richard and I have decided to postpone the wedding trip so that you will have time to get to know me,' Sophie said before he had uttered a word.

His father's eyes widened. 'I had no wish…'

'But we do.' Sophie darted forwards and gave his father a kiss on the cheek. 'It will mean so much to both Richard and me. You are part of my family now. And you travelled on a train for the first time. Trains can be rather overwhelming. The noise, the dirt and the steam.'

Tears came into his father's eyes. 'Bless you, child. I will look into taking rooms. There is much to admire about this city. I haven't been here since I was a young man. The pigs will have to do without me for a while. My new daughter requires me.'

Richard forced his jaw to relax. His father had never

done that for him—put him ahead of the pigs. Sophie with her impulsive invitation had just closed the one bright hope in his life—that his father would leave Newcastle quickly. His father would now stay and his own problems had grown. Somehow he had to figure out how he was going to protect Sophie and keep her from being used as a pawn.

'What do you think you were playing at, Sophie?' Richard exploded the instant he shut their bedroom door. 'Leaving like that! No note. Nothing.'

Sophie dropped her reticule on the ground. She had known something was wrong by his silence on the journey back and the way he'd marched into their bedroom. True, he'd been charming at her stepmother's, but he had insisted they leave immediately after he'd finished his cup of tea, not even waiting for Jane and her dresses.

'I don't know what you are talking about.' Sophie crossed her arms and readied for war. He'd been the one to be out when she awoke.

'You failed to leave a note.' He ran his hand through his hair. 'I had no idea where you were when I returned.'

Sophie tapped her foot on the ground. All the hurt and anger from earlier rose within her. He dared to complain about her absence when he couldn't be bothered to be there when she woke! She was the one who should be angry, not he. He should be on his knees in abject apology, rather than demanding explanations. 'You also failed to leave a note. I had no idea where *you* were. I refuse to wait around in rented rooms, hoping you might put in an appearance before nightfall.'

His mouth twisted. 'You decided to serve me back?'

'No, I let Myers know where I was and when I expected to return.' Sophie stuck her chin in the air. 'I needed my dresses which button down the front. I refuse to be stuck somewhere naked simply because all my clothing requires the assistance of a lady's maid.'

She waited for him to accept the truth.

He glared at her. 'Did you have to tell my father about how we met?'

'I had little choice.' Sophie met his gaze with a furious one of her own. 'I could hardly lie to him. You saw how it was. Undone by a date. It had to come out sooner or later. The truth always does. My stepmother took it very well and your father as well.'

'Who else will learn of the truth?'

Sophie rolled her eyes. 'I suspect I shall have to tell Robert and Henri. My stepmother is sure to tell them in any case. They and their children are like family.'

'Shall I take a notice out in *The Times*?' he enquired in a cutting voice. 'It will save time.'

'Once you meet Robert and Henri, you will love them.'

'I prefer to make my own judgement about people. You swore only a few days ago that this Robert of yours would find fault with me and my suit.'

'Yes, but we are married now.' Sophie pressed her hands against her temples. She had only said that when she had been certain he had no desire to marry her. Everything had changed. 'It no longer signifies. They know what society demands when people are compromised. Ultimately, all they want is to see me happy. They will be delighted that you did the right thing.'

He reached out to her, but she ignored it and stood there with crossed arms. She refused to ask him where he'd been. He should tell her and explain why he had left her for so long this morning.

'This is all wrong.' He reached out again and pulled her into his arms. He rested his chin on the top of her head. 'That's better. You were too far away. Can we start today over, please? I missed you more than I thought I would.'

'I would like that,' she said. Being in his arms made everything better. He'd missed her or perhaps just her body. It had to be enough. She would make him proud of her accomplishments. She'd show him how truly worthy she was and he'd start to truly care for her. He might not love her now, but she could make love grow… if she had enough time.

'I didn't expect to see your father,' she said, concentrating on his waistcoat rather than looking him in the face. 'My dark-rose gown has easier buttons and requires no crinoline. Jane wants my wardrobe to be fit for a peeress, but I'd rather be able to dress myself. Surely both can be managed?'

'I like your way of thinking, Lady Bingfield.' Richard's eyes glowed with appreciation as he ran his hands down her back.

They had that, Sophie realised. They desired each other. It would have to be enough to build her marriage on. She couldn't suddenly wish for undying love when he had never pretended more than desire. She had to hope his feelings for her would grow. Right now, his touch was wakening the ache in her middle.

She gave her mouth up to his mind-numbing kiss. When he kissed her, she knew everything would be right with the world.

Much later when they lay in bed together, Sophie's head against Richard's chest and her body faintly throbbing, she glanced up at his face and he seemed to be far away, concentrating on the bedpost rather than on her face.

'You haven't heard a word I said.'

He placed an absentminded kiss on her hair. 'Was it important?'

She shook her head. Her question about his childhood could wait. 'What were you thinking about?'

He put his hands behind his head. 'My father took the truth about our meeting well though. Better than I had hoped. It was a simplistic, but fatal error. I never thought about his birthday.'

She ran her hand down his chest. 'We had different expectations when we decided the story.'

'I could tell he likes you.' His hand stroked her hair. 'He does have excellent taste if you can get him to talk about something more than pigs.'

'You did want him to stay. He seemed sad earlier. I couldn't quite put my finger on it.' Sophie shook her head. Now was not the time to bring up the intelligence about his mother. Not after their quarrel had just mended. She had hated how her insides felt during their last one.

'You were completely right. I was being selfish. I

wanted to start our wedding trip as soon as possible and didn't think my father would want to stay as he normally hates being away from his beloved pigs.'

'He puts his son above his pigs.'

'I live in hope, rather than expectation.' He gave a pained smile. 'Thank you for putting duty before pleasure. We will go once my father decides to depart, but it won't be long before the pigs need his attention. I want a proper wedding trip with you this summer. I positively insist on it.'

'We are still together and we will get to the Alps this summer.' She placed a kiss on his chin. 'I'm looking forward to painting you properly. A sunlit Alpine meadow will be the perfect backdrop.'

'Shall I be naked?'

'Richard!'

His eyes danced and he ran a hand down her flank. 'I keep forgetting how truly innocent you are, Sophie. Only if you desire it. Otherwise, I shall sit very still, dressed in my best hat, coat and trousers while you paint. The very proper husband for my Lady Bingfield to paint.'

Truly innocent. Sophie's heart gave a little pang. She should never forget how experienced he was. He was used to women who knew how to do all sorts of things. The cruel words Sebastian had shouted through the keyhole circled around her brain—*Men tire of innocence very quickly.* How could she ever hope to hold Richard, if she remained innocent? How could she hope to keep him from being bored? She wanted to use the desire to bring finer feelings to the marriage. She had to show him that she was worthy of taking her place beside him, so that he wouldn't regret his impulsive act of honour.

'Sophie? You appear awfully serious? Is something wrong? You have forgiven me, haven't you? I won't allow you to wake up without me again. I promise. I had no idea that it would upset you so.'

She pushed her doubts away. In Richard's arms, everything was perfect. 'Nothing is wrong. How could it be with you here?'

Chapter Thirteen

The sooner they left Newcastle, the better, Richard decided three days later. The last thing he wanted was for Sophie to encounter his mother. Rather than getting better and reconciled to the marriage and asking to meet Sophie, his mother had written to his aunt, requesting the report on Sophie.

Richard had considered something was truly wrong with her when she sent a cryptic note and so he had hurried over there this morning, only to be greeted with a litany of Sophie's imagined faults.

With Sophie attempting to create a wardrobe fit for a viscountess before they left for the wedding trip and generally showing nervousness, the last thing she needed was his mother picking petty fault. He wanted to throttle his aunt, but knew he ultimately was to blame for goading her that day.

He refused to allow anyone to hurt Sophie or twist her into something she wasn't. He wanted the passionate woman, not the mask she'd shown to the world when they'd first met. But there was no point in explaining this to his mother. Instead he had made his excuses and left.

Richard marched into his rooms with his aunt's poison burning a hole in his pocket. He would write his aunt an uncompromising and long-overdue missive about *her* behaviour and afterwards he'd consign the so-called verdict to the fire. Sophie need not worry what his family thought of her.

He stopped, confronted with the delectable sight of Sophie in her robe.

'What are you doing back here, Sophie?' Richard tilted his head, searching for signs of distress. 'I thought you had fittings for your new wardrobe all morning and were then going to have lunch with your stepmother.'

'I came back earlier from my stepmother's.' Sophie waved an airy hand. 'There was little point in me staying. My stepmother agreed with me. A woman's place is with her husband when they are first married, rather than gossiping.'

He raised an eyebrow. 'Is that so? Did you happen to see my father? Has he decided when he is leaving?'

'Next week. The tickets are all booked.' Sophie gave a little twirl, allowing her robe to slip a little. She had to hope her scheme was working and that Richard did have a little regard for her beyond desiring her in bed. But everywhere she turned these days, it seemed people conspired to make her feel awkward and as if she was a disappointment. She wanted to be the perfect bride. She wanted to show Richard that his trust in her was not misplaced. 'I have given the servants the afternoon off.'

His glance became appreciative rather than the

glower he'd worn when he first came in. 'Is there any reason why?'

'I thought I could paint you. Get started on the portrait. It might not be an Alpine meadow, but I thought the bed would do.'

Dark passion flared in his eyes. 'You want to paint my portrait now? What has brought this on?'

'Now!' Sophie put her hands on her hips. If he went, she'd never regain the courage. She had everything planned in her mind. She'd seduce him and then she'd explain about the dinner party she'd planned. She knew having a dinner party before they had done the rounds of the At Homes wasn't strictly speaking the done thing, but she wanted to show Richard and his father that she was a capable hostess. 'Myers said that there wasn't anything you had to be doing. I laid careful plans, Richard.'

He pressed his lips together and then his face cleared. A wicked glint came into his eyes, warming her. And she breathed a sigh of relief. This was going to be easier than she'd feared. 'Never let it be said that I don't do what my lady requests, particularly when it is prettily put. Do you want me in my coat and hat for this portrait of yours?'

'I would like you to sit over there on the bed.' Sophie's limbs trembled. He was doing as she asked. She walked over to the easel and picked up a brush.

'You want me seated, not reclining.'

'Whichever way is more comfortable. But you need to keep still. Don't move a muscle. I want to capture you. When it is finished, I want to hang it over our drawing-room mantelpiece. Today I want to do a preliminary study and see if you can withstand the rigours of sitting.'

The dimple flashed in the corner of his mouth. 'I assume you will insist on entertaining the worthy.'

'Precisely. I've no wish to shock.'

Sophie drew a rough charcoal sketch of Richard's head and shoulders. She did intend to paint his portrait eventually. It would give her a chance to get to know him better, but this afternoon was about more than simply painting. It was about showing Richard that she could be inventive in their love-making.

'And you intend to paint all afternoon?' he asked after a few moments' silence in which she sketched the outline and gave a rough indication of how his hands ought to go.

'Is there some problem with this?'

'My nose is starting to itch. How am I supposed to scratch if you don't want me to move?'

Sophie smiled and reached for her brush. The request she had been waiting for. She walked over to where he sat. 'I believe I have a solution.'

She leant forwards and stroked his nose with the brush. 'All better?'

He gave a slight nod rather than reacting as she expected. 'Trying not to move as my wife ordered.'

She pursed her lips. This might take longer than she thought unless… She allowed her robe to slip as she started to turn away. His hand caught her sleeve.

'Where are you going? Other parts of me itch.'

'Do they?'

He nodded. 'All over. It is deuced uncomfortable

being a model. You should have told me when I volunteered.'

'Then I shall have to see to them.'

'With your brush?' His voice held a husky note.

'I use it when I am painting and don't want to get paint on my nose.' Sophie used the brush to caress his cheeks and forehead. 'You see. Nice and soft.'

His eyes closed. 'More, please. Remember you told me not to move. I've no intention of spoiling your… portrait.'

Her hands worked at his neckcloth and discarded it. She gently stroked down the strong column of his throat, before working on his collar and the collar studs.

His coat proved a bit more problematic to remove. And he kept true to his word and didn't move a muscle, allowing her to undo the buttons and pull off the sleeves.

With a sinking heart, she saw his shirt sleeves were fastened with intricate cufflinks. Richard's clothing was every bit as fiddly as her own.

'Next time I paint you, I think I shall have to take your advice and have you in fewer clothes. I can always paint the clothes in later.'

'I am taking your instructions to heart, but I do have the most terrible itch.' A faint smile touched his lips. 'You are not drawing now.'

Sophie drew her brush along his collar bone. 'You know how this game is played.'

'I'm a good guesser.' He pulled her against his chest. 'Is it all right for me to move now? Truly?'

She gave a nod. 'It is safe. I reached a stopping point on the portrait.'

'I promise to be the most obliging of models, but it

is best to do a little at a time. It saves on the itching...'
He took off his shirt and vest, leaving his skin gleaming golden. She put out a hand and touched the warm muscle.

He fell back on the bed so that she straddled him. His hands reached up and cupped her breasts. His thumb slowly rubbed her nipple, making it become a hardened point. Sophie gasped. He bucked upwards and his arousal teased her.

'What are you wearing under this robe?'

'Nothing,' Sophie admitted. 'I wanted to see how it would be for painting.'

'A novel approach—having the artist undressed and the model clothed.'

'I can be unconventional as well as conventional.' She brushed her lips against his mouth.

'Have I ever complained, Sophie?' He caught her face between his hands.

Sophie bit her lip. He had not complained, but she felt him slipping away from her.

Rather than answering him, she concentrated on the next stage. Her hands went to his trousers and undid them, allowing his erection to spring free. Without waiting, Sophie opened her legs wider and positioned herself. She moved her hips back and forth, feeling the engorged tip of him rub her as the ache grew within her and then, very slowly, she lowered herself down on him, calling the rhythm for once.

Much later, Richard lay with a sleeping Sophie curled beside him. With a gentle hand, he smoothed a lock of blonde hair from her face.

Sophie had the unerring knack of knowing what he needed without him even having to tell her. With her curled into his side, he could almost allow himself the luxury of believing that he could protect her and keep her safe. That he would have chosen this marriage if she knew everything about him.

He watched her stir and realised his feelings for her had grown, rather than diminished. But the only reason she was in his bed and his life was that he'd used her desire for virtue. Sometimes it felt as though he was waiting for the whole house of cards to fall.

'Mmmm,' she murmured, giving a stretch. 'That was pleasant.'

'Pleasant?'

'Wonderful. It may take me an awfully long time to get that particular portrait done.'

'I'm happy to pose whenever you like.' Richard sobered. 'You said my father has set a date for leaving.'

'A week on Monday. He has booked his train ticket.' Sophie raised herself up on her elbow. 'We are going to give a dinner party, Richard, on the Sunday. For your father, my stepmother, Robert and Henri. I have sent the invitations. I was sure you wouldn't mind. Robert and Henri arrive back two days before your father leaves. It seemed opportune. My stepmother and your father agreed readily.'

Richard went cold. He wasn't ready to meet Sophie's former guardian and his wife. He wanted to have more time to bind Sophie to him, rather than encountering the two people who would find fault with him. 'Shouldn't you have asked me before you sought assurance from my father and your stepmother?'

Her nose wrinkled. 'The letter from Henri arrived while your father was at my stepmother's. It seemed like too happy of a coincidence not to organise a dinner party. I am sure my stepmother will be happy to host the party if you don't feel we have room here.'

Richard ran his hands through his hair. Dinner parties with his father were to be endured, particularly when his father decided he could comment on the food with impunity. He could see the disaster unfolding before his eyes. His father behaving badly, Sophie in tears and these friends of Sophie's judging him. He shuddered. 'Sophie, a word of advice—if you want something big, ask a man before you ask his father.'

'I did mention giving a dinner party for Henri and Robert this morning.'

'You did?' Richard searched his memory. This morning he had been distracted by his mother's latest note about her finances and her request to see him immediately. 'The only thing you asked me about was another new dress. You always look well turned out, Sophie, and you are spending your own money.'

'Before that. The dress is for the dinner party.'

Richard rubbed his eye. The dull ache in his head returned. 'I don't recall, but I believe you.'

'Then it is a no.' Her lips turned down. 'I'd hoped...'

He flopped back against the pillows. It was wrong of him. He wanted to keep what passed between Sophie and him private. This was their kingdom. Dinner parties and At Homes belonged to a life after they returned from the wedding trip, when he could be sure of her. But Sophie was right. His father needed a proper send off. He could endure the Montemorcys, knowing that once his father was gone, he would have Sophie to himself for weeks on end and no family to bother him.

He turned over on top of Sophie and caught her wrists, putting them above her head. 'You wrong me.' He nipped her chin. 'It is a yes. Have your dinner party. Buy your gown.'

She kissed him back. Enthusiastically. 'I knew you'd understand.'

'Is everything under control?' Richard asked on the morning of the dinner party.

Sophie looked up from measuring the place settings. 'Everything is fine. I have borrowed my stepmother's cook and the menu is all agreed. Jane and Myers are dealing with the flowers.'

'Why the ruler?'

'A trick Henri taught me.' She set the ruler down. Since the afternoon she had started painting Richard, something had changed between them. She had to hope that he understood how important it was that this dinner party went smoothly. She wanted to demonstrate to Robert and her stepmother that she was now an adult. Her dinner party would positively radiate virtue. They would see that despite the hastiness of the marriage, she was happy. And she was happy…most of the time.

'Surely Myers can do that.'

'It is best to do things myself if I want perfection.'

'Perfection isn't always possible.'

'With planning it can be achieved.' She nodded towards where two long red candles stood in brass candlesticks. 'I love how the red and the brass go together.

Candlelight is far more pleasant for a party of this nature than gas.'

'I shall leave you to the last-minute preparations, then, as you have things well in hand.' He picked up his hat and gloves.

'Are you going out? The party is going to start in a few hours. I thought…I thought you might want to go over the choices for port.'

'There are a few things I need to complete before we go on our wedding trip. They shouldn't take long. Myers can solve any question with the wine. It is one of the reasons I hired him as my valet.'

Sophie pasted on a fake smile. It was there again, that withdrawing. Her stepmother had warned her—men don't like to hear about domestic bother. 'Of course, how foolish of me not to have thought Myers would know.'

'I will be back before the party starts. We will greet your guests together.'

Sophie sat watching the final splutter of the last red candle. The remains of the disaster were clearly evident.

Five plates with food—barely touched, and one plate without anything—spotlessly clean.

Richard, despite his easy assurance, had not returned in time for the start of the dinner party or its conclusion. A boy had delivered a note halfway through from Richard explaining they should start and that he'd been unavoidably delayed. He had no idea when he'd return, but he hoped it would be shortly.

She had Myers start serving the food, hoping against

hope that each noise outside was Richard returning. But he hadn't, not even when the clock struck ten.

Everyone offered to stay and wait with her, but she refused them all. The humiliation was far too great.

Henri, as she was leaving, squeezed Sophie's hand and told her that she always had a place with them.

Lord Hallington muttered about horse whips and how his son ought to know better. He offered to take her straight to Hallington the next morning if she wished.

Sophie kept the tears back until after they had all gone. She had calmly gone through his desk, hoping she'd find a clue as to his whereabouts. She hated herself for doing it, for being the sort of suspicious wife she'd always sworn she'd never be.

She happened on a letter with her name scrawled halfway down, detailing all her faults. Exhibitionist tendencies, overly refined, no taste. The final page was missing as if for some reason Richard had changed his mind about sending the letter to this Marguerite, his confidante.

It was one thing to worry and another thing to see it in black and white. She'd always worried what others thought of her and now she knew what her husband thought. If it had not been for his honour, they would have never married. It was ironic. She had spent the past few years keeping away from men like Richard because of their lack of honour...

She put her head on her arms and cried. Richard had demonstrated what he thought of their marriage and her. She had tried so hard. In spite of the letter, she still cared about him. She wanted to know he was not hurt or in trouble.

'I'm sorry, Sophie. I will make it up to you. I promise.'

She looked up and saw him standing in the doorway. His eyes were red ringed and tired, his normally pristine clothes mussed as if he'd stripped them off and put them on again. There were blotches which looked like dried tears on his shirt front. She wanted to murder him for scaring her like this. She wanted to scream at him that she wasn't too fine for her manner or suffering from an overdose of gentility or given to making an exhibition of herself. Or the half-a-dozen other phrases that had been listed.

Sophie stood up and scrubbed her eyes with the back of her hand. 'Sorry does not even begin to cover it.'

'Let me hold you.' He held out his arms and beckoned to her. 'The thought of holding you has been the only thing which has kept me going through the last few hours.'

'Really?' Sophie crossed her arms and moved so that the table was between her and Richard. Her desire for him had been how all this trouble started. If she hadn't kissed him in the carriage, they would never have married. She'd still have her self-respect and illusions. 'You have a funny way of showing it. There again, I don't suppose you truly wanted to be here and see me make a disgrace of myself with an excess of courtesy.'

Sophie picked out one of the more hurtful phrases from the letter and waited for his reaction.

His hand dropped to his side. 'I brought you something, a token of my affection. And I wanted to be here…to make sure…'

'To make sure what? That nothing went wrong? That

I didn't disgrace your name?' Sophie tapped her foot on the ground. Affection? She wanted more than affection. Affection was for pets and mistresses. She was his wife. She had wanted his regard, if not his love. 'I don't want anything from you. And I don't need your help. I managed the dinner party without you. I managed my life without you before we met.'

'I bought you a necklace.' He held out a slender box. 'A necklace of sapphires to wear at the dinner party. You could never disgrace me, Sophie.'

He placed the open box on the table and the jewels winked up at her in the dim light, mocking her.

'You see, they match your eyes.'

Her stomach twisted. He'd brought her jewels, but he couldn't be bothered to show up for the dinner party, something which was important to her. She wore his ring, but he treated her like a mistress and a not very important one at that. She had thought he might come to love her and appreciate her social skills.

'Do you think I am little better than a courtesan? To be bought off with presents? I am your wife, Richard, regardless of who my father was or—'

'I know who you are, Sophie,' he said in a deathly still voice. 'I want to explain. The necklace is an important part of the explanation. When I was at the jewellers, Hannah caught up with me.'

'Hannah?' Sophie wanted to throw up. Richard was speaking of a woman she barely knew in intimate terms. 'Hannah Grayson? The woman I met at the cricket? You know her well enough to call her Hannah?'

She sat down heavily. Her entire world crumbled about her. She had thought Sebastian was bad, but Richard was far worse. Stupid, naïve Sophie for believing Richard could be different. Once a rake, always a rake. First the letter, now this. She should have trusted her head, rather than her heart. She'd stupidly believed that she had enough love for the both of them.

'Sophie. It is not what you think.'

'How do you know what I think?' She stared at the jewels. 'Do you even care what I think?'

He winced. 'I do care, Sophie. I care very much. You are my wife. It is why—'

'It is why what? I found your letter to some Marguerite detailing my faults. How many women are in your life besides me?'

'Hannah Grayson is my sister, Sophie, and Marguerite is my mother, but I have never written any letter. Why were you looking through my things?'

Sophie put her hand over her mouth. His sister! His mother! Why hadn't he told her that he had a sister? Why had he hidden it from her? Particularly in the carriage when she had teased him about Hannah Grayson's brother? 'You are the brother who enabled the engagement, the one Miss Grayson is so proud of.'

He gave an uneasy laugh. 'Hannah wasn't supposed to be there or I'd never have taken you there that day.'

Sophie went cold. He wanted to keep his sister from her. 'I wasn't to know? About your sister being in Newcastle? Ever? What was wrong with me?'

'Can you let me finish? Nothing is wrong with you, Sophie. You were an unasked-for complication in my ordered existence.'

'An unasked-for complication?' Sophie put her hands on her hips as outrage poured through her. He made it seem as though she was a burden! 'I am sorry to make your life more difficult. You didn't have to marry me. You were the one who insisted because of what happened in the carriage.'

He raised an eyebrow. 'I wasn't planning on meeting you when I came to Newcastle. I came up to vet my sister's fiancé. My mother worried. I wanted to make sure that Hannah would be looked after properly and I know how men can take advantage of women, particularly when they fail to have adequate settlements. Then I met you and certain events followed.'

The news crashed through Sophie. Before Richard arrived she'd been furious, worried and scared for him. Now, she was simply numb. Not only had he kept his sister from her, but his mother as well. If ever she needed proof that he didn't have any feelings for her, this was it. She struggled to frame the words. 'Why did you keep them a secret from me? Why didn't you trust me? Why were you ashamed of me?'

Richard gave an apologetic smile. 'My mother is terrified of my father. She worried that something might happen when she heard that we were marrying. She has become quite irrational and hysterical. She chose not to come to the wedding and I hardly wanted to give you an excuse to delay. You see, Sophie, there is a logical explanation. It is not what you thought. Imagine what would have happened if she'd been at the wedding when my father showed up. In the end, it was a minor miracle. I wanted that day to be perfect for you.'

He looked at her with lidded eyes. Even now, he wasn't trusting her with the full story. His mother had chosen not to go to the wedding because she felt Sophie wasn't good enough.

'You were ashamed of me? Is that why you wrote that letter?'

'My mother can be overly proud. She has no cause to be.' Richard rolled his eyes. 'She and my aunt are like that. She wrote to my aunt asking for her opinion, once we were wed. The letter you found was my aunt's reply, detailing what she wrote to my father after I goaded her. Now you see that this is all a tempest in a teapot.'

'No, it is far worse. You didn't trust me. You still don't trust me. You married me without trusting me. You only married because we had to, because I forced the issue by kissing you.' Sophie struggled to take a breath. Her insides were torn to tiny shreds.

'There were two of us in that carriage.' He gave a half-smile. 'I was hardly reluctant. And as for not telling you about my mother…well, my father arrived. You tell secrets readily and without meaning to. I don't blame you, Sophie, but they just seem to spill out of you. I selfishly wanted to concentrate on my marriage, rather than having the drama of my parents.'

'I tell secrets!'

'Look at how our engagement was announced to all and sundry at the Assembly Rooms, how you proclaimed it was a love match.'

'You know the circumstance.' Sophie ground her teeth. Of all the accusations, that was the most unfair. She prided herself on her ability to keep secrets. 'My quick thinking destroyed Sir Vincent.'

'I never said you did it deliberately, merely that you found it difficult to keep secrets.' Richard's tone became overly reasonable. 'Secrets spill from your lips at the earliest opportunity and then someone else has to deal with the consequences. I didn't want to deal with these consequences.'

'Do they really?' Sophie narrowed her eyes. She wanted to shake him hard. He knew nothing about her! She prided herself on being able to keep important secrets. She would never deliberately tell anyone anything which would harm them or make them upset. Above everything, it showed how mistaken she'd been to marry a stranger. 'Richard, I kept the truth about our engagement from the woman who brought me up until after we were married and I was confronted with a glaring lie. I kept the truth from my guardian and his wife. And I share everything with Henri.'

'You share everything with an unknown.' He slammed his fists together. 'There, I rest my case. Precisely why I didn't tell you. I know what my parents are like.'

'You are seeking to justify the unjustifiable.' Sophie's mouth tasted like ash. He hadn't even listened to what she was saying. Neither did he care about her feelings. 'And you obviously don't want to know me very well. I thought we were friends, Richard, but we are merely strangers who shared a bed. You should have trusted me with this. Instead, you allowed me to blunder about, not knowing what was happening or why you were distant.' Her limbs started to tremble. In another moment, she'd break down and cry. She absolutely refused to cry in front of him. 'What else have you kept hidden from me? I loved you, Richard.'

The words hung between them. Sophie covered her mouth. She hadn't meant to confess her love in that way.

'That is unfair, Sophie. Bringing love into it to suit your purposes.' He gave a half-smile and held out his hands. 'I did marry you. I do want you, Sophie, as my life's partner. Being with you has been an oasis of calm in my life. I'm selfish. I know that, but it was done to protect you.'

'Shall we be honest, Richard? Finally? You married me because you could not have me any other way. Because you wanted me in your bed, but your sense of honour meant that you had to marry me. This was about sex and desire, pure and simple on your part. But I'm not a mistress. I thought I was your wife.'

'You are making wild accusations. You are over-tired.' He put out his hand. 'I married you because I wanted you in my life. My whole life. I planned on telling you about my mother and sister when the time was right. I wanted to enjoy you without my family causing problems for just a while longer.'

His pity at her love somehow made it worse. She hugged her waist. 'No, you only wanted me in your bed. I suppose some should say that I should be grateful that you gave me your name. But you didn't want me in your life, not really. You were ashamed of me.'

He winced when she said the words, but he did not say anything. He allowed his hand to drop to his side. And she knew her words had hit their mark. She waited for him to deny it, or say something that would fill the great yawning gap where her heart had been. 'You were the one who wanted to show me off like some prize you'd won. You were the one who planned a dinner party without asking me first. Why is it so important to you what other people think about you and your life?'

The silence became deafening and she knew she had her answer.

'I'm going, Richard. I refuse to stay here in this sham of a marriage.'

'You can't abandon our marriage.'

'You already abandoned it. You never gave me a chance. You were not interested in me.'

'Don't you want to hear why I was late?' he whispered in a ragged voice. 'Hear me out before you make your decision. Once you know, you will understand.'

'I doubt I will ever understand. You are ashamed of me. You only married me because you have your code of honour. I hoped it might be love, but it wasn't.'

'Listen, Sophie, before you judge. Please. I never wanted my family problems to concern you. It is not you I am ashamed of, but my family and the way they act.'

Sophie struggled to control her temper. She was married to him. All her instincts screamed that she should grab her valise and go. If Richard touched her, there was every possibility she'd melt. 'Why were you late?'

'My mother took an overdose of laudanum. I had to get the doctor. I had to make sure she was going to live. Otherwise our trip would have to have been postponed again. Hannah was beyond hysterical. You do understand why I had to stay.'

'Why did she overdose?'

'You would have to ask her.' He ran his hands through his hair. 'I had told her about the dinner party and that my father would be leaving in the morning. You and I were going to the Continent. I would see them again when I returned and that I hoped she'd enjoy getting to know you then. I left and went to the jewellers to pick up that blasted necklace for you.'

'I didn't want a necklace. I never wanted a necklace.'

'I wanted to give it to you, to mark our first dinner party. I wanted it to be something you would always remember.'

'I shall always remember it.' Sophie clenched her fists. 'I tried so hard. All I wanted to do was to show you that I was worthy of being a viscountess. Quite frankly, that doesn't matter any more. I am who I am and I like me. I am through with tying myself in knots for anyone, most especially you!'

'Have I ever asked you to?'

'But you are ashamed of me. I read the letter...'

'I meant to burn that after I wrote to my aunt, telling her a few home truths. But I have been so angry about it that every time I sit down to write, I can't.'

He held out his arms as if he expected her to walk straight into them, lay her head against his chest and forgive him.

Sophie put her hand to her head. 'It doesn't change a thing.'

'Sophie!'

She forced herself to turn her back and walk to where she had placed her valise. She'd packed it this afternoon in readiness for the wedding trip, a trip which was not going to happen now. A huge lump formed in her throat. She swallowed hard and, when she felt in control of her emotions, turned to face him.

'The only thing you wanted to share was sex, Richard. I refuse to have a marriage based on that. Desire always fades without something real and solid behind it. You are right. I was in a dream of love. I have woken up and discovered that I am worth it. It is why I am leaving now. I am going to spend my life living it as it was meant to be lived, rather than existing and hoping for a few crumbs of praise from you.'

'I forbid it.'

Sophie kept her back ramrod straight. The old Sophie would have crumbled, but Richard had given her her self-respect back. She knew now what she wanted and why she wasn't going to settle for this second-best marriage. 'You can forbid nothing, Richard. Not any more.'

'Where are you going?' he asked in a ragged voice.

'Where I am safe,' Sophie answered, knowing he'd never guess what she planned on doing or where she was going. She would start living her life on her terms now. 'Where no one cares what my reputation is or what title I have, but what they do care about is me.'

Chapter Fourteen

Richard stood in stunned silence. Sophie couldn't really be about to leave him. Not Sophie, not when he needed to forget about today. He wanted to hold her as she lay sleeping and look into her face. But mostly he wanted her there, beside him, talking to him about little ordinary things and worrying about little details that most people never even noticed. She was his refuge from the storm which had engulfed him. He needed her.

'Don't go,' he whispered. 'Stay with me, please. I…I care about you. I need you.'

The sound of the quietly clicked door echoed through the now-empty rooms. He wandered through the rooms aimlessly, leaving the bedroom until the last. It was as if all the light and joy had been sucked out of them.

Beside the bed, he sank down to his knees and buried his head in his hands. Tears flowed down his face. Sophie had gone. She had walked out of his life. And she would not be back.

His gut ached as if it had been torn out and roughly stuffed back in. A great black emptiness filled him. Sophie had abandoned him.

This black emptiness was far worse than when, as a boy of seven, his mother had left him with Hannah in a small glade while she ran away with her lover. When the light had faded and it was clear that no one was coming for them, he had carried the crying toddler back to Hallington and told her that he would look after her. He found his father in the study, drinking. His father had engulfed him and Hannah in a big bear hug, and told him that they would be a family together.

However, one day a few months later, he had returned from a ride to find the nursery empty. He'd gone again to the study and asked his father where his sister was and had his ears boxed for his trouble. He was never to mention his sister or mother again, his father declared, going into the first of his fearsome rages. Richard had gone back to his room and cried himself to sleep. It was the last time he had wept.

Two weeks later, he was on his way to Eton and his father had always had an excuse as to why he couldn't be there. Richard had pretended at first he didn't care and in the end he hadn't cared. He wanted to think it would be the same with Sophie, but he knew that was a lie. He'd always care. He'd always want to know where Sophie was and that she was happy. Sophie was as necessary as breathing to him.

Richard looked up at the bed and grabbed a pillow. Her faint scent of lavender and citrus clung to it but it made the ache worse and he put it from him.

'Sophie!'

The word echoed around the chamber, mocking him.

Would she have gone so quickly if she cared for him? He'd been right to keep from confessing how much he needed her in his life and how much his happiness and well being depended on her. She didn't care about him, not truly.

He started to get up, but an abandoned book under the bed caught his eye. He reached out and brought Sophie's sketchpad out.

He flipped through it. Page after page was filled with sketches of him. The first ones were hesitant and obviously done from memory early in their relationship. Later in the book, she must have drawn him while he slept. His favourite was him asleep with his face turned towards her. She had sketched his back and the way the coverlet had slipped to his waist.

Each line of the drawing screamed how much she cared about him. A tiny light flickered in the black emptiness deep within him and he knew the truth he'd been avoiding. She cared for him, deeply and passionately, and he'd refused to see it before, preferring to think that she was in love with new sensations because it meant he did not have to face his own feelings for her. He didn't want to give her the power to hurt him and in doing so, he had hurt her—deeply and irrevocably.

Richard closed his eyes, knowing he had killed whatever glimmer of love she had for him. He should have trusted her with his family, with his whole being, because she was his life. He was the one who had wronged her, dreadfully wronged her. There had been no marriage to leave, because he had not been prepared to give of himself.

He tore the drawing from the book, carefully folded it and put it in his pocket. It was a slim hope.

'I will get you back, Sophie, and I will spend my life

showing you my finer feelings. I will show you that I
know where you are going. I will always be there for
you if you want me. And I do want you to stand beside
me. If you need me to say words, I will, but I am scared.'

He put his hands to his eyes. Where had she gone?
She had accused him of not knowing her and not caring. He had to prove that he did know her, far better
than she thought.

He would find her without anyone else's help but he
had to do it quickly.

'I want to see Lady Bingfield, Mrs Montemorcy,'
Richard said, keeping his voice steady as he stood on the
doorstep of the imposing country house in Corbridge
that afternoon. 'Please tell her I am here.'

It had taken him several hours and a painful interview with his father, where he'd been accused of all
manner of things when he confessed that Sophie had
left him. Richard had not given him the true reason,
but he had persuaded his father to stay until he found
Sophie. His father had given him twenty-four hours.
The instant he left his father, he knew where Sophie
must have gone.

All the way to Corbridge on the train, he had prayed
his hunch was correct. But if it wasn't, he'd keep searching. He refused to give up.

The slender brunette stared daggers at him. If looks
could kill or maim, the formidable Mrs Montemorcy's
certainly would.

'There is no such person as Lady Bingfield.'

He knew then what Sophie and the Montemorcys

intended—an annulment. Difficult, but not impossible and the last thing he wanted.

Heart thudding in his ears, he held out his hands and begged, 'I would speak with Sophie. Your friend Sophie. Let me speak to her, please.'

She tilted her head to one side, assessed him and found him wanting. 'And if she doesn't want to speak to you?'

'I am her husband.'

Mrs Montemorcy's eyebrow shot up. 'That remains to be seen.'

Richard's stomach clenched. He was expected to go, but he refused to give in to expectations.

'Sophie! Sophie! I will stand outside this house and scream your name until you come out. You decide. But you never need to hide behind anyone's skirt. You simply need to tell me to go away. But it has to come from you.'

'You are making a spectacle of yourself, Lord Bingfield. Cease it at once!'

'I want my wife, Mrs Montemorcy. I want to speak with her. I want to know she is safe.' Richard held out his hands and willed her to agree. 'My wife's well being is very important to me.'

'You presume much, Lord Bingfield.' Mrs Montemorcy started to close the door.

Richard stuck his hand and foot in the doorway, blocking her. Sophie was there.

'All I want to do is talk with her. Sophie is fully capable of telling me to go to the devil, Mrs Montemorcy. You know that as well as I do. Sophie has no need of protection from you, from anyone.'

'If you speak to her and she tells you to go, will you go? Quietly?'

'Yes, I will go,' Richard said, bowing his head, giving in.

'Henri, it is fine. You can stop standing guard over me.' Sophie came out from behind her friend. 'Richard is right. I am a grown up. I fight my own battles now.'

Richard's heart lurched. Her eyes were mere slits, practically swollen shut from crying; her nose was red and her hair hung about her shoulders like snakes. She had never looked more beautiful to him. He wanted to throw her over his shoulder and hurry away from there. He wanted to kiss her feet. He forced his body to remain completely still and devoured her with his eyes.

'Sophie,' he said.

She gave a reluctant nod. 'I'm here. Say what you like, Richard.'

'You may speak in the drawing room, unless you wish to converse outside where all might hear,' Mrs Montemorcy said.

Richard kept his eyes on Sophie. She might be capable of fighting her own battles, but he wanted to be there for her. He had to hope that she wanted to help him fight his battles. 'It is Sophie's choice.'

'We can risk the drawing room.' Sophie took two steps into the house before stopping and fixing him with her eye. 'But, Richard, if you try anything, anything at all after I tell you to go, Henri's footmen will throw you out on your ear.'

'I understand.' He gulped a breath of life-giving air. Silently he prayed, as he had not done since he was a young boy in that wood, that she'd listen and understand what he was truly saying. He was going to bare his soul and hope.

* * *

Her legs like jelly and her head throbbing, Sophie staggered into Henri and Robert's drawing room. The last person she had expected to see today was Richard, but he was here. Her traitorous body wanted to go to him and be held, but that was how the trouble had started in the first place.

She took a steadying breath. It was the shock of seeing him.

If he came at all, she had expected it to be within a week's time after he'd managed to get the probable destination out of her stepmother. She had expected her stepmother to be more closed-mouthed. She'd given Robert her assurance of that which was why he had stayed in Newcastle at his office, rather than travelling to Corbridge to be here with her. She should have remembered that her stepmother had a soft spot for Richard.

'Remember, Sophie, I am here if you need assistance.' Henri gave Richard a hard look. 'And my husband will return shortly.'

'My wife is perfectly safe with me,' Richard said firmly. 'You have my solemn word.'

Sophie motioned to Henri to go. With one last troubled glance backwards, Henri left the room. Sophie forced her shoulders back and waited.

Richard said nothing. He simply stood there, looking at her with a haunted expression as the silence grew and threatened to suffocate her.

'I suppose it is my stepmother I can thank for you finding me so quickly.' Sophie pressed her hands together to keep them from trembling. 'She has a romantic soul, but she has gone too far this time. There was no need for it.'

'I have not seen your stepmother today. In fact, I have not seen her since the day before yesterday. You wrong her and me if you think that.' A muscle jumped in his jaw. 'I knew where you must have gone. And if you had not been here, I would have kept on searching until I found you. There are things which need to be settled between us.'

Sophie's eyes widened. She rapidly sat down. He'd known where she'd run to. He hadn't seen her step-mother. 'How did you find me? How did you guess?'

'When we first conversed after the item appeared in the newspaper, you said that if things became very bad, you would go to Corbridge. Once here, I learnt where your friends lived.'

'You remembered that?' Sophie trembled. It was when she'd been so sure that Richard hadn't cared for her. *If he didn't care, why remember?* asked a little nagging voice in the back of her mind. She quashed it, just as during her train journey here she'd quashed it every time it spoke up, reminding her about the little things Richard had done. Richard had wronged her. She believed in a person who did not exist and it was time for her to stop believing in fairy stories and romance.

'I try to remember everything about you, Sophie, because you are necessary to me.'

Necessary to him. Sophie put her hand to her mouth. 'Why did you come here?'

'I took the second train this morning and came to find you. I need your help, Sophie, and I need it urgently. I am sorry that I can't pander to your tender sensibilities and allow you to revel in your hurt, but this matter refuses to wait.'

'You need my help with what?' she asked, narrowing her eyes suspiciously. Pander to her tender sensibilities, indeed. Of all the nerve! 'I will end this interview right now if you wish to be rude.'

'I need you to help put things right. I can't do this on my own, Sophie.'

'Things are never going to be right between us,' she said. 'I made that perfectly clear last night and I am even clearer on it today. We can never go back to what we had or what I thought we might have. I have done a lot of thinking.'

He paled at her words. 'Hear me out, Sophie. We are married. Lawfully man and wife. I never wanted it to be like this. I intended to protect you and keep you safe. I thought I could fight your battles for you.'

'I know our legal status to my cost. Robert has already pointed this obstacle out, but things can be done.'

He flinched as if she had struck him with her hand.

'All I ask is this one thing and I will let you go if that is what you want.' He bowed his head. 'I will even help with the annulment, false pretences or whatever is the most expedient. I will play the villain, if the law requires, but first I require this one thing of you.'

Sophie's insides trembled. Richard was not going to try to hold her to the marriage. He was going to let her go. He probably wanted her assurance that she wouldn't sell her story to the papers or some such nonsense.

She wanted to break down in fresh tears again, but she had cried herself to a standstill already. It was worse, somehow, seeing him again and knowing that his arms had given her comfort before. She'd never again be able to lay her head on his chest and listen to his steady heartbeat. And, despite everything, she loved him and cared about him.

'What is this one thing?' she asked between numb lips.

'I want you to listen to my story and then I want your advice on how to proceed.'

'My advice?' Sophie hated the way her heart leapt. 'You have never wanted it before. You kept things from me, rather than asking me.'

'I am asking now.' His voice became ragged. 'Please. You are my last hope, Sophie. No, that's not right. You are my only hope.'

Sophie sank down on the sofa. 'I will listen.'

'My mother left Hannah and I in the woods when I was no more than seven and Hannah was a toddler, barely able to walk on her own.' Richard's voice held little emotion. 'We were supposed to be on a picnic. The first picnic of the summer, just my mother and her two children. Three of us left Hallington that day, only two returned. My mother ran away with Hannah's father.'

Sophie stuffed her hand into her mouth. It was far worse than she had imagined. How could any woman leave her children alone and defenceless in a wood? 'How did you get back? Did your father find you? How long were you there?'

'Once I realised no one was coming, I carried Hannah all the way home as my mother had taken the governess's cart. Someone had to take responsibility.'

There was a wealth of information in the stark sentences. Sophie could easily imagine the frightened boy left alone with a crying toddler, far from home, expecting help and having none come. Despite his reputation for scandal, Richard always tried to protect those who were weaker than him. It was why that woman Mary's death had affected him so badly.

She wanted to gather him in her arms and tell him what he'd done that day was a brave and wonderful thing. But she hardened her heart and stayed still. He should never have treated her in the manner he did.

'How…how could she do such a thing?' she asked instead.

'Hannah's father was my mother's lover before she married my father. He abandoned her for Australia and she married my father in haste. My father adored the ground my mother walked on. She found him old and fusty. She spent money doing up Hallington like it was water and gave extravagant parties while my father became ever more absorbed in his pig-breeding. Eventually Grayson returned and the affair started again. My sister was born nine months after he returned.'

'Hannah is your mother's love child?' Sophie closed her eyes.

'My father acknowledged Hannah as his own and then, when she was two…this happened.'

Sophie remembered the tears in Lord Hallington's eyes when he said that he'd always wanted a daughter. 'You had better tell me everything so I can understand. If I don't understand, I don't see how I can give proper advice.'

She listened carefully as Richard explained about the divorce and his father's conditions. How his mother had chosen Hannah and her lover had formally adopted her.

How he'd learnt not to depend on his father appearing at any function and that he'd had to fight his own battles. Finally Richard spoke about how he always made sure that he was never hurt like that again and how if any of his mistresses wanted to leave, he let them go. He ended things before he became involved. How he never offered twice.

Sophie pressed her lips together and knew he'd broken his rules for her. More than once. Her heart fluttered, but she simply nodded her head and waited for him to finish.

'I thought I would keep my heart safe, but when you left last night, I learnt that simply denying feelings doesn't stop them from happening. When you walked out, you took my heart with you. You didn't mean to.'

'What do you want from me? Your heart back?' Sophie clenched her hands and knew she had made a decision. Every woman Richard had known had abandoned him. She had done exactly the same thing when she didn't know about his past. But now she did and she knew he was worth fighting for. 'How can I give your heart back when I didn't know I had it?'

'It belongs to you now. It has belonged to you for longer than I dare admit.' Richard bowed his head and his shoulders slumped. 'What I wanted from you was for you to listen and you have. I will go now. I wanted you to know that I am here for you if you ever need me. And I have decided that there is no longer any purpose in trying to keep my parents happy.'

Sophie knew she had this one chance to make their marriage into the sort of marriage she wanted, rather than one that others might want for her.

'I am coming with you. I need you to need me and I think you need me by your side and in your life.'

His eyes opened wide and his mouth dropped open. 'What?'

'After you leave here, you are going to see your father and tell him the truth about why you were in Newcastle to begin with and what you wanted to accomplish. Then you are going to see your mother with your father and get him to give her a promise that he won't ruin Hannah out of spite. She believes his promises because he is like you. He always tries to keep his promises.' Sophie's heart thudded. She had to get this right. 'And if I am there, it will make life easier for everyone, particularly you. You shouldn't go into battle without your heart.'

He gave a shadow of his old heart-melting smile. 'Precisely, but why are you willing to do this?'

Sophie held out her hand. 'You could do this on your own, Richard, but it is easier if you have someone who will stand shoulder to shoulder with you. Your parents are difficult people. Your father will bluster and thunder. Your mother may fly into hysterics. They both need to see that you are not on your own any more. They both failed you when you were a boy. You never failed them. You don't have to put things right for them, but if you want to, I will be there at your side.'

'Sophie!'

'Your mother in particular needs to see that we stand together. That no one can drive a wedge between us. She needs to see that she is not losing a son, but gaining a daughter. And she is having no part in our marriage or the marriage of her daughter.'

He stepped towards her. 'What…what are you saying about our marriage, Sophie?'

Sophie drew in her breath. This time he had to believe her. But even if he didn't, she'd go on telling him until he believed.

'I'm saying that I love you, Richard, and, even if your scheme doesn't work and your parents behave badly, I will stand by you and make sure that Hannah's match happens. She is my sister now. She doesn't need to have her life ruined by selfish people who should just grow up. Just as you don't deserve it, either.' She stood up and held out her arms. 'I learnt something today. Life is better when someone believes in you and I believe in you, Richard.'

'You mean to stay married to me?' He caught her hand in his.

'Until my dying breath.' Sophie bowed her head. She wanted to get the words right and explain. 'I was angry and hurt last night because I didn't understand what you were doing. You wrongly kept me in ignorance and, rather than asking, I leapt to conclusions. I don't need protection from anyone, Richard, as long as I have you by my side. I don't care what other people say about us as long as we please ourselves.'

'Always.' He folded her in his arms and put his head against hers. 'You'll always have me. I believe in you, Sophie.'

'I know that now.' She gave a little hiccupping laugh. 'I never thought you'd come out to Corbridge or face Henri down. Some people might think it isn't much, but I know you. I know what you have been through and what you believed might happen, but you still came and you were willing to fight for me. You fought for me when I tried to hide behind my experience with Sebastian. You showed me that it didn't define me. I defined me.'

He squeezed her hand. 'I do love you, Sophie. I simply was afraid to say the words before. Until you came into my life, I didn't know what happiness could be.'

'And I was too afraid to see the signs of your love. They were there but, until I started trusting me, I didn't think I was worthy of your love.'

'I forced you into our marriage. I rushed you before you were ready.' He put his hands on either side of her face. 'I seduced you, ruthlessly and cynically seduced you because I had to be certain of you. Do you forgive me?'

'Why, Richard? Why did you do it?' Sophie whispered.

'Because I needed you in my life, every part of my life. You complete my life and make me whole.' There was a new humble note in Richard's voice. 'I wanted to make sure you could become the person you were meant to be and the only way to do that was to have you by my side. Or at least that was what I told myself. It wasn't until you walked out that I knew I married you because I needed you in my life and for no other reason. You are necessary to me, Sophie, as necessary as breathing. Hopefully, some day, I will be necessary to you as well.'

'You are already necessary.' Sophie looked into his eyes. 'Robert and Henri's return was a fig leaf for my pride because I thought you would not ask me to marry you again. I remembered what you said on the night we

met. I knew I loved you when you brought me the painting materials and then insisted I use them.'

'You were very late to fall. I know I started to love
you when you refused my invitation to waltz on the first
night. Any other woman and I would have walked away,
but with you, I knew I couldn't. I wanted to be part of
your life.' He gave a crooked smile. 'I took advantage
of you in the carriage. I had promised I wouldn't, but
the temptation was far too great. I had to know you
would be in my life and I played on your need to be
seen to be good.'

Sophie gave a throaty laugh. She had been so intent
on assuming things that she had failed to consider the
obvious. Richard married her because he wanted to. Not
because society demanded it, but because he desired it.
'I was easy to seduce. Love will do that to a woman.'

He smoothed her hair back from her forehead. His
eyes looked deeply into hers. Sophie wondered that she
had missed the deep love which shone out. Now that
she knew where to look, the love was clear to see. 'If I
had asked you to marry me without seduction, would
you have done?'

'Ask me. Ask me now and I will give you the answer
I would have given then.'

'Will you marry me, Sophie? Will you spend the rest
of your life with me?'

'Always.' Sophie lifted her mouth to his. 'I will always marry you. I will always stay at your side. Not because society demands, but because you are the keeper
of my heart and I want to be there.'

* * * * *

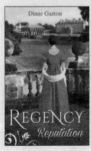